A

STRANGE

KIND

OF

COMFORT

A STRANGE KIND OF COMFORT

Gaylene Dutchyshen

DUNDURN
TORONTO

Publisher: Scott Fraser | Acquiring editor: Rachel Spence | Editor: Jess Shulman
Cover designer: Sophie Paas-Lang
Cover image: istockphoto.com/prill
Printer: Webcom, a division of Marquis Book Printing Inc.

Library and Archives Canada Cataloguing in Publication

Title: A strange kind of comfort / Gaylene Dutchyshen.
Names: Dutchyshen, Gaylene, 1958- author.
Identifiers: Canadiana (print) 2019010967X | Canadiana (ebook) 20190109688 | ISBN 9781459745452 (softcover) | ISBN 9781459745469 (PDF) | ISBN 9781459745476 (EPUB)
Classification: LCC PS8607.U877 S77 2020 | DDC C813/.6—dc23

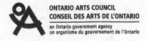 

We acknowledge the support of the Canada Council for the Arts and the Ontario Arts Council for our publishing program. We also acknowledge the financial support of the Government of Ontario, through the Ontario Book Publishing Tax Credit and Ontario Creates, and the Government of Canada.

Care has been taken to trace the ownership of copyright material used in this book. The author and the publisher welcome any information enabling them to rectify any references or credits in subsequent editions.

The publisher is not responsible for websites or their content unless they are owned by the publisher.

Printed and bound in Canada.

VISIT US AT

 dundurn.com | @dundurnpress |  dundurnpress | dundurnpress

Dundurn
3 Church Street, Suite 500
Toronto, Ontario, Canada
M5E 1M2

For my parents, Michael and Rosalene Maksymetz,
with love and gratitude

PROLOGUE

The *chudesnytsia* blends a tea of burdock root, raspberry leaves, and honey, then rests in her rocking chair by the wood stove while she sips. Usually the bitter brew eases the pain deep in her bones but today it does little to relieve her suffering. Instead, the pungent odour rising from the steam carries her off to a murky, twilight place where she drifts between wakefulness and dreams.

She is home again in the village at the foot of the Carpathian Mountains, the beloved grandmother she left behind trudging slowly up the path to a whitewashed hut, clutching the hem of a crisp white apron. It droops like a hammock with the weight of a cabbage the size of a grown man's head. And there is her mother, long dead, retching in agony as the *SS Bulgaria* rocks on an angry, endless sea. She sees herself, a small and frightened child wearing a grimy dress, woollen stockings sagging at the knees, peering up from a wooden bunk in the hull of the ship. She feels the crush of women's rough skirts against her cheek as soiled babies howl and anxious women fret over their husbands' decisions while waiting, waiting, at the port of Halifax for papers to be looked at and documents filed.

She wakes with a start to a muffled tapping she thinks might be the barn door, unhooked and flapping in the wind, or perhaps the child upstairs, not yet asleep, bumping her feet against the wall. As she comes fully awake she realizes it is someone knocking at her door. She hoists herself up, shuffles over, and opens it to find on her stoop a young, round-shouldered woman holding the hand of a child. The boy is thin and pale, with hair the colour of acorns and haunted brown eyes she senses he is afraid to close at night. The woman's face, too, bears the strain of sleepless nights. She takes a step forward as a lone wolf howls in the distant hills, a keening cry that startles the boy. "*I was told you could help my child.*" She falters over the Ukrainian words and the *chudesnytsia* thinks for a moment how like her own daughter this young woman is, the words so unforgiving on her tongue.

The *chudesnytsia* ushers them in and gestures to the table, inviting them to sit. The boy looks around the room with wary eyes, taking in the small jars of garnet-coloured jam lined up on the cupboard, the wooden print of the Last Supper hanging on the wall, the flickering candle on a small side table.

"It's a'right. You tell to me in English. What it is wrong with this little one?"

The young woman seems relieved she does not have to struggle to explain her son's condition and she speaks slowly, taking care with each word. "He doesn't sleep. He can't go a night without waking, screaming out for me. I rush in to his room and he is so scared he can't stop shaking, yet when I ask, he says he doesn't know what scares him."

In hushed tones, the old woman probes, wanting to know if the boy had been ill before the nightmares began. Had anyone died? A grandparent? A beloved dog? Had he been frightened by something? The boy's mother tells her how difficult these last months have been, lights blazing in every room throughout the night, the sheets tangled at the foot of his bed. The child has begged his mother not to leave him and cries when she does. The old woman nods, trying to make sense of it. She is familiar with such cases and has had success in the past. A cleansing read with her wax and holy water to determine the source of his buried fear together with a tincture from her wildflowers, berries, or bark should rid the child of whatever torments him.

The boy drifts to the small table with the sputtering candle and fingers a linen cloth, embellished with red and black cross-stitch, draped across a holy icon of the Virgin Mary. The boy leans in, as though for a closer look, and, with a gentle puff, blows out the candle.

"Oh," his mother says, bringing one hand to her mouth, "I told you not to touch anything."

"It's a'right," the old woman says. "We light again." She picks up the candle and a small wicker basket from the floor next to the table and holds it out to the boy. "You help me to carry?"

In the basket are a black-rimmed white enamel cup and bowl, a packet of matches, a smooth-edged knife, a small vial of water, and a lump of amber-coloured wax. The boy carries the basket, gently, as though it holds eggs he might break, and places it on the table. From a pail next to the sink, the old woman scoops a dipper of water, hand-drawn from her well, and fills the bowl.

"I ready. We start," she says, cupping the boy's chin with her right hand. The sign of Jesus had appeared on the morning of her sixteenth birthday. She had awakened to find three crosses on her palm, pulsing brilliantly red, as though they had been carved there with a pocket knife during the night. Her mother took their appearance as a sign her daughter was ready to learn the incantations for cleansing and healing that she had learned from her own mother — the same rituals handed down through generations of women in her family and brought with them to Canada. The crosses are barely visible now and she wonders if her power has diminished with them, but she reminds herself the healing comes from God's grace and the unwavering faith of those who come.

"Do you believe?" She must ask the question, but she knows the boy is too young. What does a child of six know of faith or God? He says nothing and averts his gaze so she turns to his mother, whose eyes brim with hope. "And you. Do you believe?"

The young woman nods, although the look in her eyes is wary, as though she has come not because she truly believes in the power of the Holy Spirit but out of a deep and troubling desperation. The old woman shifts the boy's chair, scraping it across the wooden floor, and arranges herself in front of him, facing east to harness the power of the rising sun as the ritual demands, although night has almost fallen. A sudden, heavy rain begins to thrum against the roof as she lights the candle and places a lump of beeswax in the enamel cup. Holding the cup over the candle, she adds a single clove of garlic and a few drops of holy water to the bowl. The scent of the melting wax brings to mind golden honey dripping from a comb and the hum of a hundred buzzing bees.

"*Vo im'ia Otsa, I Syna, I Sviatoho dukha, amin.*" In the name of the Father, the Son, and the Holy Spirit. Three times she makes the sign of the cross, preparing herself to receive

God's grace. A whisper of doubt troubles her mind and she steels herself against it, grasping the knife in her left hand. She picks up the bowl and holds it over the boy's head. He glances up at her and she senses his misgivings, too, but she closes her eyes and begins the ancient Ukrainian incantation.

"I take to the head, to the blood, to all the joints, to adjure, to summon this fear of fears; From the north and from the south, I summon you with God's lips, with God's words; And the sister-stars ..."

The sacred words spill easily from her lips. The power of the Trinity is within her — she feels it pulse with each pounding beat of her heart. The knife glints in the candlelight as she thrusts it toward the heavens, slicing the air and casting out the child's fear with the same swift strokes she uses when scraping the skin of a butchered hog.

She continues to chant in her mother tongue. "I release you beyond the mountains, beyond the seas ... disappear and vanish. I release you where people do not walk, where roosters do not crow, where the wind does not blow. Be gone! May you be buried and disappear.

"*Chrevonu krov ne pyi, bile kilo ne sushy, zhovtu kist ne lupai.*"

Do not drink red blood, dehydrate a white body, or strip a yellow bone.

The knife clatters to the table as she reaches for the melted wax. The candle flame barely flickers as she pours the thick wax and watches it move like something alive across the surface of the water, spreading until it blooms into shapes she must read. After a few moments, the shapes reveal themselves. Flames. Little greedy tongues of fire. Easy enough to see. But what confounds her is the tendril curling up and away from the heart of the blaze, stretching up toward the ceiling, unlike anything she has ever seen. Neither smoke nor flame, but separate. A tether, she senses, connecting the child to her in some way, to an event yet to happen in the distant future.

There is a sudden loud thump from upstairs and the boy and his mother look up, startled by the sound. The girl has fallen out of bed, the *chudesnytsia* thinks, and is about to explain the presence of someone else in the house when she notices the boy. His brow is smooth, his eyes clear, free of anguish, as he gazes up at the ceiling, restored.

PART

ONE

2016

SARAH

The ancient elm and the stone pile beneath it are all that remain of the fence line that once marked the boundary between their place and the Webbs'. For years it was Eldon Webb who fiercely guarded the tree but, after the old man died, it was Sarah who stood her ground and refused to let Jack cut it down. At one time, Jack and his father wanted to clean up the fence line; tear out the fence posts, knock down the tree, bury the stone pile. Open things up, make it easier for the bigger equipment they were running these days. But old man Webb wouldn't allow it. He said the fence kept the Bilyks over where they belonged and hell would freeze over before he'd let them cut down that tree. With every passing year, storm-scattered branches and quack grass crept farther into both fields. As soon as old man Webb died, before he was even cold in the ground, Jack ripped out the rotting posts, knocked down the poplar saplings, gathered up the deadfall, dragged it into a pile, and set it all on fire. He picked up the rusted strands of barbed wire and harrowed the ashes, reclaiming a couple of acres and seeding them to wheat, but at the edge of the field, because Sarah insisted, he left that elm tree standing.

Over forty feet tall, it has a canopy as wide and welcoming as a wedding tent with a natural hollow at its feet, lush with twitch grass and wildflowers: pink columbine, star-flowered Solomon's seal, droopy-headed bluebells. Sarah likes to come and listen to the nearby sound of water splashing over the river rocks and the twitter of birds. There's a peace she finds in this spiritual place, far enough away from the roar of aeration fans and equipment in the yard. It reminds her of her grand-mother's place tucked up against the foot of the mountain, where she spent so much time as a child.

She comes often, scavenging the stone pile for rocks of every shape and size, hauling them home in the box of her pickup truck. Flat ones of limestone for building garden walls and as many smaller, coloured ones as she can lift to place among her prized lilies and roses.

Today, dappled May sunshine filters through the leaves, spotting Misty's golden coat as she dozes, her head nuzzled on Sarah's thigh. Misty's heart belongs to Sarah, although she was a gift for Toni's sixth birthday. The girls squealed in delight when Misty poked her nose out of the cardboard box that morning. They promised to feed her and bathe her and teach her to sit, but it was Sarah who took on Misty's care, comfort-ing her that first night when she whimpered for her mother. Jack found Sarah in the morning, lying on the mud room floor, fast asleep with the new puppy dozing on her chest. He said it reminded him of the way she used to be with the girls, asleep in the reclining chair with a baby nestled between her breasts.

Toni is home from university for the summer; the house seems full once again. After she left, Sarah thought she'd never get used to the silence, never survive the absence of her last-born child. After thirty-two years with the frantic bustle of three girls growing up, what would she do? For the first few months, she kept listening for a door to slam or a blow-dryer to roar to life, but, over time, she grew used to the familiar sounds of the empty house. The whir of the refrigerator and the click of Misty's nails on the floor. In busy seasons, with Jack working sixteen-hour days, she often goes a whole week speaking hardly a word. She keeps the radio and television turned off during the day as she goes about her chores, relishing the solitude of her peaceful world.

Misty lifts her head, sniffs the air, growls low in her throat. Sarah catches a vague odour on the breeze, not unlike the smell of spoiled meat.

"What is it, girl?"

Misty pads toward the open field, tilts her head, looks back then barks. Sensing Misty wants her to follow, Sarah walks to the edge of the shade and stops beside the stone pile.

There is a small, pie-shaped field to the east that tapers into a shallow ravine where the field ends, and beyond that, the Makwa River, named by the Ojibway for the black bears that roam the aspen parkland. The small field had once been part of a pasture, the river a natural barrier the cattle wouldn't willingly cross. Now it's a meadow where Jack cuts and bales hay every year for the cattle.

Two calves have gone missing from their herd in the last week. Jack hoped they had just wandered off though a gap in the fence and would find their way back, as they often did. But their neighbour Shorty Cornforth is missing a calf, too, while the Nychuks have lost two calves and an old cow. Jack, Shorty, and Jim Nychuk have discussed the possibility of rustlers. They heard about some thefts in the Interlake north and east of here; prices go up, it happens, but no one has seen strange trucks and trailers on the country roads, and everyone's been watching since the cattle started to disappear.

Even though the cows are now pastured three miles away, Sarah thinks it's possible one of the missing calves has lost its way and ended up along the riverbank. She crosses the meadow and follows Misty into the ravine, sidestepping her way down, keeping her balance by grabbing hold of the branches of squat cranberry bushes and willow saplings as a shower of pebbles rains down. The sun gleams off the river as she makes her way down the steep hill toward it. She glances back over her shoulder at a stealthy rustle coming from the brush and is relieved to hear the familiar *chit-chit-chit* of a grey squirrel. Misty is poking her nose in the fallen leaves, snuffling and pawing in a frenzied way, when Sarah catches a fleeting movement from the corner of her eye. Misty, lips raised, ears flattened, barks. A primal, guttural sound Sarah's never heard from her before. As Misty prepares to lunge, Sarah grabs hold of the dog's scruff and holds her back.

There, at the bottom of the ravine along the river's edge on an outcropping of pebbled beach, is a Red Angus calf, weeks old, viciously gutted through the gaping hole where its tail should be. Its throat is torn open, too, and blood, black and tar-thick, soaks out of it onto the gravel. A swarm of blue-bellied flies hovers and buzzes above the rotting carcass and Sarah gags at the putrid stench and gruesome sight of it. She doesn't need to look more closely at the blood-stained tag in its ear to know the calf is theirs.

• • •

Jack is working in the far corner of the field. Sarah can see the dust he's stirring up as he zigzags around with the chore tractor, aiming for rocks poking from the dirt and raking them up with the stone picker. Much of their farmland lies along the shoreline of Lake Agassiz, an ancient glacial lake that once covered most of Manitoba. Remnants of rocks and stones left behind when the prehistoric lake retreated are churned up out of the earth by the tiller each fall. Every spring they must be swept up and discarded, leaving the field ready for planting.

Jack clanks across the field with a load of rocks, backs the tractor up to the stone pile, and dumps it from the picker. When he sees her, he waves from the cab and climbs down.

"Hey, you. What's up?" Jack is smiling, something he hasn't been doing much of lately. She doesn't want to give him the bad news about the calf; he's been losing sleep as it is over the rising costs of crop inputs.

"I found one of the missing calves."

"Where?" Jack looks momentarily hopeful.

"Down by the river." Sarah motions with her head. "It was dead. Torn apart."

"Damn it." Jack takes off his cap and pulls a hand through his hair. "You sure it was ours?"

"Our tag," Sarah says. "It looked to me like it was ripped up for sport and just left there. Its neck slashed open and then gutted from behind. Whatever killed it left it for the crows."

"Can you show me?"

Sarah doesn't want to go back. She'll tell Jack exactly where she found the calf, but she doesn't want to see it again. The feasting maggots. The crows swooping down, picking rotting flesh from tender bones.

. . .

Sarah gives the whiteboard a quick glance as she walks into the common room at Sunny Haven. *June 22. Beanbag toss, chair yoga, the Veselka dancers are coming to perform!* The residents themselves never read the posted agenda; it's there for the benefit of family members who, like Sarah, rarely look at it either. Chairs are lined up along the wall, most of the residents propped up like rag dolls, supported by bolsters and towels rolled and stuffed around them. They've been fed their lunch and now wait for the afternoon's events to begin. Some of the able-bodied ones, like Sarah's father, take part in the activities, although getting him to co-operate can be a challenge.

Her father is standing by the activity director's office, clutching an inflated beach ball to his chest while a young nurse's aide pleads with him to give it to her. Sarah doesn't recognize the brown polyester pants and burgundy cardigan he is wearing. The sweater is improperly buttoned and one side hangs like a small flag between his legs. An ankle monitor, meant to keep him from escaping the building, is cuffed above his left shoe. The staff lets him dress himself and Sarah is grateful, at least, that he is allowed that last bit of independence.

He turns away from the aide and notices Sarah standing in the foyer. His eyes widen as though he is surprised to see her and, for a moment, Sarah thinks perhaps he recognizes her. But just as suddenly, his eyes narrow and she realizes that, of course, her father doesn't know who she is.

"Hi, Dad," Sarah says briskly as she walks over. "Are you giving Cara a hard time?" She winks at the newest member of the staff.

"He always has to be the first at every game we play," Cara says. "Some days I don't know what to do with him."

Sarah gently eases the beach ball away from her father and speaks softly in the same calming voice she once used to settle her own misbehaving toddlers. "Dad, you can't have the ball just now. Let's let Cara have it, okay? Why don't we have a little visit first, just you and me, until it's time to start the game?" She hands Cara the ball. "I'll just take Dad back to his room for a bit while you get things ready here."

Cara looks relieved. "Thanks, Mrs. Bilyk. Addie usually has the best luck. She can get your dad to do just about anything, but it's her day off."

It strikes Sarah as incredibly ironic that her father should listen to anything Adeline Prentiss has to say. Addie and Sarah have been friends since elementary school. She was a champion at one-liners and teacher impersonations back then, often making the whole class laugh until she was sent to the principal's office. Addie was, as Sarah's father used to say, a real shit disturber.

Sarah takes her father's arm and leads him down the hall to his own small room. When he first moved in, she tried to make the room comfortable and familiar, setting up the small walnut side table, marred by a milky water stain, on one wall. Her father had picked it up from the nuisance grounds when she was a child, pointing out the paper tag stapled under it — Walberg's Fine Furniture — and saying it must have belonged to Elvina Webb because who else but the Webbs would throw out a perfectly good table? Sarah used to polish it with lemon-scented furniture oil and hide the spot with a crocheted doily. Now, the water stain is covered by framed photographs: Allison and Jason's wedding picture, Maeve and Toni's high-school graduation photos, and a baby picture of Connor. The old rocker recliner with the arms nearly worn through sits in the corner and a faded hand-stitched patchwork quilt made long ago by Sarah's grandmother is folded neatly at the foot of the bed. Sometimes, Sarah thinks she can still smell the musty odour of her father's house in it.

Her father sits on the quilt, eyeing her, as though he wonders what adventure is about to unfold. Sarah straightens the items on his nightstand and fills a glass with ice water from the pitcher. She worries that he forgets to drink enough water and the staff, as busy as they are, don't remind him as often as they should. He shakes his head, tightens his lips, and stares at the glass as though it's laced with poison.

She sighs and puts the glass back on the nightstand. "I'll just leave it here. You can take a sip whenever you like." She sits on the recliner and tries to think of something to tell him. A year earlier, he would listen carefully, leaning forward to take in her every word, forehead wrinkled, as though he understood what she was telling him about Jack — what he was planting or spraying or harvesting — or whatever the girls were up to that week. But lately, he has been sitting on the edge of the bed, legs swinging, muttering to himself, seemingly oblivious to the fact she is even there.

"Mary died," he says, leaping suddenly from the bed. His eyes widen as though he's just remembered or has been saving this bit of information until her visit. "Mary died," he says again, and Sarah wonders, *Who is Mary?* She knows her father had a sister by that name who drowned when she was a toddler, and she wonders if that's what he's remembering. He points to the room across the hall, empty now after the passing of George Feschuk, who died a month earlier. Richard, the maintenance man, was busy painting George's room last week, and earlier today Sarah noticed the furniture was back inside.

Cara pokes her head into the room and announces, "Activities starting in about five minutes."

"Mary died," he says to Cara this time, growing more agitated. Cara looks alarmed, as though she might have overlooked a dead body somewhere on the floor, and Sarah quickly says, "I think he means George," motioning to the room across the hall. "He must sense something's up."

"Oh," Cara says, looking relieved. "No, it's George, Joe," she says, raising her voice. "It's George who died."

Sarah settles her father and motions to the room across the hall. "It looks like it's all ready for someone to move in. Do you know yet who it is?"

Cara hesitates for a moment. "I'm really not supposed to say, but" — she looks over her shoulder and drops her voice — "it's Caroline Webb. Mrs. High and Mighty, that's what Addie called her."

"Really?" Sarah is startled to hear Caroline's name.

"Said the whole town used to worship the ground the Webbs walked on. Some still do." Cara gives Joe her arm and leads him to the door. "Hardly anyone sees her, that's what Addie said. Shut away in that old brick house." She looks suddenly surprised. "You must know her. The Webbs live beside you, don't they?"

Sarah nods, not quite believing the news although she did hear Caroline had broken a hip after a fall a few months ago. It was Lois Cornforth who found her, lying injured on the basement floor, when she came by with Caroline's weekly grocery order. Lois's husband, Shorty, farms the land Caroline still owns, and takes care of clearing the snow and keeping the grass mowed in the yard. Sarah can't imagine Caroline moving in to Sunny Haven where each resident and all of their frailties are on such public display.

"So …" Cara is saying. "Do you ever see her?"

Sarah used to see Caroline out in the yard tending to her flowers in a huge straw hat, her face protected from the sun and the curious eyes of anyone driving by. There were so many times Sarah had wanted to pull in, walk out to the gardens and see how Caroline was doing. It wasn't easy for her to erase the memories of that old house, to pretend the years she knew Caroline had never existed just because Jack didn't want them to.

After her husband, Eldon, died, sightings of Caroline grew more and more infrequent. Lois told Sarah that Caroline went away for extended periods of time but she'd never tell Lois where she'd been. Sarah wondered if it was her daughter, Becca, she'd been visiting and why she wouldn't want anyone to know that.

Sarah would occasionally catch a glimpse of Caroline in a window, a slight flicker of movement behind a wavering curtain, and it brought her a strange kind of comfort, just knowing she was still there.

On her way home, Sarah stops at her father's house. It's been empty since he moved in to Sunny Haven, and Jack has finally convinced her it's time to let it go. Her grandfather, James Coyle, built the house on Railway Avenue next to Coyle's Blacksmith & Repair in the 1930s and raised his family there. When Sarah's father took over the business, he inherited the ramshackle two-storey house, never leaving it until he nearly burned the place down.

Sarah never lived anywhere else; she went straight from her father's house to the house trailer on the farm after she married Jack. She was the middle child and the only girl in a family of rowdy brothers. Patrick and Paul were nearly teenagers when Sarah was born, followed right after by Brian, then Charlie, each of them two years apart. Her father liked to say the two older boys were for him, tough and hard and meant to grow up fast to work with him in his shop while the others, coming so much later, were extras for their mother. And Sarah came to believe her mother must have felt that way, too. She and her little brothers were nothing but extra work, additional mouths to feed. More babies to take care of when their mother might have believed she was free of those demands.

Her father used to tell the story of how he'd met their mother at a country dance. She was dancing a polka with a bowlegged farmer, her head tipped back and all those black curls flowing out around her; she was delicate and small-boned, nothing at all like the other Ukrainian farm girls with their wide shoulders and broad backs. Joe was instantly drawn to her and he asked her for the next dance. Wiry and fast and light on his feet, he swept her away.

Time and pain have dulled most of Sarah's memories of her mother, but there is one, still, she vividly remembers. It was July; Sarah was six years old, too young at the time to understand the impact her mother's absence would have on the rest of her young life. Sarah's father and Patrick were painting the house a turquoise blue, a colour Sarah imagined the deep sea might be. Her father was scraping the windowsills with a wire brush and Pat was high on a ladder, smiling down at her with a paintbrush in his hand. With a flick of his wrist, a drop of blue, the size of a penny, splashed on her white canvas shoe. Her mother poked her head from a second-storey window and leaned out, resting her forearms on the sill. She wore a sleeveless yellow dress the colour of daffodils, her curly hair tumbling over her shoulders. Pat tapped her nose with his paint brush and the sweet sound of her seldom-heard laughter unfurled on the wind.

Now only a tinge of that mermaid blue is left on the north side of the house where a faded For Sale sign pokes out of the tall grass in the small yard. There were a few phone calls in the first few months after Sarah put up the sign, but no serious offers. She isn't surprised; the house is too close to the tracks for anyone to want to live there. In the winter, vandals kicked in the door and littered the place with beer cans and trash. Jack's been complaining about the ongoing costs of insurance and taxes and he worries about their liability should a teenager fall through the crumbling floorboards. The time has come to tear the house down. Let the roof collapse on the scant memories lingering in the empty rooms and bury the restless spirit of her mother in the rubble.

Sarah steps through shattered glass to get inside. A faint odour of smoke still lingers, even though it's been nearly three years since the fire. She had noticed her father becoming increasingly forgetful and irritable that year so she started dropping in more often, doing all his errands and dropping off casseroles he could heat up himself. One evening she came over with a pot of soup to find the house filled with black, oily smoke. Her father had put a full carton of eggs in the oven and set it to broil. Afterward, the case worker from the Health Authority told Sarah her father could no longer live on his own. He moved in with Sarah and Jack for a while but Sarah could barely keep track of him. He was constantly on the move, slipping out of the house whenever Sarah's back was turned. Toni once found him wading through the river, not far from the elm tree, and he punched her when she tried to coax him out of the water. Sarah was convinced the safest place for him was Sunny Haven and, reluctantly, she signed the necessary papers.

Sarah makes her way up the stairs to her old bedroom at the end of the hall, the smallest room in the house. She recently remembered her father once stashing papers away in a little nook behind her bed when she was a child and she's been wondering if there might be anything still left inside.

The room is empty, except for the narrow metal bed frame. Strips of water-stained wallpaper droop from the walls and wire hangers lie strewn on the floor. Sarah pushes the rusting headboard away from the wall, revealing a panel held in place by a bent nail.

Inside are two boxes; one is filled with chipped and faded plates wrapped in old issues of the *Ross Prairie Review*, and the other is full of musty invoices and yellowed tax returns bound with brittle rubber bands. She pushes them aside. Why would he save this junk?

She is about to close the panel door when she notices a tin box, smaller than a shoe box, pushed up against the back wall. She pries off the lid and lifts out a chunky glass bottle with a pliable bulb the size of a young hen's egg. The faint scent of rosewater wafts up when she squeezes it. There are also three King George VI half dollars, their faces worn smooth, and an ivory-handled brush with strands of black hair laced through the bristles. There are a half-dozen store-bought birthday cards and as many homemade ones. She opens a card with a drawing of a woman, the same size as the house and the trees, wearing a pink triangle dress. Someone, a teacher perhaps, printed *Happy Mother's Day* inside and she added her own name. SARAH. She remembers making that card and is surprised her mother saved it. At the bottom of the box are a few pieces of rhinestone jewellery and a bright red ribbon her mother might have once used to tie up her hair. Finally, there is a small red notebook from the *Farmer's Co-operative* with a picture of an antique tractor on the cover. The first yellowed page is filled with Cyrillic script, words like the ones etched on the oldest tombstones in St. Michael's country church cemetery. On the next page, she recognizes her grandmother's hand, the cautious, cramped way she printed *For Fear,* then more pages of indecipherable words. Further on are drawings of leaves — some serrated-edged, some oblong, others variegated or round — as well as sketches of dwarf bushes and gnarled tree bark and berries coloured in with wax crayon. There are notations for various ailments: gout, lady "trubbles," colic. There is even a map with an X marking a spot along a winding creek with a large boulder and an arrow pointing to a trio of flat-topped mushrooms.

Sarah smiles, remembering the way Baba kept the best mushroom-picking spots carefully guarded secrets. She flips another page, wondering why her mother saved Baba's notebook along with the other unusual keepsakes. From what Baba told her, Sarah's mother, Olivia, rejected Baba's old ways and believed the faith-healing rituals and herbal remedies should have been left behind in the old country. She wanted no part of them. Why then, would she save the book?

Sarah keeps flipping until, on the very last page, written in a different hand, she finds this: *Save for Sarah*. There is a rustling in the walls — squirrels or mice — and Sarah shivers a little. Her mother wrote those words and it feels strange reading them, as if her mother is reaching out across time with a message for her. She wanted Sarah to have the little book.

Tucking it back in the box, she takes the book with her, leaving the old house and its memories behind.

The feud between the Bilyks and the Webbs started over the sale of Pete Tilley's land. Being right next door, Eldon Webb had expected to buy it like he did much of the land that came up for sale, by outdoing the final bid. But Jack's father, Anton, convinced Tilley to sell it to him without giving Eldon a chance to make an offer. He drove old Pete straight to the lawyer's office to sign the papers before Eldon could get wind of it. Eldon was furious at being outsmarted by a Bilyk. Eldon once shot Anton's dog, and there were other disputes over the years: wandering cows, toxic drift from a sprayer, tractor tires punctured by a set of overturned harrows left in Anton's field. Not to mention all the trouble with Jack, later. Sarah doesn't expect the news that Caroline is moving in to Sunny Haven to go over well with him, who still holds a grudge against Eldon Webb, long dead, and Caroline, too.

When she gets home, Sarah drives through the farmyard to see if Jack is there. His truck isn't parked by the workshop, but the overhead door is open and the MX tractor that was parked inside with the hood wide open that morning is gone. Anton is sitting at the front of the shop on an old wooden chair, sorting nails from a five-gallon pail into three dented coffee cans.

She pulls up in her truck. "Hey, Anton. Is Jack around?"

"No. Fixing fence. Doesn't want no more dead calves. Jack thinks maybe it's coyotes killing them, and it could be. Maybe even dogs. I told him about a pack that went crazy around here, years back. Chased down calves for the hell of it till they keeled over and died. Eldon Webb put an end to it, driving around, shooting every dog, including our Duke, whether they were guilty or not."

Anton lives in the farmhouse in the yard, the one where Jack and his sisters grew up. After Allison was born and Sarah and Jack had outgrown the house trailer, Anna, her mother-in-law, talked about retiring, moving to a house in town so Jack and Sarah could have the farmhouse. But Anton wouldn't hear of it. With the soil and the sun flowing through his veins, they all knew Anton would never leave the farm. So Jack and Sarah built a new home next to the trailer. It was handy, having Anna in the same yard to help out with the girls when Sarah was needed to run a combine or pick up seed in the spring, but she wishes they'd all stood up to Anton and insisted that he and Anna move to a place with a smaller yard and garden for Anna to look after.

When Anna died suddenly of a heart attack, life, as they knew it, folded in on itself. Eventually they got used to living without her, but it was hardest for Anton; she'd stood beside him for nearly fifty years. It was the farm — the grinding familiarity and routine of the seasons — and his three grand-daughters that finally gave him his peace. He still helps Jack with the field work, harrowing or cutting hay, simple chores that take him twice as long to complete as it would take Jack. Jack often says he catches him dozing in the tractor or finds the swather idling in the hayfield while Anton wanders along the edge of the field, filling his cap with saskatoons.

Allison's van is parked by the house; she called Sarah earlier to ask for a favour. "Do you want to come to the house for a cup of coffee and see Connor?" Sarah asks Anton as she climbs back into the truck.

He smiles, a gap-toothed grin. He adores his great-grandson and clings to a slim hope that Connor will take over the Bilyk land some day. It doesn't occur to him one of the girls might want to farm, although that's unlikely. Anton is bound to an old country tradition, believing land should pass from the heart of a man to the hands of a son. Although he tried not to show it, Anton couldn't hide his disappointment when Toni was born. They named her Antonia, to try to make it up to him, but he got the same pained look he'd had after Anna died when Jack told him they wouldn't have another. He loved each of the girls, bouncing them on his knee when they were babies, crooning a Ukrainian song about flying birds as they followed his dancing fingers with their bright little eyes. But they weren't the boy he'd hoped at least one of them would be.

• • •

Sarah comes into the kitchen and Connor, wearing his Superman cape, bounds across the room and leaps into her arms.

"Hey, how's my little superhero?" she says, kissing the top of his head.

"Mommy said I sleep over!"

Allison waddles around the corner with a sheepish look on her face. "That's my favour. Is that okay, Mom? He's just about bouncing off the walls. I don't have the energy for him in this heat."

Allison is seven months pregnant, carrying her baby straight out in front of her the way Sarah carried each of her girls. She looks like Jack, with the same acorn-coloured hair and tall, slim build, although her face and fingers are puffy from the heat.

"Sure you can stay with us, sweetie," Sarah says. "You can help Baba water her flowerpots after we have supper, okay?"

"Thanks, Mom. I am just so tired chasing after him all day. How am I going to do this when I have another one? I'll never get through it."

"Oh, yes, you will. You'll survive it. All mothers do. It's not easy, especially when all that's keeping you going is a couple hours' sleep and a strong pot of coffee."

"Survive what?" Jack asks, appearing at the back door with his grimy ball cap in his hand.

"Motherhood," she says as Jack leans down for a hug and Connor launches himself into his embrace.

"Gido! Come! See my tractor!" Connor says before rushing back to the living room, where he is using his toy tractor to cultivate the carpet.

"I guess you and Mom are keeping Connor for me tonight."

"Big date?"

"Gido! I is waiting!" Connor calls from the living room.

"I wish. No, Jason's on call this week but maybe he'll take me to the Tempo tonight and spring for an ice cream cone."

"Me having ice cream, too!" Connor pokes his head around the doorway.

Allison sinks into one of the kitchen chairs, picks up a grocery-store flyer from the table, and fans herself. "I swear, how did he hear that? I bet if I told him we were going home and he had to put that tractor away, he'd be deaf as a stump."

Jack goes to the living room to help Connor set up lengths of white plastic fence and place the cows and pigs in their pens, while Sarah tells Allison about her visit to Sunny Haven.

"I took Connor to see Grandpa last week," Allison says. "As usual, he didn't have a clue who I was. In fact, he was a little hostile toward Connor. He was looking at those photos in Grandpa's room, pointing and naming all of us, and Grandpa got upset with him. He said Connor shouldn't touch the pictures, that he was breaking his things."

"He was agitated today, too. Going on about some poor dead person. I didn't know what he was talking about but I think he meant old George across the hall."

"Has anyone moved in to that room yet?"

The back door slams. Maeve, home from her summer job in the city for a week of holidays, has just picked Toni up from work. The girls are four years apart and couldn't be more different. Toni is a dreamer, creative and eloquent, while Maeve sees the world in concrete terms. Toni wants to be a writer while Maeve is working on her MBA.

"Does it have to be so bloody hot?" Toni says, plunking into the chair nearest the fan. She gathers her black curls, holding them up with one hand away from her slender neck, and leans into the fan's weak breeze. Maeve has the fair skin and strawberry-blond hair of the Coyles, her face flushed and her hair sprung into tight curls.

"Aunty have ice cream?" Connor asks, coming into the kitchen hauling Toni's beloved old bear, Boo, by one arm.

"Hey, little man," Maeve says, scooping him up for a kiss. "Ice cream sounds wonderful."

Anton, leaning on his cane, limps into the kitchen and lowers himself into the nearest chair.

"It's too hot for June. What's the temperature anyway?"

Toni pulls her iPhone out of her jeans pocket. "Thirty-one."

"No, the real temperature. Sarah, check the thermometer," Anton says, waving to the window.

"Eighty-eight," she says automatically. She's been converting the temperature from Celsius to Fahrenheit for him for over thirty years.

"How can you know how hot it is outside by looking at that?" Anton says, pointing at Toni's phone with his chin.

"It's an app, Gido. You can check your phone for any place you want. Just click on it and it'll tell you what the weather's like there."

"App, shmapp. Phones are for talking, and only when there's something important to tell somebody. Years back, we had only one phone, hanging on the wall, not something so small, like a deck of cards, you can put in your pocket," Anton says, flapping one hand at Toni. "And party lines, six of us sharing. And a good thing, too. That party line saved the farm that time there was that big fire."

"Gido, you need a cellphone," Toni says, egging him on. "That way Dad can keep track of you, know where you are and what you're doing."

"Phhht. He knows what I'm doing. What I tell him I'm doing before I leave in the morning with the tractor, that's what," he says.

After Sarah pours the coffee, Allison gives Connor a peanut butter cookie and a glass of milk and settles him on Anton's lap. "You never finished telling me about your visit with Grandpa, Mom."

"Poor Grandpa," Sarah says, sitting down with a cup of coffee. "Sometimes I wonder why I even bother to visit. He doesn't even know I'm there."

"Sure he does," Allison replies. "He may not know who you are, but, at some level, he must remember you, your voice, the way you speak to him. He seems to relax when you're there and he calms right down."

"Poor old Joe. It was hard when Anna died, but at least she went to bed that last night with everything good as ever up here," Anton says, tapping his head with one finger. "She had the potatoes peeled, ready in the pot to cook the next morning for the *peroheh*. That's how I want to go. Quick, like that. With my workboots on."

"It seems unfair, really," Toni says, reaching for a cookie. "Grandpa's so spry, built for speed, like he used to say, motoring around the care home like he's thirty years old. And then there are the others, strapped in their wheelchairs, like Mrs. Atchison, who can't say a word, yet you know she's still in there, those green eyes twinkling, wanting to ask how we're doing like she used to when you bumped into her in the post office."

"I think it's better to be like Grandpa, actually," Maeve says, wiping a drip of milk off Connor's chin with her thumb. "Sure, it's terrible, him not knowing who any of us are anymore, but at least he's forgotten what happened to Uncle Pat and he doesn't remember that his wife ran off and left all of you."

The kitchen goes silent except for the gurgle of the coffee pot. Even though Patrick died when Sarah was a child, the girls have grown up knowing him in the same way they know their grandmother, Anna, and Sarah's own baba. She has kept their memories alive for the girls, showing them pictures and sharing stories about them. But they all know they are never to speak about Sarah's mother, although Anton once told Sarah she looked like her, with the same black curls. It might have been the way she flinched, or the dark look that surely passed over her face, but he never mentioned her to Sarah again.

"So you were about to tell me about Grandpa's new neighbour," Allison says in an attempt to change the sombre mood. "Anyone we know?"

Sarah hesitates, her heart suddenly pounding. She is reminded of the promise she made to Jack long ago, the agreement they have to keep the hurtful truth of the past buried where it belongs. She's protected him for so long but how can she be expected to continue now that Caroline is moving in across the hall from her father?

They're all looking at her, wide-eyed, waiting for her answer, when Connor tips over his cup, splashing milk all over the table. Anton shouts, "Holy geez!" and Toni jumps up, cupping her hands to catch the spill before it drips over the edge. Sarah hurries to the sink for the dishcloth and breathes a sigh of relief. In the ensuing chaos, Allison's question is forgotten.

CAROLINE

Caroline is reminded of the Tupper twins, girls she once knew from school, as she watches two of the smallest girls in the choir's front row cover their mouths with their hands and whisper. Twins, possibly, but surely sisters; they have identical turned-up noses, pointed chins, and straight black hair with bangs that need trimming. They're wearing the same navy trousers, blue T-shirts, and sashes as the rest of the girls but the uniforms of this pair look as though they've been dug out of a heap of dirty laundry at the foot of a bed. One of them points at the row of wheelchairs and they giggle behind their hands. Caroline is tempted to wag her finger at them. "Born in a barn," her mother used to say whenever Caroline was rude or forgot her manners.

While Cara, the young aide, dressed her this morning, Caroline argued that she should be allowed to stay in her room.

Why did she have to take part in these pointless social events, wheeled out into the common room and set out on display for everyone to gawk at like a heifer in an auction ring? Cara told her it would do her good; taking part in group activities stimulated Caroline's brain. There's nothing wrong with my brain, Caroline shot back. It was her broken-beyond-repair hip that had sentenced her to spend the rest of her days in this dreaded wheelchair.

A middle-aged woman, wearing the same royal-blue sash as the girls, taps two sticks together and the group starts to sing, slightly off-key, although one of the older girls in the back row has a lovely voice and is carrying the melody almost single-handedly. It's a song Caroline remembers playing on the radio when she was a girl and, after a few bars, she feels her shoulders relax from where they've been hunched up under her ears. She's thinking about a rainbow stretched across a bright blue sky when there's a commotion near the kitchen. The man who lives in the room across the hall is paddling his hands at loose air while Scott, the orderly (although Caroline's been told they don't call male attendants that anymore), has his arms wrapped around him from behind, holding him an inch or two off the floor. The old man kicks out with one foot and knocks over a small table holding a pitcher of pink juice and it crashes to the floor. The sisters quit singing and stare and, one by one, the voices of the little choir trickle out as a woman hurries across the room and takes the old man by the hand. He shakes his head the way a defiant two-year-old might and, between Scott and the woman, is led away.

After what seems like an hour, the choir resumes its song and Caroline sighs. This is what her life has come to; nothing but all this endless waiting. She is wheeled out to wait for breakfast and lunch and supper. Wheeled out to wait for everyone to be assembled and settled before any activity begins. She's been here a week and doesn't know if she can survive the tedium of this place.

After her fall down the basement stairs, she'd spent eight weeks in the hospital, a horrid place, the food tasteless and her room so close to the nurses' desk it was never quiet or dark enough to get a proper sleep without one of those small orange pills. She thought she would eventually return to her own house with the help of home care once her hip was healed (not that she wanted strangers popping in and out at all times of day) but she was told she would have to be panelled. Panelled? She was thinking of the wood-looking sheets Eldon had once nailed up on the porch walls when Dr. Boutreau told her she couldn't go home. Her injury was too severe; she would never walk again.

The woman is back, speaking to a nurse by the overturned table while the janitor mops up the juice. "May I go back to my room?" Caroline asks Cara.

"You're not enjoying the sing-song?"

"Oh, yes. The girls are very good, it's just that I'm feeling unwell."

Cara sighs. "You win." She tosses the towel she's holding onto a chair and takes Caroline back to her room, settling her into bed and handing her the remote control.

"Is there anything else you need right now?" Cara asks as she tucks an afghan over Caroline's feet.

"Just some peace and quiet, and would you please close my door?"

When Cara is gone, Caroline switches on the television. There is never anything to watch during the day; talk shows with silly celebrities, or afternoon doctors discussing bowel issues or personal family matters that should be kept within the walls of one's own home. Why would anyone willingly air such private details and bring such disgrace to their families? She turns off the television and leans back on her pillow, closing her eyes.

Life has changed so much since she was a girl. Young people marrying *after* the birth of their children or living together without walking down the aisle at all, for instance. No one bats an eye these days when a single girl gets herself in trouble. Adultery and divorce are so commonplace no one thinks anything of it. How different things were back then. Family secrets were kept in the shadows, elaborate stories woven to cover or protect the shame.

Don't think. Don't think. 'Two roads diverged in a yellow wood, / And sorry I could not travel both …' She begins the Robert Frost poem in her mind.

Long ago, she learned she could replace her troubled thoughts by mentally reciting poetry, a trick she used most often on nights when Eldon still came to her bed, his presence there weighing on her conscience. But after Eldon died, her secret finally lay dormant. Without him around to remind her daily of her transgression, she was rarely disturbed by it. It was this upheaval, the move to this horrendous place with the clatter of trays in the dining room and the constant stream of people milling around that had brought everything spewing back to mind. Never a moment's peace. A tear springs to her eye. *Don't think. Don't agonize over such things. 'And be one traveller, long I stood.' I can't bear it. Haven't I suffered enough?*

Her thoughts are a jumble as she tries to relive the summer day Becca went away. If she could just get it clear in her mind. It's so long ago; she can scarcely remember. Was it Jack or Eldon or both, facing her down with such bitter hatred in their eyes? Bilyk or Webb? Who blamed her more?

Outside of her room, she hears wheelchairs rolling down the hall as Cara and the other aides return her new neighbours to their rooms. *All of them, like me, without much use left for this world*, she thinks. *Sunny Haven: the last home for all of us as we wait to die.* She closes her eyes. She must find her peace soon before it's her time, but how will she do it?

Perhaps if she goes back to the beginning and comes out at the end of that fateful day she might uncover some clue she has missed. If she replays each detail of those long-ago years in her mind, she might remember. She must bring them all back, starting with her parents; her mother, who she loved beyond measure, and her demanding father, to whom she was bound. And Eldon Webb, who she met on a blustery spring day.

She should have been studying for a history exam but she was sitting at the kitchen table, lingering over a page in the Eaton's catalogue, admiring smart and stylish spring coats — a red, double-breasted one with silver buttons in particular — when her mother turned down the radio and peered out the window into the swirling snow. "Henry," she said to Caroline's father. "Someone's coming down the lane. Who would venture out on a day like this?"

Caroline joined her mother at the window. A man wearing a long, tan-coloured coat with the collar pulled up over his ears leaned into the wind as he ploughed his way toward the house through snow halfway to his knees. The wind had picked up considerably in the last hour — the snow drifted and swirled — and Caroline could just make out the dark shape of the truck he'd driven off the lane by the mailbox next to the road.

Her father had been reading the *Manitoba Co-operator*, commenting on the market report, which he did every Sunday afternoon. He was a man who believed in hard work, sixteen hours a day, six days a week, and he thought God intended folks to rest on the seventh day like it said in the Bible, although he, himself, didn't attend services at St. Paul's Anglican Church with Caroline and her mother. "That'll be Eldon Webb," he said, folding the paper and tossing it into a cardboard box he kept next to his chair. He made no effort to move, to look out and see where Eldon had driven off the road or to find his boots and put on his winter parka so he could head out and start up the tractor to pull Eldon's truck out of the ditch.

"And how would you know that, settin' there?" Caroline's mother took the tea towel draped over her arm and swiped at the steamy window again to take another look. "The fool's not even wearing a hat," she said, shaking her head.

"I know it because he said he'd stop by one of these days. Said he had something he wanted to talk to me about."

"Picked a fine time to drop by, in the middle of a bloody snowstorm. What's he doing coming 'round here?"

"We got business and such to discuss, if you think you need to know."

"Did you forget about the last time you crossed paths with those Webbs? Old Elvina waving her arms, complaining about that young bull you sold them. You're just asking for trouble if you plan on selling them any of our stock again."

"You just don't worry yourself about what I'm plannin'," Caroline's father said, getting up from his chair. He went to the door and threw it wide open before Eldon had a chance to knock. A blast of frigid air and the fresh, crisp smell of newly fallen snow pressed in on the heels of the tall stranger.

"Henry. Mrs. McPhee," Eldon said. His ears were pink from the cold and the top of his thinning red hair was dusted with feathery snowflakes the size of dimes. He nodded at

Caroline and said, "Hello, Caroline," which surprised her. She'd never met him before, though she'd seen him around town and passing by on the road, barely lifting one finger from the steering wheel to wave. She hadn't expected him to even know her name. Fine wrinkles fanned out from his pale blue eyes and he had a weak, inconsequential chin, despite the confident way he held his head. He turned back to Caroline's father. "It's like driving blind out there. Couldn't see where the lane was at all and steered my truck straight into the ditch there. Not the first impression I'd hoped to make."

He laughed and Caroline's father shook his hand and invited him in. Right away, Caroline's father started in on a story about an April blizzard just like this one when he was a boy, a tale Caroline had heard before — how he'd found three newborn calves, dead, all twelve legs tangled together, piled up against a fence when the snow melted — so she turned and was on her way up to her room to study when her father called out. "Caroline, don't run off. Come back here and cut us a piece of that cake you baked yesterday."

Caroline glanced at her mother, who had actually baked the lemon pound cake. Her mother pursed her lips in that angry way she had whenever Caroline's father said or did some fool thing that wasn't worth wasting her breath on. Her mother tipped her head toward the fancy covered cake plate and yanked open a drawer, rifling through the ladles and wooden spoons until she found a serrated knife and set it down on the counter. "First you'd best put the kettle on. We'll be needing some tea."

Caroline filled the kettle and put it to boil, aware all the while of Eldon watching her every move. She was conscious of her hair; the careless way she'd bunched it together and tied it into a ponytail with a frayed ribbon that morning without even brushing it when she'd found out they weren't going to church because of the storm. He was making her feel uneasy, off-kilter, the way she felt when she was called to the blackboard at school by Mr. Nott and given a difficult mathematics question to solve. She pictured herself standing in front of the class, chalk in hand, with no idea where to begin. Picking up the knife, she turned it over and looked at it hopelessly.

"Just cut four pieces," her mother said, not unkindly, and handed her four china plates. "Where is the blasted teapot?" she muttered under her breath, flinging open the breadbox and every cupboard door before she finally located the teapot next to the drinking-water pail where it always sat.

Caroline cut the cake and placed Eldon's plate in front of him. He reached for it and his hand, unusually clean for a farmer, with a palm smooth as a tabletop, brushed her arm. "How's school, Caroline? Only a few months to go, eh?"

"It's all right," she said. "I'll be glad when it's over and summer holidays are here."

"All right? It's better than all right. She won't say, but she walks away with all sorts of awards each year for high marks and such," her father said, with the same enthusiasm he had when he talked about the brand new Farmall tractor parked out in the shed.

"Dad," Caroline said, looking down at her plate. "Last year I got an award for history. It's Susan who gets all the awards."

"Don't sell yourself short, missy. Our Caroline's one smart cookie, isn't she, Mother?"

Caroline's mother stood at the sink, eating her cake standing up the way she always ate her dessert. "I will say she's got a brain in her head, which is more than some people," she said.

Caroline's father took a huge gulp of tea then shifted the conversation to the market outlook for wheat until they were finished.

"That was a fine cake, Caroline," Eldon said as he was putting on his coat. Her father had already gone to start up the tractor and her mother was clattering plates into the enamel dishpan behind them. "Maybe I'll stop by again, if that's all right with you."

Caroline didn't know what to say. She hadn't heard her father and Eldon discuss any sort of business at the table but perhaps they hadn't gotten around to talking about the purchase of bulls or yearling heifers. She wasn't sure why he needed her approval to come back and speak to her father.

As soon as Eldon was out the door her mother said, "You should have said no, Caroline. 'No, it's not all right with me.'" She dumped the tea leaves into the slop pail under the sink and rinsed out the pot. "I don't want that man coming 'round. Just wait until your father comes back. By God, he'll hear what I think about Eldon Webb sniffing 'round here." She pumped a splash of water into the dishpan, added some hot water from the kettle and took a deep breath. She turned, calmer now, and put her hands on Caroline's shoulders. "I'll wash up these plates. You go on up to your room and study for that test. I don't care, one way or another, 'bout any awards, but you *will* graduate and head off to the city this fall like we talked about."

Later, after Caroline closed her notebook and was preparing for bed, she heard the rising swell of her mother's voice coming from the kitchen and the low rumble of her father's voice as he answered. He had returned to the house after pulling Eldon out of the ditch, stamping snow off his boots and raving about the new truck Eldon had just bought at Hubley Ford. Her mother just sat there at the table with one of his grey work socks stretched over a jar, darning a hole in its heel, and didn't say a word, not about Eldon or his truck or any other thing. Caroline's father said, "Well, that's that, then," and there was nothing but stony silence between them for the rest of the afternoon and all through the evening — the only sounds the sizzle of frying pork, the rustle of newspaper pages, the scraping of forks against plates during supper. So when Caroline heard her parents begin to speak, she crept out of her room to the top of the dark stairs and crouched there to listen.

"What were you thinking, Henry? What are you up to?"

"Leave it alone, Violet. It's none of your concern."

"If Caroline's not my concern, then what is? Thirty-four years it's been without a word from me, settin' back and letting you take the reins, making all the choices for this farm, this life we set out on together. Settin' there all those years ago, quiet as a fence post, when you waltzed into the bank and borrowed money to buy Beulah's land, without the thought even entering your skull that maybe you shoulda asked my opinion. And it grieved me when you lost it, and to William Webb, no less, but I never said a thing. I kept my mouth shut, even though I knew better, when you sowed the oats that year ahead of all the neighbours so's it froze and wasted all that seed. But I'll be damned if you won't hear what I have to say when it comes to my own daughter."

A chair scraped across the floor.

"Don't you go running off to the barn like you do. I want an answer. What was Eldon Webb doing here? And don't start up with one of your fancy tales."

"Bumped into him in town yesterday, is all. And I thought maybe, instead of him sittin' up there in that big house on a Sunday afternoon, he might want to come by for a cuppa coffee."

A cupboard door slammed. "He can have coffee with that hoity-toity mother of his, the two of them, settin' there in that fancy house with their noses stuck up in the air, thinking they're better than the rest of us. When we all know she grew up poor as a church mouse, like we all did. Married for money, and flauntin' it over all the rest of us."

"What's it gonna hurt? Him meetin' Caroline? She's as pretty as any other girl in Ross Prairie, and just as smart."

"I knew you were trotting her out for a reason, you old fool. Have I been talking to the barn door these last couple years? She's decided to head off to work in the city this fall whether you like it or not. She wants an education. If you'd set aside money every year like I asked, she'd be able to start class with Susan in September instead of having to wait until she's saved up enough on her own."

"A girl her age needs a husband. With land. Lots of it. Not more schoolin'."

"What's a girl to do without schooling? Where did that get me? Bound to this farm tighter than twine to a spool, that's where. Working harder than any hired hand ever did till Caroline came along. Nothing to show for it but raw knuckles and an aching back." A lid clanked forcefully on a pan.

"I never made you stay. You could've set off down that road any time you cared to."

"And gone where?" Her mother's voice was trembling now. "With nothing more than the shirt on my own back?"

"That's the trouble with you. You were never happy. Not with this farm or any other damn thing I ever did." The screen door hit the wall then the big door slammed.

"You're wrong about that. I got Caroline, didn't I? The only damn thing you ever did right!" Caroline's mother called after him.

Soon the light would come on in the barn like it always did after one of her parents' late-night arguments. When the weather was fair, her father would often stay there all night, sleeping in the straw under a worn wool blanket. Their battles were fierce but brief, moving in like late-summer thunderstorms, over quickly after a few harsh words. Caroline wondered if everyone's parents fought that way. She couldn't imagine her friend Susan's parents saying the hurtful things her parents shouted to one another. She had spent enough time at the Wawryks' place, all those noisy brothers and sisters — eight others besides Susan — and her jolly mother with a baby in her arms as long as Caroline had known her. When Susan's father came in from the dairy barn, long after the children had been fed, he would kiss Susan's mother on the cheek and say, "How's my Missus?" And she would blush and hand him a child and set out the dinner plate she'd kept warm for him in the oven.

The next day at school, Caroline found Alice and Susan waiting for her beside the water fountain. Lurking nearby were the Tupper twins, the worst gossips at school. Caroline put her arms around her friends' shoulders and they huddled, heads together, while she told them about Eldon's visit.

"You're so lucky!" Alice said, popping up her head and stepping back.

"Lucky?" Caroline asked. "What's so lucky about that?"

"He *is* the most eligible bachelor in Ross Prairie. A real catch." Alice, with her dowdy dresses and mousy hair, was plain as a paper bag. She was always talking about boys and her main ambition in life seemed to be securing a boyfriend for herself. "Any girl would give her right arm to be married to him."

"Who's talking about marriage?" Caroline grabbed Alice's arm and steered her away from the eavesdropping Tupper twins and down the hallway toward their classroom.

"And how *old* is he?" Susan asked, following along. "I've heard my Aunt Jane mention him. They went to school together. He has to be in his thirties."

"Geez Louise," Alice said as they waited outside their classroom for the bell to ring. "He's obviously trying to court you, Caroline. You two both need to learn a thing or two about men."

Caroline rolled her eyes. As if Alice was such an expert. She lived under the strict thumb of her mother and wasn't allowed to stay out past eight o'clock, even on weekends. She'd never even had a boyfriend. Not that Caroline had much experience. She'd only ever dated one boy, Robby Mathers, when she was in grade ten. He was a town boy, cheeky and loud, but he was good-looking with that cleft in his chin like Kirk Douglas, so she'd agreed to go to a dance with him. But once he asked her to go steady, he changed, or else she hadn't noticed his annoying habits before. She disliked the way he acted, showing off in front of the other boys, tripping poor Gregory Porter and knocking him around, bragging about his father's new car, as though that might impress her. They'd broken up after two months.

"He talked to my father most of the time and we had cake, for goodness' sake," Caroline said. The Tupper twins were skulking behind them again so she dropped her voice. "I'm not *marrying* the man."

"But let's just say you did," Alice continued. Caroline could tell she was enjoying the fantasy, imagining herself, perhaps, in Caroline's shoes. "If you did, you wouldn't have to lift a finger. His mother never does. They have a housekeeper and a hired man to do the outside chores. And you could take the train to Winnipeg like Mrs. Webb does and stay at the Fort Garry Hotel and buy all your clothes at Eaton's or Hudson's Bay. Can you imagine never wearing another homemade dress and having all those shoes?"

The bell rang and Caroline linked her arm with Susan's as they proceeded to assembly. "I'm not the least bit interested in dating him," she said. "I'm going to the city with Susan in September like we planned. I'm going to work in an office or a department store while she's in class at United College." She glanced over her shoulder at the Tupper twins. "We're leaving this boring little town for bigger and better things, aren't we, Susan? And we're never coming back."

It was the middle of May and the sun lingered a few extra minutes each day, warming the earth. Tractors and drills had been rolling for a couple of weeks and Caroline's father was keeping long hours, trying to finish sowing the wheat by Victoria Day.

Caroline noticed the clothesline as she walked down the lane after the school van dropped her off, the careless way her mother had hung out the laundry — everything dangling willy-nilly, flapping towels mixed here and there among Caroline's blouses and her mother's wide skirts, her father's bibbed overalls brushing the grass next to short red-toed socks and two sets of pillow cases, not a one of them paired. A rake leaned against the clothesline pole, another job unfinished, and the wind whipped the wispy grass and crumbled leaves from a pile close to the house, scattering them back over the yard.

Old Smoky, the grain truck, its front fender tacked on with a twist of baling wire, was parked next to the house. It was her mother's job to drive the old relic out to the fields, hauling whatever seed was needed to fill up the drill, matching Henry's long hours, although lately she'd complained about the way her arms ached at the end of the day from wrestling with the steering wheel, holding Old Smoky to the road.

Caroline's old Lab, Lady, shaggy winter coat not yet completely gone, loped up and bunted her on the shin. "Hiya, girl," Caroline said, and reached down to scratch her under the chin.

Caroline opened the back door and dropped her books on the floor. The aroma of beef stew wafted through the kitchen from a covered pot simmering on the stove. The morning wash water, with its curdly film, still stood in a pail by the door and the sink was piled with unwashed dishes and pots. Half of a fat turnip, speared with a knife, sat in the middle of the otherwise empty table like a ghoulish centrepiece. There was no sound except the ticking clock and an occasional pop from the dying embers in the stove.

"Mum?" Her mother's workboots sat on the rug next to the door, her red flowered kerchief draped over a wooden chair. "Are you here?"

From upstairs, the familiar creak of the floorboard outside her parents' room and then the soft tread of her mother's feet on the stairs. She came around the corner, buttoning her blouse. Her hair — whiter than it had seemed just last week — was tousled, her eyes puffy from sleep.

"Are you home already?" she said, looking up at the clock. "I was supposed to have a box load of wheat seed at the Maxwell quarter by four thirty." She took her faded jacket from a hook by the door, put it on, and tied the red kerchief over her hair. "Make dumplings for the stew and leave the rest of this mess. I'll get to it later." She stepped into her boots, about to head out the door. "If I'm not back in an hour, come looking for me. Smoky's been acting up more than usual these last couple days and I don't need to be settin' somewhere, stranded on an old dirt road, when there's so much work to do."

A minute later, the truck roared out of the yard and Caroline glanced at the clock, then checked the stew. Her mother had hurriedly scratched out her dumpling recipe on an envelope and left it next to the breadbox. Caroline rarely saw her mother read a recipe; her cookbooks sat untouched on a shelf. She made buns and bread, white and chocolate and coconut cakes, oatmeal cookies and buttermilk muffins straight from her head, baking and cooking in the same easy way Mrs. Bell, the music teacher, sat down at the piano and played any tune. Caroline picked up the envelope and was headed to the pantry for the flour bin when she heard Lady bark. She peered out the window over the kitchen sink. A shiny blue truck bounced across the rutted yard and stopped by the house. During hard spring rains, her father — complaining about his arthritic hip and the time it took him to pick his way across the sloppy yard — often drove the tractor right up to the back door when he came in for meals, even though her mother nagged him often enough about the deep ruts it left. She had salvaged half a dozen old two-by-fours from the junk pile and thrown them over the ruts to keep mud from tracking in. Now, Eldon Webb carefully made his way across the planks, balancing with his arms outstretched, one foot in front of the other, even though the ground was perfectly dry and he could have walked right up to the house alongside her mother's flower bed if he wanted to.

Lady guarded the door, a low growl in her throat, while Caroline watched through the screen as Eldon stood outside and doffed his hat. His face was sunburned from long hours on the tractor but the broad expanse of his forehead under his receding hairline was glaringly white and it occurred to

Caroline how smooth and unlined, how free of worry, it was. He wore smartly pressed navy trousers and a cream-coloured shirt with a pale blue hanky tucked in the pocket. Even though it was a regular workday, it looked like he was headed out for a night on the town.

"Afternoon, Caroline."

"My father's not home," she said through the screen, not bothering to open the door. "He's sowing wheat at the old Maxwell place."

"I'm not here to see your father," Eldon said. "Mind if I come in?"

Eldon stayed for an hour and Caroline didn't get the dumplings made. After he left, she rushed out of the house, still in her school clothes, and raced down the country road in the family Buick, bumping over washboard and ruts, toward Maxwell's farm. She had just accepted an invitation to attend a concert with Eldon at the United Church. A string quartet from the city was coming to Ross Prairie — Maisie Stuart's grandson played the viola — on May 24. A busy time with farmers still in the fields, Caroline thought as she swerved to miss a barking dog. She had hesitated in answering him at first, knowing what her mother would have to say, but she'd kept looking at the clock, minutes ticking by, and she couldn't stop thinking about the unmade dumplings and her mother stuck along some back road in Old Smoky. Eldon wasn't showing any sign of leaving even though she'd served him two glasses of iced tea, so she finally agreed to go to the concert with him to get him out the door.

She saw her mother in the distance at the side of the road, waving her kerchief above her head, as though Caroline might not see Old Smoky pulled off the road, steam or smoke or both curling up from under the hood.

Her mother's hands were coated with sticky black grease and the smell of burnt rubber hung in the air. "Tried to get the belt off myself but I can't do it. I'll need a wrench or we might just have to come back with a chain and tow Old Smoky home. What took you so long anyway?"

Caroline could only imagine what her mother would say if she knew she'd been sitting in the kitchen, chatting with Eldon Webb about the crops he'd sown and the pleasant spring weather. Her mother looked so tired, Caroline didn't have the heart to tell her just yet that the dumplings weren't made, and she decided to wait until the time was right, whenever that might be, to tell her about her upcoming date.

Caroline was a bundle of nerves, getting ready. Why had she ever agreed to go to the concert with Eldon? She could have said she wasn't interested or had an important test to study for the next day. Why couldn't she just speak her mind and not worry so much about other people's feelings or what they thought of her? Susan, with her bright, shiny words, never held back. She came out and said whatever was on the tip of her tongue, just as she had when Caroline told her she was going to the concert with Eldon. "It's preposterous. Simply ridiculous that you consented to such a thing without giving it more thought," she'd said.

Her mother's face had grown stony and cold when Caroline finally told her. "He's too old for you," she said. She was standing at the sink, hands immersed to the wrists in a murky bucket of water.

"What's it going to hurt, just this once?"

"I know you might be impressed with his fancy new truck and the sharp way he dresses," her mother said, pointing a paring knife at her, "but there's something about him; those shifty eyes that don't seem to look right at you when he's talking, like he's scheming or thinking about some way to get the best of you even while he's standing right there in front of you. He might have your father fooled, but those Webbs, they can't pull anything over on me," she had said, and carried on peeling potatoes.

Caroline hadn't mentioned it to her father (she couldn't tell him about something as personal as a date with a man) but she assumed her mother must have, because he was in high spirits at suppertime, as chipper as he'd been in weeks, eyes shining as he talked a mile a minute about the new truck he was hoping to buy.

Caroline had two different outfits laid out on the bed. She first tried on a navy skirt with a soft pink blouse but it seemed frumpish, like something Alice might wear, so next she chose a sleeveless mint-green dress that showed off her curves, although she worried it might be too early in the season for a sundress.

She heard the creak of the stairs and turned to see her mother leaning against the doorway. She'd lost weight, and Caroline wondered why she hadn't noticed it until now. Her ample bosom had nearly disappeared and the bodice of her blue housedress was puckered in folds from the apron strings cinched tightly around her waist. "Need some help?"

"I can't decide what to wear."

"I'd put you in a burlap bag if it meant Eldon Webb would lose interest in you."

Caroline slipped into the dress and lifted her hair while her mother fastened the covered buttons. She sat at her vanity table in front of the mirror and her mother picked up a brush and pulled it through Caroline's thick golden hair.

"You look tired, Mum. Are you feeling all right?"

"I'm no spring chicken, Caroline. I'm slowing down. Can't do what I used to."

"You're not old," Caroline said, reaching back to touch her mother's hand.

"It wasn't fair to you, growing up with parents as worn out as a pair of old shoes. I hope you have your children when you're young, like I wish I could have done." Caroline's parents had been married for sixteen years before she was born, the first and only time her mother had carried a child. She squeezed Caroline's shoulder. "But not too young, mind you. Don't you be letting Eldon Webb get too close now," she warned.

Caroline laughed. "I've already told you I don't think of him in that way. But he seems nice enough."

"Don't be too sure of that. He's a sweet talker and they're the ones you have to watch out for. They know exactly what to say to sweep a young girl off her feet. He's two-faced like his mother, sweet and syrupy when they've got you face to face but just as likely to knock you flat on your arse once your back's turned. Before you know it, September will be here and you'll be off to start a new life. Don't you be letting Eldon Webb turn your head and change your plans."

"Oh, Mum." Caroline grasped her mother's wrist. "I'm not about to let that happen. Besides, Susan would kill me." She shook her head and let her hair settle in waves on her shoulders.

"Besides, there's something I need to tell you about the Webbs," Caroline's mother said, resuming her brushing. "Eldon was engaged once, about ten years ago. A city girl, someone he met when he went to agricultural college after high school."

Caroline caught her mother's eye in the mirror. "Who was she?"

"I don't know if I ever knew her name or heard it mentioned. That's the way the Webbs are. A secretive bunch. They always have been. Elvina's slick as ice, the way she controls talk 'round town, making up tales herself and dropping little bits off like bread crumbs here and there, changing how folks think. And Eldon's no better. Making themselves out to be something they're not."

Caroline twisted around on the stool to look at her mother. "What happened to the girl?"

"There was a June wedding planned at a ballroom in a fancy city hotel but in early spring it was called off. Folks wondered why, o' course, and Elvina was acting as though there'd never been an engagement, so that busybody Millie Tupper came right out and asked her 'bout it one day in the post office. The girl wasn't suited to life on a farm, Elvina said, so Eldon thought it best to let her go." She lifted one eyebrow skeptically.

"Did people believe that?"

"There was talk, o' course. Most folks, me included, believed it was the girl who dumped Eldon. I heard it was because she didn't care for the way Elvina always had her nose in his business, while others said it was something about Eldon himself that scared the girl off."

Caroline turned back to the mirror and twisted open a tube of lipstick. "You don't have to worry." She applied a coat to her lips. "I'm going to this one concert and that will be the end of it."

"You know tongues will start wagging the moment you walk into that church with him. Millie Tupper will have a story spread by the time the coffee's perked and, the next thing you know, folks'll be saying you two are planning a walk down the aisle."

Caroline stood and pecked her mother on the cheek. "Mum, it would be a frosty Friday before I'd even agree to another date, never mind letting him put a ring on my finger. I've got my whole life stretched out ahead of me, waiting for me to make my own way."

"And a sad day that'll be when we send you off." Her voice cracked and she looked down at her shoes.

"Oh, Mum. Let's not talk about that day yet. Once my final exams are over we'll have the whole summer to spend together. Just me and you." Caroline turned and fumbled through a drawer so her mother wouldn't see her eyes welling up. "Where's that yellow ribbon? Could you help me tie it in my hair?"

Millie Tupper was seated in the church foyer when Caroline and Eldon arrived. "Why, Eldon Webb and young Caroline McPhee!" she said as she handed Eldon a program and eyed his hand hovering at Caroline's waist, barely touching her.

He removed two tickets from his shirt pocket and handed them to Millie. "Judging from all the cars out there, it looks like it's a full house."

"Don't you worry about a thing. I'm sure your mother's saved you the best seats, up at the front where you always sit. Enjoy the show, you two." Millie gave Eldon a conspiratorial wink and turned to the next person in line.

Caroline spotted Nan and Fran Tupper, their necks craned and heads swivelled. They bent their heads together, whispering to one another as Eldon and Caroline made their way past the crammed pews. Four young musicians dressed in black pants and white shirts sat in chairs on the chancel tuning their instruments, plucking strings and turning keys as the discordant sounds filled the church above the low drone of voices.

Eldon took Caroline's elbow and steered her toward the pew at the front of the church. "There's Mother."

Mrs. Webb, wearing a purple flowered dress with a full skirt, stood in the aisle, fanning herself with a program. Caroline had seen her before, in Pipers' store selecting a roast from the butcher's counter or driving her Cadillac slowly down Main Street, but she had never actually met or spoken to her. Why hadn't Eldon mentioned his mother would be joining them for the concert?

"Here you are, Eldon. Finally. I was beginning to think you'd changed your mind about coming at all. I can't say I'd blame you, it's so terribly hot in here. Even with the door open, there's absolutely no breeze." She flapped the program in front of her flushed face, looking as wilted as the oversized satin rose that drooped over her ear from her small pink hat.

"Mother, this is Caroline McPhee," Eldon said.

"I know who she is," Mrs. Webb said, limply shaking Caroline's hand before turning and abruptly squeezing into the pew. Eldon slid in after her and Caroline took her place at the end of the pew on the aisle.

Mrs. Webb removed a lace-edged handkerchief from her patent-leather handbag and dabbed her glistening forehead. "Eldon, why don't you ask Millie or whoever's in charge here to open a window or two? Have they no concern at all about our comfort?"

Eldon stepped over Caroline and hurried off to the back of the church as the young minister, who didn't look much older than one of Caroline's grade-twelve classmates, spoke to the cellist before approaching the lectern, trying to get the audience's attention.

"Do you like classical music?" Mrs. Webb asked, turning to Caroline as she fiddled with one of the red gems dangling from her ear.

Caroline listened to the latest radio hits on Saturday evenings. Sometimes, when the girls were over, they pushed aside the chairs and table and jived, Susan and Alice pairing up, and Caroline coaxing her mother away from her work to be her dance partner. They would swivel their hips and twirl and laugh, sliding and swirling across her mother's freshly waxed kitchen floor.

Mrs. Webb looked at her expectantly, waiting for her reply, but luckily Eldon was back, standing in the aisle, and Caroline didn't have to admit she never listened to classical music. Marvin Tupper tugged at a hook at the top of an arched window with a long-handled stick while the minister tapped at the lectern with a pencil to get their attention. Millie Tupper bellowed, "Quiet!" from somewhere behind them and the chatter died as Eldon sat down beside Caroline and she slid closer to his mother. The quartet began its first piece, a haunting melody by Brahms in C minor.

Caroline closed her eyes, pleased at the way the music painted vivid, moving pictures in her mind and she wondered if this was what Brahms had intended; for a girl like her, sitting in a church hundreds of years later, to be reminded of two birds, soaring in wide, languid circles through a pale blue sky. She'd once seen two hawks in flight above one of her father's fields. They dipped and rolled beneath the clouds — at play, she thought — until the larger bird pitched steeply then climbed through the sky again, higher and higher, as though pursuing the smaller, more vulnerable bird. He dove upon it from above and, together, talons clasped, they plummeted in a spiralling crescendo toward the earth until, at the last moment, they'd released one another and swooped back up into the sky.

She opened her eyes and glanced at Eldon. He drummed his fingers on his knee, the tapping out of time with the music.

He was frowning — there was a deep pucker between his brows — and it made Caroline wonder what he was thinking about. He seemed to have no real interest in the music at all. After a few shorter numbers the audience applauded politely while the musicians took their final bow.

"Just wonderful, wasn't it?" Mrs. Webb said, standing in the aisle. "We should hurry downstairs so we're at the front of the coffee line. I noticed Maisie Stuart carrying a plate of her raisin tarts when you dropped me off, Eldon. I know they're your favourite."

"I don't think we'll be coming down for coffee," Eldon said. "Caroline needs to be home by nine thirty."

"Why, it's just eight o'clock," she said, frowning at him. "Do you need to go just yet? And how am I to get home if you leave now?"

"I've asked the Cornforths to give you a ride."

"Very well, then. I see you have this all arranged. You might have had the courtesy to tell me about it before the concert." Mrs. Webb huffed and turned to glare at Caroline.

Caroline felt herself blush. "It *is* early." She turned to Eldon. "There's time to have coffee first if you'd like."

"What I'd like," Eldon said, leaning in close so his mother couldn't hear, "is to take you for a short drive. There's something I want to show you."

On their way out of town, Caroline reached up and pulled the ribbon from her hair. The unmistakable smell of the end of a blistering hot day — a lazy scent that reminded her of summer holidays — swept through the open windows. Eldon had something to say about every one of his fields they passed, explaining what type of crop he'd planted or telling her how he or his father had come to own that specific piece of land. Caroline wasn't particularly interested. What did she care if

Eldon's father had won a hundred and sixty acres of scrub trees from Walter Nychuk in a poker game? They turned down another gravel road then slowed and rolled up to the Webbs' huge brick house. The front yard was dotted with a number of flower beds, splashed with the crimson red and vibrant yellow of dozens of tulips. A man working in a bed nearest to the road leaned on his spade and waved when they drove by.

They stopped in the yard and Eldon came around to open her door. "I'd like to show you where I live."

With none of their own land nearby and her school van on a different route, Caroline had only been past the Webb house a few times. She remembered the size of it because her mother had once commented that Elvina Webb might lose a few pounds if she had to hustle around that big house and do the cleaning herself.

Instead of walking in through the kitchen door like Caroline's family did at home, Eldon led her into a foyer through a massive front door with a stained glass inset as fancy as one of the windows at church. The foyer was bigger than the McPhees' living room with hardwood floors and a curved staircase off to one side. Through an arched doorway to the left was a sitting room. Every piece of furniture was polished to a gleaming shine.

"Have a seat," Eldon said. "I'll get us something to drink."

Caroline didn't feel right being alone with him in this big house without his mother or anyone else there but she settled in on a cream-coloured chesterfield with a tufted back. Oil portraits of a younger Eldon and his parents hung on the wall and she wondered why they'd had their pictures painted, why they wouldn't have just gone to a studio to have their photos taken like everyone else.

When Eldon returned with two glasses of red wine, Caroline wanted to tell him she didn't drink wine, but she took it anyway and let him clink their glasses together. "To a wonderful evening," he said, which surprised her. She didn't think he'd enjoyed the concert at all.

"So, what do you think of it?" Eldon leaned back on the chesterfield next to her and took a long sip.

She thought he was referring to the wine so she said, "It's not very sweet," and he tipped his head back and laughed. "I meant the house. What do you think of my house?"

"I thought this was your mother's house." Again, she'd said something without thinking, and she blushed when he chuckled.

"This house is meant to be mine someday," Eldon said, growing serious. "My mother keeps saying all these stairs are getting to be too much for her and she'd like a house in town."

"So why doesn't she move?"

"We're very close, my mother and I. You must know what it's like to be an only child. She has my best interest in mind and she's always said she won't leave until I'm married and settled, with a wife and a family of my own."

As a clock began to chime somewhere behind the stairs, it occurred to Caroline that Eldon might have had a family by now — a son nearly reaching his shoulder and maybe a little red-haired girl — if his engagement hadn't been broken off all those years ago.

"Have you thought about it?" Eldon asked.

"Thought about what?" The last of the chimes echoed through the empty house.

"Becoming a wife. Starting a family."

"Oh, eventually, I suppose. But I want to see a bit of the world first before I do that. There are so many things I'd like to do — dip my feet in an ocean, see Buckingham Palace, tour the ruins of Pompeii. And go to college, work at doing something I love. I want to make my own way before I become a wife and a mother."

Eldon frowned. "Farm girls didn't have such notions when I was in high school. Few of them even finished school."

Caroline felt her face grow hot. What was wrong with wanting a bit of a life before settling down to the same endless routine as most girls? "I'm not the only who thinks that way," she said. "Take my friend, Susan, for instance. She wants to be a linguist, or a professor, or the editor of a publishing house. I'd be happy enough to be a teacher working in a small town or even a country school, if it came to that."

Of course, there were many girls, like Alice, who didn't even consider other possibilities. They were content to finish school and just as quickly slip into a white dress and go straight from their father's house to a pulpit, coming out the church door as some man's wife, without knowing who they really were, or what it was that mattered to them. Without taking any time at all to listen to the singing in their own hearts. But that would never be enough for Caroline.

"Married life worked well enough for my mother and yours," Eldon said.

Isn't it wonderful that it's 1954 and, in this day and age, not all girls want to do what their mothers did? She could see there was no sense explaining things to Eldon. He was just like her father; one foot still rooted in the first half of the century with his outdated ideas. She wanted to tell him so, but what was the point? Instead, she put her empty glass on the small side table, smiled politely and asked if it was possible for him to please drive her home; it was getting late and tomorrow was a school day.

SARAH

Most of the seats around the table set up in the middle of the dance floor at the community hall are taken when Sarah arrives. Lorna Marsden, from the *Review*, is standing by the coffee pot, scribbling in a notebook, talking to Sam Wawryk, chair of the committee. He looks up and, when he sees Sarah, he waves. It is her first meeting of the committee set up to save the local emergency services. The Health Authority is planning to close the emergency room at the Ross Prairie hospital and replace the ambulance with service from Locklin, where the regional hospital is located. Local residents are worried about response times — the thirty minutes it will take for the ambulance to drive the extra distance — and they aren't willing to let go of the sense of security they have knowing the ambulance is parked nearby and ready to go. The committee was struck to convince the board to keep the service in town.

Lorna tucks her notebook into her purse and finds a spot at the table while Sam walks over to Sarah. "Thanks for coming. We're glad to have you on board."

She hasn't been on a committee since the girls were in school and, even then, it was only for groups they belonged to. She's kept her distance from the town since she married Jack. It wasn't easy to forget the way some of the townspeople treated her family and it bothered her when the rumours about Jack persisted. All heads would turn and a hush would fall over the coffee shop whenever she or Jack walked in, so they just quit going. They were content to busy themselves with the farm and their family; everything they wanted was there within the broad spread of their arms.

But when she and Jack attended the public meeting to save the emergency service last month, and they asked for volunteers to sit on a smaller committee, it seemed a worthy cause. "Glad to be here. Hope I can help."

There is one empty chair left, facing the door. She walks around the table and sits down directly across from Cady Rankmore, who is deep in conversation with a bleary-eyed Ted Hammond. Cady looks up, a furtive, sweeping glance, meant to look as though she's checking the time on the clock or something else of significance above Sarah's head, then turns back to Ted with an exaggerated flourish of her head and carries on with her story. It's an art Cady has perfected over the years, this skill of looking through people.

Heidi Dixon, a young mother of two, finishes scrolling through her phone and puts it in her purse when Sarah sits down beside her. "Hi, Mrs. Bilyk. I hope Sam gets this meeting started," she says, with a discreet nod across the table.

The meeting is called to order and, after Heidi volunteers to take notes, Sam takes off his reading glasses and parks them on top of his head. "Now, then. Tonight we need to decide the best way to present to the next meeting of the Authority board. Any ideas?"

"You'll present, won't you, Sam? With maybe one other person to attend for support?" Heidi says.

"I think we should all show up and let them know we're not going to be pushed around," Cady says, curling her lip like a Rottweiler with a warning. "There's strength in numbers."

"They already know we have the numbers behind us," Ted says. "Their chairperson and a few other board members were at the community meeting. They saw how this place was packed."

"They just nodded and listened," Cady cuts in. "Typical. We have to go in to their meeting and let them know we mean business. We pay taxes. They can't tell us what to do."

"Actually, they can," Sam says. "And it is meant to be a formal presentation. I don't think we need to show up with too many people and overtake the boardroom."

"I agree," Sarah says. "We need to come in with two or three people and a well-articulated presentation. Maybe a PowerPoint?"

"What do you all think of that idea?" Sam asks.

Ted and Heidi and most of the others nod in agreement. Cady presses her thin lips together and scribbles on her agenda with a ballpoint pen. After a lengthy discussion about the content of the presentation, it is decided someone will need to go over the video footage the local-access television station recorded at the public meeting and summarize the comments from those in attendance, and Sarah volunteers.

"Once we have that summary, would you be able to spend some time to help me put it all together?" Sam asks, and Sarah agrees.

"Who will be going to the meeting with Sam?" Heidi asks.

Cady's hand shoots up so quickly she knocks the pen she was doodling with onto the floor. "I can go."

Eyes blink. Ted Hammond clears his throat. The coffee pot sputters in the corner. Finally, Sam says, "Anyone else?"

"I think Sarah should go," Heidi speaks up. "After all, if she's made the notes and helped Sam put the presentation together, she'll be the most familiar with the content."

Again, everyone except Cady nods in agreement. "That's decided, then," Ted says, slapping the table with one hand. "Are we adjourned here?"

Sarah is tossing her coffee cup in the trash when Cady corners her. "Your first meeting and suddenly you're picked to represent the committee?" She pushes her glasses up on her nose with a manicured finger and stares down at Sarah. She is taller by six inches and outweighs her by thirty pounds.

"It appears so."

"Sam didn't even call for a vote."

"You could have volunteered to make the notes," Sarah says, trying to step around her. Most of the committee members are gone and only Sam and Lorna, with her notebook once again in hand, stand by the door.

"I think I'm a little better prepared to present to a board of directors than you are."

"That may be your opinion, Cady, but it's not what the others decided."

"What does Heidi Dixon know? A city girl married to a wannabe farmer. She's not even from here." Cady takes a menacing step toward her. "I think they made a big mistake."

"I don't really care what you think, Cady," Sarah says. She won't let Cady get the best of her so she pushes past her, clutching her handbag to her chest, and doesn't even stop at the door to say goodbye to Lorna and Sam.

. . .

Sarah sits bolt upright, patting the bed until she locates Jack beside her and hears the soft puffs he makes when he sleeps. Before the girls were born, she used to wait up for him when he worked late, but after Allison was born she could never stay awake that long so Jack always told her not to worry, to just go to sleep; he was fine. Instead, she developed a habit of waking in the middle of the night when she'd gone to bed without him, feeling for him in the dark, to reassure herself he'd made it home safely.

She glances at the luminous numbers on the clock radio: 3:36. The lamp is off, her book closed beside her glasses on the nightstand. She came home from the meeting hoping to tell Jack about her run-in with Cady, but there was a note on the table saying he was at Shorty's, helping him replace the transmission in his tandem. She intended to wait up for him but, as happened so often lately, she fell asleep with a book in her lap and the lamp still on.

She knows what he'd have said if she'd told him, anyway. What he always said. Not to waste a moment worrying about someone like Cady Rankmore. He would've kissed the top of her head, then rolled over and been asleep before his pillow was warm and she'd have lain there, replaying the scene with Cady over and over in her mind like she is doing right now.

Cady and Sarah are the same age; their birthdays are, in fact, only one day apart. Sarah can still remember the long-ago sting of being left out of the over-the-top birthday parties thrown at the sprawling Hubley home along the river at the edge of town; parties with pony rides and glittery dress-up clothes and, one year, a circus tent with clowns. Sarah endured Cady throughout junior high and high school until she finally left for university. Sarah wasn't rid of her, though. Cady returned four years later with Hughie Rankmore — a city boy — and a wedding ring. Hughie took over the management of Hubley Ford and her father pulled some strings to get Cady hired at the elementary school. All three girls spent a year in Cady's grade-four classroom. Sarah always dreaded facing Cady alone on parent-teacher days. The one time Jack came with her, Cady flipped through the pages in Toni's notebooks, pointing out clever things Toni had written, fawning over Jack and acting as though Sarah wasn't even there.

Now, as she sits in the dark, she pictures Cady picking up the phone the moment she got home from the meeting — no, she might have called Arlene on her cellphone while still parked in her Lincoln outside of the hall — and sharing her outrage at being passed over by the committee in favour of Sarah Bilyk. Sarah Bilyk, of all people! Can you just imagine? And Arlene (her best friend from high school) would have assured her, like she's always done, that Sarah is so unworthy. Her? Really?

Sarah turns over her pillow and sinks back into it, closing her eyes. The sound of Jack's breath is calming and Sarah feels her own chest begin to rise and fall in matched rhythm. She tries not to think about Cady, but then she is thinking about trying not to think about Cady and the last thing she remembers before she drifts off is Cady behind her desk in Toni's classroom, the buttons of her too-tight blouse straining as painfully as the smile on her face while she looks at Jack as though he's the only man in the world.

Sarah clutches the oversized gift bag and hurries through the parking lot at Sunny Haven. For the last hour she's been listening to a troublesome ping coming from under the hood of her truck, no doubt from the air conditioning struggling to keep up with the relentless heat. When she pulled up to the end of a long line of traffic, a police officer walked over and told her there'd been an accident; the highway ahead was temporarily closed. She sat, waiting impatiently as she texted with Allison.

I'm going to be late.
Why? What happened?
I'm stuck in traffic.
It's starting!
Still not moving.
On your way yet? Grandpa's acting weird.

She steps through the main doors into air so blissfully cool, she shivers. On the main wall of the common room, a colourful banner (*Happy July Birthdays!*) is draped above a long banquet table covered with crumpled napkins and the plastic domes from three store-bought birthday cakes. Beneath the banner, the names Melvin, Joe, and Hazel, cut from blue construction paper, are taped to the wall. Four listless helium balloons tied to two empty chairs sway restlessly in the air-conditioned breeze.

She has missed the entire birthday party — the songs and games, the cakes and the candles. The room is empty, except for Melvin Hodgson, dozing in a wheelchair, and her father, on his knees, peeking out from under the table behind the plastic tablecloth.

"Geez, Dad. What are you doing under there?"

There's a smudge of chocolate icing on his cheek and his cardboard party hat has slipped to the side of his head; it pokes out like a cow's horn. Furtively, he brushes scattered cake crumbs into a pile on the floor, scoops them up, and licks them off the palm of his hand.

"Oh, Dad," Sarah says. "Don't eat that." She reaches down and pulls him out from under the table. The front of his shirt is smeared with jam, raspberry by the look of the tiny seeds stuck to the breast pocket.

Sarah leads him back to his room. Across the hall, a new sign has been placed on Caroline's door with her name on it, and Sarah wonders if she was wheeled out for the birthday party. She's been here two weeks and, although Sarah has paused in the hallway a few times, she has yet to go in and say anything to her. Now, the door to Caroline's room is closed and, behind it, Sarah hears a man's voice.

When she has her father settled on his recliner, she hands him the gift bag. "Happy birthday, Dad. Sorry I missed your party." He fingers the tissue paper, then he places the bag on the floor and looks at it.

"It's a gift, Dad. For your birthday. From Jack and me and the girls," Sarah says, plucking out the tissue.

He pulls out the gift and turns it over. It's a replica of a 1960s vintage Mustang, cherry red, with a silver grill embedded with the iconic charging horse. It was always her father's dream to own and drive such a classic car. He narrows his eyes and stares at it, before putting it back in the bag.

Just then, Addie appears in the doorway, holding an empty tray. "You made it. Finally. Allison left early. Connor was so antsy, she took off before we served the cake."

"I can't believe I missed everything. Who'd have thought it would take me two hours to get here?"

"You didn't miss much. The same old," Addie says, coming in and perching on the edge of a chair. "Maybe it's the heat, but everything seemed off today. The power was out for about twenty minutes, Linda couldn't keep up on the piano during the sing-along, no one touched the coffee, and we ran out of iced tea."

Sarah's father kicks off his bedroom slippers, folds his hands across his chest, and squeezes his eyes shut like a child feigning sleep.

"How was he?" Sarah asks.

"His energy must have rubbed off on Connor, or vice versa. It was all Allison could do to keep them sitting in their chairs. She finally gave up and went home."

"Oh, great," Sarah moans. "Why did I think I needed to give him his gift today? He doesn't know the difference anyway. I should have skipped the shopping and been here for the party."

"Cut yourself some slack, for God's sake. Hazel Marley's daughter hasn't shown up for the birthday party once since Hazel's been here and what's her excuse? She's retired and has a lot more time than you do. You'd think those brothers of yours would show up around here once in a while."

"Charlie's coming next month," Sarah says in defence of her youngest brother, who at least shows up every couple of years to visit their father. "He'd come more often if he could but it costs so much to fly here from the East Coast."

"Good excuse," Addie says. "It's not fair, the way you've always had to hold things together for your family. You did it as a kid and you're still doing it now." She shakes her finger at Sarah the way she does when she's trying to make a point. "It's time your other two brothers got over themselves and stepped up."

Sarah doesn't want to get into it with Addie, who is very aware of her family's history. Her father disowned Brian fifteen years ago when he found out Brian had forged a cheque for five thousand dollars from the retirement fund he'd set up from the sale of the repair shop. Sarah thought they should report Brian to the police and try to recover the money, but her father didn't want to send him to jail again. Brian had already spent three years at Headingley in the eighties for fraud.

And Paul. She hasn't seen him for nearly twenty years, although she calls him from time to time, just to hear his voice. Their father never forgave him for the accident that took Patrick's life and Paul finally gave up trying to make amends.

"I don't mind taking care of Dad," Sarah says, taking the afghan from the chair and tucking it around her father. "I've never minded." She watches the slight rise and fall of his chest. "Isn't that what daughters are supposed to do?"

"Monica Marley doesn't seem to think so. And what about our old pal Becca?" Addie says, motioning to the closed door across the hall. "I wonder if we'll see any sign of her now that Caroline's here, or if she'll be like Monica, too wrapped up in her own life to spare any time for her mother."

Becca. There. Addie's said it. Becca, who's been on Sarah's mind ever since she heard Caroline was moving in. She's been thinking about what she'll do the first time she sees her after all these years. Imagining how awkward it will be sitting in the same dining room for the holiday dinners the kitchen prepares for the residents' families. Wondering if Jack will come if he knows Becca might be there.

"I've been thinking the same thing. What'll I say to her? And God only knows how Jack will react. I haven't even told him Caroline's in here yet."

"It's been two weeks. Don't you think it's time you did? And sooner, rather than later, I'd say. You don't need Jack showing up and finding either one of those two here."

"How's she doing, anyway? Did she come out for the party?" Sarah asks, tipping her head toward Caroline's door.

Addie nods. "She tries to act like she isn't interested in what's going on, but it's impossible to slip anything past her. She's as sharp as a tack."

"I'm not sure she knows who I am. I've stopped at her door a few times and looked in but I don't think she recognizes me."

Addie takes off her glasses, puffs then wipes the lenses with the hem of her uniform.

"I don't think she sees very well but she's too stubborn to admit it."

From the hallway, Cara pokes her head into the room. "Can you help me get Melvin settled? He wants to get into his pyjamas. Because of the birthday cake, he thinks he's had his supper and now he wants to go to bed."

Addie heads to the door. "Don't forget what I said. You need to tell Jack that she's here. You can't put it off forever."

Her father has fallen asleep in the recliner, his eyelids relaxed, fluttering lightly. Sarah sighs and sits down on his bed. She knows she should tell Jack about Caroline. She just can't imagine what his reaction will be when he finds out there's a chance he might come face to face with Rebecca Webb again. Sarah was so close to her once, the kind of friend she thought she might have forever.

Becca came into Sarah's life just as unexpectedly as she left it. It had been a hot day in July, much like this one. Sarah was twelve, standing alone in the midway at the Ross Prairie summer fair, mad at Addie's father for taking her friend home because she had chores to do. She was fingering the last ticket in her pocket, trying to decide if she should use it to ride by herself, when Becca appeared, grabbing her hand and pulling her through the gate of the Ferris wheel to where a skinny young man in grubby jeans was loading the cars. Before Sarah knew it, they were jerking to the top of the wheel.

"Cady didn't want to come up again. Sometimes she's such a pain," Becca said, pointing at the small group of girls who were standing close to the gate. "Don't you just love it up here? I think this is what a bird must feel like every time it leaves its nest."

Sarah had never thought about it although she supposed it must be; birds could see the tops of leafy trees and brick chimneys and the spire of St. Paul's tiny stone church any time they wanted to. They just had to lift their wings, flap, and set off. "It would be nice to be a bird," she agreed.

After the ride, Becca marched up to Cady and announced they were off to watch the chuck-wagon races. Cady's eyes grew wide when Becca linked her arm through Sarah's and pulled her off toward the bleachers. Sarah didn't know what to make of it; she'd seen the way Cady and her little group operated at school, casting one girl out while the others whispered and pointed at the poor girl standing alone on the playground. She knew she'd have to pay for Becca's unexpected attention when they got back to school in September.

Sarah was used to long, lonely summers on her own. Addie lived on a farm and her mother always had so many jobs for Addie to do — picking vegetables and berries and helping with her little brother — that it was a welcome distraction when Sarah was invited to Becca's house. Caroline drove into town to pick her up, chatting all the way back to the Webb farm, telling her how wonderful it was for Becca to have a new friend.

Over that summer, Becca and Sarah's improbable friendship grew. Sarah spent many afternoons at the Webbs', listening to records in Becca's pretty room. Even though it wasn't her birthday and for no apparent reason that Sarah could see, Becca's parents bought her a brand new two-wheeled bicycle, which meant that Sarah could use Becca's old one whenever she came. They biked down long country roads, and sometimes took a grass trail to a pasture near the river. The river was low that summer and there was a little sand ridge jutting into the water where they could walk and skip rocks or sit and splash their feet. Sometimes they brought a picnic — Kool-Aid and cookies, apples and cheese.

Her father is snoring lightly now and, down the hall, a television comes on. Caroline's door opens and Neil Lewis, a lawyer from Locklin, walks out, carrying a briefcase. When he sees Sarah, he nods. Caroline is sitting in her wheelchair, head turned away, looking out the window. A crocheted shawl, the same crisp white as her hair, is draped around her shoulders, her thin legs and long feet visible in pantyhose and flat-heeled black patent shoes.

Sarah's phone buzzes in her purse, a text message from Jack.

You still in town? Stop at Agro Centre.

She still has groceries to buy so she gets up, kisses her father's forehead, and steps into the hallway. Just then, Caroline turns and looks at her. The skin of her once graceful neck hangs in loose folds and her deeply lined face, so pale and white, looks as though she's over-dusted it with powder, the fragrant kind that used to sit on her dressing table. She squints then turns away with a look of resignation, realizing, perhaps, Sarah isn't one of the nurses or aides.

She doesn't recognize me, Sarah thinks. *She has no idea who I am.* Hesitantly, she walks into Caroline's room and extends her hand. "Caroline? I thought I'd stop and say hello."

Caroline's looks at her blankly and blinks.

"It's Sarah Bilyk. Sarah Coyle?"

Caroline peers at her more closely. A satisfied look slides over her face in the same way a child's might when he receives his mother's praise; there is a spark that brightens her eyes. "It *is* you! Sarah Coyle. Addie told me your father's room was across the hall. I was wondering when I'd see you."

Caroline reaches for her hand and gives Sarah a faint squeeze. Her hand is as dry as paper, her bony wrist so thin Sarah could easily circle it with her thumb and forefinger. And in that touch, there is something else. Sarah feels her heart well up as she senses the old connection, the feeling she used to get when she was around Caroline — that she was safe. That she mattered. That Caroline cared. That she was worthy of a mother's love.

After she's been to Family Foods, Sarah stops at the Co-op. She backs up through the gate and waits while young Matt Bewski throws open the tailgate and loads the mineral tub for the yearlings into the box. "Stay cool, Mrs. B.," he says, swiping at a bead of sweat over his brow.

Sarah opens her window, letting in air only slightly less humid than the scorching heat inside her truck. "Thanks, Matt. Let's hope this heat wave breaks soon and we get some rain." There is a deafening squeal from a reluctant belt when she cranks the air to high and heads out of town.

Once she's on the road, heading home, she remembers Addie's parting words. She can't put off telling Jack about Caroline forever. Addie is right. Of course, she is. She seems to have a sixth sense when it comes to knowing and doing the right thing. She's always been that way.

Over the years, Sarah has tried to soften Jack's opinion, hoping time might have changed his mind about Caroline, but whenever she mentions the Webbs he turns and walks away, refusing to talk about it. He can be incredibly pigheaded, as stubborn as his father sometimes, and all the talking in the world can't convince him to change his mind. He can't seem to let it go, blaming Caroline in every way for what happened that summer.

When Sarah gets home, Jack isn't there, so she puts the milk and eggs in the fridge and takes a walk to the river with Misty. Talking about Rebecca has made her remember a particular April day, nearly forty-five years ago, when they were both thirteen years old.

As happened so often, Sarah was spending a lazy Saturday with Becca at the Webbs' farm. They were biking and had stopped to tie their jackets around their waists, the midday sun beating down. Nearby, they could hear the rumble of the Makwa river. Before Sarah knew it, Becca was pedalling away and she raced to catch up with her, down the grass trail along the fence line toward the meadow, past the big elm tree with the stone pile beside it. Sarah called for Becca to wait up, but she just kept pedalling as though she didn't hear her until, finally, she stopped at the top of the rise and waited until Sarah caught up.

Chunks of ice, some as big as pickup trucks, battered tree branches, and the splintered roof of a small shed churned by on the swollen river beyond the meadow. The sound was as deafening as the trains that rolled past Sarah's house a couple times a day.

"I don't think we should get any closer," Sarah said. "Your mom just told us to stay away from the runoff water, even in the ditches. We'd be in big trouble if she even knew we were out here."

"My mother worries about everything. What's it going to hurt to take a look?" Becca ran across the meadow without looking back until she reached the top of the ravine and turned around to wave.

Sarah cupped her hands around her mouth and yelled, "Come back!"

The river was high, just behind her, and Becca took a small step backward. Before Sarah could call out again, Becca slipped and disappeared. Gone.

Sarah barrelled toward the river. One of Becca's red rubber boots swirled by and she saw Becca's head — that wet, fairy-tale hair — shooting down the river. If Becca screamed, Sarah didn't hear her. At the bend, the river made a sharp turn where the meadow ended and a thick wall of maple trees began. There was no chance of following the river after that. If Becca didn't get out of the water by then, she would be carried out to the lake, her body trapped under two feet of winter ice.

Sarah raced for the bend. Becca flailed her arms, struggling to keep her head above water. A tree trunk as big as a canoe shot past her and she tried to grab hold, but the current was too strong and too fast, and Becca's head went under again.

Sarah reached the bank, slick with muck, panting now but not slowing down, jumping over branches and sticks and dodging a busted five-gallon pail. She stumbled over a black and rotting fence post lying in her path, reached for it, picked it up in one fluid motion, and kept running. Becca's head again, her body churning around the bend, the angry current tossing her toward the riverbank where a large, gnarled oak branch was stuck against the twiggy maples.

"Becca! See there! Grab the branch!" Becca — her wide, staring eyes, her hair like a cape floating around her shoulders — battled against the current that threatened to suck her back toward the middle of the river. She was exhausted, Sarah could tell, yet she reached for the branch, trying to grab hold, hands grasping at air until she finally caught it and hung on.

When Sarah got close enough, she fell to her knees, dragging the post along under her arm, and flung herself close to the edge. Sarah grabbed the post with both hands and reached out over the edge of the bank as far as she could, plunging the post into the bone-numbingly cold water. "Hang on to the post. I'll pull you in."

Becca clung to the branch, eyes closed, body heaving. "I can't."

"You have to." She was so close, just a few feet away, Sarah couldn't lose her now.

Becca lunged for the post and caught it. Her sudden weight yanked Sarah in deeper and her arms seemed to twist in their sockets. Hand over hand, she hauled Becca in, both of them spitting icy, grey water. Sarah reached out a hand but Becca was too far away to grab hold and her hand slipped from the post. She thrashed, kicking and splashing, and was about to go under again. Sarah lurched forward and grabbed hold of the wide cape of her hair. With one mighty heave, she toppled backward, dragging Becca with her, up and out of the water.

They lay panting on the grass, Becca coughing up water, her lips the same metal grey as the river. Sarah untied her hooded jacket from her waist, slightly damp but not soaked, and draped it around Becca's trembling shoulders. She wrapped her arms around her, cradling her head to her chest, their hearts thumping in tandem. "You're all right now," she whispered.

The sun was as high as it would be in the sky that day and it warmed them as they lay there awhile. Overhead, Sarah heard the melancholy honk of Canada geese and she looked up as a small flock flew by, headed north, a V like the black tip of an arrow against the clear and cloudless sky. The geese followed their leader, trusting in his judgment, as he fearlessly shouldered the wind, taking them home.

Sarah closes her eyes. She can almost hear the call of the geese, smell the fruity scent of Becca's hair, feel it in her fist — the heft and weight of it — in that last desperate heave. She remembers every detail of that day, including the aftermath. Becca's altered version of the truth when they were questioned about it: that it was Sarah's idea to go. The blame that was laid at her feet. Eldon Webb's fury and the doubt that lingered in Caroline's eyes. She wonders now why she didn't recognize that first bald-faced lie as a clue to Becca's true nature. Becca hadn't given a second thought to implicating Sarah and saving herself. *Why was I so trusting, so easily manipulated into forgiving her?*

And now, a thought she'd once harboured comes to mind. What if she hadn't grabbed hold of Becca's golden hair? What if she'd let the river sweep her away? How much different would their life — hers and Jack's — have been if Becca had drowned in the river that day? Her bloated body found down-river, tangled among the twisted arms of the silver willows or discovered, months later, washed up on the shore of the lake.

That awful thought is something she's kept all these years in the back of her mind, dangling there to torment her whenever she allowed herself to think about it. She used to imagine herself in a story where Jack was hers first and Becca hadn't betrayed her. She knew it was wrong, wishing someone out of this world, but she can't deny she used to think about it. Thinks it still, sometimes.

As much as she loved Becca, there were times she hated her, too.

Jack is in the office, at the computer, when she comes in. She's surprised to find him in the house. Maybe it's the heat. She's noticed since he turned sixty he's been coming in early more and more often, sometimes well before dark, and after he's showered up he often asks her if she'd like to go for a drive, check the crops. Now, he swivels around in the office chair, pinches the bridge of his nose, as if to staunch whatever worry is creasing his brow, and leans back in the chair. He stretches out his legs, long and lean and nicely muscled in blue jeans the same size he wore when she married him, his stomach hard and tight, shoulders broad and strong. Except for his hair, which has gone completely grey, he hasn't changed a bit. Her heart tilts a little at the sight of him.

"You get it?" he asks, referring to the mineral.

"It's in the box."

"How was the party?"

"I missed it. There was a head-on between a van and a motor home on the highway. I was held up over an hour. Allison and Connor were gone before I got there."

"She called. Thought you'd be home by now."

"I had a few stops after I left Dad. What are you doing in the office at this time of day?"

"Checking the market. Thinking of selling the calves this fall. Might not be enough hay and the prices are decent." He clicked the mouse, then stood up and sighed. "Sooner I move those young calves, the better. Found the second one. Shorty and me were out on the quads and we came across it, and another of his, both of them torn apart worse than the one you found. We figured coyotes, but talking to Natural Resources, they say it's more likely a wolf. A lone male, cast out of the pack. Not usual for it to come this far out of the mountain, though."

"What are you going to do?"

"We had our rifles, but we didn't see it."

Sarah shudders. She is afraid of Jack's rifle, with good reason. If her father hadn't taught her brothers to shoot, Patrick would still be alive. When Sarah and Jack were first married, she told him she didn't want a gun in the house. He promised to keep it locked safely away in the gun cabinet, explaining he used it only to shoot animals that threatened their livelihood in some way. He took her out to the pasture once to show her how to use it in the event there was ever a time he might not be around to protect her or the girls. She cocked it and loaded it the way he explained and then pulled the trigger reluctantly, firing off in the distance at nothing in particular, hoping she never needed to aim it at any living thing.

They walk to the kitchen and Sarah pulls a can of coffee from a grocery bag and puts it in the pantry. "I hate to think there's a wolf nearby, prowling around."

Jack piles four boxes of apple juice next to the coffee. "Better not be walking alone. Misty would try to protect you, but she'd be no match. Stay in the yard until we hunt him down."

She has never felt anything but safe living in the country, walking or biking the gravel roads. An occasional rustle in the ditch grass might be a raccoon or a skunk, a harmless snake even, slithering through, but there was no reason to worry. She considers how she left herself exposed by the river just now. Who knew what was lurking along its banks?

"So no walks for a while." Jack flips through the mail on the kitchen table, sorting it into two piles. "Did Addie mention anything to you about volunteering for the Community Foundation barbecue? Tom just called and wondered if I'd help him flip burgers."

Sarah nods. "It's the weekend Charlie's here. Addie asked me to bring a salad." She pulls a pan of leftover lasagna from the fridge. "Speaking of Addie ... there's something I've been meaning to tell you. Addie and I talked about it today, actually."

Jack looks up from his stack of envelopes.

"You heard that George Feschuk died. Across the hall from Dad?" Sarah lifts out two slices of lasagna and puts them on plates. "Someone's finally moved in." She places a paper towel on one slice, pops it in the microwave, pulls the romaine lettuce out of the fridge then fusses with each piece as she pinches it into a stainless steel bowl.

"And …" Jack says, tearing open an envelope, "who is it?"

Sarah squeezes in a dollop of dressing, tosses the salad, adds a handful of croutons. "It's Caroline," she finally says.

Jack doesn't answer and Sarah can almost hear the dark thoughts in his mind. When she turns to look at him, he is tapping a leaflet against the edge of the table. "Do I look like I give a shit?" She was expecting this reaction but, even so, his barely contained anger and the look on his face catch her off-guard.

Sarah puts the second plate in the microwave. "Just thought I'd mention it, is all."

Jack pushes his chair back, goes to the fridge, gets himself a beer. "Heard she broke a hip." He sits back down. "You see her?"

"I did and I finally said something to her today."

Jack grunts and takes a long swig of his beer.

"It's got to be a huge change for her," says Sarah, "living in there after keeping to herself all these years."

"Hope you aren't feeling sorry for her," Jack says sharply. "The mighty have fallen, is all I can say. Always thinking she's better than the rest of us, but she's not. Ask Addie. Bet she'll tell you Caroline's shit stinks, same as anybody else's."

"Honestly, Jack. Isn't it time to get over it? You can continue to hate Caroline if you want, but that doesn't mean I have to." She slides Jack's plate across the table. "She was never anything but good to me. Stepping up, standing in, when I needed someone. Sometimes I think Becca resented me for that."

At the mention of Becca's name, Jack pushes away from the table. "You're defending her? After what she did to Becca? To me?"

"I'm not defending her. I agree with you. It was a terrible thing, what the Webbs did. I'm just saying, let it go."

"Swore I'd never forgive her and I won't. Don't expect me to." Jack grabs his beer, drains it, then stalks out the door, the pane rattling when he slams it harder than he has to.

Through the window, Sarah watches him stride across the yard. She can hear him swearing, awful words he never uses in front of her or the girls. He kicks a plastic sand pail Connor has left out, sends it flying. It narrowly misses Anton, who is making his own way slowly across the yard, and he stops, says something to Jack, and an argument starts between them.

Sarah turns away and closes the window. Her head is spinning; she hasn't eaten since breakfast, so she should be hungry, but she's lost her appetite, too. She feels nauseated, a churning sort of queasiness at the back of her throat that reminds her of the way she felt during the first months of all six of her pregnancies. She puts a hand to her mouth and heaves. The air in the kitchen is suddenly too dense, too thick to breathe, and she adjusts the thermostat until the air conditioner clicks on, then she goes to the bedroom and stretches out on the bed.

She tries to imagine what Jack is thinking. He'll be banging on some piece of equipment in the workshop, pounding a hammer against steel, or maybe searing a shovel or a shank with a red-hot weld, his helmet on, visor covering his face. She's exposed a long-festering wound but she hadn't expected it to bleed like it is; a torrent of anger and pain, still as raw as it was when Becca went away.

Shorty called her that day, told her to come. Jack was acting crazy; he didn't know what else to do. When she arrived, Jack was pacing, smacking at the tears and the snot flowing freely down his face with the sleeve of his shirt, downing shot after shot of rye whisky straight up. She tried to calm him down and find out what was going on, but he peeled her hand off his shoulder and pushed her aside. She stumbled and Shorty caught hold of her arm. He wouldn't tell them a thing about what had happened when he'd gone to the Webbs', but at least Sarah convinced him there was no point in going back over.

He lost Becca that night, and so did Sarah. Becca had packed her bags, left town, gone away without another word, ever, to either one of them. Jack blamed Caroline and Eldon blamed Jack. It was the tinder that erupted the smouldering feud between the Bilyks and the Webbs, set it off like a runaway fire. And it would be years before Sarah learned the truth, before she knew what, between them all, they'd really lost.

CAROLINE

Caroline plucked the whistling kettle from the hot plate, filled her mother's old teapot, and replaced the lid (broken, but glued together and still completely serviceable). She set out two biscuits and opened a jar of her mother's raspberry jam.

"Breakfast's ready," she called as she poured the tea.

"Oh, botheration!" Susan said. "I can't find my other penny loafer. Have you seen it?" She came out of the bedroom wearing a red plaid skirt and white blouse, waving one black shoe. When the girls had arrived in the city in the middle of August, Susan had cut her long dark hair into a shoulder-length bob with bangs, a style she believed more sophisticated for a college student, although Caroline thought she looked younger and even more fresh-faced than usual with it pinned back in barrettes like that.

"Did you look under my bed? I think I remember seeing them shoved up against the apple crate."

Susan sat on the only other chair and slipped on her shoe. "There aren't many places it can hide," she said, sweeping her arm around the tiny apartment.

"Our chickens have more room in their coop than we do in here. That bedroom seemed so much bigger before we put the beds in," Caroline said.

"It's small and it's quaint, but it's ours." Susan slathered a biscuit with jam and took a bite. Susan had always shared a room with two of her sisters, but for Caroline, listening to her roommate's restless tossing and turning during the night took as much getting used to as the eerie cries of police sirens or the constant wash of yellow light on the bedroom wall from the street lamp outside their small window.

"Do you have study group tonight, or can we plan to do something?" Caroline asked.

"I have to do some reading, but I'm sure after I've spent time with *King Lear*, I can join you for a walk in the park this evening. We have to take advantage of this exquisite weather while it lasts. Before we know it, winter will bluster in and we'll be stuck inside with nothing to do but listen to the radio."

It surprised Caroline how quickly Susan was turning into a city girl, with city ideas, just like Monique and Patsy, Caroline's new friends from the bank. They talked about the weather with little regard for the actual consequences of an early frost or a week of heavy rain in September, as though blackened marigolds in window boxes or cancelled plans for a picnic in Assiniboine Park affected their futures in the same way frozen kernels of wheat impacted Caroline's. When she walked home from work on mild days, Caroline's heart soared at the sight of a clear blue sky and radiant sunshine beaming down and she welcomed brisk westerly winds that flapped her skirt. She pictured her parents, working long hours at home, her father combining the last of the wheat, abundant this year, while her mother hauled it home and augered it into the empty bins, knowing it meant the bills would be paid with some money left over for her, finally, this year.

Before Caroline had climbed aboard the train in August, her mother had pressed five silver dollars into her hand and promised they would find the money to pay for her college tuition. She buried her face in her mother's embrace, taking in the familiar scent of her, while her mother stroked her hair. "I've talked him into it," she whispered. "If the crop comes off like we hope, we'll hold off on the new grain truck for another year and you can start school after Christmas. You'll be behind Susan, but it'll give you time to work and maybe save up a little so's you can have some extra stored up for when you're in school full-time." A sob rose up in Caroline's throat, knowing it would be her mother doing without — another season steering Old Smoky over dusty roads, another year setting out pots to catch raindrops in the attic, another winter tucking newspaper into the soles of her worn-out boots. The conductor called, "All aboard!" and Caroline pulled away. Tears poured freely down her mother's cheeks, too, and the sobs they'd both been holding broke free, making heads turn, but they didn't care. Let them look. Her father handed her mother his handkerchief and she wiped her nose and tucked it into the sleeve of her dress before taking one last look at Caroline and turning away. Even her father had pulled her into a rare hug. "Off with you, girl. Go on and start your new life."

Caroline picked up the empty mugs and plates and placed them in the dishpan. The sky had darkened to the colour of tarnished silver above the neighbouring apartment building and, over the morning hum of the wakening city, she heard the low rumble of thunder. She turned to see Susan crouched near her bed, poking and fishing about with the broom handle.

"Ah ha! The missing shoe," she said triumphantly, sitting up with the loafer in her hand. She picked a webby blossom of dust and hair off her skirt and sneezed.

"I have to get to work," Caroline said, heading for the door. "Don't forget your umbrella like you did last week or you'll get soaked again. See you after work."

Caroline stepped through the glass doors into the bank. Monique stood in the foyer, shaking the rain off her umbrella. Monique was a tall, strapping girl in her late twenties, still unmarried and seemingly uninterested in men altogether, unlike Caroline's other friend, Patsy, who routinely flirted with men of any age who came to her teller's window.

Patsy was already at her window, counting a thin stack of ten-dollar bills. She wore the same navy skirt and white blouse as Monique and Caroline, the standard uniform of all the tellers. Caroline took her place at the wicket between her two friends and opened her cash drawer.

"He looked over here on his way up to his office to see if you were at work yet," Patsy said, nodding to the stairs near the front doors.

Caroline glanced at the grand staircase that led to the second-floor offices for the managers, and half expected to spot him there looking down at her. Patsy was referring to Michael Wickstrom, a junior manager who approved small loans for automobiles and household appliances. He'd introduced himself to Caroline in the lunchroom on her very first day and then stopped at her window a few days later to ask her to change a twenty-dollar bill, pausing to chat about the weather and comment on the way her cardigan set off the colour of her eyes. Patsy kept looking over at her and when he left she squeezed Caroline's hand, convinced he would ask her to the Labour Day ball game and picnic that weekend. As it turned out, he didn't ask Caroline to go with him, but he spent the whole afternoon smiling at her helplessly from the outfield while softballs sailed over his head and, later, during the picnic, fetching her glass after glass of iced lemonade.

Monique grunted as she tore open a paper roll of dimes and dumped them into the proper compartment in her drawer. "For all the fuss he made over you at the picnic, we haven't seen much of him since then."

Caroline slid the elastic band from her twenty-dollar bills. "I think Michael's afraid he made a fool of himself, carting over all those lemonades at the picnic."

"You coulda told him to buzz off instead of taking them and then pouring them out."

"Oh, Caroline's too polite to say anything like that," Patsy said. "Besides, the way she blushes every time we mention his name, I don't think she really wants him to buzz off, do you, Caroline?"

"He seems like a very nice young man, even if he did act a little overeager at the picnic," Caroline said as she piled the last of her bills into her drawer. "I've tried to catch his eye in the lunchroom, but he doesn't even look my way. Maybe he's just not that interested."

"Of course he is. Who wouldn't be? Maybe he thinks you're not interested. What have you done to show him you are? You may not have noticed how many men queue up for your window even when Monique and I have much shorter lines." Patsy sighed and shut her drawer. "You may be from a farm in the middle of nowhere, but you look like you stepped off a train from Hollywood," she said enviously. "It's got to be that glorious hair."

Caroline blushed. "But it's so easy for you, talking and laughing with everyone who comes to your window. I just get on with business and hardly know what else to say except, 'What can I help you with today?' What could I talk to Michael about?"

"Just try to relax and imagine yourself talking to one of us, or Susan or Alice, and try not to think about how amazingly gorgeous he looks," Patsy said.

"That's the problem. The words are there, locked away behind my teeth, but when it comes time I can't seem to say a thing."

"You need to make the next move. Put the ball back in his court, so to speak."

"But how?"

"It's up to you to figure that out. If you don't talk to him and he gets away, you'll always regret the chance you didn't take," Patsy said.

"Well, then, I'll do it," Caroline said, snapping shut her drawer. "Today, I'm going to go right up to Michael Wickstrom and strike up a conversation. What do I have to lose?"

On her morning break, instead of going to the lunchroom for coffee, Caroline headed up the curving staircase. Her hand skimmed easily over the polished banister and, when she reached the top, Patsy gave her a wave from her window below, as if to reassure her that she was doing the right thing, although Caroline was curiously aware of every step she took on quivering legs.

The door to Michael's small office was open at the end of the hallway. He sat at a desk stacked with piles of paper, bent to his work, making notations in a document with a pencil. His sculpted hair was thick and sleek; thin rows from the teeth of his comb showed through like the swerving lines in a freshly harrowed field. His sleeves were rolled up, his striped tie loosened, tweed jacket hanging on the back of his chair.

"Hello, Michael."

Michael looked up from his paperwork, startled, yet seemingly pleased to see her.

"Good morning, Caroline. How are you today?" He stood, fumbling a little as he cleared a stack of books from the only other chair in the room and motioned for Caroline to sit.

Without a window, the room was airless and warm, although a small fan whirred from the top of a narrow bookcase.

"I have a question for you, something I've been thinking about, and I thought you would be the one who could help me with it."

"I'd be happy to," Michael said, a smile instantly stretched wide. "What can I do for you?"

"It's not for me, I'm not in the position to borrow any money," Caroline said. "It's my mother I'm thinking about."

"I see," Michael said, shifting a pile of papers from one side of the desk to the other.

"And I wondered," Caroline continued, "if she were to take out a small loan, say for one hundred dollars …"

"Would she like me to set something up for her here?" Michael interrupted, a puzzled expression on his face. "Wouldn't it be easier for her to take out a loan from a bank there in Ross Prairie?"

"Oh, no. I'm just inquiring about the rates and the terms for repayment. She wants to buy an electric stove — she still cooks on a wood stove and my father doesn't see the need for a new one — but I've been telling her she should have one and I need to have some idea of what she's getting herself into. Borrowing money, that is," Caroline said hurriedly. "Before she goes to the bank at home." She felt her face grow hot at the elaborate story she was telling, making her mother sound like the kind of woman who would go behind her husband's back, when in reality she kept telling Caroline she was perfectly content with the stove she'd cooked on for thirty years, that there was no point in wasting good money on a stove when the roof needed fixing.

"I understand," Michael said. He opened a drawer and rifled through it until he found the paper he was looking for and handed it to Caroline. "Here's a listing of our latest interest rates and the different terms she could choose from."

"Thanks so much," Caroline said, taking the sheet from Michael. She folded it in half on the only empty space on the desk. Somewhere nearby, a door slammed.

"Is there anything else I can help you with?" Michael asked. His green eyes were curious; there was a sweetness and openness about them.

"I wanted you to know, too, how much I enjoyed your company at the picnic. It was one of the most pleasant days I've spent since I moved here."

Michael chuckled and seemed to relax, tipping his chair back and propping his shiny shoes on the pulled-open bottom drawer. "I would have liked to have chatted with you more than I did, but I appear to have been preoccupied with keeping you refreshed that day."

"It was very kind of you to ..."

"Bring you six glasses of lemonade?" Michael grinned.

"You seemed a little nervous, as was I, but maybe another time, we could just enjoy each other's company." Caroline paused and smiled. "With fewer beverages involved."

"Absolutely." Michael stood up and came around to Caroline's chair. "I've been thinking exactly the same thing but I wasn't quite sure how to ask you. What are you doing this weekend? There's a party one of my friends is throwing. A farewell for our friend Thomas, who's off to study in Toronto. There'll be music and dancing and enough food to feed a small army. Would you like to come?"

"I'd love to," she said, standing up. "If you can promise me one thing."

"What's that?"

"Absolutely no lemonade."

Patsy was more excited about Caroline's upcoming date than she was and taking more credit than she should for having convinced Caroline to speak to Michael that day. Monique didn't see what all the fuss was about, but by Friday she was caught up in the excitement, too. Caroline had purchased an autumn-toned dress with her mother's five silver dollars and Patsy was going to go home with Caroline after work to fix up her hair like a photo of Marilyn Monroe she'd clipped from a movie magazine: swept up and back with a fat ringlet cascading over one shoulder.

Just before closing, Mrs. Miner, who was in charge of the tellers, strode purposefully from her small office next to the vault and tapped Caroline on the shoulder.

"I need to have a word with you in my office, Caroline," she said. She turned to the stout man who was next in line at Caroline's window. "My apologies. We have to close this window for a few minutes but I'll be with you shortly, if you don't mind waiting."

Caroline followed Mrs. Miner to her office where the woman gestured to a chair and picked up the telephone receiver from the top of her desk. She covered the mouthpiece with one hand. "There's someone who would like to speak with you. I'll finish up with your customers and close up your station for the day, so don't feel like you have to hurry back out. Take all the time you need," she said kindly.

The lead-coloured sky pressed against the high window in Mrs. Miner's office and the relentless rain, which hadn't let up for three days, tapped steadily against the pane. Mrs. Miner never worked directly with the customers. Why did she offer to take a turn at Caroline's station?

"Hello?"

"Caroline? Is that you?" It was her father. His voice sounded detached, as though it clung to a balloon suspended somewhere above and away from her in the vaulted ceiling near the grand staircase. Ridiculously, it occurred to her that she had never spoken to him on the telephone before; it was her mother who always answered when she phoned home from Susan's or Alice's or, lately, from the pay phone in the lobby of her apartment building. Her legs folded and she crumpled into Mrs. Miner's chair. "What is it, Dad? What's happened?"

She pictured him standing in the empty kitchen, the stove cold behind him, her mother's jacket flung carelessly over a chair.

"It's Mum. I came home after lunch and found her on the kitchen floor. She couldn't say a word, her face twisted up, and the one arm flopping back down on the floor like a sack of rocks when I lifted it. I carried her out to the truck and got to the hospital quick as I could. Dr. Alden says she's had a stroke."

Caroline's breath caught in her throat. There was a sudden stuttering of her heart and she would remember that moment later, riding home on the train, the way she could feel herself looking down, as though she was seeing herself through the rain-blurred window, blinking and blinking, unable to clear the wash of tears from her eyes.

"Caroline? Are you there? Did you hear what I said?"

"Yes. Is she going to be okay? Did Dr. Alden say?"

"He told me to call you. He said you ought to come home, quick as you can get here. Can you do that, Caroline? We need you here. Your mother needs you. Can you get on the next train home?"

Her father met her at the station when she arrived just after nine o'clock the next evening, late by nearly an hour due to a problem with a switch at a rail crossing in Neepawa. On the way to the hospital, he told her Dr. Alden was worried about the length of time that had passed before he had found her mother. They assumed she had suffered the stroke early in the morning; the cream was still out among the dirty breakfast dishes. It was one thirty when he drove back to the yard with the tractor, wondering why she hadn't brought his lunch out to the field, and found her on the kitchen floor. She had not opened her eyes or uttered a word, had not even stirred all the long day as her father waited by her hospital bed. Dr. Alden had told him the first seventy-two hours were the most critical, that he wouldn't know how serious the damage might be until she woke up, if she woke up at all.

When they got to the hospital, Caroline insisted her father let her off at the front door while he parked the truck. She dashed up the front steps and had to stop at the front desk. In her panic, she'd forgotten to ask her father for her mother's room number.

Dr. Alden and the night-duty nurse were there when Caroline ran in. The curtain was drawn around the bed and, as Caroline was about to pull it back, Dr. Alden stepped forward and grabbed her hand.

"I'm sorry, Caroline," he said gently. "There was nothing we could do."

The nurse, a pained expression on her face, placed her hand on Caroline's shoulder. "Perhaps we should just wait till your father gets here."

"What is it? What do you mean?" She wrenched back the curtain. There was her mother; her freckled, worn-out hands crossed on her chest, face pale on the white pillow, eyes closed. "I have to talk to her," Caroline cried, hysteria welling up inside her. "Dad told me you said it would do her good to hear my voice."

"I'm sorry, Caroline. Your mother passed about half an hour ago," Dr. Alden said.

Caroline collapsed on the floor. She felt her father's arms lift her and her legs move unsteadily toward the door. She didn't remember the ride home. Later, shivering in her coat at the kitchen table, she watched while her father brought in an armload of wood and got the fire going. They were too numb to speak and sat there in silence, each of them pondering their own heavy thoughts, as they listened to the wood crackle in the stove. How would they live without her?

After the funeral, Caroline stood at her bedroom window looking out at the garden. The pumpkins were not yet completely turned; dabs of orange poked through the blackened vines that stretched across the far end of the garden. There'd been a killing frost the night her mother died, spoiling the last of the tomatoes and cucumbers. Her mother would have saved them all by covering them with old sheets she kept in an apple box in the woodshed.

She watched as Anna and Anton Bilyk walked to their car. Anna carried a roasting pan she'd brought with a pot roast earlier in the week but Caroline couldn't remember if she'd tasted it, or if she, in fact, had eaten anything that day or any of the days that followed, although she must have. There was more food than Caroline knew what to do with — cakes and casseroles, fried chicken and meatballs, plates of muffins and squares. She was grateful when Betty Cornforth arrived and took over the kitchen, directing Caroline to carry the food that would keep down to the cold floor of the root cellar, making coffee and tea, and setting out lunch for the neighbours and friends who kept stopping by.

Anna had hugged her at the cemetery after they'd lowered her mother's casket into the ground. "No one knows how hard this is, and don't let anyone tell you any different. You have to get through this in your own way, on your own time," she said. "You have all those precious memories to hold on to. Never forget them." Caroline was grateful Anna hadn't said the things everyone else had said and she wished she'd told her so. *Oh, your mother is better off with the Lord* or *She would never have wanted to be a burden* or *She was such a wonderful person.*

How do you know? Caroline wanted to shout. *How do you know how wonderful she was?* Only Caroline herself knew how it felt to be loved by her mother, safe and protected, like nothing in the world could ever do her harm.

There was a tap on Caroline's door. Susan stood in the doorway, a concerned look on her face. "Is everything all right? You've been up here a long time." She had come home for the funeral, arriving the day before on the same evening train as Caroline had taken nearly a week earlier. Caroline hadn't yet had a chance to speak to her.

"I needed some space. If someone offered me another egg sandwich I would have screamed. But I see people are leaving. This whole thing has been so exhausting."

Susan sat on the edge of Caroline's bed. "Quite frankly, you look terrible. Have you slept at all this past week?"

"I didn't for the first few nights. I kept dozing off and dreaming that I was running to catch my train, that I missed it completely, kept missing it day after day. And then I'd wake up, sick with guilt for not being there with her at the end. Like it's my fault she died. That maybe if I'd never left for the city, she might still be alive."

"You can't think that way." Susan stood and took hold of Caroline's hands. "There's not a thing you could have done to change this. It could have happened a few months ago while you were still at home, going to high school. You mustn't blame yourself."

"I know I shouldn't, but I do. I'm just not sure how we'll carry on without her. Yesterday, I didn't fall asleep until the sun was coming up, and when I came downstairs at ten o'clock my father was still sitting at the kitchen table, staring at his coffee cup. He hadn't been out yet to do the milking or the chores. I shook him by the shoulder and he looked at me and said, 'Violet, is that you?'"

"You poor thing. This is so much for you to deal with on your own. Sometimes I complain about that huge family of mine, but if something ever happened, at least we'd have each other." Susan sat on the bed again. "Have you thought about what you're going to do now?"

Caroline sighed. "I suppose I need to go down and help Betty and the ladies clean up and decide what to do with all that extra food."

"No," Susan said gently, "I mean, what are your plans? When are you coming back to Winnipeg? To your job?"

Until that moment, Caroline had not considered what she would do next. She'd put one foot in front of the other, going with her father to make the funeral plans, picking flowers for the casket, selecting her mother's favourite hymns. She hadn't given any thought to the weeks that would follow. What would she do? Leave her father and go back to the city and carry on as though her mother was still alive?

She'd phoned Mrs. Miner the Monday after her mother died and was reassured she could take a few weeks before she needed to come back. But a week had already passed and Caroline realized the bank wouldn't wait for her forever.

"You can't believe how incredibly quiet the apartment has been without you. I have no one to remind me to take my umbrella to class."

"I don't think I can just up and leave Dad alone. He doesn't even know how to fry an egg." Caroline sighed and turned to look back out the window. "The harvest isn't over, either. That rain put a stop to everything and he'll need someone to drive the grain truck to get the last of the crop in now that the sunshine's returned."

Susan stood and came up behind Caroline, wrapping her arms around Caroline's waist. "I'll be waiting. Before we know it, you'll be back. The harvest will be over and before we blink, it'll be Christmas. Just think of the fun we'll have, skating in the park, attending all those holiday parties. I spoke to Patsy and she told me Michael's been asking about you. You still need to go on that first date."

Caroline could not turn around to look at her friend. Tears filled her eyes. She could not picture herself skimming along a pond on ice skates or laughing with Michael at a party. A dark hopelessness rose up inside her, along with the grim realization that she did not want to laugh or dance or act as though she didn't have a care in the world. Her mother was gone and things would never be the same.

. . .

Old Smoky belched a puff of black smoke from under its hood as Caroline cranked hard on the steering wheel and pulled into the yard. She shifted the truck to neutral and coasted down the lane, pulling up twenty feet short of the grain bin before Smoky died with one last resounding clunk. She'd just picked up the last load of oats, stained and light from standing for weeks in the rain, but still good enough to feed the pigs through the winter. She would have to wait for her father to return to the yard with the combine and get Smoky running again so they could unload. Her arms and shoulders felt like they were on fire; she had to concentrate just to wrestle with the door handle and open the door. She slid one foot to the running board and jumped to the ground. How her mother drove Old Smoky all those years, she couldn't imagine. She walked to the house, scooped a dipper of water from the pail and took a long drink. Her throat was raw, the water smooth and cool going down.

The kitchen was a mess. A mountain of dishes was stacked by the sink, and globs of grease from the frying pan she'd used for last night's pork chops floated on top of the cold dishwater. It had been days since she'd swept the dirt from under her father's chair. Two weeks had passed since her mother's funeral, the days running together in a blur of cooking and washing and farm chores. The wringer washer was as temperamental as Old Smoky and she'd ruined a good blouse — a smudge of grease on the shoulder — when it jammed in the roller. She'd found a box of ripe tomatoes in the root cellar and it shamed her to phone Betty Cornforth and ask what she should do with them. It had never occurred to her to pay attention when her mother made the preserves. All those years she'd taken for granted the jars of pink crabapples and beet pickles and plump red tomatoes lining the shelves in the cellar. And her mother had never shown her what to do or asked her to help, spoiling her, Caroline could see now, hoping Caroline would have a different life, one without the tedious jobs demanded of every farm woman.

It was only three o'clock but Caroline was starving. She'd barely had time to eat her lunch, running back and forth to the field with all those bushels of oats. She was shoving an oatmeal cookie into her mouth when Lady barked twice, scarcely a warning. "Hello, old girl. You remember me, don't you?" she heard Eldon say.

There he stood, looking at her through the screen door. Caroline tore off her mother's red kerchief and plumped up her hair. She looked a fright, she knew, her face and arms coated with oat dust and her mouth full.

"Sorry, did I catch you at a bad time?"

"I just got in from the field. We've only just now finished the oats," Caroline said.

"I can come back another time. I'm here to speak to your father," Eldon said. He took off his hat and held it over his heart as though he had a favour to ask. "And I was hoping to see you, too, of course. I didn't have a chance to speak to you after the funeral service."

"Come in," Caroline said. "Dad should be along shortly. He's likely moving home now with the combine." She was too tired to make a pot of tea so she sat down across from him and hoped her father wouldn't be too long.

"How have you been managing?" Eldon asked, glancing about the room.

"Running a house is much more work than I thought," Caroline said. "Yesterday, I had to throw away a box of apples.

They went soft before I had a chance to get to them so I fed them to the pigs. I don't know how my mother did it all."

"A woman's work is never done, there's certainly truth to that. Vera is often still in the kitchen at eight o'clock, especially when there's all the pickling and canning to do."

Vera Kalyniuk was Elvina Webb's housekeeper, a spinster who lived with her unmarried brother on his farm a few miles away. She was frail and thin, older than Elvina, and Caroline wondered how she kept up with all the chores, as well as keeping house for her brother. She imagined Vera bustling about the expansive rooms with a dusting cloth, bent and stooped, while Elvina sat in an upholstered chair.

Just then the Farmall came putt-putting down the lane pulling the combine and, a few minutes later, her father came through the door. There was a thin band of dust on his forehead and a smudge of dirt down the bridge of his nose.

Eldon stood up and extended his hand. Caroline's father wiped his hand on the front of his overalls before he shook it. "You get all finished up, then?"

"I did. A couple of days ago. It was a good year, up till that last bad spell of rain."

"Yep, it was. One of the better crops I've had in a while." Caroline's father pulled out a chair and sat down. "Where's the coffee, then?" He frowned at Caroline, as if he expected his cup to be filled, waiting for him on the table with the cream and the sugar.

"The fire went out. And I used the last of the wood this morning," Caroline said.

"That's fine, Henry," Eldon said. "I can't stay long, anyway. I wanted to finish discussing the matter we were talking about at the elevator last week. I've had a chance to think about what you proposed."

Caroline's father was about to stand up, then changed his mind and sat back down, fidgeting for a moment with the buckle on his overalls. "Caroline, run out to the mailbox, why don't you? I see you didn't pick up the mail today and there's a letter I'm expecting."

He didn't fool Caroline with his ruse. She didn't care one way or the other about whatever it was her father didn't want her to hear. Following Lady down the lane to the mailbox, she felt her spirits lift now that she was out of the house. It was still warm, even though the sun was starting its descent on this brilliant Indian summer day. The trees were mostly bare, the yellow leaves padding the ditches on either side of the lane, the field next to the house still not worked and golden with stubble. Harvest was over and there were only carrots and tur-nips to dig out of the garden. She'd have time to give the house a good cleaning, maybe even get out the ladder and wash the windows like she'd seen her mother do.

She was anxious to get back to her job; Mrs. Miner had allowed her another week before she was expected back and there was the money she owed Susan for this month's rent. Tonight, after supper, she would talk to her father about returning to the city. If she was lucky, the unusual fall weather would stretch out for another few weeks and she and Susan, and maybe Patsy and Monique, would have a chance to go for one last picnic in the park before winter set in and stayed. Maybe she would soon have a chance to wear the rust-coloured dress to a different party, or maybe out to dinner with Michael at a restaurant with candles flickering on the tables.

For the first time in weeks, she felt a lightness, a shifting of weight, a faint glimmer of something stirring in her heart she couldn't quite recognize or name.

SARAH

Sarah wakes to the patter of rain on the roof. Through the window, she can hear it splashing from the eaves into the rain barrel and, behind it, the low rumble of thunder. It's the middle of August, the lull between haying and harvest, and Jack is still asleep although it's eight o'clock. He must have turned off the alarm. She's surprised she didn't hear Toni getting ready for work. In a couple of weeks, she'll be gone back to university and harvest will be in full swing. Sarah knows she should get out of bed and begin her day. There are cucumbers to pick and dill pickles to make, and Charlie is going to be here later today, flying in from Halifax. By the time he rents a car and drives out it will be nearly suppertime. It's the second time he's been home since their father went to live at Sunny Haven. Last time, Charlie stayed for nearly a week, going to town every day to spend time with their father, sitting with him outdoors in the gazebo, pushing checkers around a board. Their father remembered him then, his face lighting up when he saw him, although he'd forgotten that Charlie was married and had two grown boys. It saddens Sarah to think how devastated Charlie will be when their father looks him over with that blank, open-mouthed stare.

Sarah has always been close to Charlie. Her mother ignored him when they brought him home from the hospital. She stayed in her room with the door closed even when Charlie was wailing right across the hall. Sarah remembers Patrick coming home after school and thundering up the stairs to lift Charlie out of his crib, Charlie's hiccupy sobs while Patrick patted his back and jounced him around the room.

Patrick spent that whole summer holiday in the house, making meals and washing clothes, while Paul helped their father in the repair shop. He showed Sarah how to heat a small pot of water on the stove before taking it off and putting the bottle in to warm. He taught her to squirt the milk on her wrist — it reminded her of the way Baba shot milk from Lou Anne's teat to the waiting cats in the barn — before they gave it to Charlie. Before the start of school in September, Baba came with her basket of candles, vials of holy water, and herbs. She ripped open the curtains in her daughter's room, roused her from bed, and sent Sarah and Brian downstairs with Patrick before firmly closing the door. Later, she blended a tea and forced Olivia to drink it. Even though Sarah's mother eventually came around and began to function again, Baba's ritual was unable to rekindle any motherly surge of love for Charlie or any of them. In the years that followed, it was Sarah who took on most of Charlie's care.

Sarah believed that of all her children, her mother loved Patrick best. He was her first-born and the only one of her sons to look like the Petrenkos. Sarah used to think their mother had used up all her love on Patrick, with none left for the rest of them, and it made Sarah worry when she was pregnant with Maeve. Whenever she felt her roll or jab an elbow in her womb, she was reminded that another life, another human being, would soon be demanding her love. She found herself unable to imagine sharing the intense love she felt for Allison with another child. But when Maeve was born and Sarah saw her serious little face and that shock of red fuzzy hair, she fell in love all over again. How could she not have known that her love needn't be doled out between both of her children in a measured way? Allison, Maeve, then Toni, and now Connor. So much love for each of them. Such was the infinite capacity of a mother's heart.

"Hey, you," Jack says, rolling over and noticing she's awake. He's never used any sort of pet name for her — not *babe* or *honey* or *sweetie* — and she often wonders why he can't bring himself to use any such term of endearment. Sarah knew he was the strong, silent type when she married him but she wishes he would unlock a little piece of himself and reveal his feelings once in a while.

"Hey you, too," Sarah says, sitting up and combing her hair with her fingers. "Eight o'clock and you're still in bed on a Wednesday morning. Your dad will be pacing around, thinking there's something wrong over here."

Jack draws her in close and she nuzzles into his chest with his chin on her head. "Tough shit, what he thinks. Got something else in mind." He brushes the top of her breasts with the tips of two fingers and, in that slight touch, Sarah's body is on fire. He rakes her hair with his fingers and his lips find hers in a long, sweet kiss. Jack's always been this way, gentle and slow to start, letting his passion build as though he has all the time in the world.

Sometimes, when she used to bring his supper out to the field in the early days before Allison was born, he'd idle down the tractor, climb down from the cab with that irresistible grin, and spread a burlap sack he carried around in the tractor onto a patch of earth. He'd slip his hand under her shirt and press himself against her then ease her down, taking care as he deliberately unfastened each button and slid off their jeans before moving over her then into her in the same languid way. She used to try to hurry things along, worried someone might see them from the road or Anton would happen by with the other tractor. But Jack would quiet her with a kiss. Time stood still and waited when they were together. It still does.

Afterward, as Sarah puts on the coffee, Jack comes into the kitchen, zipping up his jeans.

"Charlie's coming today?"

"He should be here around five. Mid-week and no rush-hour traffic when he leaves the city, so he should make good time."

"How long's he staying?"

Sarah pops two slices of bread into the toaster. "He has to go back on Sunday. It's a short visit, but it's not like Dad's going to know he's here anyway. And at least he comes."

"It'll be good to see him. We can take him to the Foundation barbecue this weekend."

Sarah nods and pours Jack's coffee. "Addie and Tom will be glad to see him."

Just then Anton appears in the doorway. "You're finally up? I came and knocked on the door after Toni drove out of the yard." He whacks his cane against the door jamb a few times. "Nobody up around here except Misty."

Jack grins. "I was … up. Wasn't I, Sarah?"

Sarah rolls her eyes and hides her smile from Anton. "You might as well sit down, Anton. Have a cuppa coffee."

"You got any of those cinnamon buns left to go with the coffee? It's been nearly three hours since I had my breakfast."

Charlie arrives earlier than expected, pulling into the yard by four thirty. When he drives up in his rental car, Misty gets up and barks. Glancing out the window, Sarah sees Charlie fold himself out of the driver's seat and open the rear door to reach into the back seat for a wheeled bag and a Styrofoam cooler. Charlie's put on a few pounds and his reddish-blond hair has receded, exposing more of his broad forehead, and from a distance it looks as though a younger version of their father is strolling up to the house.

Sarah greets him at the door, Misty tangling around their legs. She takes the cooler from him and puts it on the table. Charlie pulls her in for a hug. "Hi, sis," he says and Sarah can almost hear the lisp he had as a little boy, the way he used to call her *Tharah*.

"Get a pot of water on," Charlie says, motioning to the cooler, which contains lobsters chilling on ice. "Fresh from the Atlantic. I'll boil them up for supper."

"The girls are going to love them," Sarah says. "Jack … not so much."

"He's gotta figure out there's more to life than steak and potatoes." Charlie laughs.

"But you know he's going to ask what kind of meat I've got to go with the lobster."

"Even if it's wieners, you're bound to serve us all a gourmet-style meal. Only you can make magic with a handful of ingredients. Sometimes I wonder how you kept us all fed."

Sarah wonders, too, remembering the usually empty fridge and sparse cans on the pantry shelves. It used to shame her to ask the butcher at Pipers' for knuckle bones, telling him they were for the dog, when, in fact, she used to boil them up for broth. Baba had taught her how to stretch a few handfuls of pot barley and root vegetables into a hearty soup that, together with the two-day-old bread she bought for pennies from the bakery, could feed her hungry brothers.

It seemed to Sarah that her brothers had grown up impervious to the taint of the Coyle name. They didn't seem to notice how the rich town kids looked down their noses at them and laughed at their second-hand clothes. Perhaps it was because they were boys; they were more likely to bloody a nose or blacken an eye if they were teased at school. Fists first, Paul had taught them, and they'd gained a reputation.

"You ever hear from the boys?" Charlie asks, as though he's read her mind.

Sarah shakes her head. "I never hear from Brian and I've never tried to contact him. For all I know, he could be in jail. I guess eventually we'll have to track him down. The day will come when Dad is gone and we'll have to let him know."

"Doubt he'd show up for his funeral, anyway, unless he expected there might be some money left to him. What about Paul? Do you think he'll ever come back home?"

Sarah shrugs. "I've been trying to convince him to see Dad before it's too late. Not that it's going to change anything, but I think it would be good for Paul."

"Did you ever wonder? Do you ever think how things might've been if Patrick hadn't died? Maybe we would have been a half-assed normal family."

"It wasn't Patrick dying," Sarah snaps. "It was Mom who tore this family apart." When she says this, Sarah feels her scalp tighten as though someone's come up behind her and grabbed a handful of her hair. It's a visceral reaction she has whenever she thinks about the way they were abandoned. "She's the one who took off."

Charlie shrugs. "You ever think maybe she had a reason? Dad says she never was happy and things just got worse … after Patrick. She couldn't forgive him for giving the boys that gun."

Sarah doesn't answer.

"We all buggered off eventually. Except you." Charlie walks over and wraps his arms around her. "Our big little sister, the one who held our screwed-up family together."

Their mother walked out two months to the day after Paul killed Patrick. The brothers had been hunting elk along the park line not far from Baba's little farm. Joe had taught them how to shoot when they were just boys, thinking it was a skill they ought to know and one he couldn't teach them in the confines of town. They'd drive out to the farm on weekends to practise, aiming at tin cans on fence posts. Olivia was dead set against it. She didn't trust guns and didn't see the need to shoot for sport, although she didn't complain about the meat they brought home.

Although Sarah was only seven years old when it happened, the details of that day are burned in her mind. It was November and Paul and Pat, seventeen and eighteen years old, set out early, intending to set up in the blind they'd built in a tree on Baba's pasture. It was illegal to enter the national park to hunt, illegal, too, to shoot elk without a licence, but it was done all the time by the farmers who lived along the mountain. It was their due, they thought, for the damage the elk did to the crops during the growing season. The boys had discovered a trail the elk and deer used to venture out of the forest. They had seen small herds there during the summer grazing on the groomed pasture.

Paul climbed up the blind while Patrick walked a ways down the trail, looking for tracks in the slight skiff of snow. While Paul loaded the rifle, waiting for Patrick to return, a female elk, fat from summer grass, emerged at the mouth of the trail, head up, sniffing. Paul couldn't imagine what Patrick had done to force her out, and he couldn't believe their good luck.

They'd made a bet on their way out that morning. Bragging rights to whoever bagged one first, along with the chance to ask Katherine Watts on a date. They both had been eyeing her up for months now and he wondered about that, as he lifted the rifle and took aim. Which one would take credit for the kill and go out with the pretty new town girl? Paul looked past the sight, scanning the woods for any sign of Patrick in his bright orange cap. Their father had taught them never to fire without knowing the other's whereabouts, but where was he?

Just then, he caught a glimpse of his brother, downwind of the elk, behind her on the trail.

Pat had his arm up, waving it in the air, and Paul took this as a sign that Patrick wanted him to take the shot. His finger trembling on the trigger, he lined her up in his sight. A head shot. A perfect kill if he pulled this off. He fired and the elk went down. Her legs flailed, blood spurting from her neck, but, unbelievably, she rolled to her side and stood up. Staggering, she turned and fled into the thick stand of trees. Still momentarily stunned by the recoil, Paul cocked the rifle again and heard it click as the next bullet slid into the chamber. He quickly took a second shot and heard the *ping* as it ricocheted off a tree.

By the time the roar of the gunshot and the ringing cleared from his ears, the elk was gone. He could hear her in the distance, crashing through the underbrush. He waited a moment, expecting Patrick to emerge, ready to take the ribbing he was likely to get for letting such an easy target get away.

The rest was pieced together by the RCMP and the coroner. Paul, dazed and in shock, had driven himself to Baba's, his shirt slick with Patrick's blood. Eventually, they determined Patrick was struck by the errant second bullet and the shooting was ruled a tragic accident. Their mother never forgave their father for teaching the boys to shoot, and, in turn, their father held Paul responsible for taking Patrick's life. Their lives spiralled downhill from there. Their mother left and their father hit the bottle more than ever, staying at work late, jabbering on to whomever would listen about the old days when their family was whole.

Charlie kisses the top of Sarah's head. "Water under the bridge. We can't rewrite history. Mom did what she did and Dad did his best with us crazy little buggers after that. It was hardest for you, I know that."

"But if I just knew why. Why she never showed up, not once, in all these years. No phone calls. No letters. Wouldn't any mother want to know how her own kids turned out?"

"You gotta let that go, Sarah. You'll never know and you have to make your peace with it."

She's tried. She knows there must be a reason in much the same way she realizes she'll likely never have the satisfaction of knowing what it is. Leaning into Charlie, she feels the beat of his heart, the warmth of his arms around her, and, for now, she lets it go.

Sarah is setting out a large Tupperware bowl of potato salad when Addie arrives with her coleslaw. Hughie Rankmore is flipping burgers on one of the huge grills they've borrowed from the Lions Club and Cady is hovering nearby, peeling paper wrappers from between the burgers before handing them off to Hughie.

"Where's that baby brother of yours?" Addie asks as she plants a wooden spoon into her salad. "I've had two days off and I missed seeing him."

"He's around here somewhere. Lots of people have been coming up to talk to him. Friendlier than I ever recall toward one of the wild Coyle boys."

"Everyone knows it was Brian who came up with the shit that got them into trouble." Addie walks over to the galvanized trough full of ice and soft drinks and pulls out a Coke.

Hughie steps away from the grill and whistles through his teeth. The conversations die down as he welcomes everyone to the annual fundraiser and thanks the sponsors for the donations. Cady is at his side trying to keep her balance as she teeters on the rain-soaked turf in her ridiculous high heels. Hughie's the chair of the Community Foundation but everyone knows it's Cady who runs the show. She's gazing off, staring at someone, and Sarah can tell she's not paying any attention to what Hughie is saying. Suddenly Cady's face lights up and she cracks a sly smile. When Sarah looks, she sees Jack has noticed Cady staring at him and he acknowledges her with a slight nod.

Later, after most of the crowd has drifted away and the food's been cleared up, Charlie makes his way over to Sarah, who is tossing paper plates into a garbage bag. "I think I'll head over to Sunny Haven to say goodbye to Dad. I'm planning to leave early and I won't bother driving back to town in the morning."

"It's been good, having you here this week. It gave me a nice break."

"I wish I wasn't so far away and could do this more often."

Addie comes over and gives Charlie a hug. "Next time bring out that wife of yours and those two boys. I haven't seen them in ages."

Cady is standing nearby and, overhearing this, hurries over. "Don't run off before I even have a chance to say hello." She extends her hand to Charlie. "You remember me, don't you? Cady Rankmore?"

Charlie seems puzzled.

"Cady Hubley," Sarah offers.

"Yes, you might remember me from school. I was a friend of your sister."

Addie shoots Sarah a look and Sarah shakes her head. *Unbelievable.*

"Are you the one who was in jail?" Cady blurts out. "You Coyle boys looked so much alike, no one could ever tell you apart. My mother used to say that's how you got away with so much. Who knew which one of you was getting into some sort of trouble?"

Charlie's face reddens. "No, that would be Brian. But Paul and me, we've come a long way since those days." He grins. "Haven't raided a garden since 1974."

"I heard you say you're stopping at Sunny Haven to see your father," Cady continues. "I suppose you've seen Caroline Webb since you've been here. And I wondered how that might have gone."

"Why would that be any of your business?" Addie speaks up.

"Oh, considering the history, you know," Cady says, with a slight shrug of one shoulder. "I heard that Caroline's lawyer's been to see her and I wonder if that's got anything to do with Becca." She glances at Sarah with a smug look. "I'm sure I'm not the only one who's wondering what will happen when she comes back."

Sarah can't breathe. She feels as though the last bit of air has been squeezed out of her lungs. She reaches for Charlie's hand, just to feel something tangible, but in her mounting distress, she can't find it. It's something they've all surely thought about, but no one's said it out loud. What *will* happen when Becca comes back?

"What's your reason for bringing this up?" Addie starts in. "There's nothing …"

"When Becca comes back," Sarah interrupts. She forces the words from her lips and it seems she's listening to herself from a long way off, hearing her voice, foreign-sounding, like someone else is saying the words, careful and watchful of what comes out next. "When Becca comes back, we'll all find out what she's been up to all these years, won't we?" She's trembling now, the garbage bag rustling in her hands.

"And all those old rumours can be put to rest once and for all, can't they, Sarah?" Cady's face is impassive and Sarah realizes Cady is choosing her words, too. Picking the ones that can hurt her the most. "You know what I'm talking about, don't you? The stories about the baby? Were they true?"

The panic rises up over Sarah again. She needs to stop this now.

Charlie's looking at her. He's heard the same rumours as everyone else in Ross Prairie, although he's never asked her outright if they were true. It was a small town and there was so much speculation when Becca went off so suddenly. Lots of people didn't believe Elvina's story that she'd left early for college.

"What will you do, Sarah?" Cady looks down at the manicured nails on one hand. "What will Jack do?"

A scream is about to edge out, and Sarah wants so badly to let it but she steels herself against it. "Don't you have anything better to do than spread rumours like we're back in high school?" She drops the trash bag and takes Charlie's hand. "That's all those stories ever were. Rumours." She wants to say more. Do more. Slap that self-righteous grin right off Cady's face. Tell her to go straight to hell. But there's no winning with Cady Rankmore, so she just walks away.

When she gets home, she wanders along the stone garden paths among her flowers until she settles her seething anger. She doesn't know why she still lets Cady Rankmore get under her skin. She notices her favourite pink lilies need dividing so she finds her garden fork and sinks it into the soil, carefully extracting the main bulb. Tiny bulblets fall away and she replants each of them nearby. Only a few will catch and emerge next spring as hopeful shoots. The others will wither and die under the rich prairie loam.

CAROLINE

Caroline held her mother's white gloves to her nose and breathed deeply, the scent of the cream her mother used to wear so familiar it brought tears to her eyes. She laid the gloves gently on top of the folded dresses, skirts, and blouses in the cardboard box. There were only two indulgences her mother had ever allowed herself at the end of a long, hard day: the brushing of her thick white hair with a silver-handled brush and the application of Noxzema cream to the cracked skin on her knuckles. Caroline's tears welled over as she recalled catching a glimpse of her mother sitting on the edge of the bed in a white nightdress, lost in thought, kneading the medicinal cream into her hands. It was the night before Caroline had left to start her new life in Winnipeg. She'd walked right past to her own room, thinking about what she had left to pack, not pausing to say good night to her mother. Oh, how she wished she could have that moment back. If only she had one more chance to hug her, to bury her head in her mother's shoulder, to take that work-calloused hand in hers and feel its warmth.

She folded the flaps on the box and piled it on top of the other box she'd already packed. That morning, her father had instructed her to go through her mother's things. They were destined for the church rummage sale where her mother's few good dresses might be sold and cut up for swatches in someone's patchwork quilt.

The task had taken less time than Caroline expected. She'd thought she would find old letters or a journal but there was nothing of the sort in the chest of drawers with her mother's clothes, just a few bits of jewellery and some hair clips. It was in the kitchen where she found her mother's life. Caroline had come across a stack of old calendars, piled on a high shelf in the pantry. They were filled with notations — the first day of seeding, an early autumn frost, estimated wheat yields, reminders to herself to order chicks or bake pies for the fall supper — each one an accounting of her mother's busy days.

After she was finished, Caroline went downstairs and out to the yard where her father was lying on the ground under the belly of the Farmall, a steady clang ringing out every few seconds. There was a chill in the midday air, although the sun was making a valiant attempt in a clear sky brushed with thin, wispy clouds.

"I got all of Mum's things sorted through. Is there anything else you need me to do?" Her father kept coming up with new jobs for her whenever she mentioned she needed to get back to the city. She'd already cleaned out the hen house, scrubbing it down with Pine-Sol, painted the outhouse with a half gallon of leftover paint, and finished making the preserves.

He shimmied out from under the tractor, squinting into the sun. "You've got through it all already?"

Caroline shrugged. "There wasn't much to go through. There are only two small boxes and one box of old, worn-out things for the burn barrel."

He stood up, putting both hands on his hips and stretching backward. "Arthritis is acting up. Must be rain coming."

"Everything's done in the house. I've even mended your shirts Mum hadn't had time to get to during harvest. There's really nothing else I can think of doing before I go back."

"I've been meaning to talk to you about that," he said, stretching his neck from side to side. "There hasn't been a good time and I've been putting it off, I admit." He reached down and picked up a wrench that was lying at his feet. "There's no easy way to tell you this, I'm afraid." He tapped the wrench nervously against the palm of his other gloved hand.

Caroline felt her heart skip a beat just as it did in Mrs. Miner's office when she heard his voice on the phone. "What is it?"

"Listen," he said, looking away. He tugged off one glove and scratched furiously at the back of his neck. "The money's gone," he finally said.

She took a quick, deep breath. "What do you mean?"

"I thought about it long and hard before I spent it, I really did." He looked at her then, a pleading sort of look. "It was Old Smoky. This last harvest really did him in. I talked to Joe Coyle; he says there's no more patching and fixing that will keep that old truck on the road. The motor's shot. There's nothing to be done but replace it."

"You've bought a new truck?" Caroline managed to ask, her voice cracking with disbelief.

"It's sitting at the dealership in town. I've been waiting to bring it home until I told you."

Caroline let the news sink in. There was no money for her to start school after Christmas after all. It felt as if a heavy window blind had been drawn on the possibilities she'd envisioned for herself this year. But it was just a temporary setback, wasn't it? "I suppose I can work a whole year and start class next fall like I originally planned."

Her father tossed the wrench back on the ground. "I need to talk to you about that, too." He climbed up on the tractor seat and stared at the steering wheel, not meeting Caroline's eye. "It's your place to stay home, now that your mother's gone. Take care of the house and such."

Caroline couldn't believe what she was hearing. "What are you saying?" He wasn't talking about a one-year delay. He was telling her she couldn't go to college. Not ever. "I have to go back!"

Her father stomped on the clutch and started up the motor.

"You can't do this!" Caroline cried. "Mum wanted me to go to college!"

"Your mother's gone, Caroline. And it's up to you to take her place here on the farm and in the house. Leastways till I get you married off. It's a hard pill for you to swallow, I know, but your mother would agree with me." He pulled his cap lower on his forehead and backed away from the shop.

"But, Daddy, please," Caroline cried, trotting alongside him as the tractor puttered down the lane. "What will I tell Susan?"

"You'll tell her to find herself another roommate. Before winter sets in, I'll give you some money to travel to the city and pick up your things."

"She's expecting me back," Caroline shouted. "You can't just decide this on your own without even talking to me about it!"

Her father frowned and cupped his hand up to his ear. "No use carrying on 'cause I can't hear you anyways. Back to the house with you, now. This is the end of it." He throttled up and shifted to high gear, and, with a puff of black smoke, the tractor sped down the lane.

"Dad. Wait!" Caroline yelled, running after him. The tractor hit a deep pothole too fast and her father nearly bounced out of the seat. "Daddy!" she screamed again, stomping her foot as he turned at the end of the lane and headed down the road.

She couldn't believe it. Her mother was likely to roll over in her grave. It wasn't enough that her mother had abided by every questionable decision he'd ever made, now Caroline was being made to give up on her dream, too, just because her father had declared it so.

Her heart was beating so hard she thought it might pulverize to bits inside her chest. She was an adult now, and couldn't be told what to do. How dare her father break his promise to her and her mother! Well, she just wouldn't take this lying down. An idea was already taking shape in her mind. She would take care of the yard and the house chores until her father gave her the money to return to the city to collect her things. When the time came, she would say goodbye and board the train. She would reunite with Susan, go back to her job, save every penny she could, and take night classes if she had to; she didn't care if it took her ten years. She had no desire to ever come back home. There was no way her father, or any man, for that matter, was going to tell her what she could or couldn't do.

Caroline had ignored the spindly tree for nearly a week after her father brought it home in much the same way she had avoided him the last two months. She couldn't care less about Christmas and decorating the tree; her heart just wasn't in it. She planned to attend Christmas service, but, other than that, she hoped the holiday would pass without any fuss.

Every year for as long as she could remember, she and her mother had bundled up and climbed up next to her father on the sleigh, bells ringing on Molly's harness as she plodded through the snow. Some years they spent hours searching the woodland surrounding the pasture for the right Christmas tree, while other years, when the frigid air was so cold their scarves stiffened like cardboard under their noses, they returned quickly with a less-than-perfect tree. Her father had no business bringing home a tree this year without asking her if she wanted one, although since when did he care about her opinion?

This morning, with only two days until Christmas and Eldon sure to ask why there wasn't a tree, Caroline had finally hauled the box of Christmas decorations down from the attic. She strung garland loosely in swoops to fill in some obvious gaps and attached all the familiar coloured glass ornaments. Stepping back, she tossed a handful of icicles into an empty space near the top.

Her father was in the kitchen, listening to Christmas carols on the radio and reading the paper. Caroline checked the gravy she'd left bubbling on the stove. The potatoes were mashed; the pie she'd made with the last of the pumpkins was cooling on the table. She glanced at the clock. Eldon was expected any minute. "It's already dark. Surprised Eldon's not here yet," her father said, looking up from his paper.

Eldon, like the weather, was one topic safe enough to talk about. He'd made things bearable the last few months, visiting often and acting as a buffer between them. He tried to make peace, telling Caroline how hard it was for her father — a man from his generation — to be left alone without a woman to care for him. He tried to explain how much her father needed her. And she'd overheard Eldon tell her father that he should allow Caroline a little more freedom, more time to go out and enjoy herself. He told him he couldn't understand Caroline's desire to go off to the city any more than her father did but that she needed time to get over the disappointment of it. He often played a few hands of rummy with her father when he came, sharing his attention between them, before he'd ask to take Caroline for a short drive or to a movie in town.

"He'll be here shortly, I'm sure," Caroline said. She took three plates out of the cupboard and set them around her father's newspaper. "I think I hear his truck just now."

A minute later, Eldon came through the door, his eyes unusually bright, his face flushed from the cold. He took off his boots, hung his coat on a hook by the door, and then took Caroline's hands in his own. They were surprisingly warm. He wanted to kiss her, she could tell by the way he looked at her, but he could not, not with her father sitting right there. She sensed the passion rising out of him like July heat from a stone, and she felt herself blush as she always did when she realized how much he desired her.

"Come in and sit down. Supper's ready."

Eldon and her father started in on a lively conversation about the unexpectedly cold temperatures. Her father liked Eldon and perked up into a more buoyant mood whenever he dropped by.

Caroline would never forgive her father completely. Not only had he spent the money, he'd also tricked her into believing he would allow her one last visit to pick up her things. She'd waited and waited, still holding on to a small bit of hope, asking each week for the money to go. Finally, in late October, he brought her large suitcase and a cardboard box home from the train station. He'd had Susan pack up her things and send them home on the train.

Caroline had unpacked the suitcase, hanging the dress she'd bought with Mum's silver dollars in the back of her closet.

She would never wear it on a date with Michael Wickstrom; she'd very likely never see him or Patsy or Monique again. The memories she'd made in Winnipeg in that one short month were starting to fade and all of it — the bank, the picnic, the tiny apartment — seemed like something she might have dreamed or seen in a movie.

At about that time, Eldon had started dropping in two, sometimes three times a week. He brought her small gifts to cheer her up: fine stationery for her to write letters to Susan, clips and bows for her hair, a box of Swiss chocolate. He'd kissed her for the first time on the night of the first big snowfall in November. He'd just driven her home from a pie auction at the Legion, a fun-filled night where he bid ten dollars for her lemon meringue pie and the right to share it with her and spin her around the floor for the first dance of the evening. Thick, lazy flakes of snow had swirled down, piling up on the windshield as they sat in his truck out in the yard. The heater fan squealed away, working hard to pump warm air into the cab.

"My toes are freezing," Caroline said.

"Take off your boots," Eldon said, and she did. She swung her legs up on the seat and he massaged her feet between warm palms then lifted one of his legs and tucked both her feet high between his thighs. Her breath caught in her throat when she felt him grow hard. "Oh!" The word escaped her and Eldon moaned, taking it as an invitation, and pulled her toward him.

His lips pressed against hers, desperate and demanding, and she wasn't quite sure how to respond. She was rather disappointed, expecting something more from his first kiss. Heroines in novels grew weak with desire after a passionate kiss, but she had no one to ask if her lukewarm reaction was normal. She liked him well enough, though. Maybe the swooning would come in time.

She'd continued to see Eldon, liking the way she was treated when she stepped out with him. Businessmen and farmers as old as her father tipped their hats when she walked by on his arm. Being courted by Eldon Webb brought with it a sort of prestige, and she no longer felt like a teenage girl when she went in to Bud's Mercantile for groceries or picked up a parcel at the post office. Caroline had to admit she enjoyed her new status and all the attention Eldon lavished on her.

"Mother asked if you and Caroline would join us for Christmas dinner," Eldon said now. "Vera's cooking a turkey, and it's really too much for the two of us."

"I can't see why not. What do you think?" said Caroline's father.

Caroline was dreading that long, empty day. Her mother had never tired of making a spectacle of Christmas morning, filling three stockings with Japanese oranges and nuts and sticky, striped candy and then pinning the socks with safety pins to the arm of the chesterfield. They'd all play along, acting as though Saint Nick had left them there during the night. There was always one special present for Caroline with a tag marked *From Santa* — a baby doll or a miniature set of porcelain dishes when she was younger, skates or a sweater or skirt she'd been pining for from the catalogue as she got older, even when she was too old to believe. Caroline had found a ball of yarn in her mother's closet and knit a pair of mittens for both her father and Eldon. It wasn't much, and she felt a little ashamed of her gift for Eldon but what could she possibly give a man who seemed to have everything?

The distraction of company would be welcome on Christmas Day, and she wouldn't have to cook, even if it meant spending time with his dour-faced mother. "Of course, we'd love to come."

Eldon reached for her hand and squeezed it under the table. "I'll clear the snow off the river. Build a bonfire. We can go skating. Maybe you can invite Alice. And Susan, if she's home."

Later, when the dishes were cleared away, Caroline's father went out to the barn to tend to the evening chores and Eldon and Caroline retired to the living room. Caroline plugged in the string of lights on the Christmas tree, switched off the glaring overhead light, and settled next to Eldon on the sofa. A rainbow of light shimmered off the glass ornaments and dangling silver icicles. The tree, while not perfect, looked fine in the dim light.

"I saw Clarice Hubley in the Farmer's Store yesterday and she's invited us to a party at their house on New Year's Eve. I said we would come," Eldon said, stretching out his legs and propping one up on the coffee table.

"A party? I'm not sure I'm up to it," Caroline said, annoyed that he hadn't asked her first. "Who would I know at a party the Hubleys would throw? Everyone is sure to be so much older than me. Married women with children, all chatting to one another. What would I possibly talk to them about?"

Eldon frowned. "You need to make friends with other women beyond the girls you knew in high school. It will be good for you to meet new people."

"I suppose. I just don't know if I'll be in a very festive mood, considering the turn my life has taken in the past few months."

"All the more reason to celebrate the start of a new year. You have to keep your chin up, look forward to better and brighter things in 1955," Eldon said, stroking her knee. "Your future could be more than you'd ever hoped for."

It bothered Caroline when Eldon said things like that — dismissing her feelings, as though attending a cheery gathering and flipping the page on a calendar would diminish the gaping hole her mother's death had left in her life. "I don't know, Eldon. My life's on hold, really. What is there to expect or look forward to?"

"You're young and more beautiful than you know," Eldon said, brushing one finger gently up and down her cheek. "Your whole life's ahead of you." He slipped one hand in his pocket and just as quickly pulled it out. "But you have one glaring fault that I've noticed, if you don't mind me saying." He sat up straighter.

"And what is that?" Caroline said sharply. She didn't need another lesson from Eldon, telling her to buck up, as though he, like her father, knew what was best for her.

"You focus on what you don't have and forget to notice the good things right in front of you."

"What's that supposed to mean?" She disliked when Eldon spoke in riddles, making her try to figure out what he was trying to say, as though she was being tested in some way.

"Oh, hell," Eldon said. He stood up and reached into his pocket again. "I was going to do this on Christmas Day, but now seems as good a time as any." He dropped down on one knee and pulled something from his pocket. On the palm of his hand was a small, black velvet box.

"Caroline McPhee," he said, flipping open the lid, "I can't give you a life in the city like you wanted, but I can offer you a life where you'll have everything you need right here in Ross Prairie. I want you to be mine forever. I promise to love you and keep you always, if you'll have me."

A droplet of radiant light, the size of a seed pea, was nestled in the box and Caroline gasped at the sight of it. Eldon removed the diamond ring and took her hand. "Will you, Caroline?" he asked, gazing up at her. "Will you be my wife?"

PART
TWO
CAROLINE,
1957

MAY

There it is, the crimson stain. Each time, month after month, Caroline is crushed by disappointment at the sight of it. Eldon keeps track of her cycles on a chart in the barn, plotting her courses with the same precision he uses to graph the rainfall and log the births of the calves. He is sure to ask if she's caught — as cool and dispassionate as if he were asking whether she'd ordered starter for the chicks — and she will have to make another shameful admission. No, she has not.

She married Eldon in April of '55 after taking a few months to consider his proposal. She couldn't imagine herself a spinster, caring for her father the rest of her life, and both Eldon and her father convinced her that would be her fate if she didn't marry well. Besides, there were worse things than being a rich farmer's wife, she reasoned; it would be a comfortable life, at least. They went to Winnipeg on the train in March to celebrate their engagement and stayed at a fancy city hotel (in separate rooms, of course). She chose a stunning gown from a bridal shop on Portage Avenue and he bought her a pair of Italian leather wedding shoes soft as a baby's cheek. At a restaurant where he took her to dine, the waiter pulled out her chair and placed a white linen napkin on her lap, the table laid out with as many forks and spoons at her own plate as she used to set for the three of them when her mother was alive. In the first months of their marriage, he was ravenous in his desire for her, pampering her, letting her stay in bed each morning for as long as she wanted.

But after six months, when there was still no sign of a baby, he grew short-tempered and impatient. He tacked up a calendar next to the mirror in the bathroom, marking the days he determined held the best chance of success with an *F*. For fertility, he told her, an unspoken reminder to both of them he would come to her those nights. Caroline, however, sees Failure screaming at her every time she notices those bold, black *F*'s. She does everything he asks of her, holding completely still afterward, lying with her legs propped against the headboard, head turned away in humiliation. She swallows the foul tasting herbal remedy he's procured from Halya Petrenko, mixing it with sweetened tea each morning and then chewing a sprig of mint she grows in a pot on the windowsill. Eldon, she's noted, does nothing to enhance his own success. She alone bears the burden of her empty womb.

Two weeks ago, she prepared carefully for the prescribed night, brushing her hair until it shone before climbing between the sheets wearing nothing but a dusting of the rose-scented talcum powder he liked between her breasts. He came to her in the moonlight, dropping his trousers on the floor and sliding into bed. He did not take her in his arms or even brush his lips against hers as he used to. Instead, he pressed a cool palm to her breast, cupping and prodding in the same disinterested way Dr. Alden does during an examination, then mounted her and commenced the measured thrusts. Caroline closed her eyes and willed her body to accept the coupling, conjuring in her mind's eye the precious child she so desperately craved, a baby she would hold to her heart and treasure.

She straightens her dress and fastens the outhouse door. Sport, one ear perpetually cocked, sits outside the door thumping his tail on the worn dirt path. She reaches out to scratch the downy fur under his throat.

"I guess it's just going to be you and me for a while yet, boy," she says softly and Sport, with a deep canine understanding in his eyes, nuzzles her shin. Together they walk back to the brick house, through the huge yard intersected by a row of towering spruce trees.

A new barn for the stock and a row of freshly painted granaries are set well back from the house, behind the trees. A series of large perennial flower beds are scattered about the yard closer to the house. Their hired hand, Bert, used to tend to the gardens, but after Eldon and Caroline were married, Elvina suggested Caroline take over their care. Vera came each day to do all the household chores, she reasoned. What was there for Caroline to do? Caroline happily agreed if only for an excuse to get out into the sunshine and away from Elvina's watchful eye.

The first September, she stuck wooden clothespins into the ground, marking the location of the Maltese cross, the tiger lilies, and the brown-eyed Susans. Their startling colours reminded her of Elvina; the red too garish, the orange too loud. The next spring she dug and chopped and hauled the thick roots away, taking a certain amount of pleasure in the flowers' demise. In their place, she transplanted delphiniums, lilies, and cranesbills from her mother's garden and they swept the yard in turn with calming hues of violet, pink, and blue. Elvina disapproves, of course, complaining the garden lacks spunk, whatever that means, but, in the garden, at least, Caroline has free rein and is able to tend to the flowers of her choosing.

Eldon's truck is parked next to the house, the passenger door wide open. He comes out of the house, dressed in a clean blue shirt, neatly pressed with sharp creases in the sleeves the way he likes, and his Sunday shoes. "Why aren't you dressed? I'm ready to go."

"It can't be two o'clock yet. I've only just finished washing up the lunch dishes."

"You won't go at all if you're not waiting in the truck by the time I get back from checking the sick calf," Eldon says, gesturing to the open door. "I have three plough shears that need sharpening at Coyle's and I want to get there early."

Caroline hurries into the house and up to her room. Why couldn't he have told her he wanted to leave early while he was eating his lunch? She looks forward to her trips to town on Saturday afternoons, when most farmers and their families come into town to shop, and to her weekly visits with Alice at King's Café.

She quickly slips on her sanitary belt and attaches a napkin, pulls on clean underwear and a buttery lemon sundress with an eyelet collar she's sewn herself. She doesn't have time to brush her hair so she gathers her blond curls with one hand and fastens a tortoiseshell clip at the nape of her neck. Eldon, especially quick-tempered today, is revving the truck's engine, a warning he's about to leave without her, so she races down the stairs. He is already pulling slowly away when she leaps into the truck, reaches for the flapping door, and slams it shut.

The tires spit gravel as Eldon roars down the lane.

Caroline steadies herself as he careens past the mailbox. "How's the calf doing?"

"Not likely to make it. I should have just given his mother a bullet between the eyes for rejecting him like she did," Eldon says darkly.

"Well, she *is* young. It's her first calf. Maybe she's not sure what to do."

Eldon looks at her with disdain, in that superior way he has when he thinks she's said something stupid. "There are good mothers and poor ones and there's no amount of beating that can make a mother out of a cow that doesn't have it in her."

His comment makes the hairs stand up on the nape of her neck. Last week, she was planting potatoes in the back garden when she heard a commotion coming from the barn. She walked over and stood by the door, watching as Eldon and Bert roped and tied the frightened young cow to a stall. Bert held the bawling calf as Eldon grabbed the cow's swollen teat and squeezed out a trickle of milk over the calf's nose. The cow balked and lashed out her left hind leg. Eldon cursed, then grabbed a grain shovel leaning against the stall and struck the cornered beast across the back. The outraged cow bellowed in pain at the sickening thud of steel on hide.

Caroline knows better than to speak to Eldon when he is in one of his black moods so they ride the rest of the way to town in silence, passing by field after water-logged field. The morning's heavy rain lies pooled in all the low spots. Emerging shoots of yellowed wheat, struggling against rot, search for the sun. Anton Bilyk's tractor, sunk to the axles, is abandoned near the road.

They pull into town and cross the tracks. Two boxcars sit on the siding by the Pool elevator, waiting for the next train to haul their cargo of wheat to Thunder Bay. Main Street is already packed with parked cars and trucks and there is a long line of teenagers and children standing in front of the Star Theatre, waiting for the afternoon matinee. Caroline asks Eldon to drop her off at the library, where she can browse through the stacks before she buys groceries at Pipers' Lucky Dollar and tends to her other errands.

"I'll meet you at our usual time," Eldon says as Caroline climbs out of the truck.

"I'll just wait for you at the café. Even if you're running late, there's always someone there to talk to."

He eyes her suspiciously. On their trips home he always wants to know who she's been visiting with, which women exactly, and everything they've talked about. Caroline has come to understand he is not really interested in whatever gossip Alice may have overheard on the telephone lines or anything else that is happening in Ross Prairie. Rather, this is his way of accounting for the time she's spent when she's been on her own.

"Five thirty, then," he says. "Maybe we can stay in town for supper."

Caroline smiles at him in spite of his bad mood. She hadn't expected him to treat her to supper, which he does so rarely. In spite of the show he puts on, he is incredibly tight-fisted when it comes to his precious money and it pains him to part with it, especially for a meal he thinks Caroline is entirely capable of cooking.

"Five thirty, it is," she says, and her heart sings in anticipation of the hours that lie ahead, when she's free to go where she likes and speak to whomever she pleases.

Alice is already sitting in a booth at King's when Caroline rushes in, her arms weighed down with packages and books.

She found a table in the corner of the library after she checked out her books and, thinking she had some extra time, turned to the first chapter of Willa Cather's *My Antonia*. Before she knew it, she was lost in Antonia's world, and, when she glanced up at the clock, it was already three thirty; she still had to get her shopping done before meeting Alice.

"Geez, Louise, look what the wind blew in!" Alice swings her long, sleek legs under the table as Caroline slides into the red vinyl booth across from her. Alice is wearing a white blouse, unbuttoned provocatively low, a tight black skirt, and more rouge and lipstick than she usually wears. As soon as she took a job as an operator at the telephone office and moved out of her mother's house, she started dressing like women in movie magazines and launched an active campaign to secure a husband — definitely not a farmer, as she would often point out — although finding anyone else in Ross Prairie quickly began to seem next to impossible. Alice currently has her sights set on Bill Reynolds, the new banker in town, and she was chatting with him when Caroline came in. He is sitting at a table across the aisle from Alice, alone, a table for two.

"Sorry, Alice. I lost track of time."

"Busy, busy, rush, rush. Every time you come to town, you're always in a hurry."

"I don't have the luxury of living here like you do, able to walk to the Lucky Dollar or the post office whenever I want to," Caroline says sharply. She is tired and thirsty, having just rushed through her shopping.

"If Eldon would buy you a car or bring you to town more than once a week, you'd have more time for your friends," Alice says. "And we could have a little crazy fun, like we used to in the old days." She winks at Caroline as she says this in a voice loud enough for Bill to hear, implying they were party girls in high school, which couldn't be further from the truth.

"There's a nice blue Fairlane parked right now at Hubley's lot, and even though I've been dropping him hints, Eldon keeps telling me I don't need one yet. I've pointed out that his mother had her own car when she lived on the farm and was able to come and go as she pleased."

"Eldon just wants to keep an eye on you. It's pathetic, the way he makes you ask to be driven wherever you need to go. As though you need his permission. Besides, he's been promising you a car for two years."

"He says he'll buy me a family car," Caroline says, dropping her eyes, "when the time is right."

"It's a bribe, is what that is," Alice says, dropping her voice. She reaches across the table and touches Caroline's hand. "How's that going, by the way?"

Tears spring to Caroline's eyes and she shakes her head.

"I'm so sorry," Alice says softly. "Who would have thought getting pregnant could be so difficult?"

"Eldon's losing patience. And his mother's even worse. Last week I found another layette, a pink one this time, left on the dining-room table. I'm not sure if she'd been skulking around the house while I was out in the garden or if she'd given it to Eldon to plant somewhere I was sure to find it. As though I need to be reminded of my duty, as she puts it."

"I thought when the Queen Bee moved out of the house, you'd loosen up. I mean, being on edge with her hovering around all the time wasn't helping."

Caroline thought so, too. After their wedding, instead of moving out like she said she would, Elvina stayed on. She found fault with every house that came up for sale in town; too small, too old, she didn't care for the neighbours. That fall, she finally decided she wanted a new house overlooking the river at the edge of town on Park Street, so Eldon set about hiring someone to build it.

Caroline and Eldon had first settled into Eldon's old room, across the hall from Elvina. It made Caroline uneasy to have her so close at night, and she couldn't relax. She imagined Elvina lying there, stiff in her bed, eyes wide, listening to the thumps and creaks of Eldon's frequent enthusiasm coming from their room. Caroline was so relieved when the new house was ready and Elvina finally moved out. They moved in to her room with the dreary brocade wallpaper and overbearing furniture, and resumed their attempts in Elvina's old four-poster bed. But even with Elvina out of the house, a baby did not come.

"I don't want to talk about her," Caroline says, and orders a soda. "Have you heard from Susan? I haven't had a letter for weeks. I phoned and left a message with her landlady, but she hasn't called back."

"Me neither. Maybe she's met someone and she's too caught up in her new romance to give a care about the two of us country bumpkins. She's likely dating some dreamy city fellow with a house along the river and all kinds of money. Who knows?" Her eyes light up the way they used to in high school.

Caroline marvels at Alice's wild ideas about romance, how taken in she is by the stories she reads in romance magazines and the fantasies of Hollywood movies. She has no idea what life with one man — the everyday sameness, the effort it requires — is really like. Over time, Eldon has made Caroline's purpose and place in the marriage perfectly clear. She is expected to be pretty and good-natured, at all times, and pregnant, too, and she is beginning to resent Eldon for it. Each day is a tedious chore, inventing lighthearted conversation to stroke his swollen ego and keep him happy. There are times when she's tired and miserable and it's just too much to ask of her at the end of a long, hard day, all that pleasantry and sweetness. Sometimes she just wants to be left alone.

"She's more likely to be studying for some exam than taken up with a mysterious man. You know our Susan."

Alice takes a sip from her soda, leaving a greasy smear of red lipstick on the rim of the glass. "She's not likely to ever find a husband if she doesn't get her nose out of those books."

Bill Reynolds tosses some change on the table and is about to head for the door when Alice stops him. "Hey, Bill. Where are you off to all by your lonesome?"

"The Silver Creek bridge is washed out south of town. I thought I'd drive out there."

"Seriously? I hadn't heard about that." Her eyes are open wide with a childlike innocence that Caroline knows she's putting on; Alice and the girls at the phone office know all the news in town.

"Would you like to come with me and take a look?"

Alice springs from her seat, grabs her purse, and is halfway to the door before she stops and looks back. "It's all right, isn't it, Caroline? Leaving you here? Eldon will be along shortly, won't he?"

"Go ahead," Caroline says. "I'll be fine. I'm sure he'll be here any minute."

The café is nearly empty, except for a trio of elderly women she doesn't know, one with black curlers rolled up under a net in her hair, and a small group of high-school boys, smoking at the counter. One of them is Susan's younger brother, Gerald.

He notices Caroline and sidles over, looking down at her through a hank of black hair hanging over his eyes.

"Hi, Caroline. Long time no see."

"Hi, Gerry. Did you see Alice leave? We were just talking about Susan and saying we haven't heard from her in a while. How is she, anyway?"

"She's just finished writing exams and she's starting a summer job at the university as a research assistant for one of her professors."

"How exciting! She's always been so curious."

"That's what Dad says, but Mom's a little concerned, having Susan working so closely with one of her teachers all summer. She thinks Susan should take a break from campus, maybe find a job selling shoes or cosmetics or something. All Susan can talk about is this professor of hers."

Just then the bell rings above the door. The boys at the counter look over their shoulders and a hush falls over the café. Eldon is standing there, a greasy smudge across the front of his shirt, and he surveys the room, glaring at the old women who look up from their coffee.

Eldon strides across the café to Caroline's table. He stops and looks Gerry up and down before turning to her.

"You ready to go?"

"I thought we were staying in town for supper."

"I'm in no mood for supper. I had to wait at Coyle's all afternoon to get the damn shears sharpened. Old Jim Coyle used to get my work done soon as I dropped it off. But now that Joe's running the place, he said I had to wait my turn. There were six other work orders come in before mine. Six! And I was expected to wait. Just got the shears picked up and the groceries collected from Pipers'. We're heading straight home." He glowers at Gerry. "If you're all done here, that is."

Gerry is standing off to the side and he ducks his head sheepishly. "It was nice talking to you, Caroline."

"You, too," she says, scrambling to gather her books and parcels while Gerry hurries back to his friends.

"So who was your young friend there?" Eldon says through clenched teeth. "I thought you were meeting Alice."

"Oh, for heaven's sake. That's Gerry Wawryk, Susan's brother. Alice just left a few minutes ago, and he stopped —"

Eldon grasps her arm, clenching his fingers so tightly it makes her wince. "Maybe you should have joined the ladies over there after Alice left instead of inviting that hoodlum over here to your table."

"I did no such thing," she says defiantly. "He stopped by on his own and I asked about his sister, is all I did. I didn't know I needed your permission to inquire about an old friend."

Eldon squeezes her arm even harder and lifts her to her feet. The woman with the curlers swivels around on her chair to look as Caroline fumbles, drops two books. Eldon stalks out the door. Caroline picks up her books and rushes after him, too ashamed to look up, knowing Gerry is watching.

Eldon backs out onto the street without a glance in the rear-view mirror, guns the motor like a teenage boy with something to prove, and peels out of town. It is raining again, white sheets pouring down, and Eldon, refusing to let the rain get the best of him, doesn't switch on the wipers. Once he's on the road, he hammers his foot on the gas and the truck bucks forward. He floors it for a mile and takes the next corner too fast. The truck fishtails wildly and the paper bag of groceries at Caroline's feet topples over, spilling tin cans.

"Slow down, for heaven's sake," she says, bracing her legs. The rain hammers on the roof like pellets on metal and she can hardly see the road through the window.

He barrels on, the truck careening through slick gravel, and Caroline steals a look at him. He grips the steering wheel, his eyes intent on the road. When they get home, he overshoots the spot where he usually parks and slams on the brakes. Instinctively, Caroline cowers against the door.

Eldon heads for the barn and Caroline waits for a moment until her thundering heart begins to slow, then leans down and picks up two tins of Aylmer tomatoes from the floorboards. Outside, Sport is pacing, wiggling his rump, waiting for her to open the door, and he barks twice, a distressed sort of yelp, sensing something is wrong.

"It's okay, Sport. I'm okay," Caroline says as she eases out of the truck, checking over her shoulder to see if there's any sign of Eldon out in the yard. A swath of turf, roots pointing toward the dark sky, lies torn up on the ground. She holds her purse over her head and runs to the house.

She'll go back to bring in her things later, after the rain has stopped. For now, she'll set out the Sunday plates, make Eldon a nice supper. Cube the leftover potatoes and fry them with chopped green onion and lots of butter until they're crispy and brown. Open a jar of canned chicken and another of pickled beets. She won't say a word to him while he eats his supper; she'll wait until he's ready, until the storm of his anger has passed. She should have known better, sassing back like that at the café, when he'd just told her how rude Joe Coyle had been. Eldon Webb should not be expected to wait for anyone or anything. He was upset, and she made it worse, and now she has to make it up to him.

She'll bring up a jar of wild plums from the cellar. He will take a spoonful of syrupy sweetness, bite into a soft, red plum, the fruit a tart explosion. The hard, rough stone hidden inside will grate against his tongue.

JUNE

A pot of beef barley soup simmers on the rear element of Caroline's white electric stove. Her father never fails to point out how fortunate she is to have it, and a refrigerator, too. At her father's house, the wood stove still stands in the corner of the kitchen, though now it is cold for most of the day, stoked and lit only in the evening when her father fries himself a couple of eggs or cooks a potato.

Caroline removes the lid, pokes a carrot with a fork, and realizes she has forgotten to add potatoes to the broth. She makes her way to the root cellar down the narrow, dark staircase and waves her hand around in the middle of the pitch-black room until she locates the string attached to the single light bulb. Weak yellow light illuminates the cavernous space where her preserves are stacked on narrow shelves along one rough wall. She reaches into the potato bin and fumbles blindly, imagining spiders brushing her fingers. Outside, Sport barks — not his frantic barking that alerts her to danger but the familiar, happy bark that lets her know he's surprised or excited about something. She grabs two potatoes and hurries up the stairs.

Through the screen door, she sees Sport stretched on his back, wiggling in delight as a man crouches beside him, rubbing his belly. The man stands and removes his cap, revealing a thin, white band of skin on his forehead beneath thick, walnut-coloured hair. It's Nick Bilyk, who lives on the farm next to theirs. His shirt sleeves are rolled up past his elbows and she notices his well-muscled forearms are deeply tanned, unlike Eldon's and her father's, which are covered in long sleeves, summer and winter.

"Hello, Mrs. Webb. I think I've made a new friend," he says.

"Caroline, please," she says as she holds open the door. "Mrs. Webb moved out of this house and into town a while back, in case you hadn't heard."

"Caroline, then." Nick steps through the door, holds out a calloused hand, and smiles. "Is Eldon around?" he says, looking past her as though he expects to see him sitting at the table. Caroline shakes his hand, then tucks a stray piece of hair behind her ear and flattens the creases on the front of her faded housedress, wishing she was wearing a better one, or had at least tied an apron around it to cover the coffee stain on the front. It surprises her to see Nick at their door. A grudging sort of feud has brewed between the Bilyks and the Webbs since Nick's older brother, Anton, bought the farm next door right out from under Eldon's nose five years earlier. Eldon had naturally assumed he would buy that piece of land someday when old Pete Tilley retired or died, but Anton approached Tilley first. Anton allowed Pete to stay on in the old house in the yard and he built a new house for himself and his family. When Pete died, Nick and his mother moved to the farm and settled in Pete's old house.

"He's gone off to town to pick up a part for the mower. Can I help you with something?"

"His cows got through the fence and are over on our side of the river. We let out the bulls and, well, you know how Eldon is about mixing Hereford blood into his line."

"And he'll blame you, surely, for your bulls enticing our cows through the fence," Caroline says with a nervous laugh.

"You got that right." He smiles and ducks his head, as though he is embarrassed at the mention of his lustful bulls.

"That will be quite a job, separating the cows out in the open like that," she says, moving across the room and pulling a chair away from the table.

"Guess I should wait for Eldon and I'll give him and Bert a hand. He'll be mad as hell, but they'll need an extra man getting the cows back over."

"Sit down while you wait. There's still some coffee. And leave your boots on. I'm used to sweeping up Eldon's dirt a dozen times a day."

She retrieves the coffee pot from the stove and fills Nick's cup with an unsteady hand. She is so close to him she can smell the earthy scent of freshly turned soil on his workboots.

"Cream? Sugar?"

"Just sugar."

She sits down across from him and imagines what Eldon's reaction will be when he comes through the door, hungry and expecting his meal laid out, and instead finds Nick Bilyk sitting at his table. She considers getting up and peeling the potatoes to add to the soup, but decides against it and pours herself the last of the coffee.

Nick is the youngest of the Bilyks, a big family that started out on stonier land further north of town. He is older than Caroline and had already quit high school, like many farm boys, by the time she got to grade nine. When Caroline sees him, he always smiles or tips his cap. Before today, she hadn't noticed his broad shoulders, or the way his chest strains against the thin fabric of his shirt. He has a thick scar — a smooth, pink welt — that protrudes from the stubble of his chin — and, unexpectedly, she wonders what it would feel like to trace it with her finger.

"Where did the cows get across anyway?"

"I noticed the fence is down closer to the dirt road, near the stone pile and that old elm tree."

"My reading tree," Caroline says. "There's a natural hollow there where I like to settle in with a good book."

"I've seen you," Nick admits. "When I'm working the piece at the top of the ridge, I've watched you making your way through the wildflowers along the fence line."

Caroline takes a sip of coffee, studying him as he adds a teaspoon of sugar to his cup. She is intrigued by the notion that Nick has watched her as she steals away to her secret place — a place, as far as she knows, Eldon doesn't even know about.

"Do you go there often?" There is an inquisitive honesty to his face; he seems genuinely interested in what she has to say.

"I used to go more often, when Elvina lived here and Vera came by all week. But I still like to walk out there every now and then when I need a quiet place to be by myself. I like listening to the birds and the sound of the river."

"We all need a place like that. Somewhere to think. I climb up into the hay loft. It's quiet up there, no one's around, except for the cats. I like to look out through the loft doors at the whole, wide world." There is a childlike innocence to the way

Nick says this and Caroline can almost see him standing in the opening on the upper storey of a huge red barn, hands on hips, surveying the cows and pigs, the chickens and the ducks, in that self-contained world.

"I heard you bought the Morgan place."

Nick takes a sip of coffee then adds another half teaspoon of sugar. "It's close by. Buying my first piece of land is just the start. I'd like to set out on my own eventually. I'm thinking of expanding my herd, concentrating on cattle instead of grain crops, like Anton. As I get older, with ideas of my own, Anton and I are starting to butt heads, if you know what I mean."

"I do. I can't imagine Eldon farming with a brother or any partner, for that matter. He's so set in his ways, he'd never want anyone else telling him what to do."

"I used to think about pulling out and moving to Alberta, actually. Buy a big ranch somewhere along the foothills, hundreds and hundreds of acres all in one uninterrupted piece. It's a crazy dream, I know," he says, smiling so earnestly Caroline feels a little pull, like the tug of a stitch, on her heart. She'd forgotten what it felt like, having a dream of her own, a secret ambition to do something other than what everyone expected of her.

"It's not the least bit crazy. You should never give up on your dreams," she says. She finishes her coffee, puts the spoon in her cup. "I can picture you on some wide, open range, sitting tall in a saddle on a Palomino." She smiles. "Cowboy Nick."

"Guess I'd have to brush up on my riding and roping skills if I moved out west. Here, you're more likely to see me bouncing around on my tractor than riding my horse. How about you? Do you ride?"

Caroline shakes her head. "We just had old Molly, my father's chore horse, when I was growing up. I always wanted to, but my mother was afraid of horses and wouldn't let me near them. Her brother was bucked from a horse and killed when she was a child. And Eldon thinks horses are a relic of the past. He won't have one on the place."

"Our mare, June, is as gentle as a kitten. If you'd like, I could teach you to ride. There's a great trail, once you get to the edge of the mountain, past the old sawmills, leading all the way to Bride's Lake."

"I'd love that," Caroline blurts out, without thinking. She is caught up in the moment, imagining herself cantering along a sun-dappled trail, birds trilling in the treetops, Nick ahead of her on his own spirited horse. As soon as she says it, she realizes how foolish it is. Of course she can't go riding with Nick Bilyk. What was she thinking? She blushes furiously, reaches for her empty cup, hands trembling, clatters it against the saucer. It's the loneliness gnawing away inside her and the softness in Nick's eyes that made her say such a silly thing and now there's no way to unsay it. What would she do if Nick showed up someday on horseback, leading June?

By the screen door, Sport stands and stretches and huffs a warning as Eldon's truck pulls in the yard. Caroline straightens her skirt, pats down her hair. Her heart is aflutter. Her mouth has gone dry. She feels like she did when she was in grade five, caught by the teacher passing Susan a note.

Nick seems to sense her distress. He stands up, picks up his cup, twists it around in his hands.

Eldon, his face shadowed by his cap, appears in the door. "Bilyk," he says, but he is staring directly at Caroline. "What the hell are you doing here?"

The following Sunday, the sky is dark and a low rumble of thunder threatens rain.

"I'm leaving to get Mother," Eldon says as he puts on his cap. "She'll have had her rest and is sure to be sitting there, watching the clock, dressed and waiting. Be sure that mutt is gone by the time we're back." He gestures to Sport, who sits by the screen door on one of Caroline's mother's colourful rag rugs, as he walks out.

"Off, boy," she says to Sport, and picks up the rug. "Out you go." Sport tilts his head and whines. He is afraid of thunder and Caroline usually lets him stay inside whenever there's a storm. Lady stayed with her father after she married and Caroline missed having a dog of her own so, two years ago, the Wawryks gave her a puppy, the runt of the litter from their golden Lab, Gem. Susan thought he'd be good company for Caroline, a small and helpless thing to care for. Eldon wasn't in favour of Caroline getting the dog; Elvina didn't approve and he didn't want his workboots chewed or knuckle bones lying around the yard. She begged him to go against his mother, just this once, and he finally gave in and allowed her to bring the pup home.

"Elvina's coming," she says to Sport, by way of explanation. "You can't imagine the fuss she'd make if she knew you were allowed to stay in her house."

The kitchen is filled with the aroma of roast beef and fresh-baked rhubarb pie. Just before he left, Eldon noticed the pie cooling by the window, and asked Caroline if she'd forgotten his mother didn't like rhubarb pie. She remembered, of course, but she loved the taste of spring rhubarb, and it didn't make sense, she explained, to buy apples that were out of season, or raisins that cost so much. Eldon gave her one of his stony looks and told her she'd better have something else in mind for his mother's dessert.

She opens the refrigerator, takes out a chubby pint of cream, pours some into a bowl and sets about spinning the crank on the mixer until the cream thickens to stiff peaks. She adds two heaping tablespoons of icing sugar and a scant splash of vanilla and whisks it again, hoping the whipped cream will have the desired effect and moisten the chocolate cake she baked on Tuesday so Elvina won't notice it's gone stale.

During the week they eat in the kitchen, but on Sunday she sets the dining-room table with her only good dishes, three of four Royal Albert china plates that belonged to her mother. When Elvina lived with them, Vera always laid out a lace tablecloth, English bone china, and a set of fine silverware she polished on the first day of each month. Elvina took them all with her, and Vera, too, when she moved out. Neither Elvina nor Eldon suggested hiring a girl to help Caroline with her chores and it is now Caroline's duty, this Sunday supper ritual, although she never complains. It's a small price to pay for having her own kitchen.

She is mashing the potatoes when she hears the crunch of gravel as Eldon's truck pulls into the yard. Peering through the curtain over the kitchen sink, she sees Eldon dash around to open the truck door for his mother. He likes to make a great show of gallantry in front of his mother and Elvina revels in the fuss he makes over her. To see them, you'd think they were Prince Philip and the Queen. Eldon no longer opens Caroline's door, she's noted, stopping the practice shortly after the wedding ring was placed on her finger.

"I've just told Eldon he must speak to his councillor about that washboard road," Elvina says after they've come in. "Who is it now? Oh yes, didn't these people re-elect that Ukrainian fellow, what's his name again, Eldon?" She wrinkles her nose as though she's detected an unpleasant odour in Caroline's kitchen. "Kalinoski, Kalinochuk, some such name, who can know? None of them are easily pronounced. Anyway, something must be done about the road. It's rough enough to rattle one's teeth out of one's head."

"Only if they're not properly attached," Caroline mutters under her breath. Eldon raises his brow and frowns but Elvina does not seem to have heard Caroline's reference to the false teeth of which she is so proud.

"I'm parched," Elvina says. "Be a dear, Caroline, and bring me some water. Ice-cold, mind you. I don't care to drink dishwater."

Eldon and Elvina retire to the dining room while Caroline spoons out the potatoes and carries them to the dining room along with Elvina's water.

"Reverend Williams's sermon was painfully dull this morning, didn't you think so, Eldon?" Elvina is saying when Caroline returns with the roast beef and beans.

"Not particularly," Eldon says, and Caroline is surprised. He rarely disagrees with his mother. "How so?"

"Oh, he went on and on and on. Love thy neighbour as thyself. I mean, really, how can one truly do this when our neighbours these days are so overreaching?"

Eldon seems relieved by his mother's words. "Oh, of course. Now I know what you're getting at. I agree with you completely, but I would hardly call his sermon dull. It actually got my blood boiling a time or two. There are some people who just don't realize they must be kept in their place."

Caroline puts a serving spoon in the potatoes and Elvina reaches for them, heaping a generous helping on her plate while Eldon helps himself to a sweet pickle, eating it with his fingers. Neither one of them waits until all the food is served or for Caroline to join them at the table.

"Precisely. Take that young Bilyk, for instance. Who do they think they are, buying up more land around here? Before you know it, more of their kind will move in and you'll be surrounded by them. Ukrainians as far as the eye can see!"

"The thing is, Morgan didn't even come to me so I could make him an offer, no different than Pete Tilley did all those years ago. When I asked him about it, he said he'd given his word to young Bilyk in March. I told him I'd have offered him a hundred dollars more for it, but he didn't seem to care."

"People don't give us the respect we deserve," Elvina says, glancing at Caroline as though she's as guilty as the rest of the neighbours. "What kind of fool wouldn't want more money?"

Eldon shakes his head. "Morgan told me I don't need the land anyway. Young Nick is just starting out, he said, and could use the extra acres for pasture. It seems the boy has a way with cattle and an easy hand with birthing. Bilyk helped him deliver a healthy set of twins during that last winter snowstorm and didn't take any money for doing it, either."

Caroline takes her place at the table. Her face feels flushed and it may be, considering the way her heart skipped a beat when Elvina mentioned Nick Bilyk. She was unaware that Eldon had spoken to Morgan about the land and was glad Nick bought it before Eldon had a chance to outbid him. She passes the beef roast to Eldon to carve, bows her head and silently offers thanks. For all their haughty ways, Elvina and Eldon don't say grace at their own table.

She looks up and senses Elvina watching her as she fills her plate.

"I smell fresh paint. What have you been up to now?" Elvina has the same disapproving look on her face she has every time she discovers some small change Caroline has made to the house. She still seems to consider it her domain.

Caroline painted the kitchen cupboards a glossy white last summer and, at the time, Eldon told her there was no need to paint them on the inside. But the paint was chipped and worn and she didn't care for the old colour, a yellowish green that reminded her of dugout algae, so she brought home a quart of paint without Eldon knowing and started repainting them.

"I thought they needed freshening up."

"It seems you're spending much of your energy changing things that are just as well left alone," Elvina says curtly. "The painting and papering of the upstairs rooms, for instance. Pink walls and rose-patterned paper for Eldon's old room? It's hardly the choice I would have made. I'm surprised you allowed it, Eldon."

Caroline looks up to see Eldon concentrating on his dinner plate, scraping his beans into a pile. He doesn't want his mother to know they often sleep in separate rooms. A few months ago Eldon told Caroline her tossing and turning was keeping him awake; it was important he be completely rested, working with dangerous machinery all day, he said, so he suggested she move back into his old room. Caroline didn't mind in the least. His snoring disturbed her and she preferred the room at the front of the house, where she could look out to the road and see the neighbours come and go. She packed up his old trophies from the shelves, replaced them with her books and trinkets, and spread a bright quilt, hand-stitched by her mother, on the bed. Eldon moved in her dressing table and bought a leather chair to put in its place in his room.

"It was about time to pack up those old trophies. Gone are the glory days," Eldon says.

"That may very well be, but I don't see why she needs to dress your room up so, with pink flowers on the walls. And besides, it's meant to be a boy's room. It will only have to be redone when your son is born. And heaven only knows why that's taking so long. You would think I'd have a grandson to bounce on my knee by now." She puckers her lips and looks Caroline up and down, as if she's some sort of defective brood mare Eldon has purchased and cannot return.

Caroline grips the seat of her chair and bites the inside of her cheek, breathing hard. *It's not helping, this pressure you're putting on me.* Her father's been harping at her, too, suggesting it's something she's doing wrong, making it impossible for a baby to grow inside her. "Just like your mother for all of those years before you finally came," he's told her.

"Henry McPhee said there'd be a son and there's still no sign of one," Elvina continues and dabs her lips with a napkin. "You McPhees aren't keeping up your side of the bargain."

Caroline pushes away from the table, legs shaking, lips pressed together so tightly she can feel the blunt edge of her teeth. How she would love to give that woman a piece of her mind! Eldon's secretive deal with her father infuriates her.

She found out about it in the spring of '55, right after her wedding. She was helping her father as she often did, making meals and running errands for him when he needed a hand on the farm. There'd been a note on her father's kitchen table that day, asking her to bring the new grain truck to Beulah's field.

Beulah's? The Webbs owned that farm, at least they had for as long as she could remember. Her father had a pining for that land and she distinctly remembered the heated arguments between her parents over the years about Jacob Beulah's place.

"What are you doing here?" Caroline asked when she pulled up with the truck that day.

Her father opened the seed box and jumped down from the seeder. "What does it look like I'm doing?"

"Well, I can see what you're doing, what I meant was, what are you doing here, in Eldon's field?"

"Sowing wheat," he said, kneeling down on the ground and brushing aside the soil to check the depth of the seed. "This is my farm now."

She felt her blood grow hot, rush to her face. "Your farm? You're telling me you had the money to buy —"

"Don't go flying off the handle," her father interrupted. "No one's saying I bought it." He glared at her, as if she had no business questioning him about such matters. "Eldon signed it over to me before your wedding, if you need to know."

"He just *gave* it to you?"

"Temporarily, I suppose," he said, turning away. He stepped behind the truck and began removing planks from the end gate. "It'll be his again anyway, one day, when I'm gone and I've left it to you. God willing, your son will farm this land someday."

"What?" Caroline said. What he'd done — he and Eldon — suddenly dawned on her as she remembered that Indian summer day, after her mother had passed, when Eldon stopped by to speak with her father. She'd taken her leave willingly when her father had asked and set off for the mail, never thinking the business Eldon had to discuss with her father was the gifting of Beulah's land to her father in exchange for her hand.

Jacob Beulah's property had been the first piece of land her father had purchased as a young man; her grandfather had mortgaged the home place so he could buy it. When the crops were ravaged by consecutive years of grasshoppers and drought and the price of wheat fell during the Depression, her father couldn't keep up with the payments and the bank threatened to take not only Beulah's land, but the homestead, too. He was forced to sell it to keep the rest of the farm afloat, although it pained him to no end to see it slip out of his hands. It was Eldon's father who'd bought it; rich and well-established, he had the means to hang on and prosper during the tough times that threatened to sink more vulnerable farmers.

"I remember hearing Mum say, come hell or high water, you were bound and determined to get Beulah's land back someday."

"And so I did," he said. He untied a metal pail from the tractor hitch and climbed up into the box. "I've wanted this piece of land back my whole life."

"And this is how you did it," Caroline said. The enormity of the deal he'd brokered stretched out before her like a vast, furrowed field — a section, a township, a range. He had bartered her away for one hundred and sixty acres.

Eldon pushes away his plate and leans back in his chair. "I don't know about you, Mother, but I'm ready for my rhubarb pie. Caroline's made something special just for you, haven't you, Caroline?"

Caroline spears a bean with her fork, tastes it. It is cold, like the rest of her supper, and it lodges, like a plum pit, in her throat when she tries to swallow.

"Oh, what could it be?" Elvina asks excitedly. "Strawberry shortcake? I've been thinking the June berries might be ready."

Caroline gets the whipped cream from the fridge, chooses a small saucer from the cupboard, takes the glass dome off the cake plate, and cuts out a small square of chocolate cake. She sees that it has a thin crown of furry mould and she considers scraping it off but changes her mind. Scooping out a dollop of whipped cream, she covers the bloom of blue mould and tucks a spoon in beside Elvina's dessert before she carries it to the table.

"Here it is." She smiles sweetly. "Something special. Just for you."

JULY

"Wrap the bar soap in paper before putting it in with the rest of the groceries," Ida Piper says to the box boy. He wraps and packs the soap then pushes aside a box, discreetly wrapped in brown paper, and packs a package of soda crackers into the cardboard box instead. He is new to the store, pimply faced with a shadow of fuzz above his lip, and he seems puzzled by the challenge of fitting all of Caroline's items into one box. Ida shakes open a paper bag with a quick snap of her wrist and tucks the package the boy's been avoiding into the bag herself. Caroline wonders what Ida thinks as she packs it; two years married and still needing the Kotex.

"Don't load that box up with too many cans, the bottom will bust out before Mr. Webb gets it to his truck. That's happened to him before and he was none too pleased." The cash register chimes. "Twelve dollars and eighty-two cents." The box boy reaches for the charge account cards sitting at the end of the counter. "No need for that," Ida says. "The Webbs don't charge."

Caroline pulls two ten-dollar bills out of her wallet. Eldon insists on paying cash for everything. He thinks it beneath them to put anything, especially the weekly groceries, on credit. Caroline's family shopped at Bud's Mercantile, on the opposite side of the street, charging groceries and even goods like her school supplies and new winter boots, paying Bud up in the fall, when the crop came in.

"Here's your change," Ida says. "You're in town earlier than usual. Hope that doesn't mean you'll miss the parade this afternoon."

"No, we're coming back in later just for the parade. Eldon wanted to get all the errands done first thing this morning, before it gets busy later, with nowhere to park."

"Busiest Friday of the year in Ross Prairie, for sure," Ida says. "And I heard it's supposed to be the best parade in a while. Twenty-six floats and three marching bands."

"I'm looking forward to it," Caroline says. She puts her wallet back in her purse and heads out the door.

It is only eleven o'clock and already the temperature is above eighty degrees. The air is so thick and soupy she can almost taste it and, by the time she reaches Mavis Baylor's dry-goods store at the other end of Main Street, she feels droplets of sweat trickling down the small of her back.

Caroline's been looking forward to the parade and summer fair for weeks. It's a two-day event, starting with a colourful parade and the opening of the exhibition hall. On Saturday, all the action takes place on the fairgrounds, with horse shows, chuck-wagon races, bingo, ball games, and a pig scramble for the children. There are concession stands selling hot dogs and popcorn and a small midway, with games of chance and a few rides. Caroline's favourite is the Ferris wheel. She always went up with Susan and Alice, the three of them swinging their legs when they stopped at the very top, making the little car rock and Alice squeal and cover her eyes. Caroline loved to look out at the town from so high; miniature cars and trucks, lined up like a little boy's toys, parked all the way down Gilbert Street as far as you could see. Last year, she asked Eldon to take her up, but he said it was pointless, riding around and around in circles like hamsters on a wheel.

A small bell rings above the door as she steps inside Mavis's store. Bolts of brightly coloured cloth — ginghams, plaids, florals — are displayed on low tables and piled on shelves, and, on a rack at the back of the store, Caroline finds buttons on hundreds of cards. Mavis, the widow who owns the store, is busy at the catalogue desk, helping Anna Bilyk select a pattern. Mavis's husband was killed by a freight train while crossing a track on a country road ten years ago and Mavis, nearly forty and childless, has never remarried or even been courted by anyone again, as far as Caroline knows. She has often wondered what Mavis's life must be like, happily independent, running her own business with no one to answer to except herself. No one demanding meals on time or shirts pressed just so. Caroline reaches into her purse to find a swatch of fabric from a blouse she is sewing and sets about trying to find buttons to match. She is so busy at her task that she doesn't notice the bell ring when the door opens again.

"Eldon told me I might find you here!" Elvina marches up to Caroline, her face flushed. She is wearing a royal-blue blouse, stained by half moons of perspiration under her arms, and a navy skirt with box pleats that reminds Caroline of the hideous drapes that once hung in Eldon's room.

"Where did you see Eldon?" Caroline says, attempting a smile. "I thought he was at the elevator picking up his grain cheques."

"And so he was. I bumped into him as he was coming out of the bank. He's not too happy with the boys at the elevator, let me tell you. It seems there was a problem with the way the last loads of wheat were graded. Davis seems to think there was a touch of bran frost, although Eldon is certain there's not. We didn't get that early frost last fall that most others did."

"It was quite widespread, from what I remember," Mavis says. She is at the cash register, ringing in Anna's pattern. "I covered my tomatoes, and lucky I did, too, because just next door, Judy Eberhoff's tomatoes and cucumbers were black by the next afternoon. Didn't you tell me you'd lost all your tender flowers that night, Caroline?"

Elvina is glaring at Caroline, demanding solidarity, Caroline knows, although she can't be expected to lie about the frost. The wheat in question was planted on the home quarter and it took the same hit as the rest of the fields in and around Ross Prairie. No one had expected a hard frost on the first day of September, but the sky had been clear that night, a black canvas of shimmering stars, and the temperatures had been unseasonably cool for days before. Caroline had covered as much of the garden as she could, the sheets glowing like recumbent ghosts under the white light of a full moon, but she was unable to save it all. There was no sweet corn last season at all; the slim ears failed to fill when the leaves turned brittle and silvery brown.

"Eldon is certain our wheat was too ripe to have been affected by the frost," Elvina continues. "Nevertheless, those bandits at the grain elevators will do whatever they can to squeeze another nickel out of Eldon to keep for the company. They expect us to get by on less and less every year, it seems."

"There are many others in that same boat, Elvina. The whole town's been feeling the effect of last fall's poor crops," Mavis says. "You'd be surprised how my business falls off when the farmers are hurting."

Elvina looks surprised. Clearly, she has never considered the town's fortune is linked to the whims of nature in much the same way as the farmers'. "At any rate, I was glad I bumped into Eldon so I could tell him I'd like you both to watch the parade with me from my front yard. Those lovely elms along the street will keep us comfortable and there will be fewer children scrambling about."

Caroline's heart sinks. She's been looking forward to mingling with the crowds on Main Street. There is an atmosphere of excitement and anticipation at the top of the parade route that can't be matched by the thinner crowds as the parade passes by the residential streets. And she was hoping she might see Nick in the crowd, although she knows she could never speak to him with Eldon and Elvina standing beside her. But it would be enough to catch a glimpse of him — those strong, wide shoulders and that endearing smile — across the street. "I thought we could all watch from the same place we did last year, across from the post office," she says.

"We didn't have a finished house along the parade route last year, did we? And it's much too hot to be corralled among the crowds on Main Street," Elvina says dismissively. "There's no sense pulling that long face, Caroline, or trying to get Eldon to change his mind. He's already agreed."

Caroline quickly selects a package of plain white buttons, hands it to Mavis and searches in her change purse for a quarter. "I watch the parade from the front of my store every year and there's always so much commotion on this corner. Just as well to visit and see folks at the fairgrounds tomorrow, anyway," Mavis says, a look of sympathy on her face as though she fully understands what it must be like having Elvina Webb for a mother-in-law.

Caroline blinks quickly and slips the slim package into her purse. "You're right, Mavis. Thank you. I must get going. I told Eldon I'd meet him at eleven thirty and it must be getting close to that time and he really doesn't like to be kept waiting." She is rambling, she knows, but she cannot get away from Elvina fast enough. She doesn't want her to see the disappointment that is surely written all over her face. It was wrong to think about seeing Nick all week, getting her hopes up. She'd convinced herself that she would see him wandering up and down each side of the street with the same thought in mind, searching for her among the crowds, hoping to see her, too.

The next afternoon, Caroline fans herself with the pamphlet she was given at the gate. The cruel sun bears down, so unforgiving it has leached the brilliant blue right out of the sky. They are sitting on the bleachers, facing the dirt track, waiting for the races to start. Behind them, on the ball diamond, there is a splintering crack and an umpire bellows, "Foul ball!"

"I really can't take this heat," Caroline says. "I'm feeling a little light-headed."

"I told you to wear a hat." Eldon looks down at her from under the brim of his own straw hat. "You should have listened to me."

Caroline doesn't like to cover her hair. Today, she's rolled it up into a sleek French knot and adorned it with a rhinestone clip shaped like a butterfly. "Well, I didn't and now I don't think I can sit here under this sun another minute. I'm going to the ladies' room. Maybe if I splash my face and have a drink of cold water, I'll feel a little better."

"The race is about to start," Eldon says, nodding at the six wagons pulling up to the gate.

"I won't be long. I'll be back before you know it." She gets to her feet and steps around a broad-backed farmer in bibbed overalls and a cowboy hat, sitting in front of her. He smiles and lifts his hand to help her down the first wide riser.

"And come straight back. I didn't bring you to the fair to sit in this damn bloody heat by myself," Eldon says as he glares at the farmer until he abruptly drops her hand. "Stop at one of the booths on your way back and bring me a root beer." He reaches into his pocket, pulls out a few coins and hands them to Caroline.

She palms the money, continues down the steep risers, and hurries to the newly built high school, where the exhibition hall is located, taking a shortcut through the parked cars.

The gymnasium is blissfully cool and full of people escaping the heat. They stroll past long, skirted tables, examining jams and jellies, cookies and cakes, crocheted doilies and handiwork, children's school work and hand-stitched quilts. She'd taken her time in the exhibit hall yesterday, admiring all the entries and noting the winners in each category. One of Polly Garwood's dresses won the red ribbon for the second year in a row. Caroline had won the first-place ribbon in the junior category for four consecutive years. In the first year she was married she had intended to enter a two-piece suit she'd made, but Eldon forebade it. No wife of his was going to put her garments on public display, he said, and it irked her, being told what she could and couldn't do with her own suit. Even through the wire cage that covers the table, Caroline could see the sloppy workmanship on Polly's buttonholes and knew she could have won first place if she'd been allowed to enter something.

She feels better after she has a cold drink at the water fountain and pats her neck and arms with a damp paper towel in the washroom. In the hallway, across from the principal's office, Betty Cornforth, Millie Tupper, and Margaret Farley are sitting behind a long table along the wall.

"Well, if it isn't Mrs. Eldon Webb," Millie says when Caroline walks by.

Caroline stops to say hello. For as long as she can remember, Margaret Farley has planted herself at a table in the old exhibit hall for both days of the fair, handing out the prize money. She is blind as a badger and she peers at Caroline over eyeglasses pushed down on her nose. "Isn't that Caroline McPhee?"

"Well, she's Caroline Webb now, you remember," Millie says.

Mrs. Farley bends her head inches from the sheets spread out in front of her and runs her finger down a long list of names. "Webb, Webb. I don't see it."

"Of course you won't see it," Millie says impatiently. "She's not here to collect prize winnings. She doesn't even have an entry."

Mrs. Farley sits bolt upright. "She's not?" She looks at Millie and frowns. "Then why did you have me look up her name?"

Betty smiles and winks at Caroline. "Are you back today for a second look? Seems a lot of folks have escaped in here, out of the heat."

"I had to get out of the sun. I felt faint and a bit sick to my stomach."

Millie looks up from the quarters she is stacking in piles of four. "Oh, I know what that means. First comes love, then comes marriage, then comes Caroline with a baby carriage," she says in a sing-song way.

Caroline feels herself blush. It's such a private matter, this business of creating a baby; she wishes people wouldn't comment so freely about it.

"Good heavens, Millie, that's not necessarily so," Betty says. "It could just be this blistering heat. Howard insisted on standing in front of Pipers' for the parade yesterday and I nearly collapsed myself after an hour."

At that very moment, Caroline glances down the hall toward the exit door and sees a dark figure against the white light by the door. Her heart flips with a sudden pump of adrenalin. It's him; there's no mistaking those broad shoulders.

"I have to go," she manages to say and rushes away from the women so they can't read her face; a delightful feeling of elation and joy is bubbling up inside her. When she gets closer, she sees that Nick is grinning, walking quickly toward her.

"It *is* you. I couldn't be sure until my eyes adjusted for the light. It was your hair that gave you away. Even twisted up like that, I knew it was you."

He is wearing a white T-shirt, the kind Eldon wears under his work shirts, so tight it reveals each rippling muscle on his chest. His hair is tousled and she is filled with a desire to reach up and tame it down with her hands.

He is all she's been able to think about since that day in her kitchen. She walked to her reading tree countless times, hoping to find him mending fences or working with his cattle down by the river, but he was never there. She considered leaving him a note pinned to the tree or a fence post in the remote chance he might come looking for her, but she couldn't take the chance Eldon might find it. She lies awake at night, kicking away hot, twisted sheets, wondering if he is thinking about her, too. And now here he is and she doesn't know what to say.

"I was hoping I would bump into you on the fairgrounds, or at the parade. I walked up and down Main Street from the tracks to the post office yesterday, twice both ways, and couldn't spot you anywhere."

"Eldon's mother had us come to watch the parade with her in front of her house."

"That explains it. When I couldn't find you, I knew I had to come back to the fairgrounds today and keep looking." He seems emboldened by this admission. "I wanted to talk to you again."

A long silence stretches between them; Caroline is thrilled he was looking for her, just as she hoped he would, but she doesn't know if she should tell him so.

Caroline is keenly aware of Millie Tupper's prying eyes. "Let's get out of here," she says and they step out of the busy hallway into a deserted side corridor. She walks briskly alongside him, keenly aware of the long, hard plane of his thigh brushing against her leg. They turn a corner into a small alcove across from a locked exit door, a space where, during the school year, a rack for outdoor footwear might stand.

When they're completely out of sight, he swivels his hand to her waist and draws her in to his chest. Her arms go up and twine around his neck so naturally it shocks her. Her heart is racing, whirring away like her sewing machine when she pumps hard on the treadle, and she's not sure if it's from the danger of being discovered or from the feeling of him pressing against her. His chin rests on the top of her head and she feels his chest swell when he breathes in the scent of her hair. After a moment, he pulls away and studies her eyes.

"I haven't been able to stop thinking about you. I tell myself it's wrong, you're his wife, but it's your face I see every waking moment."

"I think about you, too. I can't begin to tell you how disappointed I was yesterday when I didn't see you during the parade. I go to my tree nearly every day, hoping you might be nearby," Caroline admits. "I don't allow myself to think about the right or the wrong of it and I don't care. I just want to see you."

Nick tips his head back, laughs out loud. "I've done the same thing, thinking maybe I'd catch you out there reading, but we must keep missing each other. It *is* a good place to meet, close enough for you to walk to, and out of sight."

Caroline doesn't feel the need to be coy, she might as well come right out and say what she wants. "Can you meet me there one day this week?"

Nick answers with his eyes. He wanted her to ask, she can tell. Of course he will. "When?"

"Wednesday?" she says, then wishes she'd said tomorrow, or Monday. Four days is too long.

A couple of boys round the corner, jostling each other and laughing. Caroline drops her arms from Nick's neck and he leans into the wall, shoving his hands in his pockets. The boys go quiet when they see them. It's the box boy from Pipers' store and the younger one is Joe Coyle's boy; she'd know that red hair anywhere. There is no exit from the hallway, no reason for the boys to come this way unless they're up to something — pulling a prank like setting off the fire alarm or hiding out to have a smoke — and they stare guiltily at their shoes until the Coyle boy turns on his heel and they slink away.

"I have to go," Caroline says when the boys are out of earshot. "He'll be wondering where I am." She turns and is hurrying away when she hears Nick call out, "Time?"

The boys are loitering at the end of the corridor and she acts as though she didn't hear him. She holds up one finger behind her back — one o'clock — and keeps walking, head down, averting her eyes when she passes Millie and Betty and Mrs. Farley. She hurries back through the gymnasium and, once she is on the fairgrounds, breaks into a run, Eldon's coins jingling in her pocket. His root beer! She's completely forgotten.

The food booths are just ahead, she can smell the fried onions, and she is about to stop when she sees Eldon stalking toward her through the rows of parked cars. "Where have you been? I look the fool sitting there by myself for so long." He is red-faced, his forehead slick with sweat.

"I'm sorry," she says quietly, hoping no one passing by will notice the way he's grabbed hold of her wrist. "I stopped for a few minutes to speak with Betty Cornforth and the ladies. You know how Betty can be, getting carried away with her stories." The sharp edge of suspicion eases from his eyes and he lets go of her hand.

"You still haven't got my drink, I see. I'll have a box of popcorn, too, and be quick about it. The finals are about to begin."

Later, in the truck as they ride home, Eldon lights up a cigarette and Caroline slides over and rolls down her window. He likes her to sit beside him, as close as she can without the gear shift knocking her knees. She thinks it's ridiculous, a married woman sitting up next to her husband like a lovesick teenager, but she humours him, although she draws the line when he puffs smoke in her face.

"You don't need that window open," Eldon says without taking his eyes off the road.

She does as she's told and cranks the window back up.

"So what did Betty Cornforth and the ladies have to tell you?"

"The usual things. We talked about the number of fair entries, down this year by twenty percent they said, especially in the baking section. No one wants to be stuck in the kitchen baking pies and muffins when it's this hot." She surprises herself with the easy way this made-up story slides off her tongue.

"Hmm," he says, tapping ash into the tray. "See anybody else? Stop to talk?" He asks this casually, but she can tell from his tone he is fishing for something, possibly setting a trap. Could he have come in another door? Seen her talking to Nick?

Her heart flutters. "Well, of course I *saw* lots of other people."

"Hmm," Eldon says again and drives on another mile. "Like who?"

Her mind races, trying to think of someone else she might have stopped to talk to. She pictures Emily Poloski lifting her little girl to the water fountain, one hand boosting that frilly, diapered rump. She could make something up, tell another story, but she stops herself.

"Like I said. Lots of people. What does it matter?"

Eldon takes another long, thoughtful pull on his cigarette, contemplating an answer. They drive the rest of the way home in silence and pull into the yard. Sport gets up from the porch and ambles over to greet her. She squats down and gives him a good rub on his belly, and he whines with pure joy.

Eldon is blocking the door when she gets to the house, one arm stretched out with his palm on the jamb. He lifts the burned-down stub to his lips and takes a long drag, exhaling the smoke in her face. "Just so you'd know," he says, "it *does* matter to me. Who you see. Who you talk to. Every single thing you do matters to me, Caroline."

Caroline tries to duck under his arm, push open the screen door. "You're being ridiculous," she says. "Now let me in the house."

He rips the nub away from his lips and crushes it on the porch under the toe of his boot. His face is inches from hers; she breathes in the rank, smoky smell of his breath.

"You'll go in the house when I say you go in the house."

Caroline turns away, sinks into the cushion on the old rocker beside the screen door. "Why are you doing this, Eldon? Why do you care who I talk to?"

"It's not that I care who you talk to, Caroline," Eldon says quietly. He wraps his fingers around her wrist like he did on the fairgrounds, squeezing harder this time, tighter and tighter until Caroline imagines she hears a soft snap, like an egg cracking on the edge of a pan.

"I care so much more about who talks to *you*."

On Wednesday, Eldon is late for lunch. *Of all days,* Caroline thinks impatiently, as she stirs the soup. It has stuck to the bottom of the pot from simmering so long. A fan blows uselessly in the corner. It has to be ninety degrees by now and she feels like she's melting away. She took such care with her bath this morning and now, here she is, sweating as though she's just spent an hour hoeing the garden.

The screen door squeaks open and Eldon walks in and goes straight to the table, flinging his cap on the chair by the door, not bothering to wash his hands.

"There you are," Caroline says, ladling out a bowl and setting it in front of him. "It's not like you to be this late."

"Your father stopped me on the road just now. He asked if I'd heard about Walter Nychuk's dead steer. It seems he found it dead in the pen, trampled or chased down until it collapsed from exhaustion, so I drove out to the pasture to check on the calves."

"You wouldn't expect that, would you? Right in the barnyard? How are the calves?"

"Everything looked normal in our pasture but I'll have to keep the rifle loaded, just in case." He slurps up a spoonful of soup. "Aren't you eating?" Eldon asks as he crushes a handful of crackers into his bowl.

"I've eaten," Caroline says quickly, although she hasn't had a bite, not even a piece of toast for breakfast, her stomach all knotted up from nerves and excitement. She busies herself at the counter, spooning out a small dish of fresh strawberries and cream. "What do you have planned for the rest of the day?"

"I have to drive out to the west Conway field to check up on Bert. He's working the summer fallow and he should've been back by now."

Caroline is relieved. She was hoping Eldon would be away from the yard for the afternoon, although she plans to set out with a small bucket and say she is off to pick berries, should he ask.

Eldon dawdles over his soup while Caroline watches the minutes tick by on the clock. She pours the leftover soup into a two-quart jar and puts it in the fridge. Eldon pushes away his empty bowl, tips back his chair and runs his tongue over his teeth, making that sucking sound that grates on her nerves. *Why won't he leave already?* She washes his bowl and the pot and puts them away.

"Back to work for me," she finally says as she hangs up the tea towel, encouraging him to go. "I'm putting the finishing touches on that skirt I've been sewing."

Eldon slides away from the table and pulls on his cap. "And I'd better go see what the hell Bert's broken this time."

Once he's gone, Caroline races up the stairs. She washes her face and under her arms with a cool, soapy cloth, changes into her new ivory blouse and runs a brush through her hair. She applies the faintest blush of pink rouge to her cheeks and picks up the bottle of Evening in Paris from her dressing table, then reconsiders. Nick seems like the kind of man who would like the natural smell of a woman. Through her bedroom window, she sees Eldon's truck slowly turn out of the lane. As she dashes through the kitchen, she notices it is a few minutes to one. It takes at least ten minutes to walk to her tree.

She is halfway there when she realizes she's forgotten her pail. "Damn," she says, and Sport looks up, surprised she's spoken out loud. He trots along at her heels, stopping to sniff at the edges of the grass path every few minutes then loping along to catch up. It's a perfect day, the sky a cerulean blue with lacy white clouds painted on, and a cooling summer breeze has sprung up.

Nick is already there, standing under the elm tree, its canopy laid out like a beach blanket on the broad blue sky. "Hey," he says.

She comes to him, suddenly shy, and he takes hold of her hands.

"Sorry I'm late."

"Don't be. I'd wait by this tree all day, all week if I had to, just to have a chance to see you." He is wearing a silver-green shirt, the colour of willow leaves, buttoned down the front, with the sleeves rolled up the way they were when he first walked into her kitchen. He lets go of her hands and touches her face, brushing away a stray tendril of hair. He sweeps his sweet fingers across the curve of her lips, cups her chin then leans in and kisses her. It's a chaste kiss, as considerate and amiable as he is, his lips soft and smooth and pliant.

"I knew you would do that," Caroline says, when he finally pulls away.

"I knew you wanted me to."

It's true. She can't deny the constant flush of desire she feels whenever she thinks about him. She wants Nick Bilyk, has wanted him to kiss her since she felt his breath on her hair in the alcove. She leans into him again, feels the hard press of his body against her breasts and knows he can feel her, too. She wants to fall inside of him, be encased by the heat of his body, stay there forever.

They sink to their knees in the grassy hollow under the tree. "You're the most beautiful woman I've ever seen," he half whispers and tilts her chin up, bringing his mouth to hers, not moving, just holding it there for a few moments until he parts her lips with his tongue and she feels its curious tip graze her softness inside. She hardly knows what to do with her own tongue during this gentle exploration, so shocked is she by the strange sensations his circling tongue inflames. With trembling fingers, she draws his tentative hand to her breast until he cups it the way a thirsty man might cherish a handful of water. He moans, an unintelligible sound that may have invoked God's name, and he pulls away, looking at her in the midday light. "Are you sure? We can stop, if you want to."

She could turn her head away, apologize shamefacedly for agreeing to meet him, tell him she's made a terrible mistake, she can never do this again. But he's stoked a fire inside her, awakened a need she hadn't even known existed before she'd met him and she doesn't want it to stop. She reaches up, unfastens the top button of her blouse and lays back into the thick cushion of grass in the hollow. The sun slants through the boughs and filters through the leaves, scattering like honey-coloured coins around them.

AUGUST

The landing is cramped and poorly lit, with barely enough room to turn around. Caroline makes her way cautiously up the narrow staircase, bracing herself with one hand against the dingy wall. Someone is boiling cabbage, the smell masking the underlying odour of mildew and unwashed clothes Caroline noticed in the stairwell the last time she was here.

Alice's room is next to the communal bathroom, a bachelor's suite, she calls it, although it's really just a square box with her bed in the kitchen and not even a proper closet to hang up her clothes. Her door is slightly ajar and Caroline raps gently then pushes it open. Alice is sitting on the bed, propped on the heels of her hands. Susan is standing in front of her and she turns to the door when Caroline knocks. Her eyes are swollen and she's holding a wadded tissue up to her nose. She looks a fright. Her hair, usually as brilliant as a raven's wing, hangs in dull strands around her pale face.

"Caroline," she wails.

Caroline drops her purse by the door and draws Susan in, hugging her close. "Oh, Susan. I'm so sorry." She lets Susan weep on her shoulder while Alice stands up and motions to the clock on the wall, flashing ten fingers twice, then tracing a finger down each of her cheeks.

"Who wants tea?" Alice asks.

"Come, let's sit." There is only one chair in the suite, pushed up under the table, so Caroline leads Susan to the bed and sits next to her, folding her arm around her shoulder. "You'll feel better once you have some tea. Then you can tell us all about it."

Susan shakes off Caroline's arm, springs from the bed and paces around the small room. "I can't sit! I can't drink tea. I can't eat." She pulls another tissue from the box on the table and blows her nose.

"I've told her she just needs to get over it and move on. There are plenty of fish in the sea," Alice says as she empties the kettle into the teapot.

"I don't want another fish," Susan says, and begins sobbing again.

"He's a barracuda, that's what he is," Alice says sharply. "Any man who preys on a young girl's feelings like he did …" She slams the teapot down on the table and the lid clatters off and falls on the floor.

Two days earlier, Caroline received a phone call from Susan's distraught mother. Susan was on her way home. She'd quit her summer job and was moving back, giving up on school, Mrs. Wawryk said, and it all had something to do with the man she'd been seeing. Would Caroline and Alice please try to talk some sense into her because there wasn't a thing she or Susan's father could say to make her listen to reason.

It troubled Caroline to see sensible, level-headed Susan like this, falling to pieces over a failed romance. What had that man done to her?

"I know whatever's happened seems like the end of the world right now. But you'll get through it. You've had your heart broken, and I can't begin to understand how that feels, but it will mend in time. You can't drop out of school over this."

"But how can I ever go back? I'm registered for another one of his classes this fall, and even if I drop it, I'm sure to bump into him on campus. I couldn't bear to see him. Not after the dreadful things I've found out about him." She blows her nose pitifully into the tissue again. "And I'm just so ashamed. I feel as though everyone will know; gossip spreads like wildfire around such an intimate campus."

"You're making too much out of all of this," Alice says, pouring the tea and handing Susan a cup. "I'd march right back into his class if I were you, show him he hasn't got the best of you. What do you think, Caroline?"

Caroline takes a sip of tea — too hot — and puts her cup back in the saucer. "I think Susan needs to start at the beginning and tell us the entire story."

Susan met John Talbott in her second year. He was much younger than her other professors; she was surprised on the first day when the attractive young man wearing a smartly cut jacket stepped onto the dais at the front of the class. He was a gifted lecturer, his voice melodious. When she got a C on her first essay, she was horrified by such a bad mark. He'd pencilled a note on the last page, asking her to make an appointment to see him. He charmed her at that first meeting and offered extra instruction outside of class. And so began a two-year romance, simple and sweet in the beginning, not even a kiss until Christmas that first year. He was married, he made that perfectly clear to Susan from the very beginning, with two small children not yet in school. But he was dreadfully unhappy; his wife — the daughter of his mother's best friend he'd been coerced into marrying — was a shrew.

As time went on, he tempted Susan with the possibility of a future after the dissolution of his floundering marriage. He told her he loved her, he wanted to be with her and only her, forever. He couldn't live without her.

"Oh, Susan. What were you thinking, carrying on with a married man?" Alice says as she plucks another tissue out of the box and pushes it across the table.

This sets Susan sobbing again and Caroline takes hold of her hand. Susan was as innocent and guileless as she had been, believing like she did in every promise Eldon made in those early days, falling for the show he put on, never suspecting the malice that lay beneath the facade. If only she'd been as perceptive as Eldon's first fiancée must have been and caught on to his true nature before it was too late.

Susan takes a deep, shuddering breath. "There was always some reason he couldn't tell his wife it was over — the baby was teething, her mother was sick — on and on it went. On some level, I considered he might never leave his wife, but he made me feel I should be content with what we had and I convinced myself I could carry on that way, as his mistress, and I kept it up. I was there for him whenever he wanted me."

"Why didn't you tell us any of this before?" Caroline asks gently.

Susan covers her face with her hands. "I was ashamed. He was married. And he insisted we keep our affair a secret so I did, even though it was gnawing away at me from inside."

"Uh oh," Alice says. "I know where this is going. You know that saying, your secret's safe with me? It doesn't happen, someone always slips up. A secret's next to impossible to keep." She nods wisely.

"A few weeks ago, I got a letter from a girl named Etta Winters," Susan continues. "She's a graduate student, studying Victorian literature. I'd seen her come out of John's office once or twice. She said she'd found out about me from John's teaching assistant and she wanted to meet with me."

"You don't even have to tell me ..." Alice says, a look of indignation sweeping across her face.

Caroline knows what Susan is about to say, too. This man of Susan's is even worse than she imagined. The two young women met and the stories they'd been told were remarkably similar. John loved Etta, he couldn't live without her, it was impossible to leave his wife, if only she'd wait. He'd already been having an affair with Etta for two years when he invited Susan, so young and naive, to his office. They confronted him, threatening to tell the dean he'd taken advantage of them, but he laughed and said he would deny it. They were infatuated, hysterical girls; he, a tenured professor. Who would the dean believe?

"I've been sitting in my room for the last two weeks, trying to decide what to do. Mom and Dad don't know the half of it. They think it's just a boyfriend who's dumped me. Mom, especially, thinks I've lost my mind, throwing my life away over a man."

"Well, aren't you?" Alice says, standing up and clearing away the cups. "There's no reason for you not to go back to school in a few weeks, waltz straight back into his classroom, and stare him in his two-timing face!"

"But how can I face him without falling apart? I love him and I want him to choose me." Susan crumples to the bed, her face covered by a curtain of hair.

Caroline reaches for her hair, pushes it away from her eyes.

"I tried to talk to him, to convince him it's me that he loves. He called me a foolish little girl," Susan whimpers. "He said I knew he was married and I didn't seem to care so why should it matter now that I knew about Etta?"

There is a soft pop, then the gurgling of water on the other side of the wall. Caroline's head is spinning, swirling like water flowing down a drain. *How easy it is to ignore your own moral compass when you're hopelessly in love.* She knows it's wrong to carry on an affair with Nick while she's married to Eldon, but she, like Susan, finds it impossible to stop.

"I still don't see why this means you have to quit school." Alice sits cross-legged on the floor and hands Susan another tissue.

"There's no way I can avoid seeing him on campus. He teaches in the same building as most of my classes."

"So what?" Alice says.

"It'll take time, but you'll get over this. You have to go back to school in September," Caroline says.

Susan's face is grey, and blue-black circles stain the hollows under her eyes. "I'm just so tired. I can't even think about this anymore."

Caroline and Alice stand up, settling Susan's head onto the pillow. "Why don't you rest here awhile?" Caroline says. "I have to get going. Eldon's likely waiting. Alice, can you walk me out?" She hugs Susan and tucks a blanket up under her chin. "I'll get Eldon to drive me out to see you in a few days."

"I think it's helped her to tell us," Alice says when they're out on the street. "She should have told us about this man long ago. That's the trouble with secrets; they eat at you if you keep them bottled up inside." She laces a tissue she's holding through her fingers, up one and down the other like a running stitch, and avoids Caroline's eyes. "There's something I've been keeping from you, too, and I've been meaning to tell you but the time never seems right. We're either at the café and there are people nearby, or I've been avoiding the topic altogether."

"What is it? Is everything all right?" Caroline is alarmed. She can't take much more bad news in one day.

Alice looks away, her eyes bright. "It's Bill. He's been avoiding me. The first few dates were fine, but he seems to have lost interest in me. It's not a wife he wants. He's just putting in time here at the bank before he moves on to a bigger and better town ... and he's shown me what he's really after while he's here." Her eyes brim over and a tear trickles out from behind her glasses and down the side of her nose.

Caroline pictures Bill, with his manicured moustache and that perfectly coiffed hair. She had her reservations about him, thought him too slick for a decent girl like Alice. "I didn't care for him when I first met him, to be honest," she says. "Someone better is sure to come along. You'll see."

"I didn't give in to him and that's why he's ignoring me. Why did we all think this falling in love business would be easy?" Alice is still looking across the street and she gives a weak wave. "There's Eldon," she says. "He just came out of the drug store. He doesn't look happy you've kept him waiting."

He is standing in front of Clarice Hubley's parked Crown Victoria, lighting a cigarette, when he sees that Caroline has noticed him. He points at his watch then beckons her over.

Tomorrow she has another rendezvous planned with Nick for when Eldon takes his mother to church. They've met four times now, the passion mounting with each encounter, but it's the conversation she waits for; hearing Nick reveal bits and pieces about himself, learning about the sort of man he is, and noting his attentive eyes when she does the same. Sundays, church day, are the best days to meet. She can slip away, guaranteeing herself a full hour, and be back before Eldon gets home. But she doesn't know how much longer she can continue this charade; Elvina is starting to ask questions about her absence from church. How much longer can she say she's feeling unwell? And what would Susan and Alice think if they knew she was carrying on with Nick behind Eldon's back? Her secret is getting harder and harder to keep. She feels the burden of it weighing her down like stones in her pockets.

Caroline balances on the edge of the porch rocker, washing cucumbers. She pulled out the vines and plucked off the last of them this morning, leaving the old, yellow ones in a heap in the garden. There are just enough to grind for one more batch of sweet relish. She reaches to the bottom of the galvanized washtub, swishes her hand around, and scoops out the last cucumber, small and curled as a snail, with spiky spines. It reminds her of a photograph from a science textbook, a human embryo floating adrift in a womb.

She stands and stretches the cramp out of her back. There is the unmistakable scent of autumn in the air even though it's not quite September. Harvest arrived early this year, with a stretch of clear, dry weather the last two weeks. The wheat is bountiful, plump, and red, and their good fortune has put Eldon in unusually good spirits, even though he's been toiling long hours. She, too, has been working like mad, especially on the days of her meetings with Nick. She picks and pickles and cans all morning, cramming a day's work into a half, so Eldon will see the jars of sweet pickles, chokecherry jam, and pink crabapples lining the countertop when he comes in at night. He just left in the grain truck to take a load of wheat to town. There is sure to be a lineup at the elevator and Caroline estimates she has an hour with Nick at the tree.

She puts the bowl of clean cucumbers on the kitchen table then sets out on her bike. She's taken it to meet Nick the last few times; it's easy to drive on the grass path now that it's tamped down, and quicker, too, than walking. Sport pads along beside her, used to her frequent visits out to the tree, where he lies, muzzle on paws, watching her and Nick without judgment.

When she gets there, she finds Nick standing at the edge of the river. It is barely a trickle at this time of the year; stones poke through the shallow surface like a handful of marbles tossed by a boy. Caroline picks up a pebble and flings it over his head so it lands in the water with a soft plop. He turns and a smile lights up his face.

"God, I've missed you. Last night it was so damn hot in my room, I took my pillow and went out to the cot on the porch. I nearly made myself crazy, thinking about you. It was all I could do to stop myself from coming to you. Not even half a mile but it might as well be a hundred. It kills me, wanting you when you're so close and knowing I can't have you, that you're with him."

"I miss you, too. I wasn't even sure I'd see you today, if you'd be able to slip away on such a perfect harvest day."

"It's not getting any easier finding excuses to get away. I told Anton I was taking a shovel to Coyle's to get fixed. He said it was a damn stupid time to do it, but I said the cultivator needs to be ready for the fall work."

"Won't he wonder what you were doing when he sees the shovel isn't fixed?"

"I ran it into town, left it with Coyle, and told him I'd be back in an hour to pick it up. Anton will think I've been in town the whole time."

Caroline takes his hand and leads him up the small rise toward the tree. "We never have enough time together, just these little crumbs we snatch when we can."

"It's only a matter of time, you know, before someone figures out what we're up to," Nick says. He takes the jacket he has slung over his shoulder and spreads it out on the grass. "I think Anton's beginning to wonder where I go when I take off. I'm not very good at lying to him."

"I don't even want to think what Eldon would do if he ever found out."

"I worry about that, too." Nick runs a hand through his hair. "Sometimes I wish we could just run off together, head to Alberta and make a fresh start."

Caroline buries her face in the hollow under his shoulder and breathes in his familiar scent, then takes another deep breath, storing up the soap-and-water smell of him. She's thought about the same thing, lying alone in her bed at night when sleep won't come; if only she could start over with Nick, put her life with Eldon behind her, chalk her short marriage up to a hasty mistake. But it will never happen. Divorce is out of the question. Eldon will never let her go.

"What do you think about that?" Nick asks, pulling her away and putting his hands on her shoulders.

She steps back, looking up at him, not sure how to tell him leaving with him is impossible.

"I don't see why we can't just start over somewhere else," he says. "Just like my grandparents did when they left the old country with ten dollars for a homestead and a trunk-load of tools. We'll be homesteading for ourselves, crossing the prairie instead of the ocean, carrying all we need in the box of my truck. What's stopping us?"

Caroline can't bear the look of hope in his eyes. "I'd go anywhere with you, you know that, don't you?" Her fingers climb up the front of his shirt, toy with a button. "But this is all too much for me to think about just now." Her hands glide down, deftly opening each button. "We have so little time, only this moment. Let's not waste it." He's about to answer when she cups his face with her hands and kisses him, inhaling the words from his lips and swallowing them whole so she won't have to hear whatever it is he has to say. She feels his lips relax as he falls into the slow river of her kiss. She never wants it to end, this tender kiss, this spool of love unwinding.

Elvina's new car, square and ugly as a boxcar, is sitting beside the house when Caroline gets home. She rubs a hand over her lips, as though evidence of Nick's sweet kisses might be visible there, and tries to affect an innocent gaze before she walks into the kitchen. The cucumbers are still in the middle of the table, just where she left them, the kitchen quiet except for the hum of the refrigerator. Caroline gently closes the screen door and steps inside.

Upstairs, she hears the scraping of a box being dragged over the floor and then the heavy thump of Elvina's feet on the stairs. Elvina claps a hand to her thick bosom when she walks into the kitchen, carrying a cumbersome glass vase, quite likely the most hideous thing Caroline has ever seen.

"Mercy, you startled me. What are you doing here?" Elvina puts the vase on the table next to the cucumbers. "I mean, where have you been until now? I searched through the house and walked out to the garden but you were nowhere to be found. I needed your help with a box in the attic. It's hot as Hades up there." Elvina sinks into a kitchen chair and lifts the hem of her skirt to her knees, flapping it a few times.

"I went for a bike ride. The house was closing in on me and I needed some fresh air."

"Hmmm," Elvina says. "Eldon tells me you've been under the weather lately." She gets two glasses from the cupboard and fills them with water from the pitcher in the fridge. "I hope you're taking proper care of yourself."

"What's the vase for?" Caroline sits down across from Elvina and takes a sip.

"It's the Morrises' fiftieth wedding anniversary this Sunday and we're having a tea for them after the service. Vivian Waller has all those spectacular mums in her garden and we're short a few vases. You will be in church this Sunday, won't you? Millie Tupper's been asking questions, raising those painted-on eyebrows of hers; she seems unusually interested in your well-being and wonders why you've been missing services."

Caroline's missed two Sundays in a row and she doesn't need Millie Tupper spreading any rumours. "I've been feeling better this week so I'm sure I'll be there. I wouldn't want to miss the Morrises' tea."

Elvina drains her glass of water in one long swallow and swipes the wet circle it leaves on the table with the sleeve of her blouse. "There's nothing you'd like to tell me, is there?"

Caroline's heart stutters. Elvina can be so much like Eldon, trying to trick her into saying something she hadn't intended to say. What does she mean, exactly? What does she know?

"I know some women don't like to announce anything until they're absolutely sure, but if you're anything like me, I knew straight away," she continues. "I was so sick each morning, I could scarcely get out of bed, my stomach rolling and pitching until noon. William's cigars were the worst, the smell sent me running to the bucket, day *or* night. I haven't said anything about my suspicions to Eldon and he hasn't commented one way or the other so I'm assuming you haven't told him yet."

Elvina is looking at her in such a kind way that it throws Caroline off; she feels as though the kitchen floor has suddenly tilted on its joists.

"You're looking a little peaked all of a sudden, dear. Have some more water," Elvina says, getting up to refill Caroline's glass. "Of course, I didn't say anything when Millie asked, although she was hoping for confirmation, I could tell. Even Betty Cornforth mentioned the telltale glow she noticed the last time she saw you."

There is a distant rumble of thunder and Sport whines at the door, denting the screen with his nose. Within minutes, rain is pelting down on the windows and drumming on the roof. Elvina leaves with her horrid vase, wanting to get her new car home and into the garage in the event of hail. Caroline still feels unsettled, so she steps out on the porch and sits on the rocking chair with Sport's head on her lap, breathing in the fresh smell and listening to the rain from the gutters pour into the rain barrel as though a giant hand is pumping it off the roof.

There *is* a reason for the rosy glow on her face and it's these feelings for Nick, but thanks to Millie Tupper, Betty and Elvina have been fooled into believing it's because Eldon's baby is growing inside her. She knows it's untrue; she's just finished her monthly and Nick's been careful not to spill his seed inside her. She could set them all straight on Sunday after the tea, but it's a convenient ruse, and one she can use for another month, maybe two, until they discover she's not pregnant at all.

SEPTEMBER

It is raining again; the second week of endless mist interrupted by occasional bursts of rain pouring down. Eldon paces between his chair and the kitchen window overlooking the yard. The oats, cut but not yet combined, are getting soaked in the rain and he is convinced the swaths will sprout once the sun comes back out. Each morning he dresses in his slicker and heads out to the barn to check the rain gauge, coming back in a mood worse than before. His shoulder aches from the damp chill and Caroline spends an hour each evening rubbing it with liniment so he can sleep. She does what she can, trying to cheer him, but he snaps at her whenever she opens her mouth, so once her chores are done, she withdraws to her sewing room and keeps to herself.

She hasn't seen Nick since the day Elvina came for the vase. She misses the touch of his skin and the gentle look in his eyes with a pain so intense there is no balm to soothe it. The next time she and Nick were to meet, Eldon came stomping into the house, dripping water all over the floor, at the exact time Caroline was due at the tree, and he stayed in the house for the rest of the day. She pictured Nick waiting for hours, rain sluicing over his face, drenched to the skin. She had no way of communicating with him. The dreary grey-blue days plodded by and she had no idea when she'd see him again.

Yesterday, when the sun tried to break through the clouds, she escaped to the tree, slogging along the muddy grass trail, hoping Nick would read the sun's brief appearance as some sort of cosmic sign to meet her, but he wasn't there. She sank into the hollow, soaking her skirt through to her undergarments, while tears of disappointment coursed down her cheeks.

Sport's ears perk up and he looks to the door then barks as someone drives down the lane. Caroline's heart pitches forward, thinking perhaps Nick has decided to drop by, Eldon be damned; he, too, is dying without her. But, of course it's not him, only her father, and he walks right in with his muddy boots and sits down at the table.

"You talk to Howard today?" he asks Eldon, stirring three teaspoons of sugar into his cup once Caroline has filled it.

"I haven't seen him. I wasn't out today, except to check the gauge. If this damn rain doesn't quit soon, we won't get the fall work done at all."

"There'll be a good stretch of weather yet, there always is."

"October third, it snowed and stayed, that one year," Eldon says. "What's going on with Howard?"

"He lost a calf, same as Walter Nychuk. Dead in the pen. It was Betty who heard the calves bawling when she got up in the middle of the night. She woke Howard and he went out with his twenty-two. Shot it into the air and scared them off. Luckily, though, he was able to get a good look at them."

"Coyotes?" Eldon reaches for a muffin Caroline has set out on the table.

Caroline's father shakes his head. "Dogs. It was a shepherd — quite possibly the Bilyks' — leading the pack, and Howard's own dog, Jip, among them. Guess that's why he didn't bark. He was up to no good with the rest of them."

"I can't believe it," Caroline says quickly. "Jip's such a gentle soul. He wouldn't hurt anything, let alone calves in his own yard."

"They say a dog gets turned once he has a taste of it. The chase, the hunt, the kill. It's instinct, they can't help themselves, no matter how gentle they are," her father continues. "Once they start to pack, there's no going back. It happened to a dog we had when I was a boy. My mother feared for the little ones so we had to put him down."

Sport pads up to Caroline, plants his muzzle in her lap. She strokes his head and he sweeps the floor with his tail.

"I still don't believe it," Caroline says. "Jip's so old and he has that bad hip. I can't imagine him chasing down a calf."

"Believe it," Eldon says. "There's a primitive need in every living creature. A mother's need to protect her young, for instance, or man's urge to survive."

"The rain's let up," Caroline's father says, clapping his hand against the table. "Time to get going. Would you come out and take a look under my hood? The carburetor's been acting up."

After the men leave, Caroline cleans up the kitchen and wanders upstairs, fingering the carmine gabardine she's laid out on her sewing table with the pattern pinned on. The stack of library books she picked up last week sits on her bedside table, untouched. She's been planning to start a new skirt but she has no desire to sew, no interest in reading; there's nothing to do but sit in her rocker and think about Nick. There's a need she has, and the last two weeks of confinement have made her realize what lies beneath it. She's tasted the sweetness of desire and it is growing inside her. It is love that she craves — to love and be loved — and she can't live without it; that soft, endless falling.

Caroline looks up from the garden as a gusty wind scatters the swaths of thin clouds, making way for a honking flock of Canada geese to pass over. She is digging muddy potatoes, the size of pint jars, and tossing them into the furrow to lie in the sun. They will have to be washed then spread out to dry before they can be collected in burlap sacks and carried to the cellar. Extra work, she knows, but there's no guarantee the soil will dry up this late in the season and who knows when winter will arrive after this late surge of Indian summer.

There have been four consecutive days of sunny weather with temperatures soaring and hot, eager winds. Combines once again lumber through the fields, collecting the last of the grain. Eldon's been in and out of the yard, hauling the oats instead of running the combine like he usually does. She had only one brief chance to walk to the tree but Nick wasn't there. She wants to hang on to this last bit of summer, knowing that soon her trips to the tree will end and she might go weeks, if not months, without seeing him. She doesn't know how she will survive the emptiness of her mundane life all winter; waking up each morning to the monotony of everyday chores and Eldon's dark moods.

He came to her bed last night, his hard lips prodding and tugging, and she hiked up her nightgown to allow him his pleasure. She bit her lip in the darkness until she tasted the sharp tang of blood. His visits are getting harder and harder to bear.

Sport barks at a squirrel he's chased up one of the spruce trees. The squirrel scolds back and Sport circles, yapping and digging his front claws into the trunk, trying to scale the tree.

"I don't know which of them has the upper hand but young Sport seems to be living up to his name," Betty Cornforth says. She is standing at the edge of the garden, dressed for town, wearing summer shoes. Through the trees, Caroline sees Howard's truck parked by Eldon's workshop.

"I'm leaving mine for another few days," she says, referring to the potatoes. "Maybe this heat will dry things up."

"I thought it best to get them off as soon as I could." Four curious hens are scratching for worms where Caroline's dug up the soil and they scatter when she spears her fork in the ground.

"Are you sure you should be doing that? The garden's still so wet and it must be hard work, fighting with that mud. I surely hope Eldon is going to carry the potatoes into the cellar for you."

"Would you like to come inside for a glass of something cold to drink? I know I could use something," Caroline says, remembering her manners.

"Oh, no. We're just on our way to town. Howard just had to return some tool he borrowed from Eldon."

Caroline pulls out a hankie she's tucked under the sleeve of her blouse and pats the sweat from her brow. "Can you believe this heat for mid-September? It was eighty-three degrees yesterday afternoon."

Sport has stopped tormenting the squirrel and comes over to sniff Betty's hem and nose the heels of her shoes.

"You've heard about the dogs, have you?" Betty asks, leaning down to scratch Sport behind the ears.

"Yes. I was sorry to hear about Jip."

"Howard didn't have the heart to put him down so we've been keeping him chained, though that's no way for an old dog like Jip to spend the last of his days." There is a sudden honk from Howard's truck horn, two short toots. "That's my signal," Betty says. "Take care in this heat and don't do more than you should." She looks Caroline over then nods her head and makes her way back through the trees.

The open screen does nothing to stir the sultry air and it settles on Caroline like a counterpane, weighing down her limbs. Her legs swim restlessly against the damp sheets and she bunches the top sheet into a ball with her toes and slides it to the foot of the bed. *'Two roads diverged in a yellow wood, / And sorry I could not travel both ...'* Outside her window, she hears the crickets. One, two, three — she counts their frenzied song, calculating the temperature outside using a trick her mother once taught her. Seventy-two degrees, even though it's 2:00 a.m.

She remembers what Nick told her about escaping to the veranda to sleep on hot, humid nights like this and she pictures him there, less than a mile away, asleep on his mother's screened-in porch. Considering her own porch an improvement to the airless bedroom, she takes her pillow and steps into the hallway, listening for the rhythmic sound of Eldon's snoring from his room, and creeps down the stairs.

Sport rises from his rug and brushes her leg with his tail. A hint of a breeze through the screen on this side of the house slides over her body like silk and she thinks about Nick again, imagining his hands on her skin. She misses him so much she feels the ache of it deep in her bones. If only she could see him tonight. She brushes her lips with her fingers. All she needs is one kiss.

A frisson of excitement shudders down her spine. What's stopping her from going to him? She'll take a chance he's asleep on the porch and, if he's not, she'll toss a pebble at his window like some lovesick teenager in a movie. Eldon sleeps like the dead; if she's back before dawn he'll never know she's been gone.

She opens the closet, steps into her garden shoes and slips out the screen door. Dew soaks the grass like heavy rain and her canvas shoes are soaked by the time she gets to the lane. The weak light from the yard post is no help at all in illuminating the road past the mailbox so she follows the gravel road by putting one wet foot in front of the other. There is only a sliver of moon and few stars in the deep, black sky. The ditch is alive with a chorus of crickets and indistinguishable rustlings and Caroline shivers, reminded suddenly of the roaming pack of dogs. Sport bounds to the side, pouncing at something he hears in the grass.

Sport. She'd forgotten all about him. "Home, Sport. Go home." He whines and circles her legs. She rubs him reassuringly behind the ears. "It's all right, boy. You have to go back." He whines again, as if he's telling her he disapproves of her risky plan. He trots a few steps back down the road, stops then tilts his head. "Get!" Caroline turns and continues walking. After a minute she looks back. Obediently, Sport has done as she said.

As she nears the Bilyks' lane, a frenzied barking starts up from somewhere near Anton and Anna's house. Caroline stops, frozen in her tracks. Why hadn't she thought about the Bilyks' dog? As she draws nearer, she sees him, a shadowy blur on the steps leading up to the porch, barking furiously, straining at the end of a chain. The porch light comes on, the door opens, and Anton steps out on the porch holding a rifle. Caroline leaps into a hedge lining the lane.

She hears another door slam then Nick shouts, "Duke! Easy!" And gradually the dog stops barking and, afterward, she hears the sound of raised voices.

"For Christ's sake, there's nothing out there," Nick is saying.

"Like hell there isn't," Anton says. "It's those damn dogs."

"It's likely a fox or a skunk and it's sure to be scared off by now. Leave me the gun and go back to bed. I'll take a walk and look things over."

Caroline's heart is racing; she's lucky she wasn't shot at or discovered by Anton, lurking in the bushes. She hears the crunch of footsteps on gravel and, through the low branches, she sees Nick standing on the lane with the gun propped on his shoulder. She is weak with relief to see him and creeps out of her hiding place. Her nightgown is soaked from the hem to her knees and spiny caragana stems are stuck in her hair.

"Caroline? Is that you? What are you doing here?" He pulls her into the warm haven of his arms. "We're damn lucky Anton didn't fire a shot into the dark over this way. You took an awful chance coming here."

"Don't be mad," Caroline says, her voice husky from the lump pinching her throat. "I just needed to see you so badly I didn't think of the danger."

Nick leads her to his mother's small house, under a sheltering maple tree on the far side of the yard, and ushers her onto the porch. A cot, washed in yellow light from a kitchen window, is set up at one end of the long veranda next to a small table. Taking her hand, Nick directs her to sit down then wraps a tattered patchwork quilt, still warm from his body, around her shoulders.

"I was at the tree every day this week," he says. "You were never there."

"I tried once, but you weren't there, either. And, after that, I couldn't get away. I might as well be chained to the porch. You'd think after two weeks of rain Eldon would have something to do but he never leaves the yard! It's as though he's staying home to spite me. I can't stand the sight of him or the sound of his voice, telling me what to think and say and do every waking moment." Crying softly, she leans into his shoulder.

He wipes the tears from her cheeks with the pads of his thumbs and brushes aside a lock of her hair. "I've been thinking about it ... and I've decided I'm going to take you away."

"Take me away? Where?"

"Alberta. Anywhere. I've thought it all through. We can leave right after harvest."

"He'll never let me go." Caroline can't even look at him. He looks so hopeful.

"We'll run if we have to, go somewhere he'll never find us."

"He won't stop looking until he does."

"Then we'll keep moving." He tips up her chin and kisses her. "We're going to be together and no one is going to stop us. I love you, Caroline, more than you know."

His words stir a need like blue flames in her belly. "I love you, too," she whispers, surrendering, finally, to the voicing of this undeniable truth. She unties the satin ribbon at her neck and slips her thin nightgown from her shoulders while Nick peels off his shirt. Her hands roam over the smooth, hot skin on his back while he enters her gently, rocking in a measured, patient way. He takes her to a sweet and glorious place Eldon has never shown her and she surrenders, again, to a pleasure she never knew existed before him. Nick is close to release himself; she can tell by his shuddering breath, but, this time, she doesn't want him to leave her. "Stay," she urges.

"Are you sure?" Nick groans. She holds her hands tight to the small of his back.

"I want every part of you inside me," she whispers, and he arches his back and moans.

Afterward, she lies folded in his arms, motionless, unable to move, the only sound in the cooling night air the rustle of leaves on the maple.

"Caroline? Are you awake?"

She murmurs and snuggles deeper into the shelter of his arms.

"Baby, you have to go." He reaches for her discarded night-gown and picks his jeans off the floor. After they dress, Nick draws her into one last embrace.

"When will I see you again?"

"How about Thursday?" Caroline sits on the cot and ties her shoes. "I'll try to be at the tree at ten o'clock."

Nick walks her along the lane and down the road until they are almost at Caroline's lane, then kisses her one last time before letting her go.

As Caroline heads down the lane, a night creature on the hunt cuts through the damp air above her with a ponderous flap of wings so close Caroline feels the hair stir on her head.

In the distance, a singular, ear-splitting gunshot shatters the still night air. Someone is shooting, quite likely at the wandering pack of dogs. Sport bounds down the lane, his coat a dull silver in the scanty moonlight. Rounding behind her, he nudges the back of her knee with his nose, urging her on.

"I know, boy. It was risky. But all this sneaking around will come to an end soon enough."

The porch light glows like a beacon over the screen door. Caroline gives Sport a quick rub then slips inside.

OCTOBER

Caroline has just measured the coffee and put it to brew when she notices an envelope with Susan's sprawling handwriting sitting on the kitchen table next to Eldon's newspaper. She tears it open and sits down to read.

September 21, 1957

Dear Caroline,

I'm sorry I was so evasive when you phoned but I couldn't be sure my neighbour wasn't standing in her door, eavesdropping on our conversation. I suppose you're curious about John, so here goes. I caught a glimpse of him on campus one day at the start of the semester. He looked terrible, pale and gaunt, and I'd be lying if I said I didn't feel a perverse sort of pleasure seeing him like that. Needless to say, I dropped his class and enrolled in another. Etta was waiting for me outside class one day and we went to the cafeteria for tea. She told me that before classes began she met with John's wife (a very sweet girl, she said, and nothing like the sort of harridan she expected) and told her about the lengthy affair she and John had been having. She also told her John was involved with a second girl, although she didn't mention me by name. Etta didn't know what came of her revelation, but I can't imagine it's good.

I'm better now. I'm so glad you and Alice convinced me to face up to John and carry on with school. How are you? Dad told me harvest has been on hold because of the rain. I hope you were able to get finished. Thank you again for being such a good friend and being there for me when I was home. You and Alice are the dearest friends anyone could ask for. I won't be home for Thanksgiving, but plan to make it back sometime before Christmas. Hope to see you then.

Yours,
Susan

Caroline tucks the letter back into the envelope, tears stinging her eyes as she thinks about Susan, and she blinks them away when Eldon comes into the kitchen, pulling his suspenders over his shoulders.

"I see you found your letter. It was hidden between the pages of the classified ads. I didn't notice it there until last night when I was reading the paper."

Caroline gets out a pan and adds a sliver of butter, considering the possibility he's kept the letter from her by hiding it himself; it's been at least two weeks since it must have arrived and it's unlikely the letter wiggled in between the back pages of the *Co-operator* by itself.

You're not the only one capable of deception, she thinks. She's hidden her own letters — ones she's written and addressed to Susan and Alice explaining the reasons she's leaving and begging for the girls' forgiveness — in an old trunk in the attic. They are stamped and ready to post tomorrow before she and Nick leave for Alberta.

"What's new with Susan?" asks Eldon, tapping his foot against the leg of the table as Caroline scurries between the stove and the table, setting the plates while keeping an eye on his egg sizzling in the pan. "I hope I don't have to haul you all the way out to the Wawryks' to see her again. She should be in better spirits by now, you'd think," he says sarcastically.

"She's back in school so you don't need to concern yourself," says Caroline curtly and pours him a cup of steaming coffee. Eldon complained both times Caroline asked him to drive her to Susan's in August, acting as though doing her that small favour was a major imposition on his busy life. "She missed coming home for Thanksgiving but she'll be here this weekend so we're planning to meet at Alice's on Saturday afternoon," she adds.

The lie tumbles out as easily as the rest of the stories she's made up since she met Nick; the truth is she's not likely to see Alice and Susan again for a very long time, if ever, and it pains her to abandon her two best friends in the world. She's leaving tomorrow at midnight, meeting Nick a mile down the road where he'll be waiting in his truck in the moonlight. It should be her father she'll miss most, but she won't; she'll never forgive him for tricking her into trading her freedom for a piece of land. He's bound to be furious when he finds out she's run off and he's sure to take Eldon's side, although she can't help but wonder how civil they'll be to one another when it comes to discussing the fate of Beulah's land.

She fretted for days about leaving Sport behind, imagining him cowering under the table when Eldon discovers her betrayal. When she told Nick, he insisted they take the dog along. She threw her arms around his neck, both crying and laughing with joy, picturing Sport on the open road with his head out the truck window, ears flying in the wind, the three of them together heading off to a life she never would have dreamed possible six short months ago.

"Bert and I are bringing the cows and calves in from the north pasture this afternoon. Can you make an early lunch?" Eldon asks.

"Of course," Caroline answers quickly. "What time?" She's planning to meet Nick one final time at the tree this afternoon to go over the last-minute details and she's relieved to know Eldon will be out of the yard.

She has an hour before she has to meet Nick so she digs her battered old suitcase out of the attic and stops at the bathroom for a damp cloth to wipe off the dust. In the mirrored medicine chest over the sink she catches sight of herself — her untamed hair, the ripe flush on her cheeks — and she tells herself it's true what Betty Cornforth said: she does appear to be glowing. She is running water over the cloth, looking at the calendar tacked next to the mirror, when another thought nudges into the edge of her mind. It occurs to her that her monthly hasn't yet arrived, and she's never been late. Heaven knows, she's been jumpy as a wet cat since she and Nick put their plan in motion, all that nervous tension, worrying that somehow Eldon or Elvina would read her guilty mind and their plot would be discovered. But could it be? She falls to her knees, rifling through the trash basket for the torn-off calendar page for September. There they are; bold black *F*'s marking her most fertile days, and the night she spent with Nick on the porch is among them. Could it really be? Her knees are too weak to stand as a tremor of hope threads its way through her and she folds up September with its magical *F*'s and slips it into her breast pocket to show Nick.

A gust of wind snatches the door and whips it out of Caroline's hand as she steps out on the porch. Yesterday, leaves in hues of ochre and crimson and copper still dressed the trees, but the blustery north wind has stripped the branches bare during the night and fallen leaves skitter like mice across the yard. There is a light dusting of snow in the clefts left behind in the flower bed where she's pulled out the bachelor's buttons and love-in-the-mist and there is a sharp bite to the air. She goes back inside and digs deep in the closet for mitts and a knitted hat before she sets out, her head bent to the wind.

She looks around the yard, wondering where Sport could be, but there is no sign of him, no sign of life at all except for sparrows tittering on the hydro wire and a few daring hens strutting about near the coop. "Sport! Here, boy," she calls and he doesn't come bounding up like he usually does. Thinking it odd, she resumes her brisk pace.

Nick is not there when she gets to the tree. She waits for an hour, her toes numb in her shoes, and she wishes Sport were curled up next to her, his warm body cutting the wind. She can't imagine where Nick could be. He had a couple of errands to run that should have taken an hour — clearing the scant bit of money out of his bank account and leaving the title to Carl Morgan's land with Fred Dunbar, the lawyer in town. Last week he loaded up and delivered six of his best heifers to a farmer from Locklin, pocketing the cash to hold them over until he secured a job and they found somewhere to live. He would send his mother a letter once they were settled; his face twisted with anguish when he told Caroline he couldn't yet bring himself to tell her why he was turning his back on the farm and the family. He would send Fred Dunbar a letter, too, permitting Anton to sell his land and the rest of his stock. Nick reassured her that Anton would send the money on and never disclose their whereabouts to Eldon, no matter how much he threatened. Caroline can only imagine the ill will between them when Eldon discovers Anton's complicity in their plan.

Caroline finally grows tired of waiting and heads home. Their plans are clear enough; she will meet Nick on the road at midnight tomorrow. Her news about the baby will have to wait until they're headed west. Maybe she'll wait to tell him until they're settled in bed at the first motel. She can't wait to see his face, the delight and joy in his eyes when he learns he's going to be a father.

Feathers, like hundreds of tiny, rustling flags of surrender, are strewn around the yard amid the bodies of battered, bloodied hens when Caroline gets home. Some are still alive, squawking pitifully, dragging torn wings along the blood-soaked ground.

Eldon's truck is parked near the chicken coop, the door wide open, and Caroline runs across the yard to find him inside the fence, wringing the fragile neck of each dying bird before throwing it onto a pile.

"Where the hell have you been?" he shouts when he sees her.

"I ... I went for a walk," she stammers.

"Where'd you walk? All the way to town? Couldn't you hear the racket of this bloody slaughter? Wait until I get my hands on your fucking dog!"

"What do you mean?" She assumed the destruction in the yard was the work of the stealthy pack, gone now after they'd had their fill of chasing and killing.

"Just what I said," Eldon snaps. "It was Sport and half a dozen others, with a shepherd like Bilyk's at the head of the pack. I saw them tear out of the yard when I drove up."

"It can't be," Caroline cries. "He would never do something like this. He's never bothered the hens, never shown any interest in them at all."

"He would and he did. I saw him myself. Dropped the bird like it was a burning stick when he saw me jump out of the truck."

"I don't believe you! Sport! Come, boy. Sport?" She looks helplessly around the yard, expecting to see him bounding toward her from the other side of the barn.

"He ran off with the others," Eldon says. "He'll be damn sorry, too, when and if he ever comes home. There'll be a bullet with his name on it, waiting for him." He strides away, leaving her with the carnage. Already, blue-black flies buzz around the dead birds and a pair of turkey vultures circle in the sky. She cannot bring herself to lay her hands on the flopping birds so she finds a sledgehammer in Eldon's shop and drags it out to the yard. A screaming hen with a severed foot looks up at her with a beseeching eye before she lifts the hammer and swings. Raw, ripe blood spatters her white canvas shoes.

Her mind is numb, a frozen wasteland, as she goes about her task, silencing the birds one by one. She cannot believe Sport had a part in this. He isn't accustomed to other dogs and he must have been surprised when they showed up, barking at them at first, trying to act fierce and in charge before following after them, sniffing and circling, as they roamed about the yard. The gate to the chicken fence was open and a few hens were out, she'd seen them herself before she left. When the dogs flushed the other hens out of the pen and started to chase them, Sport was likely to follow along, thinking it a game, gambolling next to the others, nipping and yapping, with no ill intent. He couldn't have known what the dogs were going to do. It was a one-time mistake; she must convince Eldon of that.

Soon it is over, the yard now still except for the odd call from the circling vultures, and she returns to the house, wishing she had a wood stove like her mother's with a greedy fire inside so she could burn her blood-soaked shoes. She leaves them by the door and washes her hands then washes them again, scrubbing with a brush under her nails. She can't rid herself of the stench of fresh blood or the sticky feel of it under her feet.

The next morning, Eldon's rifle is leaning against the wall by the door, the stock resting on Sport's rug. Sport still wasn't home when Caroline went to bed. She searched the yard after supper, looking under the granaries and in each of the stalls in the barn, hoping to find him. Wherever he was, he was afraid to come home, knowing he'd done wrong, but what he couldn't know was that Caroline would forgive him, that no mistake he made was too great to absolve. She wants him to be safe from Eldon's rage, but she needs him to come home. She'll do her best to protect him for the rest of the day, hide him somewhere if she has to; there's no way she'll leave tonight without him.

She was awakened during the night by Eldon prowling around downstairs, opening and closing doors, taking no care at all to be quiet for her sake. She could not fall asleep again, thinking about the eventful day ahead and about Sport, alone and afraid somewhere in the dark. She thought about the final visit she planned to make to lay the last chrysanthemums from her garden on her mother's grave. It is one of her greatest regrets, knowing the gravestone will be left untended when she goes away. Quack grass and thistles will sprout up around the cold granite stone and grow tall enough to eventually obscure her mother's name. That's what troubles her most, thinking her sweet and gentle mother might be forgotten once Caroline's gone.

Eldon comes in from outside, digs a box of shells out of the closet and throws it on the table then reaches for the gun.

"Where are you going with that? Did Sport come back?" She runs to the door and looks out. "You can't shoot him for this one mistake. I won't let you."

Eldon drops a shell in the chamber and cocks it. "It's that dog of Bilyk's that's the ringleader. The other dogs, Jip and Sport included, are just following along. You said so yourself. If Bilyk had put him down after Howard's heifer was killed, the other calves and our chickens would still be alive. I'm going over there to make it right."

"You can't just drive into their yard and kill their dog!"

"Just watch me. I'll walk into their kitchen if I have to and drop that dog right where he stands," Eldon says, clenching his jaw so tightly a thick blue vein bulges on his temple next to his eye. He's been stewing over this all night, Caroline thinks, and it's burrowed into him like a tick under his skin. He thinks he's been wronged by Anton Bilyk and he can't let that happen. Eldon Webb does not lose.

"I'm going with you," Caroline says, opening the closet and pulling out her coat "You'll go nowhere near their house, raving like a lunatic, waving that gun around. She has children, for God's sake. If you have a bone to pick with Anton, you'll do it out in the yard."

"You'll stay right here at home where you ought to." Eldon props the rifle up on his shoulder as casually as if he's off to shoot gophers in the pasture. "This is business I'm discussing with Bilyk and no wife of mine is meddling in my affairs."

Caroline races for the door, skirting around him, and she feels her blouse jerk off her shoulder, hears the split of a seam when he lunges, but he is unable to stop her. She runs to the truck, pulling on her coat, and clambers in. She has to go with him so she can communicate to Nick in some way. He's sure to think Eldon has discovered their secret when he sees him stalking across the yard with the gun. She feels a gut-wrenching danger tumbling toward her as she pictures Nick half running across the yard to confront him.

Eldon yanks open her door, grabs hold of her arm. "You're not coming with me. Now get out of my truck."

"I won't!" Caroline braces her feet on the floorboards and presses her back to the seat. She feels something rise up, a match that's struck and lit up inside her, and when Eldon leans in, she strikes out with her fist.

She half expects Eldon to lash out but he is stunned, his eyes wide, shocked at the nerve of her, or maybe she hit him just right and she's punched out his air. "Have it your way. I'm not about to drag you out," he growls.

Scant drops of rain spatter the windshield then turn into pellets of sleet on their way over. Howard Cornforth's truck is parked close to Anton's house and beside it is a black car Caroline has never seen before. No one is out in the yard, the barn door is closed. No wild barking, no lunging dog at the end of a chain.

"What are you going to do?" Caroline asks.

Eldon is staring at Anton's front door as if he's reconsidering his plan. Caroline's eyes slide over to the other house under the bare-limbed maple and she wonders if Nick is inside. Her world seems to be twisting apart, changing direction, and she feels as though she's lost her place, skipped over a page in the book of her life. She doesn't know what she's doing here, how it's come to this, sitting in Nick's yard with Eldon and a gun, and she needs to see him, if only for a moment, to ground her again.

"Going in to talk to Bilyk like I planned," Eldon says, reaching for the gun.

Caroline grabs his hand, stills it. "Leave it."

Eldon grunts, an acknowledgement of sorts, and takes his hand off the barrel.

"I'm coming with you." There's a chance Nick might be in the house and she wants to let him know, if only with her eyes, that everything's all right; she'll be waiting for him at midnight like they planned.

Eldon grunts again. "Suit yourself. I can't very well stop you but you're not to speak. Not a word. This is between Bilyk and me."

It is Betty Cornforth who answers the door. "Oh, you've heard," she barely whispers when they step inside. "I meant to phone you but it was so early. It was Millie Tupper who let me know. Phone ringing at six in the morning, I just knew it had to be bad news. He passed on shortly before midnight, Millie said. Lay eight hours on that hillside before he was found. Such a shock for someone so young," she says, shaking her head. "Howard always said it was too dangerous to plough up those steep hills."

Caroline feels the room begin to spin — too warm, too bright — and she braces one arm against the door jamb. A simple question is pinging off the edges of her mind; she has to ask it but she can't compel her lips to form the puckered O, can't force her lungs to exhale that faint puff of air.

And then Anna appears in the doorway, dead-looking eyes in her ashen face. Little Jack is hefted up on her shoulder, too big to be carried, but whimpering nevertheless into a pale blue blanket, and Caroline thinks please, please, let it be Anton, let this agony, this razor slicing my heart be Anna's burden and not mine to bear but then Anton is standing behind her, his huge calloused hand weighing down Anna's narrow shoulder, and Caroline tastes bile at the back of her throat and a moan rises up from the pocket of her soul but she holds it inside. She doesn't need to ask her simple question, *who*, because she already knows.

PART
THREE
SARAH,
1975-1976

SEPTEMBER

They are hanging around outside the pool hall when Eddie Reston and another boy they don't know drive up in a cherry-red Camaro. The street is mostly deserted, usual for this end of Main Street on Saturday night when most of the cars are parked farther down the street in front of the hotel. It's warm for the end of September; every car cruising down Main has the windows cranked wide, tunes blaring from eight-track stereos, the laughter of teenagers — recently back at school but free once again for the weekend — riding on waves of moist end-of-summer air.

"Hey, girls. Wanna go for a ride?" Eddie is in the driver's seat, his arm dangling loosely out the window, drumming his fingers on the door to Led Zeppelin. He's wearing sunglasses, big as half his face, even though the sun's ready to disappear over the brow of the horizon. "Hop in the back," he says around the cigarette hanging off his lip as he guns the engine.

"Like we'd go anywhere with you," Becca says, flipping her hair and looking away down Main as though she's waiting for someone better to pull up.

"C'mon. Don't be like that," he says. Eddie is in grade twelve like they are, an awkward boy with few friends and an unfortunate tic, a sporadic jerking of his head, which has earned him the nickname Pecker.

Becca leans in, propping her elbows on the door. "Pretty nice," she says, turning on the charm and smiling at the new boy. "Who's your friend?" she says to Eddie.

He folds himself out of the passenger seat, a tall, stocky guy with dirty blond hair curling past his shoulders. He is Eddie's cousin, Steve, from the city, and they learn the car doesn't really belong to him; it's his older brother's.

"Whaddya say?" Eddie says as Steve folds down the front seat so the girls can crawl in the back.

"Well?" Becca asks, turning to Sarah and Addie. "You want to go?"

Sarah doesn't think they should; her dad's warned her about climbing into the back seat of cars with strange boys. "We don't even know his cousin," Sarah says quietly enough so the boys don't hear. "You really want to ride with Pecker?"

"Oh, lighten up. It'll be fun," Becca says.

Addie walks around to the passenger side where Steve is standing. "Where are we going exactly?"

"Just cruise out of town a couple miles. Show you what this thing can do."

"Sure. Why not?" Becca says and hops in, her golden hair bouncing.

There's a two-four of Canadian on the back seat and Becca shoves it over when Addie climbs in. "What're we supposed to do with this?"

"Drink it, what else?" Eddie says and revs the engine again.

"There's no room for me," Sarah says, looking in. "That's really okay, I'll just walk home."

"Oh, for God's sake," Becca says, rolling her eyes. "Shove over, Addie, and give me that beer." She takes out a bottle and turns the box on its side, jamming it in front of her legs on the floor. "Got an opener?"

Steve reaches back for the beer and cracks the cap off with his teeth. "You comin' or not?" he says, and Sarah reluctantly crawls in.

They make a few laps around town, stopping long enough to talk to Bobby Boychuk, who's cruising in his beat-up old farm truck with the rear bumper hanging off. He tells them there's a roadside party north of town on Boot Hill Road, so Eddie floors it in front of the post office, squealing the tires, as Steve hoots and bangs his outstretched hand on the roof. Becca and Addie squeal as they head out of town.

Sarah braces her legs and hangs on, wondering how she got railroaded into this, trapped in the back seat with a dipshit she doesn't even like at the wheel, off to a party she doesn't want to go to in the middle of nowhere at the side of a deserted road.

"Want a sip?" Addie asks, holding out the beer. Sarah shakes her head so Addie downs another gulp and hands it back to Becca. Addie's going along, Sarah sees, forcing down the beer because Becca wants her to. Addie was hurt when Sarah first started hanging around with Becca, until Sarah made it clear that she wasn't being replaced. It hadn't taken long for Becca to take control of the trio, however. She made all the decisions about where to go and what to do, and Sarah and Addie found themselves following along.

"So you got a boyfriend?" Steve asks, looking over his shoulder, asking no one in particular but both Sarah and Addie know he means Becca. Every boy loses some level of control around her. It's her hair, Addie always says, and Sarah thinks that's part of it, but there's something more. It's like Becca is friends with the sun and uses it to her advantage, tilting her head so it catches in her hair, weaving flaxen threads through it, turning her into some kind of golden girl. That radiant sunshine seems to seep into her pores, fill her up, and she knows just when to use it. She can manipulate anyone, picking the exact right time to laugh at Mr. Strump's pathetic jokes in math class and keeping Cady Hubley in check with nothing more than a strategic lift of an eyebrow.

Becca doesn't answer him. She's staring out the window at the trees whizzing by.

"Okay, girls, ready for a real ride?" Steve taps a drum roll on the dashboard with the palms of his hands. Eddie grins and guns it. The Camaro lurches forward and the girls' heads snap back. Addie's front teeth connect with the lip of the bottle with a distinct clink and a splash of beer sloshes onto her lap.

"Holy shit, you made me chip my tooth!"

The car jets forward, a satisfied hum coming from under the hood, then Eddie shifts it to high.

"Whoa! This baby can go!" Becca's enjoying this, a look like rapture spread across her face.

Faster and faster they go until Sarah feels the tires shimmy against the blacktop and the car fishtails a bit. A tragic accident last year suddenly comes to mind — five kids killed near Locklin — and the photo she saw in the newspaper, that one girl's shoe, lying on the highway. The fields and trees are nothing more than blurs of orange and yellow, blending together now out of the corner of her eye. They hit a dip in the road and go airborne, sailing up then slamming back to the pavement as the car rocks on its wheels.

"Slow down!" Sarah shouts, patting and poking her hands into the crevices of the seat around her, searching for a seat belt tucked away. It's time to put it on. Just then there's a terrible screeching and she pitches forward, smacking her forehead on the back of Steve's seat, and the car skids sideways, tires squealing. Becca screams.

When they finally come to a stop, the smell of burnt rubber hangs in the air. "Fuck, man," Steve says and Eddie just sits there and stares, hanging on to the wheel. A grain truck sits at the edge of the highway, its front end angled into the ditch, and a young guy is walking toward them, waving his arms.

"He's pissed off, man," Steve says and they all crawl out of the car.

There's something familiar about him although Sarah isn't sure who he is. He's not much older than they are, but she notices the way his eyes take everything in, looking things over, seeing them all for what they really are, a bunch of crazy kids with a case of beer and nothing to do on a Saturday night except try to get someone killed.

He is glaring at Steve and Eddie, his chin jutting out. It's a rugged chin that matches his strong cheekbones and the confident line of his jaw. Sarah doesn't want to stare but she can't help herself. His face is perfect.

"You're damn lucky I swerved over or they'd be picking pieces of you up off the road. You think that tin can is any match for my grain truck?"

"You were going too slow, man," Eddie mumbles. "And I didn't see that other car coming."

"You're fuckin' lucky I didn't roll." He takes a step forward, lifts a fist like he's going to lace Eddie between the eyes but then he stops himself, clasping the knuckles of his clenched fist with the other and looks away. "You girls okay?" His face softens as he looks at Sarah with real concern and she feels something reach up and grab hold inside then roll and pitch in her stomach. She feels almost sick, but in a good and glorious way.

"Scared shitless, but we'll live," Becca says, stepping out from behind Steve. She gathers her hair with one fist and drapes it over a bare shoulder. "Heard you were back from college but I haven't seen you around."

"Hey, Rebecca." He seems caught off-guard, as though he's surprised to see her. "Been busy with harvest, same as everyone else."

"Heard you're back to stay and farm with your dad," she says, smiling sunshine at him. "We're going to a party. You wanna come?"

He shakes his head. "No, gotta get back with the truck." He takes a sidelong look at Sarah again, as though he, too, might know who she is. "Make sure you idiots take it easy," he says with a frown to Eddie and Steve, then he climbs back into his truck, backs onto the road, and pulls away.

After the close call, they ditch their plan to go to the roadside. Sarah and Addie want to go back to town, although Sarah knows she can't go straight home — her dad will kill her if he sees her drive up in that fancy red car — so they drop her off at the pool hall. She takes the long way home, walking briskly along Park Street, swinging her arms, breathing hard, working out her duelling emotions — the bright fear she felt in the car and the warm flush that washed over her when the guy in the truck first looked at her. She slows down when she nears the luxurious brick houses with two-door garages and backyards overlooking the valley, the ones with the perfect families living inside. She imagines mothers and fathers behind the walls, playing canasta at dining-room tables while children sleep in comfy bunk beds or eat popcorn in front of flickering TVs. Maybe she'll have a life like that someday with a husband who'll adore her and beautiful children with fine-featured faces. If she closes her eyes tight and wishes really hard, she can almost believe it.

They're in school on Monday morning, waiting for the first bell beside Addie's locker, when Sarah finds out who he is. Cady Hubley is standing beside the biology lab with a crowd of girls around her. "It was so fun!" she is saying, telling them all about the Saturday night roadside, loud enough so Sarah and Becca and Addie will know what a great party they missed. Eddie is rummaging at the bottom of his locker across the hall. When he stands up, he looks over, trying to catch Becca's eye, and she looks away as if she doesn't know him.

"What a loser. We're lucky he didn't get us all killed," says Sarah.

"Whose idea was it to go anywhere with that peckerhead?" Addie asks, digging out her algebra text from a tumbled pile. "If we would've slammed into the back of that grain truck, we'd all be toast."

"The guy driving the grain truck, who was he anyway?" Sarah tries to keep the tremor out of her voice and act as if she's just curious and not dying to know.

"Oh, him?" There's a small mirror hanging on Addie's swung-open door and Becca leans in, dabbing her lips with gloss. "He's my neighbour, Jack. I rode with him on the bus for years."

"I thought he was going to drift Eddie. He should have. One punch and he would've sent Pecker flying all the way back to town," Addie says.

Becca pats the excess gloss from her finger onto her cheeks and blends it in with her fingertip, making her whole face shimmer. "He's changed a lot since I last saw him. He used to be skinny but, wow, did you see those shoulders?"

"You mean Jack Bilyk? From the farm next to yours?" Sarah remembers something about him, something he once did and what Becca's mother said afterward.

They were down by the river behind the Webbs' farm. The water had dried up to a trickle that summer and they had taken their sandals off and were having a contest, jumping from stone to stone, trying to make it across without stepping into the shallow water. Some of the stones were slippery with green slime and once, Sarah almost went in. From the bank on the other side, they heard a low rumble, like a log being rolled, and then the sound of splintering twigs, as though some enormous creature might be ploughing through the underbrush and deadfall. Sarah stopped where she was, one foot raised in the air. A thunderous roar cut through the air; Becca screamed and leaped off her stone. She thrashed through the water back toward the bank. Sarah followed, stumbling over loose stones, splashing muddy water as high as her back.

When they were safely across they heard the sound of laughter. Two teenage boys emerged from the stand of poplars on the other side of the river, one as tall and scrawny as the other was short and round, chuckling and pointing at them.

"You assholes!" Becca shouted, reaching for a small rock and hurling it at them. It landed in the water with a feeble plop. "I'm gonna tell my dad!"

"You just go ahead and do that!" yelled the tall boy. "I'm not scared of your old man!"

When they got back to the house, Becca told her mother how Jack Bilyk and Shorty Cornforth had tried to scare them. "And I'm telling Dad just because he dared me not to," she said indignantly.

Mrs. Webb nervously straightened the gathers in her apron, plucking at each little pleat. "They're just teenage boys, having a little fun with you. There's no need to stir your father up over such a harmless prank. You know how he can be when it comes to those Bilyks. He's apt to storm over there and start something. You just stay away from Jack Bilyk."

Afterward, Becca told Sarah there was a feud going on between her father and Jack's, something from long ago regarding a dead dog. There was more to it than that, she said, but her mother wouldn't talk about it and her father only swore under his breath whenever the Bilyk name came up.

Becca screws the lid onto her lip gloss and shoves it in the back pocket of her jeans. "Yep. He's lived right next door all my life and I barely know him. He's cute, though, don't you think?"

The bell rings and the girls fall into step behind a moving throng of students. *He's more than cute*, Sarah thinks, following along. He's the most handsome boy in the world and she thinks she might be in love with him.

Sarah's basket is nearly full — they've been at this for nearly two hours — skirting the woodlands, wandering trails, and even searching along the gravel road. Baba seems to know every tree, every blade of grass and wildflower, every wild rose growing on her land, and her first basket is already full, waiting to be picked up later along a path they'll pass over on the way back to her house. She is stooped to her work, fingers thick as sausages, skillfully plucking red rosehips the size of fat peas from the tips of the prickly branches. One of her wool socks has slipped down and is pooled at her ankle while the other, secured with a red rubber ring, sits tight at her knee. She's wearing a green flowered *babushka* with a nearly identical skirt and a bright yellow blouse, so the bears will be sure to see them, she jokes. Sarah's always on the lookout, jumping at every cracking twig and rustle she hears in the bushes, but Baba just laughs. She isn't scared of anything. The bears are after the berries, same as we are, she says. There are lots to go around.

"How you doing?" Baba comes over and looks in Sarah's basket. "Good," she says, and Sarah smiles; good rhymes with food when Baba says it. "You finish that basket, we go back after that."

When they return to the house, they wash the rosehips and sort through them, throwing out the blemished ones and picking the brown sepals and stems off the others. The rosehips will dry on white tea towels spread on Baba's kitchen table and she will gather them up later and store them in glass jars, where they'll glow like precious rubies.

Baba settles in on her rocking chair beside the wood stove with a cup of tea when they're done, sighing deeply and lifting one leg then the other with great effort onto a footstool. "You want something to eat?"

There are cinnamon buns, freshly baked this morning, sitting on the table, and Sarah tears one apart and devours a gooey bite.

Baba's house has four rooms: a small closet off the kitchen large enough for a washstand and a galvanized tub that she drags into the kitchen each Saturday, a tiny bedroom and living room, and a large kitchen with two stoves. Above, there is a half-storey, where Sarah sleeps when she stays over.

There's an outhouse out back and a commode in the basement. She finally gave in and let Sarah's father move an electric stove in about five years ago, but she insisted on keeping the wood stove in the corner. She still uses it to bake bread and brew her tinctures and teas. An unlit candle and an icon of the Holy Mother, draped with a cross-stitched cloth, sit on a small table next to her bedroom door. She lights the candle each night before bed and sits in her rocking chair to recite her rosary, the beads sliding through her gnarled fingers, one at a time.

Baba Petrenko was there for them after Sarah's mother left. It shamed her that her own daughter would do something like that — Sarah was sure of it — but she never spoke a harsh word about her youngest daughter. Olivia couldn't be tamed, Baba said, and was born with the same restless nature as her father. He had up and left them all for Alberta after the war, saying he wasn't cut out to be a farmer. Baba helped as much as she could, bringing over roasters of *peroheh* and *holoptsi* whenever some neighbour drove her to town. She gave them sacks of potatoes and tubs full of carrots, jars of fruit and pickles and jam. Sarah, especially, spent as much time as she could with her grandmother even when they were older and the boys no longer wanted to come.

"Baba? Do you remember how you felt when you fell in love?" Sarah asks, taking another bite of her bun.

"Ya. My head feels like full of sawdust and I would do stupid things. He was all I could think about. And my stomach, too. Like bird wings flapping in there when I see him." She clasps the arms of her chair and shifts her swollen legs, wincing in pain. "Why you want to know?"

"Just curious, I guess," Sarah says. "I've been thinking about what it might be like."

"Oy," Baba says, taking a sip of tea and smiling. "So there's a boy. You want to tell me about him?"

Sarah finds herself opening up and telling Baba about Jack and the near-accident and the way she felt when she first saw him.

"Bilyk, you say?" Baba puts one finger up to her lips and furrows her brow. "How old he is? Twenty, something like that?"

"Maybe a little older. Why?"

"His mother, she brought him to me. Was raining hard that night, I remember."

Sarah sits up straight in her chair. "Do you remember what was wrong with him?"

"Couldn't sleep. Bad dreams. Scared to go to bed at night." She pauses then glances at the blessed icon on the small table. "Is God's will, what the wax shows, but that night, I don't know." She shakes her head and makes the sign of the cross.

"Why? What was it?" Sarah pictures Jack, a scared and helpless little boy, sitting in this very room, maybe in the exact same spot she's sitting right now.

"Most times, I see one thing in wax, only one, and I know right away what it is, but that time, I see two. The one, I knew right away it was fire. Flames, like little tongues across the water; easy to see. But then I see something else in water, a string curls out, reaches up to ceiling. Up, up. Maybe six inches. How wax can do that?"

"What did it mean?" Sarah is on the edge of her chair.

"I explain about fire and his mother, right away she says there was grass fire on farm, the boy, he had to run for help. Can hardly reach crank from chair. But he rings. Someone answers and neighbours, they come and help put out fire before barn burns down. But that wax standing up like that? I say nothing." She raises one arm and pushes the air with her upturned palm. "So I chase away boy's fear, the way my mother show me."

"Holy," Sarah breathes. This story about Jack is something special she'll keep. She feels closer to him somehow, just knowing it.

"First and last time I see him. They never come back." Baba is looking at Sarah, her eyes narrowed. "I remember something else. You were here, upstairs sleeping. Maybe that's why wax point like that to ceiling?" She nods her head. "Ya, that's why." She pauses, nodding her head with more certainty. "You know how I say everything happens, happens for reason? This boy, this Jack Bilyk, it was God put him on that road in that truck. To protect you. Someday, he will be yours."

OCTOBER

Step on a crack, break your mother's back. Sarah and Addie used to play that game. The sidewalk at school had hundreds of cracks, some shoestring-thin and some wide as their arms. They would leap and hop along the sidewalk, avoiding the cracks, seeing who could make it the farthest. What Addie didn't know was that Sarah came back after school and played a different game, twisting it around to suit herself. It was her secret. She aimed for the cracks, reciting a revised chant in her mind. *Step on a crack, bring your mother back.* Sometimes she hopped for hours; the more cracks she laid her foot across the better the chances of her mother's return. She longed for a mother, someone to sit in the audience during Christmas concerts or visit with her teachers on parents' day, all dressed up in a swishy skirt, ironed blouse, and bright, shiny shoes. She would be so proud of Sarah's neat scribblers and all those pointy *A*'s on her report card. Her father came as often as he could, but there always seemed to be a farmer with something to fix at the last minute before the shop closed, and he was usually late or didn't come at all. When he did show up at school for the concert, he wore his grimy coveralls and stood at the back of the gym, leaning against the wall.

Sarah remembers this as she sits at the dining-room table with Becca, watching Caroline in the kitchen. A few years ago, Caroline insisted Sarah start calling her by her name. "It seems so odd, you calling me Mrs. Webb," she had said. "Especially since we've come to be such good friends."

Caroline is baking pies for Thanksgiving. There's a heavenly smell — pumpkin, cinnamon, and nutmeg — and she's working on the pastry, rolling it gently, back and forth, back and forth, then flipping it with one hand like it's a rare and delicate parchment. A scarf is knotted on top of her head and she's wearing an apron over her pale pink button-front dress. It looks as though she's stepped back in time — she could be Richie and Joanie's mother from *Happy Days* — in the old-fashioned kitchen with its sturdy chrome table and bright yellow chairs.

"Are you ready to take a break yet?" Becca pushes aside the encyclopedia she's copying notes from and sticks a pencil inside to mark her place. They're working on essays for English class, researching William Shakespeare's life and trying to relate it to one of his works. "Like it's going to say anything in here about whether or not he was feuding with some other family. Romeo and Juliet didn't even live in England."

"I think we're supposed to think about the social context of the time and see how that may have influenced his work." Sarah closes the biography she borrowed from the school library and looks down at her notes. "I don't think we'll find answers in these books. Miss Fletcher wants us to come up with our own theories."

"My theory is I never should have taken university-entrance English." Becca is drawing hearts with a red pen on a loose leaf. "I wouldn't have, if I were you."

Sarah is not going to university after graduation like Becca. She's going to get a job, maybe stay on full-time at Pipers', and wait until Charlie graduates. Even then, if she goes to school, it'll likely be community college for some sort of diploma. She's taken all the UE courses at high school, though, to prove she can do it.

Caroline comes into the dining room and sets down a plate of cookies. "Looks like you girls are ready for a snack. Would you like some milk?"

Becca rolls her eyes. "Really, Mom? Cookies and milk?" She pushes away from the table and goes to the kitchen. Sometimes she's so mean to her mother. Caroline looks embarrassed, and Sarah thinks Becca's a jerk for treating her like that. If Caroline were her mother, she'd never act that way.

"*Romeo and Juliet*?" Caroline sits on one of the chairs next to Sarah and picks up her book. "This was always my favourite. Two star-crossed lovers. Such a tragic end."

"I like the tragedies, too. I don't find his comedies funny at all."

"I agree, they're rather silly, aren't they? Of course, we have to remember we're reading them in 1975, or in my case, nineteen fifty-whatever-it-was. But the themes, comedy *or* tragedy, are universal and they stand the test of time. You know what they say, the more things change, the more they stay the same."

Becca hands Sarah a glass of Pepsi and sits down. "You can say that again." She props her feet on one of the dining-room chairs. "Take that stupid feud between us and the Bilyks. I bet no one even remembers what it's all about."

A few stray hairs have fallen onto Caroline's forehead and she tucks them back up under her scarf. "I'm sure your father does, and he has his reasons; it's not up to us to question him about them."

"Well, it's just stupid. To live your entire life beside someone and not know anything about him?"

There's a visible jerk of Caroline's head. "Him?" Her voice sounds tight, strangled, as though something's pressing on her windpipe. "What do you mean by that?"

"Oh, nothing," Becca says, picking up her glass and one of the cookies. "C'mon, Sarah, let's go up to my room and hang out for a while. Shakespeare can wait."

Later, while they're lying on Becca's bed listening to the Eagles, Sarah thinks about the way Caroline reacted when Becca referred to Jack. Her own heart jumped, too, the way it always does when the thought of him comes to mind. She's kept her secret crush to herself, savouring the taste of Jack's name on her tongue. She's been meaning to tell Becca and Addie how she feels about him but she's afraid. She's not sure if Jack would ever consider dating a girl like her. But if she doesn't tell, how will she ever know?

"Bec?"

"Yeah?" Becca is on her back, feet in the air, toes tapping to the bass from her stereo.

"Do you ever run into Jack? See him around anywhere?"

Becca's toes stop moving. "Why?"

The only way to do this is to just come right out and admit it, get it over with quickly, like ripping off a Band-Aid. "Because I sorta like him." Sarah feels herself blush, a wave of heat laps over her face from her roots to the base of her chin. "I mean ... I think he's cute and I wish I could get to know him. Meet him sometime, you know?"

Becca sits up. "Seriously?"

Sarah sits up, too. "I mean … you know him, at least. I wondered if you could introduce me to him or something. Sometime."

"I don't see how I can." Becca gets up and goes over to the record player, flips over the LP, and sets the needle down again. "I mean, when would I introduce you? He doesn't come to any of our lame high-school parties and my dad sure doesn't want him coming around here."

"I know," Sarah says, flopping her head back down on the bed. "It was a dumb idea."

"Seriously," Becca says again, "you really like him?"

"Forget I ever said anything," Sarah says, covering her face with her hands. "I only saw him that one time. And he's way too old for me and probably has a girlfriend, anyway."

"I've been wondering about that myself," Becca says quietly.

"You'd get into trouble with your dad if he found out you were talking to him. He likely wouldn't be interested in me, anyway."

"He would so." Becca's mouth curls up at the corners but her eyes aren't smiling. "It's just impossible, you know? For me to help you."

"That's okay," Sarah says. "If it's meant to happen, it will. That's what my baba always says."

Becca nods and there's a distant kind of look in her eyes like she knows something she's not telling. Like maybe she, too, thinks Sarah doesn't stand a chance with a guy like Jack.

The kitchen table is covered with newspaper and the stringy innards of a pumpkin. The pumpkin itself, now a one-eyed jack-o'-lantern with a lopsided grin, is perched at the edge of the table. A tower of dishes is stacked in the sink and the milk jug is sitting out on the counter. There's no sign of Charlie or Brian, but the TV's blaring from the other room.

"Guys!" Sarah shouts, poking her head into the living room. "When will you learn to put the milk back in the fridge when you're done with it? And turn that down!"

Charlie's sitting on the couch, his feet propped on the coffee table between stacks of old hot-rod magazines. "What if I want another glass?"

"Then you'll go back to the fridge and take it out again." Sarah stomps across the room and turns the volume down herself. "And what's with that mess you left on the table? Who's supposed to clean that up?"

Charlie grins and points at himself, an overdramatic circling of his thumb to his chest, and Sarah tries not to smile, but she can't help herself. He can be a little pain in the ass, she knows, and she's spoiled him; it's her fault he gets away with as much as he does. Charlie was only three years old when their mom left and Sarah's mothered him ever since. She taught him to print his name and how to tie his shoes. She used to let him climb into her warm bed when he was up too early on Saturday mornings and she never made him eat his canned peas. Even though he's thirteen, she still sees him as that freckle-faced little boy with the sparkling blue eyes that had her wrapped around his little finger.

"Where's Brian?"

"He's at Mikey's house. They're planning to find someone to cruise around with tonight."

"What about you? Is Terry's mom taking you out in the country again this year?"

"Nah," Charlie says. "We're just going in town this year."

This will be Charlie's last year trick-or-treating. She knows he says he's going out for candy, but she imagines he'll get himself into some kind of harmless trouble. Knock over a few garbage cans, soap a few windows. She remembers when Charlie used to tag along with her and Addie; she can still feel his sticky little hand in hers, hear the swish of his pillowcase, loaded with candy, dragging on the ground. He was a ghost for more years than she can remember, the only costume she could easily make: an old pillowcase torn up the seams and draped over his head then two circles cut out for his eyes. She always dressed up like a hobo. Colourful patches sewn on an outgrown pair of jeans and stuffing from an old pillow stitched into a square, cut from one of her father's old shirts, and tied to the end of a stick. Becca had a new costume every year — Little Red Riding Hood in grade three, several fairy princesses, and a cheerleader with shimmery pompoms one year when she was older.

Sarah is making supper when her father comes home. She hears the door slam and the *thump-thump* as he kicks off his boots. He looks tired, as he often does, and she wonders how long he can keep it up, hefting around that heavy steel. He shrugs off his coveralls and leaves them by the door.

"I noticed a couple shingles in the backyard," Sarah says as she opens a tin of mushrooms. "That strong wind last night must have blown off a few more."

He sits down heavily at the table and rubs the back of his neck. "I'll need to crawl up there and put a proper patch on it. It's always one damn thing after another around here."

The house is getting more rundown with each passing year. Her father stopped caring when her mother walked out and the weight of his despair has crippled the house — scoured the paint off the siding and wrenched the front porch right off its foundation. Sarah is ashamed of it, that quick-put-your-head-down-and-don't-look kind of feeling she gets when she walks up. Last year, she heard Cady Hubley bragging about the eighty-six trick-or-treaters who showed up at their house on Park Street. No one, except the kids who live nearby, goes trick-or-treating on Sarah's side of the tracks. She handed out to only twelve kids last year (including her brothers), two suckers each plus a popcorn ball she made herself, so brittle Brian and Charlie batted them around like softballs with two wooden spoons the day after Hallowe'en.

She dumps the mushrooms into six whisked eggs and adds it all to the onions and chopped wieners frying in the pan. Omelettes-on-toast, she calls this creation, one of Charlie's favourites.

"You going out tonight after you hand out the treats?"

"I guess so. The girls are coming to town and we'll hang out for a while."

As if on cue, the phone rings. It's Addie. "Hey, I just talked to Bec and she's not coming with us tonight. She was acting all mysterious and she wouldn't say why. Did she say anything to you?"

Sarah agrees to call and find out what's going on. Becca answers the phone on the first ring. Dishes clatter in the background; it's suppertime at the Webbs' and she can almost see Caroline bustling around the kitchen in her apron, pulling out a pot roast with oven-mitted hands.

"Just a sec," Becca says. Sarah hears the receiver banging against the wall, a pause, then a click, then Becca's back on the line. Becca has an extension in her room (she and Cady are the only girls in their class who have them).

"Mom? I'm on. You can hang it up now." Becca waits for a click and the kitchen sounds go quiet. "Hey, what's up?"

"Addie says you're not coming with us tonight."

"I got stuff to do."

"What stuff? It's Hallowe'en!"

Becca skates around Sarah's questions, half answering them with vague explanations. Becca didn't come out the weekend before, either, although she showed up at school on Monday with her eyes all sparkly like she'd had the best time in the world sitting at home doing nothing. Something is going on with her. Sarah wonders if Becca has found a new group of friends, girls who are popular and more fun to be with than Addie and her, and it bugs her to think about it.

"Why don't you come and sleep over tomorrow?"

Becca hesitates again, a long empty pause. "I'll have to see if Mom will let me."

Again, Sarah is puzzled. Becca doesn't usually need Caroline's permission; she tells Caroline what she's going to do, not the other way around.

Sarah is taking her last bite of omelette-on-toast when someone pounds on the door.

"Trick or treat! Hallowe'en apples!"

Sarah hurries to the cupboard where she's hidden the bubble gum, licorice, and peanuts and finds the licorice bag torn open, the candy half-gone. Three little masked faces look up at her when she opens the door. One of them, dressed like a pirate, is holding a flashlight nearly as long as his leg. She tosses a handful of peanuts and three pieces of bubble gum into each of their bags and hesitates before throwing in a couple sticks of licorice (stiff as pencils but what else can she do?). The smallest one, Herman Munster, she thinks, keeps holding his bag out, waiting for more, until the tallest one in the middle mumbles thank you from behind his mask and nudges the other two to do the same before they turn and scurry off to better, more generous houses, following the bouncing beam lighting their way.

NOVEMBER

Sarah is in bed, sick with the flu, listening to sleet pepper her bedroom window and a gusty wind flap the porch door, a rhythmic bang keeping time with the excruciating pain throbbing in her head. Every muscle in her body aches, even ones she didn't know existed before today. She wishes Baba were here to brew one of her healing teas.

Downstairs, the telephone rings. Five, six, seven rings and it stops then starts up again. *Where are those boys and why aren't they answering it?*

Sarah struggles out of bed, every muscle screaming, and wraps an afghan around her shoulders then hurries downstairs.

"Sarah? Did I wake you?" It's Caroline, sounding all chipper. She's likely been awake, baking cookies or something, since the crack of dawn.

"No, I'm just sick," Sarah croaks.

"November's such a nasty month, isn't it? Not quite yet winter, but acting like it, with all those cold north winds and everyone coming down with the flu. If I'd known you weren't well, I wouldn't have allowed Becca to spend the night. Is she there? I need to speak to her."

Sarah's heart skips a beat and she feels a little queasy. The hammer in her head feels like it's smashing the backs of her eyeballs. She has no idea where Becca is.

"Uh … she's in the shower right now. Can I give her a message?"

"Get her to call me back as soon as she can."

Sarah sits on a chair, stretching the telephone cord as far as it goes from the wall to the table. Now what should she say?

"On the other hand," Caroline continues, "just tell her she's to stop in at her grandmother's house. She's been so busy lately — there's more homework and extra projects this year than I can recall her ever having before — that she's missed the last two Sunday visits with Elvina. I'm the one having to listen to her complain that Becca never comes to see her."

"Sure, I'll tell her as soon as she's out of the shower," Sarah says.

"Very well. And don't be a stranger. I've missed you. I keep asking Becca why you girls don't come to our house to work on these projects of yours anymore, but she says she gets more accomplished at your house, although I don't see how, with those little brothers of yours running around." Caroline laughs, a strained, put-on sort of laugh. "She says she works better amid chaos. I suppose it's good training for the dormitory next year."

After she hangs up, Sarah pours herself a glass of orange juice and taps two Aspirin out of the bottle. She considers phoning Addie to see if Becca is there but she remembers Addie and her family are away for the weekend, gone to Saskatchewan for her aunt and uncle's fortieth anniversary. Where else could Becca be? Her toes are cold from the icy kitchen floor so she goes back upstairs, slips on a pair of socks, and climbs into bed.

Outside her window the sky is flat and grey, as bleak as everything else in November, and it makes Sarah feel out of sorts, as though she's misplaced something valuable that wasn't hers to begin with. Becca's up to something, she's sure of it now. She's been different, quiet and aloof, as though she's guarding a secret, and it bugs Sarah to think Becca's keeping something from her. And using her, too. Telling Caroline she's been doing homework and spending nights at her house when she's off having fun with other girls. A hot wave of anger rolls through her when she pictures Becca, laughing at some party, maybe even at Cady's house, flitting around the room with a beer in her hand. And it's shame she feels, too, when she thinks Becca's finally figured out that Sarah, with her runaway mother, quick-fisted brothers, and shabby old house, isn't quite good enough to be friends with her. It hasn't been enough, *she* hasn't been enough or done enough to do better than the rest of the Coyles, and now it's cost her a friend.

On Monday morning, Sarah squats by her locker, turning binders and notebooks and textbooks upside down, killing time, pretending she's looking for something. She is giving Becca the silent treatment, although Becca doesn't seem to notice; she's waiting for Sarah to stand up and talk to her like she always does. Addie's telling Becca about a second cousin she met for the first time over the weekend.

"He was such a hunk. I'd date him if I could."

"Eww," Becca says. "That's sick."

"It's not like we did anything," Addie says defensively. "He was just interesting, you know? And I just thought it's too bad he lives in Saskatoon and we're related."

"You can't date your own cousin," Becca says.

"He's not my *first* cousin. Besides, cousins married cousins all the time in royal families; we learned about it in history."

"Well, the whole idea is gross. Don't you think so, Sarah?"

Sarah stands up and shuts her locker. It makes her mad to see Becca acting as though everything's the same between them, as though there isn't a secret she's keeping, one Sarah isn't worthy of knowing. She's dying to know where Becca was on Friday night and what happened at home when she showed up without stopping to visit her grandmother, but she's not going to ask her. Becca's sure to have lied to her mother, coming up with a story on the spur of the moment, and Caroline, as usual, likely believed her.

Sarah cradles her chemistry text in the crook of her arm, drapes her purse over her shoulder, and heads off to class, Becca and Addie following behind. She imagines the look — *What's up with Sarah?* — that passes between them.

Mr. Lawson is away for the morning and there's a substitute teacher, a grey-haired woman with more wrinkles than Baba, and she tells them to work on their own, no lesson today. Immediately the class starts to buzz as students turn around in their desks, heads bent, talking to each other. Becca is sitting behind Sarah and she pokes her, but Sarah ignores her. She flips open her notebook and considers going back to her locker to get her unfinished history assignment but Becca pokes her again, a blunt tip nudging her back. Then Becca comes around and sits in the empty desk in front of her, planting her crossed arms on Sarah's desk. "What is your problem? Are you mad at me about something?"

And all the irritation that's been churning inside her comes bubbling forth. "I thought I was your best friend. I thought I meant more to you than a handy excuse to use when you're off sneaking around with your new friends. You've been telling me you're at home and you've been telling your mom you're with me. So, yeah, I'm just a little pissed off."

Becca is stunned. "When did you talk to my mom?"

"On Saturday morning. And I didn't appreciate having to lie to her. I had to cover for you without even knowing where you were. What if something had happened to you? If you'd been hurt or in an accident? Where were you anyway?"

Becca gets up and grabs Sarah's hand, pulling her out of her desk. She drags her across the room while the substitute shouts, "Girls! You must have a hall pass if you're leaving the room."

In the washroom, Becca lets go of Sarah's hand. "I'm sorry. I know I've been awful, putting you and Addie off every weekend, but there's something … I didn't know how to tell you, so I've been keeping it to myself, and I wanted to tell. I really did."

"I'm listening," Sarah says. Becca sounds like Charlie, making excuses after she's told him he has to do his homework and turn off the TV. "This better be good."

"I've been seeing someone." Becca's voice quivers a bit. "I didn't tell you because … No one else knows, just the two of us. I can't risk Mom and Dad finding out."

Sarah feels like she's been kneed in the gut, the air stripped from her lungs. She knows, without Becca saying it, that it's Jack she's been seeing. She pictures them all on the road that day, the Camaro spun around facing town and Jack walking toward them, staring them down, until there was a softening in the hard line of his jaw. She thought his concern was for her, but of course it wasn't. He must have been looking at Becca.

The little conversations Sarah's composed in her mind for her first meeting with Jack, rehearsing them over and over before she falls asleep, float off in her mind like bits of paper blown away on the wind. She'll never use them now, never get to know him as anyone else but Becca's boyfriend.

She remembers the day she told Becca she liked him, the sudden way her foot stopped moving in the air, the look on her face when she told Sarah she couldn't help her. "Were you already seeing him when I told you I liked him?"

Becca has a pained look on her face. "I met him on the road one day not long after Eddie nearly ran his truck off the road. I stopped and we talked for a while and then went for a drive. I could tell he really liked me. We decided to meet at the elm tree by the stone pile and things kind of went on from there." Her voice trails off.

Sarah nods, trying to hide her crushing disappointment. "Why didn't you say something and stop me from making a fool of myself?"

"It was so awkward. I didn't know what to tell you. I thought it might just be a passing thing, you know, but he wanted to keep seeing me. We met all through the fall and when it got cold out, I'd take my car and we'd meet somewhere in the country," Becca continues. "I'd tell Mom I was at your house, or Addie's, and she always believed me."

It makes Sarah almost physically sick to think about Jack and Becca together, and angry, too, realizing how Becca fooled her. "It was risky, don't you think, using me and Addie like that without letting us in on it. How was I supposed to know what to say when your mom called?"

Becca nods her head knowingly. "Now I know why she asked me if I'd seen my grandma when I came home on Saturday. I wondered what she meant by that so I said

Grandma wasn't home. That seemed to satisfy her." A visible look of relief steals across her face. "I'm lucky she fell for it. It's because of you, you know. She trusts you. She'd never suspect you weren't telling her the truth."

And Sarah feels the troubling weight of it, the burden of having to keep Becca's secret. How will she be able to look Caroline straight in the eye from now on? Cady and Arlene Mills burst through the doors just then and, when they see Becca and Sarah, they look at each other and start giggling.

"Did you two have a fight?" Cady leans in to a mirror and fluffs her hair with her fingers. "Are you breaking up?" she asks in a mocking way.

Arlene snickers.

"As if we'd ever tell you what we're talking about." Becca stands next to Cady and stares her down in the mirror.

"What will you do without Sarah? Following you around, hanging on every word, doing whatever the hell you tell her to do. Huh, Becca? Everyone knows you only wanted to be friends with her so you could be the coolest one in your new little group."

"Shut up, Cady," Becca says. "C'mon, Sarah, let's get out of here."

Cady blocks their way, putting one hand on the door. "You couldn't stand to stay friends with me because I was the most popular girl in town and you couldn't handle the competition. So you found yourself a charity case to be your new friend."

Sarah is stunned. She knows Cady is mean but she never expected her to actually come right out and say such terrible things in front of her. Worse yet, could what she was saying be true? Sarah always wondered about the ease with which she'd fallen into the sphere of Becca's world, not by any choice Becca made, not really, but by convenience. A matter of being in the right place at the right time, standing alone by the Ferris wheel. Had Becca grabbed her hand, breaking away from Cady and her other friends to ride the wheel with Sarah, just to spite Cady Hubley?

"It's easy to be the top dog with such a pathetic loser for a best friend." Cady waves her other hand dismissively at Sarah. "Someone who lives across the tracks and has a drunk for a dad and a mother who couldn't stand her miserable life and ran away."

Sarah feels a deep shame burning inside her and a rage, too. She yanks Cady's hand off the door and shoves her aside. She wishes she had the guts to knock Cady over and beat the shit out of her, like her brothers would do. Hot, angry tears well up and she forces her eyes wide open, unblinking, so they don't spill over. She won't give Cady the satisfaction of seeing her cry. Pulling open the door, she runs down the hall and back to the classroom.

MAY

"Hold still." Caroline is fussing with the armhole on Sarah's jacket, pinning on a sleeve. She pokes her with a pin — a sharp peck — and Sarah flinches. "Sorry, I'm almost done."

Sarah's standing in Caroline's sewing room, arms out-stretched like a scarecrow, wearing a partially constructed gown Caroline is sewing for her graduation. They picked out the pattern and fabric together at Mavis Baylor's store, a simple A-line dress, sleeveless, with a bolero jacket in plum purple satin. Becca's gown is already finished and hanging in her closet; a pale pink chiffon halter-style gown with a full skirt, so light and airy it looks like it could float off the hanger and dance by itself.

"I've been meaning to ask you about Becca," Caroline says as she starts to pin on the second sleeve. "What's going on with her?"

How am I supposed to answer that?

Sarah stayed clear of Becca for a few weeks after Cady said all those hurtful things about their friendship last fall. She needed time, too, to get over the crippling news about Becca and Jack. She avoided Becca's phone calls and ignored her at school, unable to find it in her heart to hear Becca out; she wasn't sure she wanted to know the truth about the real reason for their unlikely friendship. Becca was persistent, however, and finally left a note in Sarah's locker.

> *I've never had a friend as true and loyal as*
> *you. Cady's jealous because I chose you over her.*
> *Please believe me.*

And eventually Sarah did. She allowed Becca back into her life, carrying on as though nothing had ever happened.

Becca and Jack eventually let Addie and Shorty Cornforth in on their secret and they all swore not to say a thing. Becca couldn't risk her parents finding out. The five of them even hung out together a few times at Addie's house when her parents weren't home. It wasn't easy seeing Becca curled up in Jack's arms. Sarah told herself that Jack was no different than any other boy who fell under Becca's spell, although she sometimes noticed Jack looking at her, trying to catch her eye. When she finally allowed herself to look at him, right into his eyes, he smiled at her in a wistful kind of way, and she wondered about that. But a romance with Jack wasn't meant to be, despite Baba's prediction.

"Do you know if there's something troubling Becca? She hardly looks at me when I'm speaking to her, or else she storms off in a huff," Caroline is saying as she tucks in some excess fabric at Sarah's bosom.

Caroline's face is so open and sincere. Sarah doesn't want to keep lying to her but she can't betray Becca. "I'm not sure what's up with her. There's a lot for her to think about, leaving home and moving away to be on her own."

"I'm not looking forward to her leaving either, but you don't see me biting off her head every time I open my mouth. There's change coming for all of us. Has she considered for one moment what my life will be like when she's gone? How difficult it'll be for me?" Caroline's voice wavers as her fingers flutter over Sarah's skin, tucking and pinning.

What must it be like, Sarah wonders, *to have a mother who'd care that you're gone? Someone who might cry, even, when you packed your things in a suitcase and climbed aboard a Greyhound bus.* She studies Caroline, bent over beneath her outstretched arm, noticing for the first time the fine lines around her eyes and the threads of silver laced through her hair. She'd noticed a sadness about Caroline lately, a heaviness in the way she seemed to go about her daily chores, as though she was marking time, waiting, like Sarah, for something besides the next long day to come along. She sensed it wasn't easy for Caroline living with Eldon, who seldom smiled or even said as much as one kind word to her. While Sarah expected that one day she would go on to a better sort of life, she realized that Caroline would forever remain in this brick house.

"We fool ourselves into believing there's a plan," Caroline continues. "We think there's a pattern set out for our life that will come together like the pieces of this dress, pinned and stitched together." She jerks at the seam under Sarah's arm, spears her with another pin. "But then something happens and life goes veering off in a completely different direction without you even knowing how it happened and suddenly the dress is never finished and you're sitting there with all these swatches you're not sure what to do with." Caroline stands back and carefully pulls the pinned-up jacket from Sarah's shoulders then eases out her arms, one at a time. Her eyes are bright, on the verge of tears. "Nothing turns out like it's supposed to."

Sarah understands. Her own life completely changed course after Patrick was killed and her mother left. In time, she came to realize there was really only one thing to do when life dealt her such a blow. Just get back up and move on.

"My baba always told me if there's a hill in front of me, I'm meant to climb it. What's the sense in turning back? The hill will still be there."

"It's just that sometimes it's so much easier to stay there at the bottom," Caroline says. "It takes too much effort to go on."

Sarah doesn't agree, but she doesn't say so. She wants to know what's on the other side of every hill she comes to, even if she has to wait until the time is right to trek over.

Later that week, Sarah is at Baba's farm, helping her plant the garden, when a car pulls up. Baba puts a hand to her brow, shielding her eyes from the sun, and leans on her rake. They've almost finished planting the corn, three wizened seeds in each of sixty shallow hollows. Baba tested the soil this morning before they got started, pulling her bare foot out of her rubber boot and burying it in the dirt to her ankle. "Is good. Warm enough. We plant today," she said.

A man climbs out and helps a woman, holding an infant wrapped in a white blanket, out of the car. He walks over, stepping carefully between the rows marked with seed packets slipped onto sticks. "Mrs. Petrenko?" His voice cracks and he licks his lips. "Are you the *chudesnytsia*? The one who helps people?"

Baba nods and sets down her hoe. "Ya, that's me."

"We're here about my wife. Her mother and I don't know what to do. She cries all the time and doesn't seem to care at all about the baby. Leaves him in the cradle and closes herself up in our room, lays in bed all day without saying a word. This can't keep going on."

Baba nods. "Come," she says. "I see this before. Many times. I help her." She turns to Sarah. "You finish here then come up to house. I want you should watch."

Sarah throws the last of the seeds into the holes, covers them with a thin layer of soil then picks up the empty corn seed packet, impales it on the last whittled stick, and stabs it into the ground. When she gets to the house, the man is sitting in a chair, holding the sleeping baby, while the woman stands behind him, clutching the back of the chair. Her skin is the colour of skim milk, her lips the same bluish hue as the hollows under her eyes. She glances around the room, eyes unfocused, until she notices Sarah.

"Who are you?" she whispers and it's spooky, the way she looks. Waxy, not quite alive.

"Sarah, get my basket." Baba drags a chair into the middle of the kitchen so it faces away from the window. After asking a few questions, she leads the woman to the chair then melts the amber wax over the candle, pours it into the water and begins to chant the mysterious words Sarah's heard before.

Sarah first remembers the ritual when Baba used it for Charlie. It was after their mother left. He was three years old and had started wetting the bed. Night after night, she would hear him whimpering and her father cursing under his breath while he changed the soaked sheets. After a while, he just left the sheets until morning and made Charlie climb into bed with Sarah. She can still remember the faint smell of pee and the jarring touch of Charlie's chilly toes creeping up her calves until they nestled behind her warm knees.

One day when they were at Baba's, Sarah told her about Charlie's nightly accidents. Baba sat him in a chair in the middle of her kitchen while she melted wax with a candle, recited strange words, and waved a knife in the air. After she was finished, she took the water she used and poured it under a tree, telling Sarah it must be poured where no one could step on it. When their father came to pick them up, Brian told him about it. Their father started hollering and waving his arms, telling Baba he wouldn't have any of her hoodoo-voodoo around his kids. Baba just sat there calmly, shelling her peas until he yelled himself out, then said, "Just wait. You see how it helps." And it did. Charlie never wet the bed again.

Baba's told Sarah many stories about the ancient ritual and how it cures what she calls fear-sickness. A folk tradition from the old country, it passed from mothers to daughters for generations. Baba had hoped to teach the skill to Sarah's mother (she was the more sensitive of Baba's two daughters) and she'd expected Olivia to pass the practice on to Sarah one day. Her dream faded after Olivia left, but Baba pinned her hopes on teaching Sarah the ritual herself.

Sarah has watched the healing ceremony many times, but she can't speak Ukrainian, she's told Baba, and how would she memorize the chants and prayers? She also believes she isn't religious enough; the only time Sarah attends Mass is when she stays over at Baba's. Besides, Sarah once told her she wasn't interested in learning some ritual from the Dark Ages. Baba shook her head sadly, then resigned herself to showing Sarah which wild plants and roots to harvest from the woods. How to blend them with herbs and flowers from the garden to ease pain in the joints or the misery of a colicky baby.

When Baba is finished, the woman is as limp as a puppet on strings, her eyes closed, her head lolling to one side. The baby is awake, mewling and rooting at the man's shirt. He stands up and shakes the woman gently by the shoulder, rousing her, and she opens her eyes as if from a deep sleep. Baba shuffles to the cupboard and pulls out a small jar, then she measures crushed powder and fragrant leaves from various jars into it with a spoon before securing the lid and handing it to the man.

"One teaspoon in one cup hot water. Twice a day. Take maybe two weeks, maybe less, she be better." She strokes the baby under her chin with a crooked finger. "She be happy with this one after that."

"How does it work?" Sarah asks after they leave. "I mean, what's so magic about pouring melted wax into holy water?"

Baba frowns. "Not magic." Then she shrugs her shoulders. "Is not for me to question. Is God, working. The heart, it hears. It heals."

"Well, I don't get it," Sarah says. "That woman didn't seem to be aware of anything."

"Ah, but her husband. He did," Baba says wisely.

Sarah dips her fingers into the bowl and pulls out the molten chunk of wax. It sits on her palm, a lump still warm, the colour of mulled apple cider, shaped like a droplet of rain.

JUNE

A train rumbles by, rattling Sarah's bedroom window and breaking her concentration. She's trying to study but her mind keeps wandering. There are only two weeks left of class before exams and everyone at school's been talking about summer jobs and plans for the fall. The clap of train wheels rolling over the track reminds Sarah that everyone is hurtling forward toward bright and certain futures while she's being left behind, a single boxcar sitting off alone on the siding. Becca, like all the kids from UE, is off to university. Addie and nearly everyone else are going to community college or moving to the city to find jobs. Even some of the farm boys are leaving to get their aggie diplomas before they come back to stay. Just four years, she tells herself, four years until Charlie is as old as she is now; then she'll leave, head west maybe, the only direction it seems anyone from Ross Prairie ever goes.

As the sound of the train fades away, she hears a noise in the hallway and looks up from her notes to see Becca, eyes spilling over with tears, standing in the doorway. She's holding a dented red coffee tin in both hands.

"I hate her," she cries. "I really, really hate her."

"What's happened? Tell me! What's wrong?"

"Look at this! She found it and now she knows! She said I'm never to see him again but I won't do it. I'm not going to give him up because she says so." Becca wrenches the lid from the can and tosses out a scrap of crumpled paper.

Sunday, 10:00. Can't wait to be in your arms. B

"Jack and I leave notes for each other and hide them in this can under a rock at the edge of the stone pile. She must have followed me there." Becca puts her hands on her cheeks and shakes her head furiously. "I don't know how she knew but she was out there, snooping around, and she found it. I've never seen her so mad in my life! She was pacing in circles, breathing so hard you'd think she'd raced to town and back. She reached up and yanked at her own hair. I've never seen her like that. She's crazy!"

Becca, too, is pacing, back and forth from the bed to the door. "'Oh no, you can't. I forbid you from seeing Jack Bilyk,'" she says in a falsetto, mimicking her mother, shaking her halo of curls. "Well, I don't give a rat's ass if she'll allow it or not. I'm in love with him and she's not going to stop us from being together."

Sarah finally gets up and puts a hand on Becca's shoulder. "You better calm down yourself. Come, sit, and tell me everything."

Becca came home from school, she says, to find the battered coffee can sitting in the centre of the table, the lid off, the can empty. Her mother appeared from the shadows in the dining room, eyes fiery with rage, waving the note. She knew it was for Jack and she wanted to know how long Becca had been sneaking around with him. Since the fall, Becca said, not that it was any of her business. But Caroline kept grilling her, demanding to know where they'd been meeting. When Becca sat down at the table, refusing to speak, Caroline picked up a book and pitched it at her. Then she came over and tipped her right out of the chair. Becca cried out, threatening to tell her father, but that only made Caroline crazier.

"She demanded to know if we were sleeping together. 'You've spent the night with him, haven't you? That time in November, when you said you were at Sarah's, you were with him for the whole night. How many other times, Becca? How many?' That's what put her over the edge."

"Talk about overreacting," Sarah says softly.

"It's crazy. Why go completely off the deep end about it? Why does she care so much about an old feud between our fathers? I mean, chill out already. I don't understand. She acts civil enough to Anna; I don't know what the big deal is."

Sarah doesn't understand, either. It seems completely out of character for Caroline to get so upset about it.

"So, is it all right if I spend the night? Can I stay until I figure out what I should do?"

Sarah nods. She doesn't imagine it will be long before Caroline or Mr. Webb comes to town looking for her. She wonders what Caroline will think, what she will say when she sees Sarah and realizes she's known all along about Jack and Becca; how Caroline will feel to find out Sarah's been lying, too.

On afternoon break on the last day of exams, Bobby Boychuk is sauntering up and down the hall, telling everyone within earshot where the book-burner is going to be tonight, oblivious to a frowning Mr. Lawson, who is standing in the door to room 5. Bobby might as well be wearing one of those sandwich boards, advertising the whereabouts of the party. Sarah won't be surprised if Lawson reports it and everyone gets ticketed at the party for drinking underage and having open liquor.

"You going to the book-burner?" Addie shoves the last of her binders into a huge canvas bag and zips it.

"What do you think?" Becca glares at Addie and slams shut the locker door with her hip.

She isn't going to the book-burning party. Her father came to collect her later on the day she showed up at Sarah's with the can. He knocked on the door and told Sarah that Becca had to leave, his face stone cold, and went to wait in his truck until Becca came down; he followed her car home. Becca explained later that Caroline thought it best not to tell Eldon about Becca and Jack, but that Caroline had grounded her anyway. Becca's been begging to go to the party, insisting that Jack isn't likely to be there, but Caroline's held firm and Becca can't go.

"She's still grounded, but I'm going," Sarah says, stepping between them. "And I'm still coming to your house after school like we planned," she adds, nodding at Becca.

Addie rolls her eyes. She's been losing patience with Becca for the past few weeks, complaining she's tired of hearing her moan about Jack and how much she misses him. And Becca's been telling Sarah how she thinks Addie's selfish, rambling on about summer and fun, not caring at all about poor Becca's world turned over. Sarah's been getting a stretched-apart feeling from them, each pulling her in the opposite direction, wanting her to choose sides, pick one of them over the other, and she refuses to do it.

. . .

When Sarah gets to Becca's after school, Caroline stares at her blankly then turns back to whatever she is stirring on the stove. Her hair is fastened at the nape of her neck; the ponytail makes her look like a child, vulnerable in some way, and Sarah feels a hard finger of regret for her part in Caroline's obvious heartache. The counters are cluttered, dishes piled everywhere, and the top of the dining-room table looks as though a canister has been filled there — that puff of flour that settles after it's poured out of the bag — so thick and white is the dust.

At suppertime, Caroline dishes potatoes and peas into bowls and sets down a platter of roast pork, then turns her narrow back to them as she piles pots into the sink. While the rest of them eat, she washes, the only other sounds in the kitchen the clinking of glass and the scratching of plates. Mr. Webb asks Sarah if she is off to Winnipeg in the fall, and when she says no he returns to his plate and mops up the last of his gravy.

Later, the bonfire's blazing, red-gold sparks flaring up each time someone tosses in a scribbler or a handful of notes. The flames crackle and lick at the air. Cady Hubley is dancing by the fire, tossing her hair and seductively rolling her hips as though she's conjuring spirits. Del Foley's blue Charger is parked nearby, stereo blaring so loud Sarah's heart thumps in time with the bass. Addie's not here yet and Sarah doesn't feel like mingling with everyone else. They are huddled in small groups, the cliques from school separate and apart like they usually are, drinking beer and laughing. She feels strangely detached from everyone, all these kids she's known her whole life who have promised to keep in touch in the messages they wrote in her yearbook. She imagines leaving high school will be similar to that one time she went to summer camp with

Becca, all the girls exchanging addresses on the last day, vowing to keep writing to each other until they came back next year. Sarah didn't get even one letter from those summer-camp girls but, then again, she didn't mail one away either, and she never went back.

"Wanna beer?" Bobby holds out a bottle and Sarah shakes her head. He gave her a ride out to the party and she's hoping he's not under the mistaken impression she'll want to make out with him when he drives her home.

Sarah notices someone in the shadows past the fire, leaning against the hood of a parked car, a lone figure slouched with his hands jammed into the front pockets of his jeans. She can tell by the way he holds his head that it's Jack. She makes a wide circle around Cady and Del, who's her latest boyfriend, and other couples pressed up against one another, slow dancing to the next track on the stereo. As she gets close to him, someone feeds the fire a fresh bundle of notes and the flames flare, lighting Jack's face for a few seconds with a burst of light. He's unshaven and his hair curls over his shirt collar, longer than it was the last time she saw him. There is sadness in his eyes but a purpose in the set of his jaw and he half smiles when Sarah walks up to him.

"I haven't been to one of these in a while."

"No doubt." Sarah is suddenly shy, keenly aware this is the first time she's been alone with Jack without Becca around.

"I thought maybe Becca would be here. I need to talk to her. I guess you'd know if she's coming?"

Sarah shakes her head. "She's still grounded."

Jack pulls a mickey from the inside pocket of his denim jacket and takes a swig, then holds it out for Sarah. She takes a sip; lukewarm amber liquid skims down her throat and a rush of heat spreads through her body. "Caroline will have to give in and let Becca out sooner or later," she says. "She can't keep her locked up all summer." Her eyes don't leave his face. "Becca told me how she had to break up with you over the phone while her mom stood there and listened."

"Her old man's such a prick."

Sarah hands the bottle back to Jack. "He didn't make her do it. Caroline told Becca they couldn't even tell her father about it because of the trouble between your families, so he doesn't even know. It was Caroline who made Becca end it with you."

A shadow of anger flickers over his face. "Always thought it was Eldon who had it in for us Bilyks, but I guess she's no different than he is," he says, tipping back the bottle again. "I figured things wouldn't last between Becca and me, anyway. Because of who she is, not that she's a Webb, necessarily, but because of that way she has about her, you know? Like she says jump and she expects me to say 'how high.' I guess she's been used to getting her way all her life."

Sarah understands. She's been under Becca's spell, too.

"I thought it would just naturally be over when she went away to school, we'd just drift apart without having to make a big deal out of it. I didn't think she was really into it that much anyway, you know? Like dating me was just some kind of prize she was trying to win." He takes another pull from the bottle. "But she needs to know that I think it's best for both of us to just end it now."

A fight breaks out by the fire between Del Foley and some guy Sarah doesn't know wearing a Locklin Lions jacket. Del jabs the guy in the face and he wallops him back on the side of the head. A crowd gathers around, chanting, "Fight, fight!" as they tumble to the ground.

"Looks like it's time to get out of here," Jack says. "You need a ride back to town?"

Sarah doesn't want to ditch Addie, but she isn't in the mood for hanging around. She is mostly quiet on the way home, thinking how thrilled she would have been back in the fall to be riding alone with Jack. She takes a sideways glance at him, at the face she'd like to drift her fingers across like a blind girl reading Braille, memorizing that slight bump on his nose, the firm bones in his cheeks, the moist curve of his lips.

"Would you do me a favour?" He looks at her and turns down the volume on the radio. "Could you give Becca a message for me?" When Sarah nods, he says, "Just tell her I need to see her. I need to tell her it's best this way, for this to be over. She's not going to like it, but she needs to know the truth."

"Sure. I'll tell her tomorrow," Sarah says, as a faint glimmer of hope blooms in her heart. Becca always made her believe Jack was just as madly in love with her as she was with him, and now Sarah wonders if that was ever true. Maybe Jack was more ambivalent than Becca had let on, or even realized.

She waits for Jack to say more but he's quiet, the only sound the thump of tires against asphalt. Just before they reach town, he reaches over and turns up the radio. A song Sarah likes is playing and she listens, really listens, to the lyrics for the first time. *Let's just kiss and say goodbye.* She's glad Jack wants to do it, just say goodbye to Becca and let her go. But she knows Becca doesn't want that to happen. Becca wants him and she always gets what she wants. She will do whatever it takes to keep him. Jack belongs to Becca and she'll never let him go.

When she gets home from her job at Pipers' the following week, her father is sitting at the table, an open ledger in front of him. He takes his pencil and scratches the pale pink scalp where his thinning red hair flops over.

"Did Becca call?" she asks him. All she could think about all day as she stocked shelves and rang customers through is what Becca and Jack might have talked about yesterday. She'd waited nearly a week to tell Becca that Jack wanted to see her. She didn't want to spoil Becca's graduation, but it didn't really matter; Becca hardly smiled at all in her pretty pink gown. Jack and Becca finally met at Sarah's house yesterday afternoon while Caroline thought the girls were rafting on the river with a bunch of other kids from school. They were alone in Sarah's room for nearly an hour. When they came out, Becca's eyes were swollen and red and Jack was so serious it looked as though he'd found out he was going to jail. He didn't even look at Sarah, and she got the feeling he and Becca had discussed something more than a breakup. After Jack drove off, Sarah wanted to know what was going on but Becca wouldn't tell her; she just kept crying. Sarah was desperate to know, and before Becca left she'd made her promise to tell her soon.

Her father looks up and shakes his head. "Nope. Only one phone call and it was Hydro with a second warning that they'll turn off the lights if I don't pay the bill. Money's like goddamn water around here. Flows through those boys' fingers and evaporates into thin air."

Sarah knows how hard it is; she had to buy a box of cereal with her own money last week just so there'd be something for breakfast.

"Don't worry about making supper. Brian and Charlie aren't home and I'll make myself a sandwich later. Take the night off for a change." He smiles weakly and turns back to his work.

She goes upstairs and changes into a T-shirt and shorts then rinses out her uniform in the bathroom sink and hangs it up to dry.

"Sarah, phone!" her father shouts. She flies down the stairs, hoping it's Becca, but it's Shorty, sounding hysterical. "Can you come over to my place? It's Jack. He's fucked up, man."

"Why? What's happened?"

"He went over to Becca's this morning, wanting to see her, and her old man came out waving a gun in his face."

What the hell is going on? "Geez, Shorty. Slow down!"

"He threatened him. Said if he came around again he would beat the shit out of him or worse." Shorty's panting, short of breath as though he's run up a couple flights of stairs, and Sarah can almost see his round red face, puffing into the phone. "He told Jack they've sent Becca away and he'll never see her again."

Sarah doesn't understand. Why would Jack go over there if they'd broken up? Becca's father must have found out about them, but what did it matter if it was all over? All she can think about is Jack. "How is he?"

"Like I said, he's messed up. He's been drinking all afternoon and now he wants to go back over there. He might listen to you. Can you come over and see if you can calm him down?"

Sarah grabs the keys to her father's truck and is out the door, tires squealing as she makes a sharp turn past the elementary school. There's a little girl there, hopping along on one foot. Her pigtails bounce like springs with each little jump and her lips move as she sings. Sarah hears the high, shrill voice of a child chanting in her head.

Step on a crack, Becca's never coming back.

PART

FOUR

2016

CAROLINE

Caroline opens her eyes. A dull ache in her head has grown to a stabbing pain and she can feel a pulse there, behind her right eye, with every beat of her heart. Looking around, she wonders, *Where am I?* Then she realizes she is in Sunny Haven, not twenty-one as she was in the moment she was just remembering but eighty years old, frail and old and broken, put here to spend the rest of her days. There's no going back. Her life will end in this place as surely as Nick's ended in that overturned tractor.

She can still see herself standing at the Bilyks' front door on that crisp October morning, the shock of learning about Nick like someone chopping her down at the knees. Eldon grunted his condolences then turned on his heel without saying a word about Anton's dog and took his festering anger home. Caroline doesn't recall if either she or Eldon said a word in the truck after they left. She only remembers a mind-numbing anguish circling her throat like a noose, yet she couldn't let Eldon see it. She made herself think about the orderly suitcase stashed under her bed; the tight rows of rolled underwear and stockings, her black patent church shoes wrapped in brown paper. Sport was on the porch when they got home, waving his tail. Eldon reached for the gun and got out of the truck, and before Caroline could stop him he pulled the trigger and shot him. Her grief spewed forth in a tide of rage and she sprang on Eldon, hitting him dead-on with the full breadth of her body. His legs splayed out from under him and the rifle flew up in the air. And then she was on him, pounding and slamming, her fists raining down, connecting with hard bone and soft flesh, yet he didn't fight back. When she was spent, Caroline rolled onto her back. The sky was as blue as she'd ever seen it and it had no business being that way. The tears came then and she opened her mouth and wailed, loud and long; she didn't care if the whole world could hear. Eldon stood up and went to bury the dog.

She got by the next weeks and months speaking barely a word. She quit eating and grew thin. When Eldon would catch her crying in the middle of the day, she would turn her back to him, and he let her, without comment or concern. Elvina finally told her the histrionics had gone on long enough; she needed to get over the loss of a pet and couldn't she just get another dog? No one knew she was mourning the loss of the man she loved. She emptied the suitcase and put it away. There was no escape now. She resigned herself to the situation she had created. Before Christmas she told Eldon about the baby.

SARAH

From her father's room, Sarah watches as Addie transfers Caroline out of her wheelchair into the reclining chair by the window. Her legs are frail, so thin Sarah could circle her thumb and forefinger around one of Caroline's bony ankles. It's been nearly six weeks since she first walked into Caroline's room and told her who she was. Now Sarah stops by to say hello whenever she comes and lingers a few minutes longer each time. They were timid with each other at first, Sarah carefully choosing her words, but every visit is easier than the last, each of them opening up a bit more. Neither one of them has yet to mention Becca or Jack.

On her way out, Addie pokes her head in Joe's room. "You staying for a while?" She looks at her watch. "I'm on my break in twenty minutes or so, if you want to hang around. You can have coffee with me in the lunchroom."

"Sure," Sarah says. "I'll wait."

Her father is listening to his TV, wearing a set of big plastic headphones. The staff had been having trouble with him fiddling with the TV volume, turning it all the way up and back down over and over again, annoying bursts of noise echoing in the hallway, and they threatened to take the television away. It was Toni who came up with the idea of the headphones. A look of awe spread over his face the first time Toni placed them onto his head.

Sarah considers going across the hall but Caroline appears to be nearly asleep in her chair. In her purse, Sarah has a large-print edition of short stories by Alice Munro she thinks Caroline will like. Last week, she learned Caroline was still an avid reader, despite having to use a magnifying glass, so when Sarah was browsing the stacks at the public library and she came across the Alice Munro, she thought immediately of Caroline and checked it out. She hasn't told Jack she's been visiting Caroline; he's not likely to understand what it means to her to reconnect with the woman she was once so close to.

There were plenty of rumours after Becca left. Millie Tupper had her own theory about why she had disappeared: over the years, a few girls had gotten pregnant and left town suddenly, only to return within a year as though nothing had happened, their eyes downcast when you looked at them. But Elvina wouldn't stand by and let that sort of talk be spread around town about Becca. Elvina planted her own truth to dispel the stories, telling anyone who would listen that Becca had gone all the way to British Columbia to get a business degree at the best school there was.

Sarah chose to believe Caroline, who denied the rumours and verified the story about school in B.C., although Sarah often wondered why Becca had never called to say goodbye and tell her about the change of plans herself. Their friendship must not have meant as much to Becca as she'd thought.

She didn't see Jack again after the day Shorty called. She heard he left town early in '77 and she always wondered if he'd ended up in B.C. She assumed he hadn't been honest with her about wanting to break up with Becca, so she went on with her life and tried to forget him.

After Becca left, Sarah visited Caroline often. She seemed so lost and Sarah was lonely, too, with Becca's sudden departure and Addie gone off to college. In the beginning, Sarah asked about Becca frequently, but Caroline seemed reluctant to discuss her. She once mentioned that Becca had written to Elvina, telling her about her business classes and her new friends. It made Sarah sad to think that Caroline, herself, had not received such a letter.

Caroline and Sarah spent hours together, having tea, discussing books or playing cribbage or Scrabble. During that first winter, Caroline tried to teach her to sew, thinking it a skill every young woman should know, but Sarah was no better at it than she had been in home economics. Eventually Caroline gave up, and in the spring she shared her love of flowers with Sarah instead. They spent hours together in Caroline's garden. Caroline taught her how to lift perennials and Sarah dug up a patch of grass next to her father's house and created a bed of her own. She moved salvia and irises and phlox. Her favourites were pink lilies, which Caroline told her came from her own mother's garden. The next year, clumps of them bloomed in the Coyles' shabby yard.

Jack came back in the spring of '80 and walked into Pipers' store, where Sarah still worked. She was surprised to see him at the counter, pulling out his wallet to pay for a few things. He'd grown leaner; his skin and body toughened up as though his time out west hadn't been easy. He smiled when he saw her, his face lighting up, and told her they'd have to get together for coffee.

She didn't hear from him for a few weeks, but she wasn't surprised. The weather was good; tractors and seed drills were rolling. In the middle of June, he came into the store and asked her to lunch. He kept this up, taking her out a couple of times a week for quick meals at the Chinese café or fries and a burger at the hotel coffee shop. They avoided mention of Becca at first, but one evening, about a month later, during supper at a nice restaurant in Locklin, Jack brought up the subject himself.

"You know how I told you I was in Alberta the whole time I was out west?"

Sarah's heart skipped a beat. "You weren't?"

"I need to be honest with you. I actually went all the way to the coast at first. I hung around there a couple of months before I headed back to Alberta to look for a job." Jack pulled the wine bottle from the bucket and topped up their glasses.

Sarah felt a sharp stab of jealousy poke at her heart. "So … did you see her? What did she have to say?"

Jack looked grim. "I didn't find her. I checked out the university Elvina had told everyone about but she wasn't enrolled there. I went to a couple of the colleges, but had no better luck."

Sarah pushed away her plate. Her appetite was gone. She was angry with Jack, although she had no right to be. They were just friends, sharing a meal. He'd made no attempt to show her this new relationship was anything else. "You told me that night at the book-burner it was over between you two."

"And it was. I thought if I broke up with her, maybe I'd have a shot at dating you, like I'd hoped to from the very beginning."

"Dating me?" Sarah reached for her wine glass, nearly tipping it over.

Jack pulled a hand through his hair. "The night Eddie Reston nearly smashed into my grain truck? I noticed you right away. You looked so scared and I could tell you didn't want to be there. I was going to ask if you wanted me to drive you back to town."

"It was me you noticed?"

"Damn right." Jack smiled. "That pretty face hiding behind those black curls." He reached across the table and touched her hair.

"But Becca ..." Sarah started to say.

"Yeah, Becca," Jack sighed. "She stepped right up and made it all about her." He paused and took a sip of wine. "Just like she did that October, when was she walking down the road and flagged me down. I rolled down my window and she leaned in, all smiles, and asked me for a ride." He looked at Sarah, as though asking for forgiveness, before he went on. "She was flirting, it was so obvious. Flipping her hair, reaching down to pick up something she supposedly dropped so I could see down her shirt. She jumped in and I drove a couple miles then said I had to get back, there was work to do."

The waitress came by, asked if there was anything else she could get them. Jack shook his head and waited until she was gone before he continued. "Just before I dropped her off, I asked about you. If you were one of the other girls in the car. I thought I remembered you from when you were younger. 'Sarah Coyle?' she said, and then she got this look on her face; a darkness came over it. She stopped for a while to think, and, just like that" — Jack snapped his fingers — "she was all sweetness and smiles again and told me you were dating Bobby Boychuk."

"Why would she say that?" Sarah could hardly believe it. Becca must have been shocked to realize Jack was interested in her — plain little Jane who'd never had a boyfriend, who'd never had much of anything. She'd decided to take Jack for herself because she didn't want Sarah to have him. "Especially after I'd told her I liked you, too."

"You did? You weren't dating Boychuk?"

Sarah shook her head. "When was that exactly?"

Jack frowned. "Right after Thanksgiving. I remember because we still had a few acres to finish up after the holiday that year."

"She knew I liked you and you liked me and she went after you anyway. And she lied to me; she said you two were already together by then."

"Shit." He let out a long sigh. "Becca moved right across the seat and wrapped her arms around me. She said, 'How about me? Do you like me?' And she kissed me and ... well ... one thing led to another until ..." He drained his glass. "It shouldn't surprise me she'd backstab a friend to get what she wanted. I wish, at the time, I would've known how you felt. It would have changed everything." Jack tipped back his head and closed his eyes. "Damn her anyway."

Sarah reached across the table and took his hand. "What do you mean?"

Jack was quiet for a few moments and Sarah sensed he was struggling to keep his composure. He opened his eyes and looked at her, taking a deep breath. "I went out west because ... there *was* a baby," he said, his voice barely a whisper. "Those stories Elvina Webb tried so hard to cover up? They were true. That day at your house, Becca told me she was pregnant. We were going to take a few days and figure out what to do."

Sarah was stunned. That explained the way Becca and Jack had looked when they came down from her room. It seemed a logical explanation for Becca's sudden departure. But all these years Sarah had believed Caroline when she told her the rumours weren't true.

"I went over to talk to her parents the next morning, and her old man pointed that shotgun at me. She had obviously told them. I told him we could get married, if that's what they wanted, but he was just as likely to kill me as let me talk to her or tell me where she was."

"Oh, Jack. No wonder you were so upset that day at Shorty's."

Jack nodded. "I didn't want anyone to know Becca was pregnant. What was the point if the Webbs had already decided she was giving it up?" He paused. "She told me no one else knew and I was ashamed you'd find out I knocked her up. But it was eating me up inside, the thought they were making her give our kid away, and I went back to the Webbs' before Christmas. I needed to know where she was. Eldon said I'd never have Rebecca or the baby, either."

The restaurant was nearly deserted by then except for another couple on the other side of the room. Sarah was thankful Jack's back was turned so they couldn't see he was crying.

"I went out west about the time I figured she'd be having it, not for Becca, but for our baby. I thought maybe, if it wasn't too late, I could bring him home and raise him myself. I checked out the homes for unwed mothers and all of the hospitals. I bought a bouquet of carnations and wandered the halls on the maternity wards, asking about her, looking at the babies in their bassinets. But I never found either one of them. I guess she did what they wanted and gave him away." His voice cracked. Sarah stood up and went around and sat next to him. She pulled him close and let him cry into her shoulder, stroking his cheek and whispering his name. She promised herself she would give him her love, all of it, and babies, too, as many as she could, if that's what he wanted. They would be her gifts to him and she would cherish them, showering them with every bit of love ever denied to her by her own mother, and then some.

Jack kissed her for the first time that night when they were parked in his truck in her father's driveway. She kissed him back, deeply, with a hunger she'd suppressed for four years. The unveiling of the truth about the baby unleashed a passion in both of them and they didn't wait for their wedding. They married in September, a short ceremony at St. Michael's country church with a handful of people. Instead of heading out west or to college like she'd once planned, Sarah quit her job and they started their life with nothing but the future rolled out before them. Jack was the best and truest friend she'd ever had in the world.

The business section of Main Street consists of two blocks and between them they share two empty lots and four boarded up buildings. Ross Prairie is down to one grocery store — Pipers' has long since closed its doors — and the paint on most of the buildings is peeling. Gone are the days when, on Saturday nights, the street in front of the hotel was lined with cars and half-ton trucks, kids hanging out, waiting to convince someone of age to pull them some beer.

Sarah pulls up to the municipal office where the Regional Health Board is meeting tonight. Her hands tremble a bit as she fumbles with the Duo-Tang folder that holds her three-page presentation. The USB stick is tucked safely in her purse; Sam says the board has a laptop they can use and, luckily, he knows how to load it and queue up their PowerPoint so all Sarah has to do is read from her notes. They decided to invite Jon and Jolene Lentz to join them and tell the board their own personal story, how quickly the ambulance arrived early last year when their ten-year-old son, Carter, was mangled by a grain auger and response time was critical.

The Lentzes are waiting with Sam in a small office beside the boardroom when Sarah arrives. Jolene has regained the weight she lost in those long months while Carter recovered at Children's Hospital and she looks up, the skin wobbling on her double chin. "They've told us we're up in five to ten minutes." She glances at Sarah's folder and frowns. "I didn't write anything down. Do you think I should have?"

"Just speak from your heart, the way you did at the public meeting," Sarah reassures her. "Your words are more powerful than anything Sam or I can say in our presentation."

"I wondered if maybe we should have brought Carter along," Jon says. "So the board could see for themselves how well he's doing, after his leg was so torn up." The accident was horrendous — a bent guard on the auger and Carter stepping over it when his small foot slipped through. Jon was right there, shut everything off within seconds, but Carter had extensive injuries.

"I didn't want to have him listen to all the details of that day, how it seemed like forever before the ambulance arrived when it was really only twelve minutes." The painful memory dulls Jolene's eyes and she looks down at her hands. "I'll never forget the sound of the siren wailing as it came, the seconds ticking off while the towels soaked through in my hands."

Sarah remembers it well; Addie called from work to tell her about it. She was reminded of all the times the girls played out in the yard and all the warnings she rattled off over the years. Jack was paranoid about safety. He had told the girls the story of his uncle Nick so often they could recite it by heart: a handsome young man killed at twenty-four when a tractor he was operating on a hillside flipped over and pinned him. Jack put up a fence around the house before Allison took her first steps and he made Sarah keep the girls penned up like chickens until they were old enough for school. He wouldn't allow the girls to step foot into the farmyard unless he or Sarah was with them.

The sun slants in through the venetian blinds and Sarah twists the wand so Sam can quit squinting. The office isn't much bigger than a bedroom, tight with the desk and two filing cabinets, and it's so stuffy and warm, a bead of sweat trails down the side of Jon Lentz's face. Suddenly the door flies open and Cady Rankmore bursts through, carrying a briefcase. "Am I late?" She's dressed as though she's here for a job interview, in a tight black skirt with a suit jacket and her ludicrous shoes. Jon pops up to offer her his chair while Sam catches Sarah's eye with a pained look on his face. "We didn't expect you, Cady," he says.

"These meetings are open to the public; I could be in there right now if I wanted to." She looks at Sarah down the length of her nose. "I've come to hear how well you do in convincing the board with your presentation."

"I suppose you're welcome to come in and listen." Sam is sweating, too; a sheen from the diffused light shines off the top of his head.

"I'd also like to mention the considerable contributions the Hubleys have made to Ross Prairie." Cady reaches under her blouse at the shoulder and tugs at her bra strap, visibly hefting one pendulous breast. "My family funded many of the incentives to recruit new doctors and there's not a one of them who knows that, least of all Carol Bodnarchuk, who supposedly represents our interests on this board. I'd like to know how someone like her got on the board in the first place."

"I'm sorry, Cady, but it's not possible. They've only given us twenty minutes," Sam is saying when the door opens and the board chair, a silver-haired woman with eyeglasses dangling around her neck on a thick gold chain, invites them into the boardroom. Cady positions herself at the table next to the Lentzes instead of sitting in the row of visitors' chairs at the side of the room and makes a show of opening her briefcase and removing a yellow legal pad as though she's been asked to take notes. Someone offers Sarah a glass of water — she is so nervous her tongue clicks in her mouth — and she takes a sip. Cady's come for no other reason than to judge her so she can have something to talk about later with Arlene. Sarah is also suddenly aware of the other eyes looking her over, strangers mostly since the board is now regional, although there is Carol Bodnarchuk, at the end of the table, who catches her eye and gives a slight nod.

After introductions, Sam taps a few keystrokes and their first visual lights up the white screen. Sarah begins. She's comfortable and confident with what she's written, yet during the presentation her mind floats off and she can't help but wonder what the others are thinking, if they're being swayed by her words. She's aware of every intent face — the wide-eyed young man with thick glasses, a scowling dark-haired woman, Carol, bobbing her head, as well as the others.

She concludes her presentation and invites the Lentzes to speak. When they're done, the frowning woman is wiping a tear. The board chair, a woman named Marianne, stands up to shake hands with them and is about to turn to Sarah and Sam when Cady jumps up and pumps Marianne's hand. She beams when Marianne thanks her for coming.

"Wow," Sam says under his breath. "Can you believe that?"

Yes. Yes, she can. Cady hasn't much changed from fifty years ago, diverting all the attention back on herself in just the same way she rescheduled a birthday party so no one would attend Sarah's party when they were little girls.

"Marianne just told me Carol's stepping down. Have you heard?" Cady says to Sarah before turning back to Marianne. "I'd like to be considered for it. I'm very civic-minded; I take after my father that way."

"There's a process, forms and such to fill out, then interviews and a board recommendation of our preferred candidate we send on to —" Marianne starts to say before Cady interrupts.

"I'm a teacher, recently retired, and I have all the time in the world, and superior qualifications, too." She lifts up her chin. "Not that Carol didn't do a good job, that's not what I'm saying, but I live right in town, not out in the country somewhere, and I have my finger on the pulse of the community. I know what they're talking about."

Sarah pauses as she gathers up her things. Cady's right, no doubt. She collects and dispenses gossip as well as old Millie Tupper did back when they were girls. She turns to Cady. "It isn't a matter of knowing what people are talking about. You have to understand the issues and you don't need to live in town to do that." Sarah pulls a pen from her purse, jots her email address on a small slip of paper. "You have to actually care about the people you represent."

"I know everything about this town. I don't know what you're trying to say, Sarah," Cady says, staring her down.

"If you don't know what I'm trying to say, you're even more obtuse than I always thought you were." Sarah hands the note to Marianne. "If you wouldn't mind, Marianne, could you send me the forms? I'd like to put my name forward for the position." At the door, she turns and smiles at Cady. "We'll leave it to the board to decide," she says. "This isn't high school and it's not a popularity contest. May the best candidate win." She turns on her heel and walks out the door.

CAROLINE

Caroline shifts uncomfortably in her bed and flaps her blanket so it snaps like a sheet in the wind then looks at the clock radio on the nightstand. Eight thirty-two. They've turned out the lights, but her room glows in a pale wash of lingering daylight, bright enough to read if she could only swing her legs over the edge of the bed, stand up, and reach for the book on the side table by her chair. She has no patience for the strict rules in this place. How do they expect her to sleep when it won't be dark for hours?

Eldon was an early riser, up at dawn each day, even when the time changed at daylight savings. He always complained when they had to adjust the clocks, saying the concept was unnecessary, designed for the leisurely pursuits of city people, not farmers who worked in tandem with the rising and setting of the sun and not the hands of a clock. He insisted on a full breakfast so

Caroline was drawn from her warm bed, too, frying eggs and ham or bacon as the sun poked over the horizon. At first, after he died, she'd still felt the need to spring out of bed once her rocking chair in the corner began to take shape in dawn's tender light. But she soon realized she could linger if she chose, settle her head back on the pillow like she used to when she was a teenager and her mother indulged her on Saturday mornings. Her father used to huff about it; she could hear him in the kitchen telling her mother Caroline should be up, helping with chores, but her mother would shush him and say, "Let her sleep."

Even now, Caroline feels a timorous squeeze on her heart whenever she thinks of her mother. Dead more than sixty years and yet she can still see her standing in the kitchen, whisking a thick batter while the sun opened its sleepy eye. She has surpassed her mother's age by nearly thirty years, in robust health the whole time until she slipped on the stairs. When she turned fifty-two, she marvelled at how young she still felt and she wondered why she had ever considered her mother an old woman at that age. Had her mother, despite her tired eyes and work-worn body, still felt like she did, young and so full of life inside?

Charity, the night-duty nurse, trundles by, those horrid plastic clogs she wears clapping against the floor. She backs up and looks into Caroline's room. "Not sleeping yet?"

Who can bloody well sleep when you've put us to bed earlier than a bunch of eight-year-olds? Caroline wants to say it but she knows she must be polite, especially to this inaptly named beast of a woman. She once saw Charity pinch Simon Tuttle in the dining room when he'd purposely knocked his dinner plate on the floor.

"Would you like me to give you something to help you sleep?" Charity looms over her and Caroline can smell the nurse's oniony breath.

Caroline shakes her head and is tempted to hold her two hands crossed over her mouth the way Becca used to when she tried to give her a teaspoon of Buckley's. She won't be fooled into swallowing one of those little pills Charity feeds to residents like Simon or Joe so she can sit at the desk doing crosswords all night.

"Could I have my book? Perhaps if I read for a while I'll get sleepy."

"Lights out means lights out and rules are rules." Charity fills a glass with water, leaves it on Caroline's nightstand, and waddles out of the room.

Caroline closes her eyes. If Addie were on duty, she'd give Caroline the book. She doesn't always bother with the rules. Caroline has seen her passing Martha Gudz an extra dish of ice cream and racing out the door with John McTavish in his wheelchair when those four big red combines of Three Oaks Farms roar by, just so he can see them and be reminded of his own days on the farm. She's always soft-spoken with residents like Simon and Joe. What good does it do to get angry with someone like that? *Thank God for small graces.* She might not be able to stand up and reach for her book, but at least she can read and she knows her own name. That's one thing she thinks about so often now: the different ways to live and the different ways to die. She wants to go quickly when the time comes.

Two weeks was all it took when Eldon died. It was the spring of his seventy-eighth year. He'd had congestive heart failure for years, growing weaker and weaker as time went on, struggling to breathe, until he collapsed while eating breakfast one day. Caroline called the ambulance and followed in her car to the hospital. Day by day he failed, until all he did was sleep. Caroline sat at his bedside, watching the rise and fall of his sunken chest, holding her breath when he did, long seconds where she thought it was over, that she might be free to go home, until he gasped and started up again. On a few occasions he called out Becca's name. Caroline leaned in close, whispering into his ear. "Do you know, Eldon? Do you know where she is?"

Eldon and Elvina had always known of Becca's whereabouts and they kept it from Caroline like a pair of conspirators, even when she cried and begged them to tell her. It was Elvina who insisted they send Becca away; she was the one who came up with the plan and came over to pack Becca's things. She told Caroline that Becca wanted nothing to do with her. And besides, the shame of Becca's illegitimate child would tarnish their good name, Elvina said, so it was decided that the baby would be put up for adoption; Caroline's first grandchild given away like an unwanted puppy and raised by complete strangers on the farthest edge of the country.

There was an aunt in Victoria, a sister of Elvina's by the name of Irene, whom Caroline had never met. She guessed that's where Becca was sent. Irene had escaped her hard-scrabble life on the farm by boarding a train in the twenties and riding it over the Rockies until she came to the ocean, settling there, never to return to the prairies. As far as Caroline knew, Irene had never married. With the help of a persistent telephone operator, she called every Farr in the book until a woman, who she could have sworn was Elvina — so similar was the haughty voice of Aunt Irene — answered the phone. No, Rebecca was not there, Irene told her each time she called. Caroline assumed Irene was lying to her, purposely keeping her from speaking to Becca on orders from Elvina, perhaps. She called for weeks, always getting the same denial, and finally Caroline screamed at the woman, demanding to speak to her daughter, but Irene refused. The next day, the number was disconnected, the new number unlisted, and she never spoke to Irene over the telephone again. But she always remembered Irene's words before she last hung up the phone.

"Rebecca doesn't want to speak to you. You've destroyed her life and she wants nothing to do with you. You're dead to her. Now leave us alone."

SARAH

On a Saturday morning in late August, Sarah swings by Sunny Haven to drop off the book she's been carrying around. A few residents are already in the dining room, bibs on, waiting at the tables for breakfast while the aroma of coffee and toast hangs in the air.

"Hey, Mrs. B.," Cara says as Sarah walks in. "You're early this morning. I don't think we even have your dad dressed yet." She's standing behind the front desk, plucking half-dead red roses out of a vase.

"That's all right. It's actually Caroline I'm here to see."

Cara tosses the dripping flowers into a wastebasket and comes out from behind the desk. "Oh, about Caroline," she says quietly. "She's had a rough week; she's been so restless, awake and calling out during the night. I think she's started having nightmares, although she won't say she is or she isn't.

You know her, all prim and proper, she thinks she's being a bother if she complains about any little thing."

"Has she had any changes to medication? That happened once to my father."

Cara returns to the desk and flips the page on a chart. "Doesn't look like it."

As they make their way down the hall to Caroline's room, Cara tells Sarah how disoriented Caroline seemed this morning. "She was barely awake, and possibly still dreaming, but she grabbed onto my hand and kept asking, 'Where is she? Where has she gone?' I'm worried about her. I know I shouldn't be telling you this, but who else can I tell? You're the only one who ever stops in to visit her, except for her lawyer those few times. There's no one listed on her family contact info, either, although I gather she has a daughter somewhere."

They walk on in silence, past a frail woman bent nearly in two, clutching the wall rail, making her way down the hall on her own. Tufts of white hair poke out from her pearly pink scalp and Sarah is reminded of a doll Toni once gave a haircut to.

"Do you think that's who Mrs. Webb was calling for? The daughter?" Cara stops beside Caroline's room. She is awake, sitting in her wheelchair, an afghan tucked over her lap. Across the hall, Sarah's father is still in bed, the comforter pulled up under his chin. They medicate him for the night, Sarah knows, and she questions the necessity of the sleeping pills. "He's still sleeping like a log," Cara says, motioning to Sarah's father. "I guess I'll dress Simon first then I'll come back and wake up your dad."

When Sarah walks into Caroline's room, the corners of Caroline's mouth barely tilt up. She looks unwell; her skin has taken on an unhealthy pallor with grey-blue shadows beneath her eyes.

Sarah sits down on the bed and pulls the book from her purse. "I picked this out for you. Something you can read a story at a time, if you like."

"Perhaps a new book will perk me up. I've just finished the romance novel someone left behind in the lounge. What a waste of eyesight it was! All those heaving bosoms." Caroline looks pleased as she flips through the pages. "I love story collections. You can flip through, find one you like and read them in any order you please. And look at the size of these words! I won't even need to use my reading glass." She pauses, running her finger down the list of titles. "Have you read these? This one sounds interesting. *My Mother's Dream.*"

"I've read so many of her short stories but I can't say I remember that one."

"With all the thoughts I've had swimming around in my mind, waking me up at all hours and keeping me awake, I could write such a story myself. I wonder if dreaming night after night about your dead mother is some sort of omen that you're about to die." Caroline pauses and looks at Sarah sharply. "You've never heard that, have you?" She lays the book on her lap. "If there's one thing in abundance in this place it's too much time to think. There was a time I believed I'd be happy to have no dishes to wash or meals to prepare, no socks to darn or floors to sweep, but it's terrible, sitting here all day with nothing to do."

"But at least you're able to read and crochet, to understand what it is you're listening to on TV. And you know you're here, today, not living back in 1952." Sarah glances across the hallway at her sleeping father.

"Oh, of course," Caroline says gently. She sighs. "Yes, I should be thankful for the blessings I have. It's just that I've been thinking about my mother so often these days and then dreaming about her at night. I could swear I saw her in my room last night, sitting right where you are. It's as if she has a message for me, like there's something she wants me to do."

Sarah senses that something *is* wrong; she can almost feel Caroline's agitation. "What could she possibly want you to do?"

Caroline plucks at a loose stitch on the afghan and loops it around her finger. "The same thing I've wanted all these years, I suppose. The only thing I have left to do on this earth. I need to find her."

It's Becca she's talking about, not her mother. "You have no idea where she is, do you?"

Caroline gives Sarah a long look. "I haven't known for forty years. It was Elvina and Eldon who sent her away. I believe she was in Victoria with Eldon's aunt in the beginning. Elvina told me she had letters from Rebecca, but she'd never let me see them. She'd tell me a tidbit about her every now and then — where she was working or going to school. Finally, I decided I needed to see her for myself, so I went to B.C. to find her." Caroline pauses and shrugs her thin shoulders. "But I never did. And then Elvina died and Eldon didn't seem to care much one way or another where Becca might be, and I couldn't blame him. Why should he?" She pauses again. "I know she didn't contact you in the first few years after she left but, later, did Becca ever try to get in touch with you?"

Sarah shakes her head. "I always hoped she might try to see me if she was home. I kept waiting for her to phone or send me a letter. But eventually I figured she must have heard about me and Jack, and after that I didn't expect her to call. I knew things were over between Becca and me. Just like it was for us once Jack and I got together."

They both sit in silence for a few moments and Sarah assumes Caroline, too, is remembering the afternoon she told

Caroline she was dating Jack. They'd looked at each other sadly and Caroline reached across the table where she'd just laid out the tea things. She took Sarah's hand. "I suppose this means the end of our visits, then."

"I wish it didn't have to be this way, but my loyalty has to lie with Jack." It wouldn't be easy to give up her visits with Caroline, who had been there when she needed guidance and advice.

"I understand. There are some mistakes that simply can't be forgiven." Caroline's voice cracked.

Caroline finally breaks the long pause, bringing them both back to this moment. "Becca never came home. Not even once. I thought she might come when Elvina died, but Eldon phoned Irene to let her know, and he told me neither one of them was going to travel all the way from B.C. for a funeral. Irene had never been back to see Elvina while she was alive, why should she come now? And it was because of me, Eldon said, that Becca chose to stay away."

Sarah moves off the bed, kneels at Caroline's feet and takes hold of her hand, the skin so fragile it's almost translucent; if she squeezes too hard Sarah thinks it will crack like a thin layer of spring ice. "I don't understand. She was angry with you because you didn't approve of her and Jack. But it wasn't your decision to send her away. Why couldn't she eventually forgive you?"

"Oh, she'd seen the ways Eldon could punish me," Caroline says. "She was doing the same thing. Making me pay."

But Sarah needs to understand. When Becca married and had children of her own, surely she would have forgiven her mother and wanted to see her again. "It doesn't make sense that she would stay so angry with you. Especially as you and Eldon grew older, why wouldn't she want to come home?"

"I … I can't say," Caroline falters, bowing her head, and a few moments pass by. Sarah senses there's something Caroline's not telling her and when Caroline looks up, she is crying, tears sliding down her cheeks.

Across the hall, Sarah sees Cara with her father, shoving one of his arms into the sleeve of a checkered shirt. She reaches for a tissue and presses it into Caroline's hand. "I'll just leave you now," she says gently. "I see my father's awake. Is there anything I can do for you before I go?"

Caroline reaches up with one bony hand and clutches Sarah's jeans at the knee.

"Yes. Yes, there is something you can do. It's your help I need. I want you to help me find my daughter."

When the telephone rings at four in the morning, Sarah is immediately awake. Jason called before midnight, Allison was in labour, and about time, too; she was six days overdue. Jack grunts and rolls over, oblivious, so Sarah clambers over him and races to pick up the phone. It is Jason with wonderful news. They have another grandchild, a wee girl this time, healthy and strong, eight pounds, fourteen ounces, and twenty-one inches long. No name yet, but both baby and mother are fine.

Sarah looks in on Connor, asleep in Allison's old room. One of the socks he insists on wearing to bed has worked its way off and Boo, Toni's old bear, limp from too many spins in the washer, is wedged under his arm. Sarah kisses the bare little foot and pulls the quilt up from the foot of the bed.

A patch of moonlight is spilled on her side of the bed and she crawls back into it beside Jack. The window is open and there is a breeze; the blinds click against the casing like slow drips of rain. She tosses and turns, unable to sleep, thoughts of her own lost babies coming to mind. There were two in four years before Allison was born. She lost them both at the end of their first trimesters; the devastation she felt each time was immeasurable. Another miscarriage followed between Allison and Maeve and she started to believe her unwelcoming womb could only carry girls, that each swept-away baby must have been a boy. When she mentioned it to the doctor, she was told it was an old wives' tale, that there was no scientific evidence to support such a theory. But Sarah had heard similar stories from other heartbroken women and she believed it was true.

Sarah is dreaming, warm plump fingers holding her hand, and she thinks it might be Jack's boy, lost long ago. She's searching her mind, names flitting through, but she can't seem to find one that fits. When she opens her eyes, Connor is standing beside her, clasping her fingers with Boo tucked under his arm.

Later, as she's pouring milk into Connor's cereal, Jack comes in from outside, moving across the kitchen with wide, quick steps like he does when something's gone wrong outside.

"Everything okay?" Sarah puts the carton back in the fridge while Jack rummages in the junk drawer next to the stove.

"Need a short bungee cord to close up the gate."

Sarah frowns. "There's nothing wrong with the gate."

"The clasp is loose and it opens if you hit it just right." He motions to Connor and lowers his voice. "I saw him get through it yesterday with Misty. It's not safe for either of them to be out of the yard." He explains that Shorty had just been over to tell him he'd found their new pup, just six months old, dead near the barn. Torn open from flank to tail.

"Bad enough it's killing calves out in the pastures, now it's cocky enough to come right into a yard. The pup didn't even bark; Shorty and Lois never heard a thing."

Connor's picking soggy pink and yellow O's from his spoon and lining them up on the table. They still have the fence around the house and Sarah has always been comfortable leaving Connor to play in his sandbox under the maples, although she had no idea he knew how to open the gate.

Jack pulls a speckled green cord from the back of the drawer. "Keep your eye on him. Don't let him outside on his own."

They decide to go to the hospital to see Allison and the new baby in an hour, after Jack changes the broken sickles on Anton's swather. Sarah settles Connor with a colouring book and crayons, and brings her laptop to the kitchen table. She hesitates before typing Becca's name into the box in the middle of the white screen and hitting *images*. Immediately it flashes rows of faces, dozens of women named Rebecca Webb, although at first glance most are too young to be the Becca she's looking for. After scrolling through a few sites, she realizes she needs an account to search some of them so she opens Facebook instead and searches for Becca's name, studying all the faces of the Rebeccas she finds there. She returns to the search engine and clicks on some of the links, reading obituaries and various articles from as far away as Australia. It occurs to her Becca might have a different surname, if she ever married — few young women kept their maiden names back in those days — so she gives up and turns her attention to a search for the baby. There's a massive amount of information on adoption, pages and pages. She discovers limitations on who can request such personal information and she is overwhelmed at the complexity of the problem. This promise she's made to Caroline is going to be next to impossible to keep.

. . .

The elevator doors slide open on the third floor and a nurse asks Connor, who is holding a helium-filled foil balloon, if he's here to visit a new brother or sister.

Connor just stands and stares, tongue-tied, although he chattered all the way to town from the back seat, listing all the toys he was going to share with his new baby sister. They pass through the double doors into the ward and pause first to look through the nursery windows, but there are no babies there. When they arrive at Allison's room, they find Jason dozing in a chair and Allison holding her diaper-clad baby against her bare chest. Skin to skin, they call it, a new concept they've come up with since Sarah's girls were born. In those days, she was shown how to swaddle them properly, rolling them up snug and tight, and keeping them that way.

Allison has the blissful, lazy look of a mother drunk on love for her child but her eyes light up when she sees Connor. She shifts a little, patting the bed, and Jack lifts Connor up for a look. The baby has jet-black hair and, although Jack says it's too early to tell, Sarah thinks she looks like Allison. She has the same pretty ears, delicately shaped and flat to her head.

"What have you decided to call her?" Sarah asks.

"Emma Dawn," Allison says, stroking the baby's soft cheek. "Isn't that just perfect for her? And isn't she the most precious little girl you've ever seen?"

As precious as you and your sisters, Sarah thinks. She remembers gazing down at her own newborn daughters, thinking each of them the most beautiful baby in the world.

"Do you want to hold her?" Allison pulls the sleeping Emma away from her chest and Sarah nestles her in the crook of her own arm. Emma's tiny eyelids quiver, her mouth round and puckered as a bellybutton. Jack looks over Sarah's shoulder, his arm circling her waist.

. . .

In the truck on the way home, Jack is in such high spirits Sarah decides to tell him about her recent visits with Caroline. He doesn't take his eyes off the road but Sarah notices his jaw tighten when she says Caroline's name.

"I thought I told you I didn't want to know anything about her. I could care less what she might have told you." He looks at her sharply and the truck swerves in a ridge of loose gravel. "And I don't know why you'd care either."

"Oh, Jack. She's just so lonely. She hasn't been lucky enough to have the sort of life that we've had. Can't you remember all the crazy noise, the girls in the morning, the three of them in the bathroom at once? Or the way they used to feed off one another once they started giggling about some silly little thing. She's never had any of that, though she must have been happy enough in the years Becca was growing up."

"Caroline made her own life, locking herself up in that old house, cutting herself off." There's a stubborn tilt to his head. "Look what she did when Eldon died. Put him in the ground without anyone, not even the Cornforths, knowing about it."

It was true. The people of Ross Prairie were used to flocking to the homes of grieving townsfolk in their time of need, bearing casseroles and cakes, and the secretive way Caroline acted when Eldon died rubbed at the core of them. Calvin Potts, the gravedigger, said there'd been a graveside service under the light of a harvest moon, with only the minister, a funeral director, and Caroline herself in attendance. She hadn't shed a single tear, Calvin said, but he heard her say "fill it in" before she drew her black scarf from her head and walked away.

"She told me Becca's never come home. Not even once. They seem to have lost track of her after Elvina died. Can you imagine how hard it would be if one of our girls decided they were so angry with us they walked out of our lives and we never saw them again? It would be almost as bad as watching them die. At least that way you'd have a grave to visit and wouldn't be forever imagining them somewhere, living a life without you in it."

"I have a pretty good idea of that, don't I, Sarah? Or have you forgotten?" He's hanging on to the steering wheel with both hands. "I lost a child. Never got to even know him. The Webbs just gave him away." He takes his hand off the wheel and rubs at the moisture under his nose with his thumb. "Don't ask me to forget about that."

Jack always refers to the given-away baby as *him*. Sarah supposes that in his mind he's created an image of the son he might have had in much the same way she's imagined her own lost babies. They don't often mention the baby; long ago they promised each other they'd put that painful episode in their lives behind them.

At home, when he stops, Jack keeps his hand on the key in the ignition and stares straight ahead. They sit like that for a minute before Sarah says, "I'm sorry. I shouldn't expect you to forgive her."

"It would be easier if I just knew what happened to him. If he grew up okay. Had a good life."

Sarah wonders, too. She's heard of such reunions. Adoption records are easier to access than ever before, with websites where information can be shared so adoptive children and parents can reconnect. DNA databases to provide valuable clues. She needs to try harder to find Becca. If she does there might be a chance she can find Jack's child.

CAROLINE

There is an atmosphere of chaos in the common room. Simon Tuttle has done something to his electric wheelchair and it's spinning in circles while Cara chases after him, trying to grab the control. In the corner, the card table they keep with a scenic jigsaw puzzle is turned upside down and Martha Gudz is scolding Addie and pointing at Sarah's father.

Through the commotion, Caroline spots Sarah in the foyer.

"This place is a circus," she says crossly when Sarah comes over. "Would you unlock this chair so I can go back to my room? I've had enough of this."

When they're in Caroline's room, the first thing she asks is, "Did you have any luck finding Rebecca?"

Sarah tells Caroline about her futile search. "None of them were Becca," she concludes. "It isn't easy finding information with all the privacy laws they have these days. Have you asked your lawyer about it?"

"He told me I could hire someone, but he says it may not be easy, especially if Becca doesn't want to be found. After all, she knows where I am and could contact me if she wanted to. He said he knows of many similar cases where estranged children materialize after the parents are dead with their hands out for what's been left to them in the will. She may show up yet."

Caroline wheels to her bedside table and pours a glass of water. "When we drew up our wills, Eldon insisted there wasn't to be a cent left for her," she continues. "He wanted it all to go to the United Church and the Community Foundation, divided equally between them. I suppose he thought that would be his legacy, leaving a huge endowment to the community and perhaps having his name engraved on a plaque somewhere. But after he died, I thought about all that money collecting dust in the bank. Why shouldn't I be allowed to have some fun with it?" She gives a self-satisfied smile. "I was still young, only in my sixties, so I joined up with tour and travel groups, and started to see the world. I went to all the places I'd once dreamed about. I watched the changing of the guard at Buckingham Palace, strolled along the Champs Élysées, climbed the steps at the Colosseum. I even went on an African safari."

"I had no idea," Sarah says. "How wonderful for you!"

"There was a pile of money, much of it left to Eldon by his mother, and I spent it, which gave me some satisfaction. There's still some land I own and a fair-sized nest egg sitting in a bank account. I've been thinking about that lately. So I've changed my will, going against his wishes — after all, it's my money now — and writing the whole works over to Rebecca, or any of her children, if they can be found." She pulls a tissue from the sleeve of her cardigan and balls it in her hand. "A lot of good that will do me if she shows up after I'm dead, though, won't it?"

"All I've run into are dead ends," Sarah says helplessly. "Is there anything else you can tell me? Any hints at all about where Becca might have gone?"

"She was staying with Irene, Eldon's aunt, in Victoria. Have I told you about that? A woman as miserable as her sister, and that's the truth. I had this nagging feeling that maybe Becca hadn't given up the baby at all and I was driven by a burning desire to see my daughter and grandchild. Once I'd skimmed enough money from my grocery allowance to buy myself a bus ticket, I went looking for them." She notices Sarah's reaction and says, "Oh, don't look so shocked. I never had more than two nickels to rub together when Eldon was alive. I didn't even have a chequing account of my own until after he died. He doled out every penny I ever spent, watched it like a hawk." She doesn't tell Sarah about the way she was punished when she returned from B.C., Eldon taking away her car keys and going to town by himself for six months while he made her stay home. "It wasn't an easy life." She rolls her chair to the window and looks out. The backyard is empty, as it usually is, although she once noticed two children hopping over the low rails of the gazebo, playing some sort of game. If only this place would plant a few flower beds in that vast brown lawn to give her something to look at.

Sarah clears her throat and Caroline realizes she's waiting for her to continue.

"I arrived in Victoria with an envelope I'd found at Elvina's, with Irene's return address in the corner, tucked inside my purse. Irene's was quite a stately place, I remember thinking when the taxi pulled up — brick, with a wrought iron gate, much too large for a spinster living on her own. I sat for a moment, collecting my thoughts and my courage, clinging to a faint hope Becca might answer the door, surprised at first when she saw me then crying and laughing all at the same time and inviting me in.

"Irene was cruel, full of hate and spite even though she'd never met me," Caroline continues, her voice wavering. "I can only imagine the stories Elvina must have told her about me. She said Becca was long gone, moved out on her own, but I didn't believe her. I wedged my foot in the door when she tried to close it and I shoved my way in. There was a staircase near the front door and I took it up, two stairs at a time, calling for Becca. The bedrooms were as dark as the ones I'd first moved in to at Elvina's house, with heavy drapes, no light shining in at all. Irene was on my heels, threatening to call the police as I tore open every door. None of Becca's clothes hung in the closets; there were certainly no signs of toys or a small child. 'Where is she?' I screamed again and again but Irene kept telling me to get out. I grabbed her by her scrawny arm and, I swear to God, I could have heaved her right down those stairs."

Caroline is breathing hard, replaying the scene in her mind, her chest pumping up and down as though she is still in Victoria, dashing from room to room, frantically searching for her child.

"I told her I would go to the police myself if she didn't tell me where Becca was, but she laughed in my face. She knew as well as I did the police wouldn't do a thing. By then Becca was twenty-three years old and there was nothing I could do if she didn't want to see me."

"Oh, Caroline. I'm sorry."

"I've been dreaming about her the last few nights, you know." Caroline turns away from the window. "Becca, I mean. Not that bitch Irene." She pushes down on one wheel, swivelling the chair to face Sarah. "Now it's not only my mother coming to me during the night, it's Becca, too. The two of them together, both wanting something from me. In the dream they have their arms around each other the way young friends do and it makes my jealous heart rear up, feeling like I'm the third wheel, being left out of something." She dabs at her nose with the tissue. "I can't think straight these days after going all night without sleep. Yet, try as I might, as soon as my eyes are closed and I drift off, there they are, as real to me as if they're standing right here in my room. I'm forgetting things. Just last night I accused that Bishop woman of moving my reading glass when there it was, right on the side table where I'd left it. And I'm beginning to wonder what the point is of reading anyway, when I come back to my book and can't remember a word I've read the next day. It makes me wonder if I'm losing my mind."

"No, you're not," Sarah reassures her. "Things like that happen if you're not getting enough sleep. Maybe you should see if Dr. Boutreau will prescribe something to help."

"I won't have it," Caroline snaps. "I don't want the good sense I have left addled by any sleeping pill." She looks Sarah in the eye. "It's peace I need before I die and there's no way I can get it, besides finding my girl." She turns back to the window, gazing out again at the yard. In the gazebo, there's a withered pink petunia, neglected, watered only by the rain, in a single hanging basket. A breeze has come up and the forlorn basket sways, a barely perceptible motion, like a child's empty swing.

SARAH

O n her way home from Sunny Haven, Sarah thinks about Caroline's trip to Victoria and wonders if Jack's search for Becca might have been more successful if he'd known at the time about Great-Aunt Irene. It brings to mind their own futile search; the time she and Jack set out to find her mother.

Baba's people had settled farther west, not far from Yorkton, just across the border, and Sarah believed her mother might have gone to Saskatchewan when she left. Baba told Sarah she still had some cousins farming there and Sarah thought it would be a good idea to look them up.

It was October, right after harvest, when they told Anton and Anna they were taking a honeymoon for a week or so. Anton said he'd never heard of anyone going to Saskatchewan for a honeymoon. Besides, why go now when there was still so much work to do? But there were always chores, so Jack threw their suitcase in the truck and they drove off while Anton stood in the yard, still talking and shaking his head.

Starting at the border, Sarah and Jack stopped in the smaller towns and villages along the way, asking in coffee shops and municipal offices if anyone knew of a woman named Olivia Coyle, but no one had ever heard of her. They found some of Baba's relatives near Wroxton, and, while they might have been her distant cousins, they didn't know her daughter. Sarah scoured the phone books at motels in Yorkton and Regina, writing down numbers for both Coyles and Petrenkos and calling from lobby pay phones. A man in Moose Jaw, when he answered, told Sarah to hang on for a minute. A fissure of hope cracked open for the first time while she cradled the receiver next to her ear but when the woman came on the line she said her name was Olive, not Olivia, and she sounded too old to be her mother. They headed home after that, Jack complaining for the first fifty miles about the loss of time and good money but, when Sarah's disappointment spilled over and she started to cry, he pulled into a park — a roadside spot for campers and tents with stunted trees and a small, empty pool — and rented a cabin. She lay in his arms for two days and he soothed her the only way he knew how.

It won't be any easier to find Becca, Sarah thinks as she nears the boundary between their farm and Caroline's. Perhaps she should tell Caroline to take the lawyer up on his suggestion and hire a private investigator, someone used to tracking people down. There's a limit to the internet and how much Sarah can do.

Anton's in the field on the swather, making the outside round on the wheat, the golden swath falling on the stubble in a nearly perfect line like the stitching on the edge of a pocket. The reels spin, catching the sun, as he turns the far corner of the field by the stone pile.

The aroma of fresh tomatoes, garlic, and basil wafts through the kitchen when Sarah walks in. Connor's with Toni on the floor in the living room, backing a tractor into a large cardboard box, making the beeping sound all new equipment makes these days. Boo is sitting in a trailer, a bright red ribbon tied around his neck.

"Jason phoned," Toni says, getting up off the floor. "Emma's still a bit jaundiced and the doctor wants them to stay. He said he'll swing by about four to pick up Connor. You're good to watch him now? I have to get to work."

Sarah nods. "Go ahead. Thanks for starting lunch."

"No problem," Toni says. Before she leaves, she motions to a small tin box on the coffee table. "Oh, I found that inside the box I used for Connor's shed. He wanted me to make Boo a bow tie from the ribbon. I couldn't figure out if the stuff belonged to your mother or your baba, or both. I thought maybe you'd like to look through it."

Connor is building a fence for the toy cows and he's clucking softly to them, promising to feed them as soon as he's made a few bales of hay.

Since he's preoccupied, Sarah sits on the couch and opens the box, thinking it odd it should resurface just weeks after she brought it home from her father's and stored it away. She didn't know what else to do with it at the time, and she couldn't bring herself to throw it out. The birthday cards still smell faintly of roses and there's a postcard from Wasagaming — fin-tailed cars parked along the lake — she hadn't noticed when she first found the box. She picks up the red notebook with Baba's drawings. Broadleaf burdock, shiny purslane shaped like a fingernail, a milkweed's moppish head; Sarah recognizes all the plants from her walks through the woods with Baba.

They lost her two years after she and Jack were married. By then, she had battled cancer, her breast removed and then rounds of chemotherapy. Sarah had convinced her to take the treatments, although Baba thought she could cure herself with her cache of bark and roots and flowers. She'd been so sick from the cocktail of drugs they gave her, grown haggard and hairless and gaunt. Within a year, the cancer had spread to her lungs. No more chemo, she said, and waited to die.

Sarah flips to the back of the notebook and reads what her mother wrote. *Save for Sarah.*

If Baba were to explain it, she would say it is God's will that Sarah discovered the tin box in the cranny. Baba believed everything happened for a reason, and Sarah wonders if it *is* mere coincidence that she should come into possession of the little red book. It seems a natural fit with the holy icon and other things Baba wanted her to have after she died. The basket, blessed candles, vials of holy water, and her rosary are all stored in Sarah's china cabinet with the Easter cloth Baba once cross-stitched for her.

Sarah goes to the dining room and finds Baba's things in the cabinet. She opens the well-worn leather pouch with the rosary inside and fingers the beads. A lump of golden beeswax is also inside and she lifts it out. Baba was a woman of great faith with a resolute and unwavering acceptance of God's will. Sarah would like to be more like her but she's always had so many questions. After Baba died, she made a point of attending Mass at Christmas and Easter, and she had the girls baptized like Baba would have wanted, but she lacks the same blind faith. Baba believed so completely in the chants and prayers of the healing ritual, for instance, that she fully believed that all who came to her would be cured.

Sarah is closing the cabinet drawer when she is suddenly aware of the silence; she can no longer hear Connor talking to the cows or his equipment *beep-beeping*.

In the living room the plastic animals are lined up inside the fence but there's no sign of him.

"Connor!" Sarah runs into Allison's room, looks in the closet where the toys are stored and under the bed. He's not there. She looks in the other bedrooms, flinging open closet doors. "Connor, we're not playing hide-and-seek. Come out and I'll give you a treat." Bribery usually works with him, but not this time. She runs down to the basement, checks the storage room, her mouth dry as a sense of dread bubbles up. Where could he be? Back upstairs and out into the garage. Misty's whining, pawing at the door. Connor's shut her in, run off, and left her behind.

Sarah tears outside. The gate's open, the green speckled cord like a coiled snake on the ground. Thunder rumbles from slate-grey clouds stacked high in the sky. "Connor! Jack!" But there's no one around to hear her. She races through the yard, checking in the shop and in the cab of the MX parked next to the bins. There are a hundred places he could be, most of them unsafe for a three-year-old, but the only thing she can think of is the vicious intent of that cunning wolf, as likely to attack a small boy as it did a defenceless pup. She notices something, a flash of red, lying in the grass at the back of the yard. It's Boo, lying face down near the grass trail leading to the river. She runs back to the house, phones Jack's cell, but it goes straight to voicemail. Damn him for never answering his phone! She is drawn to the gun cabinet, some thought circling in her head, and she unlocks it, grabs Jack's rifle then flips open a box of shells. Pocketing a handful, she heads back outside.

. . .

The clouds are close and black in the muttering sky as she runs toward the river, squelching her panic, pushing it back down her throat until she stops, panting, next to the stone pile. She looks across the meadow and calls, "Connor? Are you here?"

She scrambles down the ravine. The water is only a few inches deep, just as she expected at this time of year, and she steps carefully across the first few stones, the way she and Becca once did. Stopping, she peers across to the other side into the stand of poplars, the underbrush thick, overgrown after so many years undisturbed by Eldon's cattle. A magpie squawks from the sparse branches at the top of a tall poplar then flaps off. Sarah waits, listening. From the dense underbrush, she hears a sudden furtive rustling. Across the river, a wolf slinks out of the bush, carrying a small wad of red fur in his teeth. He stops near the bank and, when he sees Sarah, he drops it, curls a corner of his lip, and growls, a menacing rumble, deep in his throat.

Fear clenches a fist in her gut but Sarah doesn't move. The wolf's body is tense, his wiry coat patchy with mange. He stares her down from only metres away. With two or three bounds, he could easily rip open her throat. His teeth sinking deep into the soft flesh where Jack kissed her this morning. She reaches into her pocket for a bullet without taking her eyes off him; she's not blinking and neither is he. Why hadn't she loaded the damn gun? She cocks the rifle — the sound like kindling splitting across a knee — and slides the shell into the chamber. The wolf lowers his head and steps forward, growling louder now, and Sarah doesn't hesitate. She lifts the rifle to her shoulder, his wide head lined in her sights. Amber eyes, unblinking. She feels the cool metal of the trigger on her finger and she presses it back in a sure, steady way. There's a thunderous roar; the kick from the gun slams into her shoulder and the blast hurls the beast into the air. A small flock of sparrows bursts out of the trees, scattering like buckshot across the sky then circling and swooping back to alight again in the scrawny poplars, this time on Sarah's side of the river.

She waits for a minute while her heart slows, watching to see if he moves, although she knows it's impossible. A brilliantly red patch seeps and spreads into the gravelly pebbles next to what's left of his head. Her bullet got him right between those gold-flecked eyes.

CAROLINE

Becca comes to Caroline during the night, alone this time, her raving hair wild, her eyes harsh and accusing. In the dream, they're in the kitchen, the calico curtains drawn across bricked-over windows. The dark is thick as tar in every corner, the only light a flickering candle in the middle of the table, and Caroline knows, without seeing, the house is empty, devoid of everyday life as if ransacked by thieves. And then Nick is standing there as young and alive as he was the day he came over to tell Eldon about the wandering cows. *Here he is. This is your father.* Caroline is relieved to tell Becca the secret she's been carrying for so long; it's like a tumour split open, releasing the poisonous truth. *Why didn't you tell me before? I had the right to know.* Caroline's not sure of the sound, a *click-click* like the sound of a gun being cocked and, when she turns to look, Eldon is standing behind her, the muzzle of his gun dripping blood. And there's Sport on the floor, the life draining out of him and pooling thick and black at her feet. *We need to get out!* She turns to take Becca and Nick by the hand and run but they're gone, although she can still see their shadows lying long on the floor. Caroline turns, crashes into the table, knocking over the candle and pitching her into complete darkness. Then the hiss of a match, the sulfuric smell of the devil himself, and Eldon holds the quivering match to his face.

You will never leave me. I'll never let you go.

Caroline opens her mouth to scream — and awakens in her own safe room. Her pillow's on the floor, the water glass at her bedside tipped over. Using her hands, she hoists herself up and leans against the headboard, heart pounding. The only thing she remembers from the nightmare with any clarity is the claustrophobic sensation of being locked away in a walled-in room.

When she returned from Victoria, her car wasn't parked in the Greyhound parking lot in Locklin where she'd left it. She assumed Eldon had tracked it down and driven it home with the second set of keys. She had no choice but to call him from a pay phone and ask him to pick her up. Where else could she go?

He didn't speak when he drove up or even ask her where she'd been. He stowed her suitcase in the trunk and, on the way home, Caroline tried to explain why she went to B.C. without his permission. He never asked if she'd found Becca in Victoria. The moment they stepped through the door, he lashed out with his fists, punching her in the stomach, then the face. "You. Will. Never. Leave. Me."

She cowered on the floor while he kicked her with his boots. After he'd driven out his rage, she crawled upstairs, the pain so intense it ached to draw a breath. She surely had broken ribs. Her body was covered with bruises the colour of raw beets, and her right eye quickly swelled shut.

She should have left him after that. But she stayed, believing her presence in Eldon's house was her penance, her suffering at his hands atonement for what she had done. She was an adulteress who gave birth to another man's child and let her unsuspecting husband raise it as his own. And so she stayed, surviving on hope. Hope that Becca would forgive her. Hope that she'd eventually come home.

Eldon didn't seem to care one way or another about Rebecca at all — discarding without thought or distress all the years he'd supposedly loved her. He steeled himself to the world as though his heart were coated with pitch, going about his daily chores as though Becca had never existed.

Nothing changed in the routine of their daily lives. She felt no different than Elvina's housekeeper, Vera Kalyniuk, forever in the kitchen, cooking and baking, washing and cleaning, as well as tending to Eldon's physical needs in every possible way. He came to her bed from time to time and she tolerated it as she did any other chore. As weeks became months and months became years, the hope of seeing Becca again began to fade, but Caroline held on to it in the same way a drowning man grasps on to a rope, thinking she might yet see her one day, walking down the lane with a suitcase in one hand and a child in the other. She often thought of leaving Eldon, finding a job in a bank, perhaps, but the brick house was where Becca would inevitably come back to, so Caroline stayed, waiting for her. She stayed until the years became decades and her eyesight began to fail and, finally, Eldon passed away.

Down the hall, Caroline hears the clatter of dishes. The early shift of kitchen staff has arrived to cook breakfast. Hopefully, later, Sarah will come by. Sometimes she brings Joe into her room, sits him down in the wooden chair she moves over from his room. He's as docile as a lump of dough if it's early in the day, smiling and nodding as though he knows what they're talking about. Such a wonderful woman Sarah has turned out to be, and lovely to look at, too. It makes Caroline wonder if Becca has aged gracefully, and whether she colours her hair. Is she a good mother, as Sarah seems to be, and happily married?

Loving Becca was not always easy; she had the same prideful, selfish way about her as Eldon and his mother, although how that was possible, Caroline didn't know. There seemed to be no hint of Nick in her at all, in either looks or in nature. Eldon spoiled her, not only with material things, but by letting her have her way. She was a self-indulgent girl who expected to get what she wanted. Caroline wishes she'd tried harder to shape Becca into a different sort of girl, one like Sarah who was gentle and kind and appreciated every single thing she had.

"Good morning, sunshine," Cara says, smiling at the door. She is always in good spirits, even as early as this. "Did you sleep well?" she asks as she bounces into the room on those squeaky sneakers she wears. There's a genuine look of concern on her face and Caroline re-evaluates her early opinion of Cara; what she lacks in competence she makes up for in goodness.

"I woke from another bad dream only minutes ago. I can't remember a thing; you know how it is with dreams, exploding into a million small pieces you'll never remember once you open your eyes. It seemed I was in some sort of jail, one with bricks instead of bars in the windows."

Cara rolls her arm under Caroline's back to help her sit up and swing her legs over the edge of the bed. "Maybe you're dreaming about this place. John McTavish calls it the Sunny Haven Correctional Facility."

Caroline has to admit, she's thought of it that way herself. "It's not as bad as all that. At least you don't make us wear those orange jumpsuits."

"Ha! That's funny. It would be a pain to dress you up in one of those." Cara's at the closet, holding up two dresses, one pale blue and one with pink flowers. "Which one will it be?"

SARAH

When Sarah tells Jack about the wolf, she credits motherly intuition. She has no other way to explain it. A powerful force drove her to the river with the rifle, knowing she had to protect Connor. After she killed the wolf and returned to the yard, she found Connor in the workshop, perched on the riding lawnmower, turning the wheel. He had heard her calling, but thought it a game to make her look, so he sat very still in the dim shop when Sarah came dashing through. In her panic, she didn't see him. She was relieved and angry at the same time after she found him, but all she could do was hug him.

Later, after Jason picks up Connor, Sarah walks back to the river. There is a bloody trail on the opposite bank where Jack dragged the wolf into the trees.

On her way back to the house, she pauses at the stone pile to select a few stones to prop among her recently transplanted lilies. A grey rock with a raised, rough marking that looks like a cross catches her eye. Jack must have picked it this spring and she hadn't noticed it on top of the pile before now. The rain has washed it clean and the sun glimmers off the silver-flecked granite. She climbs on the pile and, using her legs, dislodges the stone and pushes it off. It tumbles into the grass and lands on its flat bottom. Sitting there, with its purple-coloured cross facing east, it reminds Sarah of a tombstone. It's too heavy to move so she leaves it for Jack to pick up later with the front-end loader.

The next morning, Sarah pours three cups of coffee and pops two slices of bread into the toaster. Toni is making a sandwich for her lunch. She has just two more days of work and then, before the Labour Day weekend, she is heading back to university.

"What's new at Sunny Haven? How's Grandpa? I guess I'd better stop in and have one last visit with him before I head back," Toni says.

"He's the same as always," Sarah says. She takes a sip of coffee. "It's Caroline that seems to be failing. She can't sleep and it's taking a toll on her."

Jack is flipping through the *Country Guide* and doesn't appear to be listening.

"Why? What's wrong with her?" Toni asks.

"She's having nightmares and something's weighing on her mind. I wish there was a way I could help her."

Toni spreads peanut butter on her toast and sits down at the table. "Isn't there a story about Dad when he was a little kid? Something about your baba curing him of nightmares?"

"You're right. She performed her wax ritual," Sarah says, nodding.

"That's almost hard to believe." Toni looks at Jack. "Do you ever have nightmares, now?"

Jack glances up from the magazine. "Worked like a charm. Never had another one."

After Jack and Toni are gone, Sarah wanders into the living room to find the tin box and its contents on the coffee table where she left them. She picks up the red book and, as she leafs through it, it occurs to her she might use the wax ritual to help Caroline. She's had no luck finding Becca, but what if she can help rid Caroline of her terrible dreams? Maybe she can chase away the tormenting nightmares in much the same way Baba did for Jack when he was a boy all those years ago.

Of course I can't. I'm nothing like Baba.

She returns to the china cabinet, retrieves Baba's things, and places them into the small basket. The wax is firm and smooth in her hand and she feels a comforting warmth from it, as though Baba's spirit is contained in that fragrant lump.

It's intention that matters. And being a good person.

God. Spirit. Call it what you will, Sarah does believe there's something bigger than herself, and she taught her daughters to live with the notion of such a higher power. To be grateful and gracious and kind. She's tried to live that way herself.

She loves Caroline. She always has. Why wouldn't she try whatever she could to help bring her the peace she deserves? Taking the red book, she heads out the door.

The next morning, Sarah stands next to Caroline in the dining room, holding the basket with Baba's things.

"What on earth do you have there?" Caroline sits up tall in her chair, trying to peer inside it.

"I think I might have a way to get rid of your nightmares."

"How do you intend to do that?" Caroline asks, wide-eyed.

"I'll tell you all about it back in your room. I'll just say hello to my dad."

Addie is urging him to finish his juice but he's shaking his head, his lips pressed tight.

"What's up with the basket?" Addie asks, wiping Joe's chin.

"It was my grandmother's. It sat on a small table in her house for as long as I can remember."

"I didn't ask whose. What are you doing with it?"

Most people, including Addie, knew about Halya Petrenko and her faith healing, but Sarah has to admit she used to be ashamed of Baba's old-world ways. Once, when she and Addie and Becca were sitting in a booth at the King's Café with a couple of boys, Baba came through the door, bent over her cane. She was dressed no differently than any other day of the week, in her *babushka* and bright flowered dress. Sarah's face burned with shame and she stared into her milkshake, not daring to look up in case Baba would see her. When she finally looked, Baba still stood at the counter, peeling the foil from a stick of Juicy Fruit gum. She caught Sarah's eye then looked quickly away and followed her cane out the door.

"I'm going to light a few candles in Caroline's room. Try some old-time meditation like my grandmother used to do. I thought maybe it would help her sleep."

"Strange time of day to try to help somebody sleep, isn't it?" Addie pulls Simon's wheelchair away from the table and unfastens his bib. "But it won't hurt to try. She's too stubborn to take a pill and we've tried everything else we can think of."

Addie and Sarah take her father and Simon back to their rooms. Once her dad's settled in his chair, Sarah tells him about the wolf, holding out the full length of her arm with her finger pointed then jerking it back to show him how she killed it. He nods, with a knowing look on his face, and Sarah is thrilled when he says, "I got a jumper, too." She hopes he's remembering the hunting trips he used to take for white-tailed deer with Patrick and Paul.

When Sarah comes into her room and closes the door, Caroline skims across the floor in her chair, eyes bright. "What is it? Have you brought me something to eat?" She looks at the things in the basket. "What is all this for?"

"When Jack was a little boy his mother brought him to my grandmother. He had bad dreams — night terrors are what they call them now — and my grandmother was able to help him."

"What does that have to do with me?" Caroline lifts her eyebrows suspiciously.

"She believed many ills were rooted in some sort of trauma or fear. I've seen her cure everything from bed-wetting to post-partum depression." Sarah explains the whole mysterious ritual and shows Caroline the paper with the words Anton translated from Ukrainian to English.

She took the red book to his house yesterday and had him decipher the ritual word by word while she recorded him on her phone. It took a few hours — Anton stopped often to add his own wisdom — but eventually they got through it. Sarah spent the rest of the day painstakingly transcribing the words onto paper.

"And this will stop the dreams? Help me sleep?"

"I figure it's worth a shot. There's just one thing I need … and that's for you to believe."

"Sounds hokey to me." Caroline wheels away to look out the window. "I'm not even Ukrainian."

"I don't think you have to be. All you need is faith." Sarah places the enamel bowl on Caroline's desk, fills it with a jar-ful of water she drew from the well, and adds a few drops of blessed water. She steadies a candle in the glass holder she brought, then lights it. "And I need to believe I can do this. We need to have faith in each other. It's worth a try, isn't it?"

Caroline nods. "I suppose so. You've always been a sensible girl and I trust you."

The familiar self-doubt creeps back in but Sarah presses on, for Caroline's sake. "Why don't we just get started? See how it goes." She pushes Caroline's wheelchair to the centre of the room and stands behind it, facing the east window. The wax is warm in her hand. She drops it in the cup and holds it to the flame.

CAROLINE

How can this possibly get rid of her night visitations? It's crossed Caroline's mind more than once that the visions and dreams mean her end is drawing near, and it weighs heavily on her. Her mother's face is creased with a deep, indelible sorrow each time she comes and Caroline takes it to mean she wants Caroline to atone for her mistakes before she dies. But she's paid her debt. Isn't it enough that Nick was ripped from the life they planned, crushed into the earth beneath that tractor, before it even began? And the daughter he gave her, snatched away just as suddenly on that fateful June day?

Caroline doesn't remember Sarah turning off the light or maybe a black cloud's crossed in front of the sun but her room's suddenly as dark as a chapel with a single flickering flame. Sarah has a dull knife in her hand and she's saluting the air, chanting in a voice barely above a whisper.

"I release you beyond the mountains, beyond the seas." Strange words.

"I release you where people do not walk, where roosters do not crow, where the wind does not blow." Not godly at all.

"Do not drink red blood, dehydrate a white body, or strip a yellow bone." Blood and bones.

Sarah's face is as smooth and relaxed as someone asleep, her motions trancelike, practised, although she says she's never done this before. She places the bowl on the desk and takes up the cup she only minutes ago held over the flame. The wax slides easily from the cup into the water and Sarah leans in close for a look.

Caroline catches her breath as she feels an unexpected pressure, a slow lean against the back of her heart. It lets up in the time it takes her to swallow another lungful of air then pushes again, harder this time, behind her left breast, and she pictures her pulsing heart shattering like a china cup. She lifts her hand to her chest and takes another deep breath, and the walls in her room start to spin, the crushing weight bearing down even more. She wonders if she's having a heart attack. If only she could stand up, take a brisk walk, and get the blood pumping to where it is needed.

"Caroline, are you all right?" Sarah is saying, crouching down in front of her chair.

Caroline feels a hot wind roar in her ears, which she knows is beyond the realm of possibility, just as she knows her mother is not really here, but she sees her right there, sitting on the bed like a prim lady in church, and a fleeting thought slips into her mind: *Is she here, now, to lead me away?*

Sarah again. Hovering over her. "Should I call the nurse?"

"No, no, don't." The pressure is easing up, the tight belt around her heart slowly releasing. "I'll be fine in a moment."

She's grounded again, back in her everyday room, and, when she looks over, her mother is gone.

"Could you hand me that glass of water?" she asks, and Sarah passes it over.

When Caroline moves to give the glass back, Sarah is staring into the enamel bowl with a perplexed look on her face.

"What happens now?" Caroline asks, peering up at her.

"I have to tell you what I see."

"And?"

"There are two shapes. One looks like a tree." Sarah frowns. "But the other … I don't know … it's just a jagged lump. They both seem familiar, somehow, but there's something I'm not seeing. It's like a piece of the puzzle is missing."

Caroline's heart flips in the quick way it used to when she thought Eldon might catch her in a lie. There *is* a missing piece, and it's the secret she's hidden all these years. Hadn't Alice once said that secrets are impossible to contain forever? Like dandelion fluff, apt to drift away on a light wind to settle and bloom into someone else's truth.

"There's something I need to tell you about that last day. About Becca," Caroline says. The time has come. The Bilyks have the right to know that Becca is one of their own.

Caroline's voice cracks when she says her daughter's name. "She was in such a state that day, pleading with me to understand. Didn't I know what it felt like to be in love?" Caroline looks down, picks at a bit of loose skin at the base of a nail. "Of course I knew about love. I loved her father desperately."

There's a soft tap at the door and Addie looks in but Sarah waves her away. "Becca was furious with me. She didn't understand why I disapproved of Jack so strongly. She knew about Eldon's opinion of the Bilyks but she couldn't understand why I would be so opposed to a romance between them; she expected me to take her side against her father. She was carrying on in the kitchen that day, throwing cups from the cupboard and smashing them on the floor, insisting she would run off and marry Jack and there was nothing we could do. I told her it was impossible, she simply could not have anything more to do with this particular boy."

"Why? What did you have against Jack?"

"It wasn't Jack. It was something I'd done that Becca was being made to pay for. But I wouldn't change a minute of it." Tears flow freely down Caroline's cheeks and she makes no effort to brush them away.

The digital number flips on the clock; the usual sounds from the hallway beyond Caroline's door are muted by a spell that seems to have fallen over the room.

"Becca was hysterical so I slapped her." She looks at Sarah, her eyes begging forgiveness. "I swear, before that day, I'd never lifted a hand to her. Becca was so shocked, she stumbled back, holding the palm of one hand against her face. She sank to the floor, sobbing, then looked up and told me there might be a baby. She was late by six weeks, but, like any young girl, she didn't want to believe it. She'd already told Jack and he said they had no other choice but to get married. I couldn't believe it." Caroline wrings her hands. "I had planned to keep the secret from her for as long as I lived. What sense would there be in telling her? I thought she'd soon leave for the city, be as happy as I'd been to get away from the farm. She would make new friends. Meet someone else and forget about Jack. But I was so shocked when she told me about the baby, I blurted it out. I told her ... that Jack was her cousin."

Caroline holds her hand over her mouth, stifling a cry. She is remembering Becca's shocked face when she told her.

"Her cousin?" Sarah says, still seeming confused.

"Her father was Jack's uncle," Caroline says quietly. "Nick." She covers her face with her hands. "I wasn't able tell her how pure our love was, nothing at all like what she must have been thinking. She pushed me with all her might, called me every vile name you can think of. Told me she hated me. Then she ran off, and it wasn't until later, when Elvina showed up, that I knew Becca didn't even want to say goodbye. She never wanted to see me again. And I could hardly blame her. I turned the whole truth of her life on its head."

In the hallway, the wheels of a cart clatter by as an aide pushes it from room to room, handing out fresh pitchers of water.

There. It's done. I'm finally free of it.

"So Eldon found out Becca wasn't his child," Sarah says.

"I hoped he never would — Becca and I could have kept it between us if only I'd had time to explain — but she ran out. She must have gone straight to Eldon and told him. I stayed in the house the rest of that day, thinking eventually she'd cry herself out and come back. Eldon didn't show up for supper either, but he came back just before dark. I was in my sewing room, keeping my hands busy, hemming a skirt. He grabbed me, picked up my shears from the sewing table and hacked off my hair. Threw it in clumps on the floor. Then he held the scissors against my throat — I thought he would kill me. He knew it all. About Nick. That Becca wasn't his own daughter. And about Becca's baby. I wasn't fit to call myself a mother, he said, and he was sending Becca away. Then the next day, Jack showed up and told us he was prepared to marry her. Eldon pulled out his gun, told him he'd never see Becca again either."

Silence fills the room.

"He punished me every day for the rest of his life," Caroline finally says.

"How did you —?"

"Stay? Survive?" Caroline shakes her head. "What choice did I have? I had nowhere to go. And besides, every letter that came, every packet of mail, I was sure one day I'd find something from her. For the first few years, every time the phone rang, I raced for it, hoping I'd hear her voice. I stayed because I wanted to be there in the kitchen when she came through the door, to hug her, to hold her tight, to tell her I was so sorry."

Caroline is exhausted. She can scarcely speak. "That's all I really want. I want her to come home so I can explain. I want the chance to earn her forgiveness."

SARAH

It's something Sarah's always wanted, too. An explanation and a chance to forgive her mother. She's resented her all these years and she wants to be rid of the anger. Why would a child leave forever? Why would a mother? There is nothing that would ever keep Sarah from her daughters. No mistake or choice they could make would ever change or diminish her love for them. She could never leave them. It goes against nature for a child to forsake her mother just as it does for a mother to abandon her child. With the exception of abuse or neglect, no fight should be enough to sever those ties, no disagreement too great to not make amends. Why did her own mother leave and never come back? Why would Becca?

Sarah takes another look at the wax shapes ... and it is suddenly obvious. A place so familiar, she can't believe she didn't recognize it right away. Her tree near the river. A place that connects them both. The Bilyks and the Webbs.

But what of the jagged lump?

Impressions are flitting through her mind like frightened birds as she studies the second shape more closely. She's always wondered about Becca's sudden disappearance. Why did she leave without saying goodbye to her or contacting Jack — if she loved him so much — with a message?

She picks up the rough piece and holds it on the tips of her fingers. There is a small marking like an irregular cross on its face. Jagged. Smooth. Limestone. Granite. Fist-sized or boulders. Churned up out of the earth then cast aside in a pile beneath the elm tree.

And a thought, one that may have always been there, folded tight and stitched loosely to a dark corner of her mind, takes shape.

What if Becca never left at all?

It's a perfect harvest day, the kind you might find on a picture in one of those calendars that grocery stores once gave away. Wispy white clouds like pulled-apart puffs of cotton stretch across a clear blue sky. Golden heads of wheat rattle in an autumn wind. Shorty is on his backhoe, the huge roaring machine grappling with the biggest boulders and setting them aside. He picks off the smaller rocks, one at a time, more and more carefully as he gets closer to the bottom. Once the earth is bare, he lowers the blade and tips it, removing slices of dirt. Sarah stands beside Jack, leaning into the hollow beneath his shoulder. She thinks she can hear the beat of his heart.

Shorty continues probing, moving slowly along, removing scant bites of earth until they see a strip of tattered cloth. Jack jerks up his hand and stills it against the sky. Shorty stops and climbs out of the backhoe. Jack picks up his shovel and begins to dig, slowly, taking care with every scoop until he unearths the truth: yellowed bones, long and tapered. A human skull.

Shorty walks back to the house to call the RCMP.

"All this time, she was here." Jack shakes his head. "It's no wonder he never wanted us to knock the tree down and bury the stone pile. He couldn't take the chance we might find her. The old bastard must have used a tractor to knock the rocks off on his side of the pile. Once he cleared them away, he dug a shallow grave. Laid her in it and covered her up then loaded the rocks back into the bucket and piled them back on. No one would ever think someone was buried here."

Sarah is quiet, overwhelmed by the extent of the cover-up. "Caroline told me he was out late that night," she finally says. "Came in raging, piling all the blame for Becca leaving on her. And here he'd been, hiding his own tracks, while his mother came and packed up Becca's clothes then went home to dream up a story real enough for everyone to believe."

"And he kept on piling," Jack's voice cracks. "More and more stones weighing her down."

Only three living souls had known Becca was dead and they all went to their graves with the secret. Sarah is struck with the pains Elvina took to conceal the truth. She'd involved her sister, Irene, in her scheme, each of them deceiving Caroline, making her believe it was her fault Becca had gone away. What had compelled Elvina to do it? Was it the public shame of Caroline's secret being revealed, as Caroline was led to believe, or Eldon's guilt of his crime? Would any mother do the same to protect her child? Would she?

. . .

Later, when Sarah tells Caroline they've found Becca's body, her face seems to crack in two. Her mouth falls open. "She can't have been dead all these years!" she cries.

"I'm so sorry, Caroline." Sarah gets down on her knees and puts her arms around Caroline's fragile shoulders. She feels the old woman quake as the truth takes hold and she starts to sob.

Tears trail down Sarah's cheeks, too. Caroline needs time to mourn. All those lost years, Caroline believed Becca was alive and too angry with her to come home. Sarah's thought the same about her own mother except she's been the one holding on to the anger, blaming her mother for staying away. She never considered that maybe her mother wanted to come back but someone or something kept her from it. Maybe Mom died alone, long ago, too.

"You're absolutely sure?" Caroline is saying and Sarah leans back to sit on her heels. "The police are sure it's Becca's body you found?"

"They'll want a DNA sample from you, just to confirm it."

Minutes go by before Caroline pulls a tissue from her sleeve and dabs her eyes. "It's my fault. If only she hadn't found out Nick was her father, she'd be alive. I should have followed her out and told Eldon myself. He could have killed me instead."

"It must have been an accident," Sarah insists, still unable to believe the gall of Eldon and his mother, pretending all those years Becca was really alive. No one, not even her own mother, considered Becca a missing person when Eldon and Elvina claimed she was living on the other side of the country. "Eldon could have gone to the police and explained."

"That wasn't likely to happen. The whole sordid story would have come out and Elvina couldn't let that happen. The Webb name and status meant more to her than all her money and that fancy new house. She'd come from nothing and couldn't tarnish a reputation she'd spent her whole lifetime creating."

"So you think Eldon killed her intentionally?"

"I wouldn't put it past him," Caroline said. "Eldon had a hair-trigger temper; she surely set it off when she told him she wasn't his child. He would have flown into a rage, as he often did with me, although he'd never hit Becca before. He could have struck her, knocked her flat on the ground. She'd have meant no more to him at that moment than a stray dog.

"I have no doubt in my mind he would have killed Nick, and me, too, had he ever found out about us. He was the kind of man who would do that. Eldon could never be bested by anyone, even in the smallest way. He always had to keep the upper hand. Who's to say he didn't choke the life out of her? He might have done it to take it out on me. It's the ultimate punishment for a mother, isn't it? Taking away her child?"

Sarah can't even contemplate that despicable possibility.

"In any event, their cover-up kept me right where Eldon wanted me. When he asked me to marry him, he said he was going to keep me forever. He told me I could never leave him. But I would have if I'd known Becca was dead, and he knew that. He was my jailer and hope was my prison. Like always, Eldon got what he wanted."

The small funeral and subsequent interment is held at St. Michael's. At Caroline's request, Becca is laid to rest in the Bilyk plot beside her father.

While the priest gives the closing prayer and blesses the casket for the last time, Sarah offers Caroline another tissue. She looks up from under the veil of her black hat, her eyes red-rimmed.

"Are you okay?" Sarah asks, concerned about the way Caroline is slumped down in the wheelchair, the weight of this day more than she can bear.

"I will be," Caroline says. "Once this is over."

Addie comes up and leans down to give Caroline a hug. "She looks so tired," she says to Sarah. "I think I should just take her back." There's a luncheon planned for the few guests at Sarah and Jack's house, and Sarah agrees there's no need for Caroline to come.

"The last weeks have been just too much for her, processing all that's happened and then insisting on helping with the arrangements," Sarah says quietly. After the forensic analysis of Becca's remains, they learned the back of her skull had sustained blunt force trauma, the cause undetermined. Sarah and Addie help Caroline into the waiting van while the cars slowly leave and everyone heads back to the farm.

Jack lingers beside the grave. Sarah comes up and puts her hand on his shoulder.

"It's not only Becca lying here," Jack says. "My child died that day, too."

"I know." Sarah hugs him. "I'm so sorry. We have to mourn for him, too."

"You said *him*," Jack says, stepping back and looking down at her. "I've always felt it was a son I lost, but you've never said it before."

"All these years, in my mind, a little boy's grown up ahead of our girls. He looks like you, with the same stubborn lift to his chin. I thought about him when each of the girls was born. When I lost the others." Her voice wavers. "At every special occasion, there he was."

"I always thought losing him was punishment for getting fooled by Becca and going along with it when she offered herself up when all along it was you I really wanted. I'm so sorry for that. I'll regret it till the day I die."

She steps back and gazes up at him. "At least now we know there never was a baby born and given away, but if there had been, I know I would have loved him. Because he was yours."

Jack touches the soft pad of her cheek with a rough finger. "I know it," he says.

In the distance, combines growl in the fields, gathering up the grain, the end of another cycle like all of the others. It's the pattern of their lives, this ebb and flow of seasons.

"I need you to know something, Sarah," he finally says. "You've been the best wife I could have ever asked for. I know that everything you've ever done, you've done for me and the girls."

Tears well up in Sarah's eyes again. "I know it, Jack. You don't have to tell me."

"I know I'm not one for words. For saying what I'm thinking or feeling."

"Like, *hey, you,* instead of honey, or baby?" Sarah says in a teasing way. She's smiling up at him.

Jack looks surprised. "But it *is* you. It's always been you. You're the only one I've ever wanted."

"I know it, Jack." All the love she's ever needed has been right here in the circle of Jack's arms.

EPILOGUE

The elm is gone now. Jack tore it down with the tractor and dragged it to the river with a chain. In the spring, when the Makwa was swollen, the tree floated off until it made its way to the lake. The stone pile is gone, too, buried, the ground levelled flat in the same place it stood all those years.

Caroline lived for four more years, good years filled with long, peaceful nights. Sarah was with her at the end, holding her hand.

Jack and the girls had already said their goodbyes; Connor and little Emma, too, lifted up to give a last kiss to their Nanny. Sarah was alone, holding back tears. "It's going to be all right now," she whispered, as she laced her fingers through Caroline's silky hair. "I'm right here, beside you." Another ragged breath, then a pause, longer than the last, until Caroline struggled for another.

Caroline's eyelids fluttered, and through her cracked lips came a question. "Is it you?"

Could Caroline see Becca waiting for her? Or was it her mother she saw, standing at the end of a tunnel washed in white light? Sarah knew it was Caroline's time, but she wasn't ready to let her go. "Yes, yes, it's me," Sarah said, the sorrow she'd been holding inside rising up in a pain so intense she could scarcely breathe.

Sarah felt the faintest tremor from Caroline's hand and Caroline's eyes fluttered open one more time. "It *is* you," she said, then she gave a last gentle breath.

"Sarah."

ACKNOWLEDGEMENTS

Although *A Strange Kind of Comfort* is a work of fiction, the river rescue is based on a true story — the heroine, my mother. Thanks, Mom, for sharing it with me and for your ongoing love and support.

Dad, your memory lives on in my heart. Thanks for always being in my corner.

My children have blessed me with the fulfillment, heartache, and absolute joy of motherhood. Without them, this novel would not have its soul. Thank you for your inspiration and encouragement.

The characters of Anton and Anna were created in memory of my in-laws, who taught by example. Addie was based on my dear friend, Adeline, in her memory. She was the most forthright person I have ever known.

Much gratitude to Fisher, Linda, and Julie, fellow members of the Parkland Writer's Group, for their careful reading, honest suggestions, and continuing friendship.

The Word and Wax: A Medical Folk Ritual Among Ukrainians in Alberta, by Rena Jeanne Hanchuk, was an invaluable resource. Ms. Hanchuk's research validated my own understanding of the folk ritual and her book was the source of the healing incantation.

For believing in my story, special thanks to acquisitions editor Rachel Spence, at Dundurn Press. Jess Shulman, thank you for your insight, skill, and expertise in guiding me through the editing process. To Dundurn Press and staff who offered valuable advice every step of the way, many thanks.

Finally, for your unwavering patience and support, much love and thanks to my husband, Wayne. Thanks for answering my questions about farm equipment and methods when I was not quite sure and needed an expert opinion. I wouldn't want to share this with anyone but you.